KARA FUNCHEON

Echoes of Prophecy

Dear Reader,
I believe you.

Contents

Preface

So, they killed Cassandra first 'cause she feared the worst
   And tried to tell the town
   So, they set my life in flames, I regret to say
   Do you believe me now?
   -Taylor Swift, "Cassandra"

Listen to the *Echoes of Prophecy* playlist here: https://tinyurl.com/Prophecy Playlist

Prologue

Cassandra

The men had it wrong.

Homer. Virgil. Aeschylus. Euripides.

I did not rebuke Apollo's advances.

I loved him.

I was his priestess, his confidante. His friend.

But the gods are foolish. Apollo, most of all. His favor is fleeting. Ask any of his lovers - Daphne, Calliope, Adonis, Hyacinth, even - it was rumored - my mother, Hecuba. I counted them once, the lovers of Apollo – I got to the sixty-seventh name and stopped. I didn't want to read about any more of them.

We all had our share of tragic tales. But that's the destiny of those who love the gods, not just worship them. There's a distinction, and it's a matter of life and death.

For my love, my affection, my loyalty - Apollo both blessed and cursed me. I became a mere footnote in history, a pitiable character in other men's narratives. Many things have been said - all of them false - about me.

They said I went mad, that I was left in a temple with my twin, and that I angered Apollo.

The truth? You wouldn't believe me if I told you.

1

Cassie

Present Day

"Oh my god," I whispered, my heart heavy as I leaned back in my chair. My hands rose to my face, futilely attempting to hold back the tears. No matter how many times I revisited this character's story, it never failed to shatter me. But tonight, grief wasn't enough—tonight, I felt the spark of rage.

Awful. I adjusted myself and dove back into the article on my table. Highlighter in hand, I marked the text, focusing on a single passage—one singular woman—my namesake.

"That's all she gets?" My voice cracked into the silence of my apartment. I shook my head and reached for my battered copy of *The Iliad*—tabs, notes, years of study carved into the margins. Every time I returned to it, the same fury burned hotter. Homer had erased her. Virgil twisted her. Aeschylus and Euripides exploited her madness. They had relegated Cassandra to a footnote, a tool to advance a man's tragedy.

And me? I had inherited her name. Cassandra. The curse of truth without belief. Some days, I wondered if I had inherited the curse, too.

My laptop glowed in the corner of the table, my dissertation draft open, bleeding with comments. Dr. Hawthorne's notes loomed in the margins: "Expand beyond Homer. Compare treatments across texts. EH."

Her neat little "EH" was a dagger every time I saw it. I knew what she meant: more analysis, less anger. But how could I strip the anger out when the texts themselves dripped with it?

Fine. Let's just say it.

> *In The Iliad, Cassandra is almost invisible. She appears only once, in Book 24, crying out to summon the Trojans to mourn Hector. That's it. No prophecy, no vision of Troy's fall, nothing that makes her Cassandra. Homer takes the very thing she's remembered for—her voice—and erases it. He tucks her back into the chorus of grieving women, indistinguishable from Hecuba or Andromache. A woman who should speak the future becomes a footnote to someone else's death.*
>
> *Later authors try to fix this silence, but they do not. They just turn it into something else. Aeschylus' Agamemnon gives her torrents of speech, wild prophecy that rushes like blood from a wound. She names her own murder, Agamemnon's murder, the horror in the house of Atreus—and no one listens. The chorus looks at her like she's raving. Prophecy becomes another kind of silence: truth scripted to be ignored.*
>
> *Euripides' Trojan Women is worse. She laughs. She raves with joy that she'll be taken by Agamemnon, because it means his death is certain. The audience is meant to smirk at her frenzy. Even when she's right, her voice is reframed as madness.*
>
> *And the Romans—they just codify the punishment. Virgil has her shout about the wooden horse, and they dismiss her. Ovid makes it Apollo's fault: she said no to him, so he twists her gift into a curse. Speak the truth, but never be believed. Divine punishment for refusal.*
>
> *Across every version, the pattern repeats: Cassandra speaks, but no one hears her. Her silence is not lack of speech—it's the world's refusal to grant her meaning."*

I pause. My fingers hover over the keyboard. It sounds too angry, too personal. But maybe that's the point. I add one more line, almost as if under my breath:

She is not just a character. She is a template. An archetype of silenced women—

forever right, forever unheeded, forever rewritten as lament or hysteria.

I sit back and stare at the screen, heat pooling in my chest. It's supposed to be a dissertation, but some days it feels more like an autopsy.

When an alarm went off on my phone, I realized I had a few minutes to get ready to meet a childhood friend, Eloise, at a new wine bar in the city. Leaving my laptop open, books and sticky notes everywhere, I stretched my back before starting to get ready. I deserved a break for my research. I deserved a glass of wine.

* * *

I was almost half-an-hour early. Needing to kill time, I walked to a small bookstore in the same plaza as the wine bar. I could use something new to read this upcoming weekend.

You mean something to add to your never-ending TBR pile. I whisper to myself, thinking of the last time I sat down to read for fun.

The bell above the door chimed as I stepped inside, trading the sharp evening air for the warm scent of paper and coffee. A new bookstore—my favorite kind of refuge. For a moment, I closed my eyes and let the quiet sink in, a cathedral made of books.

I drifted toward the fiction shelves, fingers trailing spines, when a sound caught me—soft singing, a lullaby threaded with something that felt older than the store itself. Drawn to it, I rounded a corner and nearly tripped over the source.

A young woman sat at a table in the back, a guitar resting against her knees. She looked up, her smile quick and knowing, her dark curls catching the lamplight.

"Hi there," she said, her voice like honey. "Did you like my song?"

"I did," I admitted, steadying myself. Her golden eyes sparkled behind oversized glasses, warm and unsettling all at once.

"I'm Calliope," she said, as if that explained everything. "Come, have some coffee. You look like you need it."

I hesitated, glancing at my watch. Less than thirty minutes until I needed to meet Eloise, but somehow I didn't want to leave. "Maybe just a quick one."

She brought two cups from behind the counter, handing me one without asking. "Almond milk and honey syrup."

I blinked. "How did you—?"

She waved it off, the silver ring on her finger catching the light. A tiny lyre gleamed in its setting. "Old trick from somewhere I used to live a long time ago."

Something about the way she said it made the hairs rise on my neck, but her smile softened the unease. We sipped, and she spoke of books, of her sisters who were all writers, singers, performers. I listened, lulled by the cadence of her voice, until a text pinged on my watch:

ELOISE: *OMW, 5 minutes.*

I scrambled for my wallet. "What do I owe you?"

Calliope shook her head. "Don't be silly. Stories should always be shared freely."

I stepped out into the cool evening air, the taste of honey lingering on my tongue and Calliope's words echoing in my head: *Stories should always be shared freely.* I thought of my dissertation, of the women whose stories had been buried, rewritten, or silenced. Maybe that was what drew me to them so fiercely—the sense that their voices had been locked away, waiting for someone to set them free.

Shaking off the thought, I headed toward the glow of the wine bar next door, telling myself I needed a drink, not another metaphor.

The wine bar was dim and humming with low jazz, its shelves lined with bottles that gleamed like stained glass in the candlelight. I slid onto a stool, still carrying the sweetness of Calliope's coffee with me.

The bartender caught my eye immediately. His dark curls framed a smile both mischievous and knowing, and his shirt—bold leopard print, unbuttoned just enough to show tanned skin—looked like it belonged to someone who had never once cared about a dress code. When he reached for a glass, his sleeve rode up, revealing a tattoo curling along his forearm: a staff entwined with ivy and tipped with a pinecone. It looked familiar, but I just couldn't quite place it.

I tilted my head. "That's unusual. What is it?"

He flexed his wrist, making the ink ripple. "Old symbol," he said easily, offering no explanation. "For fun."

Before I could press, he leaned on the counter, eyes glinting. "So, what'll it be?"

"I'm a white wine girl," I said, smiling faintly. "Surprise me."

His grin widened, conspiratorial. He vanished down the bar, then returned with a glass that caught the golden light.

"Moschofilero," he said, lingering on the syllables like they were sacred. "Bright, crisp, Greek. A wine that doesn't behave." He winked as he set it before me. "Tell me what you think."

I took a sip. The flavor bloomed—spice and sunlight, wildflowers after rain. "It's... alive," I said, surprised at my own word choice.

"Exactly." He leaned closer, lowering his voice. "Wine should be alive. Otherwise, what's the point?"

Someone called him from the far end of the bar. He slipped away in a whirl of leopard print and laughter, leaving me with the glass, the music, and the uncanny sense I'd just brushed against something far stranger than a charming bartender.

I swirled the wine in my glass, thinking of his words. Alive. My dissertation felt anything but alive—footnotes and frameworks, neat boxes for voices that had never fit neatly into anything. Maybe that's what I was missing. Maybe rage and grief didn't belong in the margins; maybe they belonged in the text itself.

Eloise swept through the door a moment later in her signature pink jacket, her presence pulling me back into the ordinary. I raised my glass to her, but part of me still felt that wild, effervescent hum in my veins.

"Cass!" She hugged me tight. "I've missed you."

"I'm just happy you're here."

She slid onto the stool next to me. Eloise grinned. "Okay, big news.

I downloaded a dating app this morning. *Love Connection.* Already got matches."

I raised an eyebrow. "El, you're braver than I am."

"You should try it," she teased, scrolling through her phone. "You spend all your time in libraries. This way, you might meet someone under fifty."

I laughed, nearly choking on my wine. "You know how well it went with Aiden."

"Ugh, Aiden." She made a gagging face. "Still, please don't hide forever. You've got to live outside those dusty books of yours. You're always telling your students about voices being silenced—what about your own?"

Her words stung in a way she didn't mean them to. I lifted my glass, hiding behind a smile. "Maybe I'll stick to fictional men. At least they don't interrupt my writing."

We both laughed, but her comment echoed longer than I wanted it to.

Even though Eloise and I talked for hours, I couldn't help but think about the bookstore. I felt a sense of connection with Calliope that I had only experienced with one other person, which unnerved me. Shaking my head as if to reset my thoughts and focus, I raised my glass, and we clinked them together in a toast. "στην η για μας," I toasted. "To our health!"

* * *

The morning sun peeked through my curtains, painting my duvet gold. I groaned when I realized I was still in last night's clothes. How much wine had El and I drank? My head throbbed, my throat dry enough to drink Lake Tarpon dry. No time for self-pity, though—today was a teaching day. A classroom full of students was waiting for me to lead them through mythology.

"Morning comes whether we want it or not," I muttered, sounding more like my mother with every passing year, dragging myself upright. Normally, these early hours were my favorite—the quiet before the world woke, the whispers of the past still clinging to the air. But today, I dreaded it.

By the time I crossed campus, the college town had shaken itself awake:

students rushing, professors murmuring, the whole place humming with ideas. Stepping into my classroom, I felt that familiar pulse of pride, even through the haze of my hangover.

"Good morning, everyone," I said, setting my bag down and forcing a smile. "Today we continue with the silenced women in myth—the ones whose voices are lost in the roar of their male counterparts."

A murmur of anticipation rippled across the room. Eyes lit with curiosity.

"Let's start with Athena," I said, and notebooks flew open. As we talked about her contradictions—warrior, strategist, goddess of wisdom, yet complicit in silencing other women—I felt my own energy rising, my headache fading.

When the discussion deepened, I sat cross-legged on the desk. "Remember—the societies that created these myths reflected their values. And those values meant women's voices were often pushed to the shadows."

A hand shot up from the back, belonging to a young woman with sharp eyes. "Professor Bennett, do you think… if we had preserved more of these women's stories, the world would be different today? Maybe women wouldn't have struggled for so long to be heard?"

Her question stopped me cold. I'd asked myself the same thing a hundred times alone, but hearing it here, from her, hit differently.

"I'd like to think so," I said carefully. "Maybe suffrage would've come sooner. Or maybe we wouldn't have needed it at all—because women would have been treated as equals from the start. After all, women make up half the population. Imagine how much history we've lost by ignoring half the voices."

The class nodded, pens scratching, and I pressed on. "When we give voice to these women now, we aren't just reclaiming their stories. We're reshaping our world. We're filling in the silence."

From the back of the room, I hear "Professor Bennett, you sound like Cassandra herself sometimes—always warning us to listen."

The class chuckles. I forced a smile, playing along.

"Hopefully, without the part where no one believes me," I said, trying to make it a joke. But inside, the words caught in my throat.

By the end of the session, I was swept up in the rhythm of it—questions, answers, sparks of insight flying across the room. For a little while, hope burned brighter than doubt. Maybe what I was doing mattered. Maybe it could change something.

That hope clung to me long after class. As the sun dipped low and I walked home along the narrow streets, I thought of the lesson again, tangled with my own memories. Growing up, I had always felt like the mythical Cassandra—the girl who spoke up, only to be brushed aside. The only sister in a house of brothers, my warnings, my questions, my dreams were always laughed off or ignored. That bitter taste of being unheard had driven me here, into these myths. Studying those women—Cassandra, Briseis, countless others—was my way of giving them the voice I'd always wanted for myself.

My phone buzzed as I walked home, and without checking, I answered.

"Hey, Cassie!" Nik's voice burst through the line, warm and boyish, like he was trying too hard to sound carefree.

I sighed. "Hi, Nik. What's up?"

"Just wanted to check in on my favorite sister."

"I'm your only sister." My tone came out sharper than I intended.

He laughed it off. "Theo says you're still buried in that dissertation. He told me to tell you not to forget to eat sometimes."

Of course, Theo had said that. Theo, the responsible one, the steady one. The one who carried the family business like it was destiny. He always looked out for me, but it felt more like patrolling the walls than standing beside me.

"Yeah, I'm working," I said flatly.

Nik shifted, his voice softening. "You know, Cass…I-we're proud of you. Even if we don't really get half of what you're doing."

The words landed like they always did—meant as comfort, received as dismissal.

I bit my lip, the tired argument rising in my throat. "It matters, Nik. These women matter. Their voices—"

He cut me off with a teasing laugh. "There she goes again, our little

Cassandra, warning the world. Just don't expect us mere mortals to keep up."

It was a joke, but it stung anyway. If only he knew how close he was to the truth.

"Thanks, Nik," I murmured instead.

"Anyway, I've gotta run. Don't work yourself sick. Love you."

The line clicked off before I could answer. I stood there in the twilight, phone heavy in my hand, throat tight with everything unsaid.

That was always the way of it.

I may have been speaking, but I was never really being heard.

2

Cassandra

Ancient Troy

Princess Cassandra moved like a shadow through the marble halls of Troy. The mosaics beneath her feet sang of heroes and gods, but their stories mocked her with their permanence. Statues of deities loomed above, silent witnesses to her restless spirit.

Cassandra's vibrant auburn hair flowed behind her, a wild river of defiance in stark contrast to the orderliness of her surroundings. At twenty-three, Princess Cassandra was considered by many to be the most beautiful maiden in all of Troy. Her long hair cascaded down her back like a raging fire, and her eyes were as green and fierce as the Aegean during a storm. She knew that beauty was not everything. Despite her royal birth, she struggled against the societal expectations that were placed upon her. Every rustle of silk against marble reminded her of the shackles that bound her to her role as a princess. Cassandra longed for freedom, for a life outside the palace walls where she could make choices and follow her dreams. However, a woman at her station saw such desires as unacceptable.

As she walked through the halls, Cassandra's mind raced with thoughts of escape. She couldn't help but envy the birds that flew freely through the sky above Troy. Societal norms or expectations did not confine them; they could soar wherever their wings took them. But despite these feelings,

Cassandra knew she had a duty to fulfill as a princess. She was expected to marry into a powerful family and help secure alliances for Troy. It was a fate that she had been resigned to since birth, but it weighed heavily on her soul. As she reached the end of the hall, Cassandra paused before an ornate window overlooking the city below. The sun was setting over Troy, casting golden light over its ancient structures. Her heart swelled with conflicting emotions - love for her home and people and an unrelenting desire for something more. With a deep sigh, Cassandra turned away from the window and continued her duties as a princess. But deep within her heart burned a fire that refused to be extinguished - fueled by dreams of freedom and adventure beyond the palace walls.

As the eldest daughter of King Priam, she was constantly overshadowed by her brothers. Those brothers were great warriors and princes. She longed for their strength and charm but felt a deep emptiness. She could only watch as her brothers' destinies were whispered about while hers remained a mystery. But the princess was blessed with an innate wisdom that defied her royal lineage. Every movement within the majestic Palace was calculated as a delicate balance between her true self and the persona prescribed by society. Deep within, a knowingness simmered, waiting for its moment to shine.

The pull towards the outside world grew more robust with each heartbeat, urging her towards the sanctuary where she found solace from the burdens of her solitude. With a glance back at the towering columns that held up the legacy of her people, Cassandra made her decision. It was time to seek the serenity of Athena's Temple, the sacred place where whispers of the future could momentarily quiet and where she could be Cassandra—not a princess, nor a pawn of fate, but a woman yearning to unfurl the wings of her spirit.

The marbled floors of the Trojan palace echoed with the soft patter of Cassandra's footsteps, a silent testament to her restlessness. She moved with grace, each step a quiet rebellion against the unseen chains of expectation that bound her. The walls, adorned with frescoes of gods and heroes, watched over her, whispering tales of bravery and fate through their timeless gaze.

Paris appeared, his form emerging from the shadowed archway like an ill omen. His gait bore the arrogance of a prince who had never tasted the bitter gall of humility. "Cassandra," he addressed her with a dismissive wave, his voice carrying the iron weight of authority and expectation.

"Brother," she began, her words laced with a plea for understanding, "there are matters of strategy we must discuss. I think—" But Paris cut her off with a curt gesture as if swatting away a bothersome fly.

"*You* think?" Paris scoffed, his lips curling into a smirk that did not reach his eyes. "Spare me your womanly fancies, Cassandra. Strategy is a man's concern. Attend to your loom and leave war to us warriors."

The words struck, familiar as a bruise. Her jaw tightened, the flame in her green eyes now kindling with ire.

At the edge of the chamber, Aeneas, son of Anchises, shifted slightly, his dark gaze flicking toward Cassandra. He said nothing, offered no defense, but the weight of his silence felt different from the others' dismissal—an acknowledgment, quiet and unspoken.

"Very well, brother," she replied, quieting the storm within her with Herculean effort. "I shall tend to my 'fancies,' as you so kindly said."

Paris offered no further words, turning on his heel and striding away with the unearned confidence of one who has never faced genuine opposition. The princess allowed herself a moment of raw frustration as the distance between them grew. With his quick decisions and swift actions, Paris often mistook recklessness for bravery and impulse for intuition. Paris was a storm that knew no reins, a ship sailing blissfully towards hidden rocks beneath the dark sea.

As she wandered through the empty hallway, save for her ever-present guards, Cassandra felt lost and uncertain. She longed for some insight or guidance, but her mind seemed to be clouded by uncertainty. A sense of purposelessness weighed heavily on her. She had no special abilities or knowledge to give her an advantage in this world, and her voice held no sway among those in power. Her dreams were just that—distant, unattainable dreams.

She turned her steps toward Athena's Temple, the one sanctuary where her restless thoughts might quiet. Past courtyards and gardens, past guards who shadowed her without question, she walked until the oak doors of the shrine stood before her.

Carved owls and olive branches caught the dying light. She traced them with her fingertips before pushing the doors open. Inside, stillness reigned. The goddess in bronze armor towered above offerings of honey cakes and incense, her gaze eternal and unyielding.

Cassandra knelt at the altar, her eyes closed, her voice a whisper:

"O gray-eyed Athena, grant me strength to walk the path the Fates have set before me. Let not my thoughts be shackles, but weapons of wisdom."

Here, in the goddess's embrace, the mask of princess and pawn fell away. For a moment, she was simply Cassandra—seeker, dreamer, a woman aching to be heard.

* * *

King Priam found her there at twilight, sitting beneath the olive trees. Her hair glowed like fire in the fading sun.

He watched her in silence, a mixture of pride and sadness welling up within him. Cassandra had always been a source of wonder and concern, as one always is with daughters. Cassandra must have sensed someone was watching her, so she opened her eyes and caught sight of her father. Her eyes widened in astonishment, and she gave him a broad grin as she stood.

"Ah, Cassandra," he said, opening his arms. His voice was fond, his embrace tender. She was his favorite, though he never said so aloud. He caressed her hair, staring into her face that was so much like his own. "I was looking for you. I had a feeling I could find you here."

"Pappá," Cassandra replied, smiling softly. "I trust your meeting went well?"

Cassandra met with her father each afternoon after he met with advisors and other city officials. As always, she was not permitted in the council chamber, but he told her what was discussed, as if secrecy might soften the exclusion. Together they walked back through Troy's streets in silence, guards trailing like shadows. It wasn't a long walk from the Temple to the Palace, but the silence was imperative–neither wanted to share any secrets outside the Palace walls. When they reached their home, Cassandra focused on the intricate carvings that adorned the walls. It was a beautiful place, but more like a prison to her. Her father guided her towards the King's private chambers in silence. She was anxious about her future and her place at court. She wasn't sure she wanted to get married off to some wealthy lord, but couldn't quite find the words to express that anxiety to her father.

"Cassandra, my dear," her father said, interrupting her thoughts. "What is on your mind?"

Cassandra sighed. "Sometimes…sometimes, I wish to see the world beyond these city walls. There is so much more than duty and alliance. I want to know it."

Priam placed an arm around her shoulders, the weight of his crown in every word. "Someday, perhaps. But for now, be content. Few are born to such privilege."

The comfort stifled. She bit her lip, knowing he meant well, yet hearing only the echo of dismissal. Frustrated, Cassandra made a mental note to revisit the Temple of Athena the following day. The gray-eyed goddess of wisdom could help her on this journey.

Cassandra's thoughts turned to the future of Troy. She had been having troubling dreams lately, seeing the city engulfed in flames and its people slaughtered. She tried to push the images from her mind, but they kept returning, haunting her.

"Cassandra, is everything alright?" her father asked, noticing the troubled look on her face.

"I…I don't know," she stammered. Cassandra took a moment to gather her thoughts.

"I have been dreaming," she confessed as they neared his chamber doors. Her voice dropped. "Dreams of Troy burning. Of slaughter. Of ruin."

Stopping at the entrance of his chambers, King Priam looked into the face of his daughter. He was a tall man with copper hair and light eyes. Looking at Cassandra, with her identical hair and eyes, comforted King Priam. Unlike his eldest sons, Hector and Paris, who shared their mother's dark features, Cassandra was the most like him in both coloring and personality. He admired her strength and intelligence. It was one of the reasons for their daily walks.

Priam paused, his eyes soft with fatherly love. He stroked her hair, a mirror of his own. "Do not trouble yourself with nightmares. Troy will endure. It always has, and it always will."

His reassurance should have soothed her. Instead, it deepened the ache. Once again, she had spoken — and once again, no one believed.

3

Cassie

As I approached the grand, ivy-covered building the next day, my chest tightened with each step. The faces of my colleagues flashed through my mind–mostly men, all brilliant scholars in their own right. But how many of them understood the weight of the stories we studied? How many could comprehend the depth of the silenced voices that haunted our texts?

"'Sandra," a deep voice pulled me from my thoughts.

I turned to see Aiden Rhodes, a fellow doctoral candidate whose passion for mythology matched my own and, unfortunately, my ex-boyfriend. With his tousled hair, his eyes held a glimmer of excitement. Internally, I groaned.

"Are you ready for the big meeting?" he asked, stepping beside me.

"Ready as I'll ever be," I replied, trying to sound confident despite the growing knot in my stomach.

Aiden and I started grad school together several years ago—both brand-new doctoral students interested in mythology and the classics. We formed a friendship that quickly turned romantic. It had ended on absolutely terrible terms, but we had to work in the same department. But I avoided him as much as I could.

"I never realized you were capable of such in-depth research on a topic like women's voices in mythology, 'Sandra." His words sounded nice, but they were laced with ire. He placed a reassuring hand on my shoulder. I immediately shook it off. "Good for you for finally stepping outside of your comfort zone."

"Please don't call me that," I asked for the thousandth time. "God, you're the worst. How did we date for so long?"

He chose to ignore me. So I continued, knowing what buttons to push. "At least Thomas doesn't sneer when I mention mythological women. He runs numbers all day and still manages to treat people with more grace than half this department."

If looks could kill, I would have been burned at the stake. Aiden hated Thomas Sinclair. They had been best friends and roommates all through undergrad, then something happened in grad school that turned friendship into rivalry.

"Funny, I don't see him around," Aiden muttered, his jaw tight.

"He's presenting to the finance department today," I shot back. "Unlike some people, he's too busy doing actual work to loiter and insult."

"You mean crunching numbers for grants," Aiden sneered. "That's not scholarship, that's bookkeeping."

"Numbers keep this place running," a calm baritone cut in behind us. I turned just in time to see Thomas himself pushing through the main doors, tall, neatly dressed, his expression cool but firm. He didn't look at Aiden—he looked at me. "Good morning, Cassie. Ready for battle?"

Relief loosened something in my chest. "Trying to be."

Thomas gave a small nod, then flicked his eyes toward Aiden, his voice level. "Funny thing about scholarship—it falls apart when you start dismissing whole categories of voices. Ignoring women in myth is like ignoring half the data set. Any first-year knows better."

Aiden's mouth opened and closed, but no comeback came. He turned away, laptop hugged to his chest like a shield.

Thomas looked at me then, steady and unflinching. "Good luck today, Cassie. You've got this."

Before I could thank him, he disappeared into the throng of faculty offices. But his words lingered, quiet ballast against the storm brewing beside me.

I took a deep breath, drawing in the crisp autumn air as if it could steady my nerves. My thoughts drifted to the women who had inspired this journey – those who had defied convention and demanded their voices be heard, even when the world refused to listen. Women like Cassandra of Troy, whose prophetic visions were both a curse and a rallying call for change.

"Alright," I whispered, steeling myself for the challenge ahead. "Let's do this."

As we walked into the meeting room, I straightened my spine, summoning every ounce of courage I possessed. For these women, their stories, and the generations yet to come, I would make sure their voices would never be silenced again.

The classroom was a battleground where ancient echoes met modern voices, and I sat at its center, armed with nothing but my conviction. As we waited for our dissertation chair to meet us, Aiden and I tried to have a civil discussion about our chosen topics. Our weekly group mentoring session was the only time I had to interact with Aiden (among other doctoral candidates). I dreaded these meetings.

Aiden tapped his pen against his notebook, his laptop still closed, then leaned forward with that smug half-smile I knew too well.

"I still don't get why you chose to focus on women's voices," he said, unpromoted. His need to be the dominant voice, to fill up space, filled me with dread.

I didn't look up from my own laptop screen. I slowly picked up a pen, ready to take notes or doodle in the margins. "You don't have to get it, Aiden. It's between me and Dr. Hawthorne."

He chuckled, low and sharp. "People have to get it, Cassie. That's the whole point of research."

I finally met his eyes, pen pointed like a weapon. "*You* don't have to get it. My work is about reclaiming silenced women. That matters, whether you approve or not."

He pushed his laptop open with exaggerated calm. "And yet Graves already argued Cassandra's curse was just a metaphor. Symbols, not history. If I cite that on the committee floor, whose side do you think they'll take?"

Heat rose on my neck, but I steadied my voice. Of course. Graves. His shield, his excuse, his neat little escape hatch. "Graves wasn't working from primary texts. If you bothered to read Stesichorus or Lycophron, you'd see that Cassandra isn't a metaphor. She's consistently treated as a truth-teller, yet ignored. That's cultural memory, not symbol."

God, he talks like he's auditioning for the director's cut of *300*. I thought to myself.

For a second, his smirk cracked. He scribbled something down, jaw tight. I recognized that old tell—he hated being challenged, hated being reminded he wasn't as untouchable as he pretended.

"Bias," he muttered. "You're letting your feelings cloud the work."

I forced a smile. "Funny, I could say the same thing. If every woman's voice is dismissed as hysterical or allegorical, maybe the bias isn't mine."

A ripple of laughter moved across the seminar table. Someone smothered a grin behind their hand. For once, it wasn't me shrinking in my seat. Instinctively, my fingers curled into fists beneath the table. How could he not see? The air in the room grew heavy with tension.

Before Aiden could recover, the door swung open, cutting the tension like a blade. Dr. Hawthorne swept inside, her heels clicking like a metronome against the tile. She moved with the kind of precision that made the whole room straighten instinctively. Her sharp gray eyes scanned the table, lingering on me a moment longer than I liked.

"Well," she said, setting a neat stack of papers on the table, "a lively start. Miss Bennett, passionate as always." Her voice was cool, controlled, and deliberate. "But passion without discipline is a fire that burns itself out. Anchor your arguments to evidence and strategy, or they will scatter like smoke."

"Mr. Rhodes," she turned to Aiden, her tone even edged with something formidable, "your perspective seems rather limited. Would you discount the influence of women like Penelope, whose fidelity and cunning were as crucial to The Odyssey as any of her husband's exploits?"

Aiden opened his mouth and closed it, visibly taken aback by her intervention. Dr. Hawthorne's gaze held him in place, unyielding and sharp as Athena's spear. I could almost feel the ground shift beneath us, the room charged with electricity that seemed to crackle in the space between her words.

"Miss Bennett has raised an important point about representation and value in historical narratives. We must not forget that our understanding of these myths is colored by those who have told them—and those who were silenced. To ignore half the population is to see only half the picture."

I absorbed her words, letting them strengthen my resolve. Unknowingly or not, Dr. Hawthorne had just championed my cause, validating the countless hours I'd poured over scrolls and texts, seeking the whispers of those long-muted voices.

"Thank you, Dr. Hawthorne," I said, giving her a grateful glance. "The thread of women's experiences runs deep through the tapestry of history. To pull it out would unravel the very essence of our past."

"Indeed, Miss Bennett," she replied, nodding slightly, her eyes reflecting the wisdom of ages. And it is our duty as scholars to weave these threads back into the narrative, to restore the full richness of the story." She then launched into our regular meeting cadence, deftly changing the subject and avoiding all-out war.

As the session drew to a close, I pondered the irony of our discourse. We were debating the significance of ancient women's voices while I struggled to make mine heard. But with Dr. Hawthorne's support, the tide may be turning. Perhaps the time had come for these forgotten stories to emerge from the shadows.

As the last rays of sunlight faded from the room, leaving us in the gentle embrace of evening, I felt an ember of hope ignite within me. With renewed determination, I vowed to champion the voices of the past, knowing that their echoes would resonate far beyond the confines of this seminar room.

* * *

The hum of my laptop seemed to mock me as I sat on the worn couch of my tiny apartment, the cursor blinking relentlessly on the screen like a heartbeat. The words of my dissertation, once vivid and sure, now blurred before my eyes, tainted by Aiden's venomous doubt. With each echo of his disdain, the voices I sought to amplify in my work seemed to fade into silence, swallowed by the chasm of academia's indifference.

"Is this really how you want to be remembered, Cassie?" he had sneered, his past words echoing in my head. *"Peddling stories about forgotten women to an audience that doesn't care?"*

I could change it.

It would be easier, I thought to myself. I could focus on a more minor, more popular topic. Something about Loki or Hermes? I do like the trickster stories.

I looked around at the stacks of books and notes around my apartment. Years of research and tears were strewn about. I had felt confident after Dr. Hawthorne's interruption and her confidence in my work.

But.

My mind betrayed me.

But.

Aiden may be right.

I let my head fall backward momentarily, willing the female voices to return to my head.

When they didn't, I reached for the mouse, trembling as the erasure specter loomed over me. I could delete it all—every word, every reference, every footnote—obliterate years of research in one fell swoop. A cold sweat broke across my forehead as my hand hovered over the delete key, and my breath came in short, sharp gasps. In that moment of despair, I was Cassandra, screaming prophecies into the void, unheard and unheeded.

"Hey, hey, easy there."

I startled, but only for a moment. It was always like this with her. Diana had been appearing in my life at impossible moments since high school, as if she carried some sixth sense tuned only to me. I didn't question it anymore.

"Di...?" I stammered, trying to steady my breathing. "How did you..."

She pressed a glass of water into my hand, curling my fingers around it. "Drink. Then we'll talk." I obeyed, the cool glass shocking me back into my body. Her presence filled the small apartment like a shield.

"Your 'something is wrong' vibe is pretty loud," she said with a gentle smile, closing the door behind her. She crossed the room in a few strides, her presence instantly grounding.

"Talk to me. What's going on? Why were you about to send your magnum opus to the digital underworld?" Her tone was light and her dark hair caught the lamplight, a glint of silver threading through..

"What if I fail them?" I asked, the fear of inadequacy gnawing at my resolve. "What if I can't make their stories resonate in today's world?"

"Then you'll try again," she said. "You'll rework, revise, and re-imagine until you do. But you won't give up. You can't. Because you, Cassandra Bennett, are the fiercest advocate those women have ever had."

Her words renewed something within me—a spark of defiance against the shadows of doubt. The panic constricted my chest and began to ebb away, replaced by a slow, simmering determination.

"It was Aiden, wasn't it?" Diana said, arranging the couch pillows. "He said something."

I looked over at my best friend. Her dark eyes bore into my soul - it was like she could sense when I needed her the most.

"Yep." My lips formed a tight smile.

A moment passed, and I couldn't look her in the eyes.

"But... but what if Aiden's right?" I admitted, my voice a mere whisper. "Who wants to read about the silenced women of mythology? "

"Stop right there," Diana interjected, her voice firm yet soothing. She took my hands in hers, her grip both warm and reassuring. "Aiden is an egotistical jerk who wouldn't know the importance if it hit him in the face with a lightning bolt. Your work matters, Cassie. You're giving a voice to those who were voiceless by history."

"Di..."

Diana shook her head. "I could kill him. I could do it with one arrow straight to his cold, black heart."

"Di..."

"I won't," she abruptly got up and walked towards the fridge. Pulling out a bottle of wine, she continued. "But he would deserve it."

I laughed and accepted the glass she handed me. "I don't know why he gets to me so much."

"Um, because he knows how to push your buttons? You dated him for a year and a half. You might have even married him. He's trying to punish you."

She was right. I looked down at my hand, which had once held the ring Aiden had given me (and took back). Its absence was freeing, but he had possessed me so entirely at one time. I looked back up at my friend and gave her a weak smile.

"Thank you," I murmured, squeezing her hands in gratitude. "For reminding me what I'm fighting for."

"Always," she replied with a wink. "Now, take a deep breath, hydrate, and return to those mythic matriarchs waiting for their encore. They've waited centuries—don't make them wait one more night."

I laughed, a sound brittle with lingering anxiety, but the echo of resilience lay underneath it. The cursor still blinked expectantly on my screen, but now it didn't seem quite so menacing. It was a beacon, guiding me back to my chosen path—one where every keystroke was a declaration that these stories would not be lost to time.

"Alright, let's do this," I said, more to myself than to Diana. "For Cassandra and all the others whose truths deserve to be heard."

As Diana settled into the armchair with a book, her silent support a pillar of strength, I returned to my dissertation. Amidst the ancient myths and scholarly discourse, I began to weave the threads of forgotten voices back into the fabric of our collective memory.

* * *

The stillness of the apartment wrapped around me as Diana's presence receded, the soft click of the closing door punctuating our conversation. The silence was no longer oppressive but seemed to hold space for contemplation. I wandered over to the window, watching how the moonlight cast silver filigree patterns across the floor, as ancient as the myths that pulsed at the heart of my work.

I had always sought harmony to avoid the storm of conflict. Yet in Aiden's dismissive words, I heard the clash of swords, the cries of the unheard—a siren call to battle I could no longer ignore. No, I would not be the quiet scholar nodding to the rhythm of outdated beliefs. Aiden was a modern-day Paris, convinced of his prowess, unaware of the Achilles' heel in his argument—his blatant disregard for the potency of feminine narratives.

My fingers curled into fists at my sides. "You don't get to do this," I whispered into the darkness, a vow made to myself more than anyone else. "You don't get to make me feel small." With all her foresight and wisdom, Cassandra had her voice smothered beneath layers of patriarchal interpretation. But I would not let that be the end of her tale—or mine.

* * *

I must have drifted off at some point, because suddenly I was running through streets that weren't mine — stone walls, fire in the air, voices crying out in terror. The air smelled of smoke and honey, sweet and choking.

A shadow surged out of the flames, hand outstretched. When I grabbed it, the skin burned away to ash in my palm.

I woke gasping, tangled in my sheets, my chest heaving like I'd run miles. The clock glowed 3:17 a.m.

Without thinking, I reached for my phone and dialed Diana, but it went straight to voicemail.

"It's me," I whispered into the dark. "I just…needed to hear your voice."

The line clicked off, leaving me alone with the silence. For a long time, I sat there, phone heavy in my hand, wondering if she had been here at all.

* * *

I must have fallen back asleep. My sheets were discarded on the floor, and my hair was a rat's nest. From the kitchen, I could hear Diana prepping coffee and doughnuts. It was our tradition. When one of us called asking for help or advice, the other showed up with coffee and doughnuts as a kind of offering, a symbol of comfort and friendship.

Diana listened carefully as I recounted the details of my nightmare. She could tell I was genuinely shaken, and I felt thankful for my friend.

"I know it's just a dream, but it felt so real," I said, trembling slightly. "I don't know what to do with it."

Diana put a comforting hand on my leg. "I think you're reading too much into it," she said. "Dreams are just our subconscious minds trying to make sense of things. It doesn't mean anything."

I nodded but still couldn't shake off the feeling of unease. "But it was so vivid," I said. "I can still feel the flames, the chaos. It felt like a warning, like something bad was going to happen."

Diana smiled reassuringly. "Come on, Cass. You're just stressing yourself out. You're just worried about your dissertation and that asshole, Aiden, and it's coming out in your dreams. It doesn't mean you have some psychic ability."

My heart sank at the thought. Diana was my closest friend, but she didn't understand what it was like to have nightmares that felt more than dreams. I felt a sense of isolation, a sense of being trapped in my mind.

"I know you mean well, Di," I said softly. "But I can't help how I feel. Maybe it is just a dream, but I have this gut feeling there's something more to it."

Diana sighed. "Okay, I get it. But you can't let this control you. You can't let it take over your life."

I nodded, but I knew that it was easier said than done. I had always been a little anxious and a little neurotic, and I knew it would be tough to let it go. But Diana was right; I couldn't dwell on it. And I could try not to, at least for her.

"Thanks," I said, forcing a smile and sipping my coffee. "I appreciate it."

Diana's silver arrow necklace twinkled in the morning sun. "Anytime. Just don't let this consume you, okay? You're stronger than you think."

With one last hug—and a promise of Friday Night Happy Hour—Diana left my apartment, leaving me to my vivid dream but comforted by the fact that the brain is a strange thing, and it was probably nothing.

It was nothing.

Right?

4

Cassandra

Ancient Troy

The fire in Priam's war room guttered low, throwing long, jagged shadows across the table where maps, scrolls, and tablets lay scattered like offerings to strategy itself. Resin smoked in the bronze braziers, the sharp scent stinging Cassandra's eyes, but she did not blink. She stood at the edge of the table, hands folded tightly in front of her, a lone figure among men and their measures.

"Pappá," she said at last, her voice steady though her heart thundered. "I fear for Troy. The walls must be fortified, the watch doubled. Encroaching danger gathers at our borders. I have seen it."

Her words rang too loud in the chamber, swallowed by the crackle of flames. Priam raised his gaze, his face worn with years of rule, his expression one of both affection and exhaustion.

"Cassandra," he said gently, "I do not dismiss your fears. But you must trust that all is being done to safeguard our city. Your brothers and I labor day and night. We cannot live by omens and shadows."

Before she could answer, the heavy oak door groaned open. Hector entered with his soldier's stride, Paris trailing behind, his cloak half-draped, eyes already narrowed in disdain.

"Father. Sister," Hector greeted warmly, his presence filling the chamber like a steady flame. He bent over the table, studying the spread of maps.

"Let us consider every possibility."

"Indeed," Priam said, gesturing to both sons. "All measures must be weighed for Troy's defense."

Cassandra's heart quickened. Here was her moment.

"Then hear me," she said, voice sharpened by urgency. "I have seen danger. Our gates are strong, but not enough. The watch must be doubled, the rivers guarded. Darkness draws near—"

"Ha!" Paris's laugh cut her off, sharp as a knife. "Your fancies again, little sister? Dreams and shadows? This is no place for women's imaginings. The city is defended by men, not by the mutterings of a maiden."

"Paris," Priam warned, his brow furrowed, though the tone was indulgent, not stern.

"Our sister's counsel is not without weight," Hector interjected, his voice calm but firm. He placed a hand upon Cassandra's shoulder, a shield against Paris's scorn. "We cannot afford blindness."

Paris sneered, folding his arms across his chest. "And if the city learns their king listens to a woman's fears? They will riot in the streets. She is no Athena, Father. She is a daughter to be married off. Nothing more."

The words struck harder than any spear. Cassandra turned to Priam, searching his face for defense, for belief. But his shoulders sagged under the weight of crown and council. His eyes softened with sorrow — and fell away.

"Just go, Cassandra," he said. And then he turned his back.

The dismissal cut deeper than Paris's venom.

Moonlight bathed the courtyard in silver as she fled into the night, her sandals whispering across the marble. The cool air stung her face, but anger burned hotter beneath her skin. Her fists clenched until her nails bit into her palms, blood pricking her flesh.

"Cassie."

The voice stilled her. She turned. Hector approached, steady as ever, the only one who dared call her by that name.

She tried to mask her tears, but the moon betrayed her. "That was fun, wasn't it?" she said bitterly.

He sighed, settling beside her on the marble steps. For a moment, silence stretched between them, filled by the distant hum of Troy alive at night — merchants closing stalls, children's laughter echoing faintly from alleys, the rhythm of a city that believed itself eternal.

"Paris is a fool," Hector said at last.

"Paris spoke what Father dared not."

Hector studied her, his eyes soft with love but shadowed with sorrow. "Your counsel was wise. You see clearly. But the city will never follow a woman's warning. Perhaps… it is time Father found you a husband. With alliances come safety."

Her heart cracked anew. "Not you too, Hector."

"I will guard you always. That I swear," he said, placing his hand gently upon her hair. For a moment, he lingered, then rose, his tall form cutting a solemn figure against the torchlit palace. And then he was gone, leaving her in the silver silence.

Her tears came freely now, falling into her lap, dark spots upon her green chiton. Above, an owl called, its cry sharp and lonely. She lifted her gaze to the walls of Troy, proud and impenetrable — and thought how easily stone could crack.

* * *

At dawn, Cassandra walked the streets of Troy, her thoughts heavy as the stones beneath her sandals. The city gleamed around her, every detail carved with pride: the towering gates plated in bronze, the markets alive with voices, temples crowned with statues. Children darted between stalls, laughter spilling like water. To any other eye, the city was eternal.

But to Cassandra, it all felt fragile. Balanced upon the edge of a blade.

The Temple of Athena loomed before her, its bronze doors gleaming in the rising sun. Columns soared skyward, their friezes alive with painted scenes of the goddess's victories. Her heart ached to enter, yet fear gripped her chest. She longed for Athena's wisdom, yet dread rooted her feet.

At last, she forced herself inside. The air was cool, hushed, filled with the faint scent of incense and olive oil. Shadows danced across frescoes of war and wisdom. The goddess loomed at the heart of it, carved in marble and bronze, helm gleaming, spear raised, gaze unyielding.

Cassandra fell to her knees at the altar, the stone cold beneath her skin.

"O gray-eyed goddess," she whispered, voice trembling, "hear me. My words fall to dust. My father turns his face away, and my brothers mock me. What am I to do? Show me my path."

The air shifted. The torches guttered. Cassandra's skin prickled, as though the marble itself had drawn breath.

When she raised her eyes, an old woman stood beside her. Her face was lined with age, but her gaze was storm-gray, sharp as a blade's edge.

"Child," the woman said, her voice low and resonant, carrying weight far beyond her frame. "You are troubled by shadows of what may be. The future is always uncertain. But strength is not. Wisdom is not. Be clever. Be steadfast. The gods walk beside you, even in darkness."

The words sank into her bones, as heavy as prophecy. Cassandra bowed her head, trembling. Was this mortal comfort, or the goddess herself cloaked in mortal guise?

When she lifted her eyes again, the woman was gone. Only the goddess remained, unblinking, eternal.

5

Cassie

Present Day

The dream clung to me like smoke.

All week I couldn't shake it: flames licking marble walls, bronze doors buckling under heat, people running as the city burned. The air had been thick with ash and honey, sweet and choking. I tried to run, tried to scream a warning, but my feet rooted to the ground. When I woke, the screaming still echoed in my throat.

It was only a dream, I told myself. But the dread settled deep in my chest, stubborn as stone.

Usually, I liked the rhythms of my job — lesson prep, grading, the careful weaving of stories into syllabi. Today I was going through the motions, staring at the cursor on my laptop until the clock reminded me I'd lost an hour. I needed to snap out of it. I had a class to teach.

Today was my virtual class. As part of my teaching assignment, I was required to hold one lecture a week online. The faces appeared one by one on Zoom, little windows into dorm rooms and kitchens. My mythology students settled in, half with coffee mugs in hand, the other half still wrapped in blankets. I shared the screen, The Iliad staring back at us in all its blood and bronze.

"Think of Cassandra," I told them. "She knows the truth — but no one listens. What happens to a society when it silences its prophets? It's women?"

A few brows furrowed. Pens moved across the bottom of screens. One blank stare. The question hung in the digital silence.

I pushed them through the text, my voice trembling at first but steadying as I sank into it. The words felt alive, echoing through the room with an urgency that wasn't just mine. My students leaned in. For a moment, it was as if the walls of Troy weren't a story but a warning.

As the discussion deepened, I couldn't shake the feeling that there was something more going on. The words of the ancient text seemed to echo with a certain urgency, as if they were trying to convey a message beyond the surface level of the story. It was as if the tale of the Trojan War held secrets that were meant to be unraveled, secrets that could hold significance for not just my students, but for me as well.

Lost in these thoughts, I eventually noticed that one student in particular, Sarah, was silently observing me. Her eyes bore into mine with an intensity that sent a shiver down my spine. There was something about her gaze that felt familiar, as if she held a knowledge beyond her years.

After I wrapped up the lesson and assigned homework, Sarah lingered on the Zoom call.

"Professor Bennett?" she began in a soft voice.

After a pause, she continued. "I've been doing some research on my own, trying to uncover any hidden symbolism or messages within the story," she said. "And I think I might be onto something."

My interest piqued, I motioned for her to continue.

"Well," Sarah began, her voice gaining strength, "there are theories that suggest the Trojan War was not just a historical event but also an allegory for inner conflict and the battle between one's desires and responsibilities."

"Go on," I urged.

She took a deep breath and continued, her words flowing with a newfound excitement.

"These theories propose that the characters and events in *The Iliad* represent different aspects of human psychology. For example, Achilles may symbolize our own internal struggles with pride and ego, while Hector represents our sense of duty and honor. And the war itself becomes a metaphor for the battles we face within ourselves."

"I think you're onto something, Sarah," I said, connecting the dots in my own mind. "There's a complexity to this text that goes far beyond what we've traditionally understood. It's like the story is a mirror, reflecting our own struggles and emotions at us."

Sarah's eyes gleamed with excitement as she absorbed my words. "Yes! And if we can unravel these hidden meanings, maybe we can unlock something within ourselves."

"Professor Bennett," she said, her voice low. "Do you ever feel like these stories are more than stories?"

I almost laughed, but something in her gaze pinned me. "Every day," I admitted.

Her lips curved, not quite a smile. "Then you understand." And the call clicked away, leaving me staring at my own reflection in the blank screen.

After the lecture ended, I sat alone in my living room, the weight of the dream still heavy on my mind. The scent of old books and the soft glow of lamplight filled the room, creating an atmosphere that seemed both comforting and eerie.

I picked up a worn copy of The Iliad from my coffee table and flipped through its pages, my fingers tracing the faded words. As I read, fragments of the dream resurfaced in my mind, intertwining with the ancient tale unfolding before me.

The burning city, the desperate cries for help—I couldn't shake the feeling that it could be more than just a simple nightmare. What if it held a deeper significance, a connection to the stories I had immersed myself in since childhood?

I needed a break from the landscape around me, so I decided to grab my laptop and walk to the closest cafe. Caffeine always helped me ground myself.

I was so focused on the dream I had last night and my upcoming lesson plans that I didn't even notice that I was on a collision course with another person. Neither of us was apparently paying attention, and we collided on the sidewalk, his papers flying all around us. I ended up flat on my ass.

"Whoa, sorry about that," the man said, flashing me a smile that made my heart skip a beat.

I couldn't help but stare at him. He was tall, with short blonde hair and bright blue eyes. Dressed in a black leather jacket, he radiated charm and attractiveness.

"It's fine," I said, trying to gather my papers and stand back up all at once. It wasn't graceful. "I wasn't paying attention."

The man chuckled and offered his hand to help me stand up. "I know the feeling. I can get lost in my own thoughts from time to time."

"I am so sorry for running into you. Are you hurt?" I asked, shoving my planner and various papers back in my bag.

"No. I am perfectly fine. Are you?"

"Just a bruised ego. I should let you go," I went to turn away, eager to hide my flushed face.

That's alright," He held out a hand. "I'm Apollo, by the way."

"Apollo, like the god?" I asked, "Were your parents hippies, or maybe huge fans of Greek mythology.

I slapped my hand over my mouth, embarrassed at what I had just said.

"It's a long story," he said with a smile. "I'm sure you have one about your name that you haven't said."

"Cassie," I said, still staring at him. "Cassandra"

Apollo flashed me another smile. "Nice to meet you."

"My mother is Greek," I blurted out.

The corners of his eyes crinkled as he said, "Mine, too."

My brain had fully stopped working. I was a terrible flirt.

He's not flirting, you dummy. He's being nice. You almost ran him over.

"Well, I should probably get going," I said. "It was nice meeting you, Apollo."

"You too, Cassandra," he said, still smiling.

As I walked away, I couldn't help but feel like there was something different about him. He seemed almost... otherworldly.

But I shook the thought off. It was probably just my imagination running wild after the nightmare I had the night before.

I walked into the cozy corner cafe, my eyes scanning the room to check for an open table in one of the corners. I knew I'd need to be there for a few hours, so I wanted to make sure I was not in the way of anyone. Luckily, I had been coming to this cafe for a while and had found a "favorite" table, which was thankfully empty.

I walked up to the barista, ordered my tea, and paid. I made my way to "my" table and set up my laptop, planner, pens, and the rest of my space to work for a couple of hours.

Pulling up my courses, I crafted a plan of attack for my few hours outside, just as the kind barista delivered my tea. I decided that focusing on my new mythology course should take precedent, as I could teach English 101 in my sleep.

But when I looked up, Apollo was there again, striding through the door as if he had always belonged. He moved with a kind of grace that seemed practiced and effortless all at once. His presence drew eyes — including mine.

As I gazed at him, it was impossible not to be struck by his presence. He stood tall and broad-shouldered, his physique hinting at a life of physical activity and fitness. His hair was light and tousled, falling just so over his forehead in a way that seemed effortless and yet perfectly styled. His eyes were a deep, piercing blue, the kind that seemed to see right through you. But it wasn't just his looks that drew me in. It was the way he carried himself - with a confidence and grace that was both captivating and intimidating. He moved with a fluidity that hinted at a lifetime of discipline and training, and there was an intensity in his gaze that made it impossible to look away.

"Cassie," he said, smiling when he spotted me. "Mind if I join?"

I hesitated. Then nodded.

He sat across from me, filling the space like he owned it. Conversation came easily — too easily. He asked about my work, my classes, and my favorite texts. He listened, really listened, his gaze fixed in an almost unnerving way.

By the time he leaned back in his chair and said, "Friday. Dinner," I'd already agreed without realizing it. He left me his number, his smile lingering like sunlight long after he walked away.

I realized that my tea had gone cold, and I went to the counter to ask for a cup of ice, but the very sweet barista had already made a second, hot cup. So I made sure to leave him a generous tip for being so kind and thoughtful.

When I sat back down, the whole scene rushed back to my mind. Had I really met a man named Apollo? Had we really sat in this little off-the-beaten-path cafe, and *he asked me out?* It seemed so strange and totally out of character for me.

I reviewed my lesson plan, not remembering what I had written before Apollo walked in the door. But as I flitted back and forth between my gradebook and my emails, I couldn't focus. My mind kept drifting back to the unexpected encounter with Apollo. I couldn't believe that I had agreed to go out with him, especially given my reluctance to take risks such as these. I was still on shaky ground after my last relationship ended. Turns out that even smart girls can be tricked by a narcissist with a great smile.

But something about Apollo had drawn me in. It terrified me. That's how it started with Aiden, my ex-boyfriend. I was a sucker for a great smile. I couldn't stop thinking about Apollo, though.

I ordered another tea and a croissant - and tried to focus on my work as I waited for my order. But every time I looked at my laptop screen, all I could think about was Apollo. What would our date be like? Would we have anything else in common? Was I making a mistake by agreeing to go out with him?

Just then, my phone beeped with a new message. I glanced down and saw that it was from Apollo.

> **APOLLO:** *Hey Cassie, looking forward to seeing you on Friday. Can't wait to see what you'll wear.*

My heart fluttered when I saw his name on my screen. I quickly wrote back.

ME: *Oh? Is that right? Maybe I'll just show up in my PJs and you'll have to like it.*

APOLLO: You could wear a burlap sack and you'd be breathtaking.

ME: Well...then you're just going to have to wait and see.

As I hit send, I realized that I was smiling from ear to ear. Maybe this was exactly the kind of adventure I needed in my life. Maybe taking a chance on someone like Apollo was exactly what I needed to break out of my comfort zone and start living a little. Aiden be damned.

Later that day, I paced around my apartment, my phone clutched tightly in my hand. I knew I had to call Diana and tell her about the date I had agreed to go on with Apollo, but I couldn't help feeling a bit apprehensive about how she would react.

Taking a deep breath, I dialed Diana's number and waited anxiously for her to pick up.

"Hey," she answered, with warmth in her voice. "You okay? You sound... off."

"I met someone," I blurted. "Apollo."

Silence. A long one. Then: "Apollo," she repeated, flat and careful.

"Yeah. He asked me out. I said yes."

Another pause. Then her voice softened. "Don't let him think he owns you."

I laughed nervously. "It's just a date."

"With Apollo," she said again, almost to herself.

"Di?"

Her tone brightened, almost too quickly. "I'm happy for you, Cass. Really. You deserve this. Just—be careful."

I hung up, unease prickling at my skin.

6

Cassandra

Ancient Troy

The needle pierced the fabric with a soft hiss, again and again. Cassandra sat cross-legged on the floor, thread pooling in her lap, while her mother worked deftly upon a half-finished panel of lilies. The chamber was quiet, save for the rhythm of their stitching. To Cassandra, it felt like a cage.

"Mother," she asked lightly, though her eyes burned with restlessness, "what do you think my future holds?"

Hecuba's hands stilled. "Your future, my daughter, is a husband. You are nearly of age. Suitors wait at the gates."

"Not this again," Cassandra groaned, tossing her embroidery aside.

Hecuba frowned, her voice tightening. "Do not be ungrateful. A princess's duty is to bind her family to strength. Marriage is your path."

Cassandra lowered her gaze, heart still raw from the council chamber. Paris's sneers echoed in her ears, her father's silence heavier still. "And if I do not wish to marry at all?" she whispered.

Hecuba leaned closer, her shadow falling over Cassandra. "Then you deny your place in the order of things. You are not Athena. You are not free of duty. Beauty and wit are gifts the gods have given you — use them to honor your house, not to defy it."

"I was not given my voice to sew it into pillows," Cassandra murmured, but Hecuba heard and scowled.

"Be careful, child. Cleverness can be a curse for a woman. Follow your heart if you must — but remember, the gods punish those who stray too far."

Looking back up at her mother, Cassandra's smile faltered. She needed to make sure her voice was heard, even if it meant angering her mother. "But...I feel like I'm meant to do something more. Something important."

Hecuba sat down next to Cassandra on the stone floor. "Your father and I have already received offers from several noble families."

Cassandra stood up and paced around the room, trying to decide if *maybe* her mother was right. She did have a duty to her family and her kingdom, but she also knew that she couldn't deny her own desires and dreams. She resolved to find a way to balance both, but for now, she remained unsure of what that would look like.

Hecuba sighed again. "I understand your feelings, Cassandra, but you must also understand that as a princess, you have certain duties to our kingdom and to our family. Please, think about this carefully."

Cassandra nodded, but her mind was elsewhere. She was always restless, always longing for something more. As she gazed out at the gardens, she suddenly had a feeling of unease, as though something ominous was on the horizon.

"Mother, do you ever worry about the future?" Cassandra asked suddenly.

Hecuba looked at her daughter, surprised by the sudden change in subject. "Of course, my dear. The future is always uncertain."

"But do you ever feel like...like you can see things that other people can't? Like you know what's going to happen?"

Hecuba frowned, sensing the undercurrent of anxiety in her daughter's words. "What do you mean, Cassandra?"

"I don't know, it's just...Sometimes, I feel like I can sense things, like a feeling that won't go away. I can't explain it."

Hecuba put down her own sewing and took her daughter's hand. "Cassandra, you mustn't worry about such things. The future is in the hands of the gods. We can only live each day as it comes, and trust that they will guide us in the right direction."

Cassandra bent her head again, thread trembling in her hands. But her thoughts were already outside, roaming the gardens, drawn to a presence she could not name.

* * *

The next morning, Cassandra summoned her guards. "Take me to Apollo's temple," she said, her chin lifted in defiance of her own unease.

The captain exchanged a glance with another guard, sizing up the young princess before them. Cassandra was known for sneaking out of the palace on her own, and they were confused by her request. But they could not deny the princess's request, and so they acquiesced.

"Of course, Your Highness," Stratokles, captain of the guard, studied her as though weighing her intent. "You have until the sun reaches its peak. If you do not emerge, I will come for you myself."

The streets of Troy bustled with life — the smell of bread from the ovens, the call of merchants, the press of sandals on stone. Cassandra longed to lose herself in the crowd, but her heart pulled her upward, toward the shining temple that crowned the hill.

As they approached the temple, Cassandra could feel her heart beating faster with anticipation. There was something about this temple that excited Cassandra. It was one of the many reasons why she had avoided it on her own.

"Leave me here," Cassandra turned to her guards. "I wish to pray alone and make my offering in solitude."

The two guards looked at Cassandra with suspicion.

"I will come back out, I promise. I'm here to pray, not sneak away."

The Temple of Apollo rose before her in gold and white marble, its columns bathed in morning light. Inside, the air was heavy with incense, thick with song. Priests chanted, their voices weaving like smoke, their eyes sliding past her as though she were air.

Cassandra approached the altar, her offering of honey and wine trembling in her hands. "O Phoebus Apollo," she whispered, "hear me. I am torn between paths. My words are scorned. My dreams burn me. Show me what I must do."

Silence. The priests' song blurred. The god's bronze likeness loomed, impassive. Cassandra laughed bitterly, setting her jar of honey upon the altar. "What did I expect? That you would step down from Olympus and answer me like a lover?"

Cassandra left her offering of honey and wine on the altar. With one last look at the large golden statue, Cassandra turned and exited the temple.

But something stopped her. She turned back towards the altar.

Cassandra's gaze shifted to the statue. It was grand and imposing, with a stern expression etched upon its stone face.

And a voice — soft, melodic, wrapping round her like smoke — breathed her name.

"Cassandra."

She froze.

The priests were gone. The chant had ceased. Shadows lengthened across the columns, and from them stepped a figure crowned in laurel, his eyes alight with a radiance not of men.

"Cassandra," the figure repeated, his voice like a gentle breeze on a summer night.

Cassandra's breath caught in her throat as she stared at the mysterious figure before her. The air in the temple seemed to thicken, crackling with an otherworldly energy that sent shivers down her spine. Her hand instinctively reached for the ornate dagger she kept hidden beneath her robes, but something held her back.

Fear mingled with curiosity in her eyes as she studied the figure stepping out of the shadows. He was tall, his features obscured by the cloak that clung to him like a second skin. A crown of laurel adorned his head, marking him as no ordinary mortal.

"Who are you?" Cassandra whispered, her voice trembling slightly.

The figure stepped towards the gardens, his ethereal gaze never leaving hers. He said nothing.

Cassandra stepped forward, trying to catch up to the man who was walking away from her. "I ask you one again, in the name of my father, King Priam. Who are you?"

When they reached the gardens, under the shade of a laurel tree, the man finally spoke. "I am Apollo."

A gasp escaped Cassandra's lips as recognition dawned on her. Apollo, the god of prophecy and music, stood before her in all his splendor. She had prayed to him countless times, seeking guidance and understanding in her visions. And now, he was here, in the flesh.

"But… how?" Cassandra stammered, unable to fully comprehend the situation unfolding before her.

Apollo's lips curved into a gentle smile as he reached out a hand, beckoning her to come closer. "I have heard your prayers, Cassandra. I have seen the torment that plagues your soul."

Cassandra's heart raced with a mixture of excitement and trepidation. She had always believed that the gods could hear their prayers, that they could hear humanity's every plea. There was also a part of her that thought it was all made up to make humans believe in something bigger than themselves.

Tentatively, she stepped forward, her eyes never leaving his radiant face. Apollo's presence was warm and comforting as he placed his hand on her forehead, and in that moment, Cassandra felt a surge of energy flow through her. Visions flashed before her eyes, like fragments of a puzzle falling into place. She saw the destruction of her beloved city, Troy, the flames engulfing the towering walls, and the cries of its people echoing in her ears. She saw the faces of her loved ones, their fates intertwined with the tragedy that awaited them.

But amidst the chaos and despair, Cassandra also saw glimmers of hope. She saw a path, narrow and treacherous, leading towards a different future. A future where Troy might be saved, where lives might be spared. The weight of this knowledge settled heavily on her shoulders, but Cassandra knew she couldn't ignore it.

As Apollo removed his hand from her forehead, Cassandra's legs gave way beneath her, and she sank to the ground. Overwhelmed by the power of his touch, she trembled with a mixture of awe and fear.

"I will see you again, Cassandra," he murmured, and when she blinked, he was gone. Only the bronze statue remained, its eyes unyielding, the altar flickering with dying light.

7

Cassie

Present Day

Friday.

Date night.

I stood in front of the mirror, tugging at the hem of my green dress like it might change its mind about fitting me. My one "date look." Cheap Amazon find, tiny flowers, simple gold jewelry. Brown sandals. Freshly curled hair that had taken three hours of pleading with my curling iron.

"You clean up nice," I muttered to my reflection, trying to drown out the chorus of What ifs pounding through my head. What if I said something stupid? What if he didn't like me? What if he was secretly married? What if I sneezed and mascara ran down my face? The mind of an overthinker is a funhouse mirror.

The doubt kept creeping in, whispering in my ear, tempting me to cancel, to stay safe within my comfort zone. I hadn't been on a first date in a really long time. The last date I went on was a blind date that had me sneaking out the back door of the bar. It was so bad. Have you ever seen a grown man throw a temper tantrum because the server brought a vinaigrette salad dressing and not oil and vinegar? Because I have, and it's not attractive.

My phone buzzed. *Diana.*

DIANA: *You've got this, Cass! Remember — he's just as nervous as you are. Have fun. I'm rooting for you.*

I smiled. Trust Diana to sound like a coach before battle. Maybe she was right. Maybe this was just a date.

I whispered to the mirror, "I am brave. I am capable. I am deserving of love." Silly, but I needed it.

As the cab approached the restaurant, Apollo was waiting outside the restaurant, golden under the streetlight. I took one more deep breath, channeling all my courage, and stepped out of the cab. In that moment, I chose to embrace the unknown, to let go of the fear that had held me back for far too long.

"Cassandra," he said warmly. The way he said my name made my stomach flip.

Inside, the restaurant was dim and humming with low conversation. We sat across from one another, a candle between us. My pulse still hadn't slowed.

"So, Cassandra," he said, leaning in, "tell me about yourself."

I blushed, absurdly aware of how his gaze pinned me. "I love reading. Photography. Exploring new places. And..." I hesitated, embarrassed. "I have this...obsession with mythology."

His mouth curved, amused. "Mythology? That's not strange. That's destiny."

I laughed nervously. "Destiny?"

He tilted his glass, eyes never leaving mine. "You and I were bound to meet."

The words should have felt romantic. Instead, they vibrated with something heavier, as though he meant it literally.

The conversation flowed — books, music, travel. He asked questions, listened intently, his focus so total it was intoxicating and unnerving. His hand brushed mine across the table, warm and lingering.

"Which myths draw you most?" he asked.

I hesitated, then smiled. "Cassandra. My namesake."

His eyes gleamed. "The prophetess who spoke truth and was never believed. Fitting, isn't it?"

A chill rippled through me. "I suppose so."

He leaned closer, offering his hand, his voice dropping. "Maybe together, we can break curses."

He said it playfully, but when his thumb traced circles on my palm like he was writing it into me. A strange shiver passed through me — not just the normal butterflies of a first date, but something sharper, almost like static. For the briefest instant, I thought I saw torches flicker against a stone wall, shadows moving. I blinked hard, and it was gone.

Apollo's thumb brushed mine as if he hadn't noticed anything unusual.

Hours blurred. The restaurant emptied. Outside, the wind tangled my hair, and Apollo tucked a strand gently behind my ear.

"Dinner again?" he asked, already certain of the answer.

"Yes," I said before I'd even thought about it.

His hand found mine, fingers intertwining as though they'd always belonged there.

By the time the cab slowed to a stop in front of the restaurant, I was giddy, glowing, restless with questions. He kissed my cheek — lingering, soft — and whispered, "Goodnight, Cassie."

My knees felt weak as I whispered back. "Goodnight."

From the backseat of the cab, I checked my phone and saw a text from Diana:

DIANA: *Text me when you're done - I'll be up waiting, so just show up. I want a full debrief, and I have wine.*

My best friend. She always knew what to do.

"Can I change the address?" I asked the cabbie, and at his nod, I gave him the cross streets to Diana's apartment.

She opened the door in sweats, the glow of *Friends* reruns flickering behind her. Wineglass in hand, she raised an eyebrow. "Well, well. Dirty. Rotten. Stay out. Someone's radiant. Tell me everything."

I collapsed onto her couch, words tumbling out — the nerves, the dinner, the connection I couldn't explain. Diana listened, sipping, her eyes sharp even as she smiled.

"It sounds like you had an amazing time," she said finally. "But Cass…" She tilted her head, studying me. "You feel something different, don't you?"

I hesitated. "Yes. He's…charming. Intense. There's something about him I can't put my finger on. Like…like he's more than he seems."

For a flicker, her expression hardened, though her voice stayed light. "Mysterious men rarely bring peace."

"Di…" I laughed, but uneasily. "You sound like my mother."

She smirked, lifting her glass. "Someone has to. Just—be careful. Don't let him own your story."

Her words settled over me, oddly heavy. But she clinked her glass against mine before I could dwell on it. "To first dates. To mystery. And to not marry narcissists with vinaigrette tantrums."

I laughed until tears pricked my eyes. With Diana beside me, the night felt less like a curse and more like a possibility.

8

Cassandra

Ancient Troy

Apollo's touch still burned on her skin as she walked through Troy. The city lived and breathed around her — merchants crying their wares, bronze flashing like fire in the sun, the scent of roasted figs curling through the air. Children darted between stalls, their laughter piercing, too bright. Cassandra moved among them as through a dream, untethered from the noise and color, as though the world had tilted and left her standing on its edge.

Every sound felt sharpened; every shadow carried meaning. In the flicker of a torch, she saw ships on a dark horizon. In a child's cry, she heard the echo of mourning yet to come.

She did not notice the soldiers until their bronze shadows cut across her path.

"Princess," one said, bowing. "Your father summons you. He awaits in his chamber."

Her pulse quickened. The prophecy pressed like a stone behind her ribs. She followed them through narrow halls that smelled of smoke and cedar, her sandals whispering over the marble floor.

The king's chamber glowed in muted gold. Priam stood by the window, sunlight etching the lines of care into his face. He turned when she entered, his eyes softening.

"Pappá," Cassandra said, bowing low. "You wished to see me?"

He regarded her for a long moment before speaking. "Cassandra. It is time we speak of your future."

Her stomach tightened. "My future?"

"It is time for a husband. Our dynasty must be secured."

The words struck her like a thrown spear. Cassandra lifted her chin. "Pappá, I know my duty. But I cannot marry. Not yet. My path lies elsewhere."

Priam's sigh was heavy, like wind through old cypress. "You speak of paths and destinies," he said. "But I am king as well as father. The council whispers already — they ask why my daughter speaks in councils meant for men, why she lingers in temples, why she shuns every suitor sent from noble houses."

"I do not ask them to understand," Cassandra said quietly. "Only you."

Priam's eyes searched hers. For a moment she saw compassion — and fear. "You are dearer to me than any jewel of Troy," he said. "But the gods gave men order, and kings must heed it. If you speak too boldly, if you reject too much, the people will turn."

Cassandra's throat ached. "Then let them," she whispered. "Let me stay. Let me guard Troy as I can. I will not be sent away to warm another prince's hall while this city burns."

Priam's jaw tightened; his hand trembled before it stilled upon hers. "Daughter," he said, voice breaking, "love is not a shield strong enough. I cannot always protect you from the weight of men's scorn."

She bowed her head, tears blurring the light between them. When she looked up again, his face was the face of a king, not a father.

That night, sleep would not come. The air in her chamber felt close, suffocating with unspoken fate. She rose and wrapped her cloak around her shoulders, slipping from the palace like a ghost.

The streets were hushed now. Torches guttered low, their smoke twisting into thin, dark ribbons. She passed the empty markets, the still fountains, the sleeping lions carved in stone. Each step drew her upward toward the high temple of Athena, where marble gleamed beneath a blood-colored moon.

Inside, the silence was vast. The scent of oil and myrrh hung in the air, ancient and unyielding. Cassandra moved through the columns until she stood before the goddess — towering in marble, spear raised, eyes carved in unblinking gray.

Cassandra knelt at the altar, her hands trembling.

"Bright-eyed one," she whispered. "Help me. Apollo has touched me. He has filled me with visions I cannot bear. I do not know if it is a gift or a curse. Show me how to wield it. Show me how to endure."

No answer came. Only the low murmur of the wind slipping through the temple's stones.

Cassandra bowed lower, despair pressing her into the cold marble. Then — the faint rustle of wings.

An owl descended upon the altar, feathers catching the torchlight like fragments of bronze. Its golden eyes fixed on her, piercing and eternal. It did not move, did not blink — only *watched*.

The air stirred. Warmth brushed her cheek, carrying the scent of olive leaves. She felt it then — a gaze vast and ancient, resting upon her unseen.

Cassandra pressed her palm to the altar's stone. "I understand," she whispered.

The owl gave a low, resonant hoot . It was not meant as comfort, but command. Then it spread its wings and vanished into the dark.

Cassandra rose, the fire in her veins cooled, tempered. Apollo had given her flame — too bright to bear. Athena had given her silence — cool and sharp as forged steel. Between the two, she would endure.

And somewhere beyond the city walls, in the night that waited, the faintest tremor of prophecy stirred the air.

9

Cassie

Present Day

The Zoom classroom buzzed with chatter as my students logged in, little squares popping up one by one. I adjusted my headset, my reflection staring back from the corner of my screen. Hair pulled back, lipstick barely holding on. Not exactly the picture of confidence.

But the real distraction wasn't my lipstick.

It had been three days since the date with Apollo. Apollo. Even thinking his name made me want to laugh — or shiver. Dinner, laughter, the way his gaze had seemed to burn straight through me. I kept telling myself it was just a first date, but I hadn't been able to stop replaying it. And I hadn't heard from him since.

I shoved the thought aside. Tonight's lesson was one of my favorites.

"Alright," I began, smiling into the screen, "today we're talking about one of the most fascinating myths in Greek mythology — the story of Apollo and Python."

Slides flickered beside me: an image of Delphi, golden light over mountains.

"In ancient times, Delphi was sacred ground," I explained. "It was home to the Oracle — a woman who spoke with the voice of Apollo himself. Kings, generals, farmers — they all came to hear her riddles, hoping for answers."

The words were practiced, but something in my chest tightened as I spoke them. I thought of my dream — fire and screams, my voice trapped in my throat. Would anyone listen if I warned them?

Shaking it off, I clicked to the next slide. "But Delphi was not unguarded. A monstrous serpent, Python, coiled through the sanctuary, keeping mortals away. Until Apollo came."

I paused for effect. My students leaned in.

"He was the god of music, of healing, of prophecy — but also of archery. And he had fire in his veins. He would not be stopped."

As I spoke, my mind wandered — to the man across the table in a dim restaurant, smiling as he said my name. Destiny. That was what he'd called it.

When I focused back on the small Zoom boxes on the screen, I noticed that my students listened with rapt attention, their imaginations ignited by the story of gods and monsters. Unfortunately, my mind continued to wander, my thoughts intertwining with the ancient myth I was narrating.

"In the end," I concluded, "Apollo's triumph over Python solidified his role as the god of prophecy. The Oracle of Delphi became his mouthpiece, and her prophecies were sought by people from all corners of the ancient world."

As I finished discussing the myth of Apollo and Python, and my students had absorbed the tale, it was time for questions.

A virtual hand shot up on the screen. I called on Sarah, whose dark eyes always seemed too intent.

"Professor Bennett," she asked, "what exactly did the Oracle do? How did she give prophecy?"

I smiled. "Good question. She sat in a chamber beneath the temple, where sweet-smelling vapors rose from the earth. She'd breathe them in, slip into a trance, and speak riddles. Words tangled, half nonsense, half divine."

Sarah's eyes widened with intrigue. "So, did the vapor somehow help her see the future?"

I nodded. "It's believed that the fumes may have induced a trance-like state, allowing the Oracle to commune with the divine."

"So..." another student piped up, "she was high?"

The class broke into laughter. I let myself laugh, too. "Yes, there's a historical belief the Oracle of Delphi was in an 'altered state of consciousness'—which is the polite academic way of saying she was basically hotboxing the temple. During this altered state, the Oracle would speak in riddles and cryptic phrases, often in response to questions posed by those seeking guidance. However, the exact nature of the vapor and its effects on the Oracle remain a subject of historical debate. Either way, she spoke, and people listened."

I hesitated, staring into the camera at my own reflection. People listened. The irony wasn't lost on me.

Another student asked if the Oracle was always right.

"Not always," I admitted. "Her words were often cryptic, easy to twist. But kings still built empires on them. They wanted to believe."

A third student added, "And what happened if someone didn't like the Oracle's answer?"

I almost added: Sometimes truth itself isn't enough. Sometimes, no one believes you, no matter what you see. But I bit my tongue.

"There were times when the prophecies were met with skepticism or disbelief. People might consult other oracles or seek alternative answers. But overall, the Oracle of Delphi held immense sway in the ancient world, and her prophecies were highly respected."

The students continued to engage in the discussion, asking questions and sharing their thoughts. I found myself drawn into the conversation, my connection to the subject matter deepening with each query. As we explored the intricacies of the Oracle of Delphi, I couldn't help but wonder if my own encounters with the world held a connection to the ancient myths I so passionately taught.

When class ended, I lingered in the empty Zoom room, staring at the silent squares. My students logged off; I was left with my own face. Alone. Again.

I needed to get out.

* * *

Diana and I met at a bar down the street, the kind with music-you-can't-quite-place humming low and shadows in the corners. She was already waiting in a booth, wine in hand, dark hair spilling over her shoulder.

"Well," she said as I slid in beside her. "That's a face."

I laughed weakly. "It's nothing."

"Nothing named Apollo?" she teased.

I groaned. "Three days. No text, no call. And yes, I caved — I sent the 'had a great time' message. Nothing back."

Diana's expression shifted, sharp beneath her smile. "So he disappears. Mysterious."

"Mysterious doesn't cover it." I toyed with my glass. "Di, there's something about him. Like he's more than just…" I faltered, embarrassed. "More than just a guy."

She arched her brow. "You're letting mythology bleed into your dating life again."

"Maybe," I said. But her hand covered mine, warm and grounding.

"Listen. You deserve someone who sees you. Really sees you. Don't romanticize shadows."

Her words should have soothed me. Instead, unease pooled low in my stomach.

We changed the subject, both needing to lighten the mood. So we filled it with laughter, speculation, and a sense of camaraderie that only best friends could share. As I sipped my wine and Diana offered words of encouragement, my nerves lingered in the background

* * *

That night, I curled up on my couch with a book, the city lights glowing through the window. My phone buzzed. I leapt before I could stop myself.

I picked it up eagerly, and his name lit up the screen—Apollo.

"Hello?" My voice was too quick, too eager.

"Cassandra," His voice, smooth and melodic as ever, poured through the phone. "It's Apollo."

As if I could forget.

Relief flooded me. "It's good to hear from you."

"I apologize," he said, tone low, threaded with regret. "I've been... preoccupied. Family matters."

A vague excuse. But acceptable. It had, after all, been only a first date.

"I wondered if I'd hear from you," I admitted. "Our date... it left an impression."

There was a pause on the other end of the line, as if he was carefully choosing his words. "I feel the same. Our connection is...rare."

My heart skipped a beat.

Apollo's voice grew warmer, more sincere. "I'd love to see you again, Cassandra, if you're willing. How about dinner this weekend?"

My heart hammered in my chest, and I wondered if he could hear it. "Yes. I would love that."

He chuckled softly, almost possessively. "Good. And this time, I won't keep you waiting."

The call ended, but his voice lingered. I set the phone down, staring at it. Was this the beginning of something extraordinary — or a warning?

Outside, the city pulsed with neon. Inside, I traced my finger across the book in my lap, the words of prophecy staring back at me.

The Oracle spoke in riddles no one could ignore.

And I couldn't ignore the feeling that my life had just stepped into one.

10

Cassandra

Ancient Troy

The morning sun poured gold over Troy, catching on the marble columns of distant temples. From her chamber window Cassandra watched the city shimmer, every rooftop blazing like a votive flame. Her gaze fixed on Hera's sanctuary — stately, solemn — yet her heart tugged elsewhere. Some invisible thread drew tight in her chest, pulling her toward another god entirely.

Helenus found her lingering at the gates. A scroll hung forgotten in his hand. "Sister?" he said, tilting his head. "You look as though you're listening for something."

"I am," she admitted softly. "Something calls me. At first I thought it was Hera. But now..." Her voice trailed into the wind. "No. It is Apollo."

Helenus's brow furrowed. "Apollo. Cassandra—be careful. You know what Father would say. What Mother would say."

She laughed suddenly, almost wildly, the sound ringing off the stone. "Perhaps. Yet my heart beats like a drum, and I must follow it."

He stepped closer, steadying her shoulders. "Always chasing omens," he murmured, but affection threaded his voice. "If you are determined, I will not let you go alone."

Relief softened her eyes. "Then come. Perhaps the god calls for you as well."

Among the guards who trailed them, Cassandra noticed Aeneas walking a half-step apart, his face half-lit beneath the morning sun. When she laughed again — light, disbelieving — she caught the faintest quirk of his mouth, as though he'd understood a secret meant only for her.

* * *

Inside the sanctuary, golden light filtered through bronze doors, laying ribbons of brilliance across the marble floor. The air hung thick with incense and beeswax. Each breath tasted of devotion and decay.

"I'll leave you for a moment," Helenus said softly. "You need solitude. And so do I."

Cassandra touched his sleeve, gratitude glimmering through her nerves, and moved deeper into the temple.

The statue of Apollo rose before her — beautiful, terrible, and still. The sculptor had caught him mid-motion, bow lowered, the faintest suggestion of a smile carved at his lips. But in the angled light his stone eyes seemed alive, as though the god himself looked out through them.

She knelt and pressed her palms to the cold altar. "Lord Apollo," she whispered, voice trembling, "you have drawn me here. If you have words for me, I am listening."

At first, there was only silence — the kind that hums rather than fades, thick as breath in the throat. Then came a shift, subtle but immense, as though the air itself bent around her.

The scent of laurel filled the chamber. Gold light shimmered where none had been.

A voice brushed her ear, warm as sunlight and just as dangerous. "Seeker of guidance..." it murmured. "I have been waiting."

Her eyes flew open. From behind the statue, a man stepped into view. His hair glowed like molten metal; his skin gleamed with the warmth of dawn. He moved as if the air parted for him.

"Hello, Cassandra." His voice was melody and command entwined. "You returned."

Her breath caught. "Apollo."

He smiled — a smile that promised knowledge and ruin in equal measure. "I have watched you," he said, approaching. "Your mind is quick, your spirit restless. The world would bind you with thread and silence, but I would set you free. I hear you, Cassandra. I have always heard you."

Her heart hammered. "Why me?"

"Because you are unlike the rest. Fire burns in you. Truth spills from your lips even when no one wishes to hear. That fire is mine to cherish, and that truth —" he leaned closer, eyes gleaming like molten amber — "is mine to guide."

His nearness was intoxicating — sunlight made flesh, pressing warmth against her skin. And yet beneath the radiance was something vast and cold, like the hollow silence after lightning strikes.

"You feel it, don't you?" he murmured. "The bond between us. You belong to me, as Delphi belongs, as prophecy itself belongs. Come to me again — tomorrow, at sunset, by the sacred olive beyond the city walls."

Her pulse stumbled. "Outside Troy?"

"Yes. There we will speak without interruption. There, I will show you what fate binds us to."

For a moment she hesitated — but the god's eyes burned through doubt. "I will come," she whispered.

His smile curved, slow and triumphant. "Good."

He reached out, fingers brushing her cheek — a touch both tender and searing. Heat surged through her, and in its wake came a vision: fire leaping across Troy's towers, her people screaming beneath a red sky. The temple shuddered.

She gasped and fell back, the world spinning — and when she looked up again, he was gone. Only the statue remained, serene and unyielding, its marble mouth curved in that same inscrutable smile.

* * *

Helenus found her moments later, pale and trembling, one hand still pressed to the altar.

"Sister?" His voice was tentative. "What happened?"

She turned to him, eyes distant, voice a whisper scraped raw. "The god heard me," she said. "That is enough."

He frowned, searching her face. "Cassandra…"

But she only shook her head, gaze drifting toward the doors where sunlight spilled across the floor.

"Come," she said quietly. "Let us go."

Together they stepped into the morning. Troy blazed before them, bright and unsuspecting — and somewhere behind her ribs, the god's warmth still lingered like a secret brand.

11

Cassie

Present Day

I'm halfway through my first (okay, third) cup of coffee and five tabs into JSTOR when the second email lands—this time from the department admin—reminding everyone about the pedagogy colloquium at noon. **Guest presenter: Aiden Rhodes. Topic: "Evidence, Elegance, and the Limits of Interpretation."**

I choke on a laugh. Aiden talking about limits is like Zeus hosting a seminar on fidelity.

By eleven-fifty, the conference room smells like burnt coffee and dry-erase marker. Faculty cluster in polite constellations; grad students hover at the edges like satellites hoping someone will notice they exist. I take a seat near the back, notebook open, pen ready, spine straight. Professional. Composed. Unmoved.

Aiden strolls in five minutes late, all corduroy and practiced ease, the kind of handsome that knows it plays. He gives the room a genial sweep, then lets his gaze snag on me for a beat too long. A smile—thin, private—flickers and is gone.

"Thanks for coming," he says, dropping his leather folio on the table with audible gravity. "Today I want to talk about the difference between reading the text and reading ourselves into the text."

A few chuckles. I can feel the sermon building.

He warms up with safe territory: the dangers of anachronism, the seductions of tidy narratives, the way modern agendas can warp ancient evidence. All true in principle. He cites a Victorian philologist for color (of course, he does), then pivots.

"And to that end," Aiden continues, clicking to a slide, "I've included an addendum examining a persistent classroom myth: Cassandra as a silenced prophet in Homer."

My pen pauses.

On the slide: a cropped image of Iliad 24, a line in transliteration highlighted neon yellow. He's already stacked the deck: no mention of the lament structure, no mention of the broader tradition, just a single, isolated line.

Aiden smiles, almost kindly. "The evidence shows that in Homer, Cassandra is not a prophet, not a figure of epistemic violence. She's a mourner—a standard ritual role. Anything else is—" he air-sketches quotation marks "—projection."

I brace my jaw.

He proceeds with the confidence of a man who's never been interrupted. "Students love the Cassandra story where she predicts doom and is ignored. So do some instructors. But in Homer, she doesn't prophesy. Full stop. The 'silencing' narrative is a later accretion—Aeschylus, Euripides, Roman reworkings." He flips to another slide. "Our job is to disentangle the layers, not flatten them."

I stare at the highlighted line. He's not entirely wrong, and that's the problem. Half-truths spoken smoothly are harder to fight than errors.

He keeps going. "I'll go further: importing the latter curse back into Homer is not only sloppy, it's pedagogically dangerous. We train students to read their feelings into the ancient world and call it justice."

A low murmur ripples through the room. I feel my pulse in my throat. Breathe, Cassie.

From the doorway, a soft footfall. Dr. Hawthorne slips in late, as if an owl just ghosted down a branch. Gray eyes, unreadable. She meets my gaze for the briefest moment, a flick of attention that steadies me more than the coffee.

"Questions?" Aiden asks finally, palms up in mock humility.

No one moves. I count to three—to keep myself from leaping—and raise my hand.

"Aiden," I say, voice even, "two clarifications and a concern."

A few heads swivel. He smiles that cool, debating-society smile. "By all means."

"First," I say, "your slide isolates Cassandra's lament in *Iliad 24*, but it doesn't mention that she summons the city to grief before Hecuba and Andromache. It's a small thing, but position matters. The text gives her a vocal authority—ritualized, yes, but public. She's not invisible."

A couple of nods. Aiden's smile tightens.

"Second," I continue, "you're right that the explicit curse—to speak truth and not be believed—is later. But your conclusion leaps from 'not present in Homer' to 'irrelevant to Homeric reception.' Students don't encounter *The Iliad* as a sealed artifact. They meet Cassandra braided through Aeschylus, Euripides, Virgil, and Ovid. Teaching responsibly means naming the layers and the braid."

He shifts his weight, and I see it—the faint flash in his eyes when something slides out of his control.

There it is.

"And the concern?" he prompts.

"You cite a nineteenth-century essay to claim that the 'silenced prophet' reading is a modern feminist imposition." I tilt my head. "That essay also calls Cassandra 'hysterical' and suggests her value is in 'catalyzing the hero's arc.' Which is…less philology than pathology. If we're going to appeal to authority, we should interrogate what that authority is doing."

The grad students, may the gods bless them, try and fail to hide their smiles behind coffee cups.

For a beat, the room thrums.

Aiden recovers, genial again. "Important points, 'Sandra." He says my name like a warning. "But rigor has to win over resonance. The lament isn't prophecy. The curse isn't in Homer. Telling students otherwise is storytelling, not scholarship."

"Respectfully," I say, still calm, "the lament is an explicitly gendered form that frames who gets to speak and when. Naming that isn't storytelling; it's context. And ignoring the tradition that made Cassandra emblematic of epistemic violence is, frankly, its own kind of story."

A sound like a sigh moves through the room. Hawthorne's expression doesn't change, but her pen stops moving.

Aiden's jaw ticks. "We'll have to agree to disagree."

"We'll have to agree to read the whole corpus," I say lightly. It lands sharper than I intended. A small, vicious part of me enjoys that.

He closes the laptop with a soft click that feels like a slammed door. "Let's break for lunch."

Chairs scrape. Conversations explode. Someone claps me on the shoulder in passing. "Nice," a colleague whispers. "About time someone said it."

I pack my notebook slowly. My hands are steady. My knees are not.

"Professor Bennett?" a voice murmurs. I turn. It's Sarah—Zoom-square Sarah—in three-dimensional nervousness, clutching a spiral notebook to her chest. "That was…amazing. Sorry, is it okay to say that? I didn't know people talked like that in real life."

I laugh, tension cracking just enough.

Her eyes are bright. "I… there's a reading group? For women in myth? Could I…?"

"Email me," I say, meaning it. "We'll build one if it doesn't exist."

She nods, relief softening her shoulders, and disappears into the crowd.

The seminar room finally emptied, the air still carrying faint traces of the heated tension Aiden had left behind. I was stuffing my notes into my bag when a familiar voice stopped me at the doorway.

"Don't take him too seriously. Aiden's been sharpening that blade since grad school."

I turned to find Thomas Sinclair leaning casually against the frame, arms folded, a small, knowing smile on his face. His suit jacket was a shade too formal for the worn-out lecture hall, but somehow it suited him.

"Thomas," I said, exhaling some of the irritation that had been knotted in my chest. "I'm used to him by now."

"Used to him doesn't mean you should tolerate him." His gaze flicked down the hall where Aiden had disappeared. "Remember that we used to be friends, he and I. Back before his ego started needing its own zip code."

That earned a laugh from me, the first one since class began.

Thomas's smile softened. "I caught part of your argument. You were right, by the way. About the women in those epics."

My heart tightened—not because the words were dramatic, but because they were so rare. Simple validation.

"You actually believe that?" I asked, almost suspicious.

"Believe it?" He shrugged. "I think it's the only way to read them honestly. A story's not just its heroes. It's the scaffolding around them—the voices that hold up the whole damn thing. Without Andromache or Penelope, those men are just noise."

His calm conviction hit me harder than Aiden's barbs ever could.

I studied him for a moment. Finance director. Numbers guy. The kind of man who balanced budgets and faculty squabbles instead of indulging in literary debates. Yet, here he was, giving more respect to my dissertation in thirty seconds than Aiden had in three years.

"Well," I said, trying to sound casual, "I guess that makes you a rare breed around here."

Thomas chuckled. "Don't let Aiden convince you otherwise. Some of us actually listen."

And with that, he offered me a nod—not the condescending kind, but one of solidarity. The kind that lingered long after he walked away.

When I finally look away from Thomas' retreating back, Dr. Hawthorne is ten feet away, regarding me as if I'm a coin she's decided to keep in her pocket. "Walk with me," she says, already turning toward the hallway.

I fall in beside her. She moves like she always knows the shortest path.

"That could have gone poorly," she says, not unkindly.

"I know," I admit. "I tried to stay on the text."

"You did." She glances sideways, something like humor flickering. "Though you showed your spear-point."

"I'll try to blunt it."

"Don't," she says, and it's almost—almost—warm. "Sharpen it. Just learn when to sheathe it."

We reach the end of the hall. She pauses. "Rhodes lost a grant last year. He blames the committee for 'trend-chasing.' He will frame your work as that. Be ready."

"Oh," I say, the information slotting into place like a key into a lock. "So he needs me to be sloppy. It proves his point."

"Exactly." She taps her pen against her palm. "Do your work. Do it cleaner than he does. And, Cassandra—" (I blink at the way she says my name) "—don't let anyone tell you your questions are decoration for someone else's argument."

By the time I can formulate a response, she's already moving away, gray eyes back to their cool weather. I watch her go, a strange heat in my chest.

Back in my office, the adrenaline leaks out of me in a rush that leaves my hands shaking. I set my forehead on the cool wood of the desk and breathe. Professional. Composed. Unmoved. Right.

My phone buzzes. A text from Nik.

NIK: you still alive or did you finally murder someone in that ivory tower

ME: tempting

NIK: lunch? i'm near campus. theo's stuck at the site

ME: can't. faculty sparring match. Tell Theo to hydrate.

NIK: you too, cass. love you. don't let them steamroll you.

ME: they tried. i rolled back.

NIK: that's my girl

I grin despite myself. My brothers, my modern Paris, and Hector, I think, except mine don't die, and they occasionally bring me spanakopita.

The doorframe clicks. I look up. Aiden leans against it like a man in a cologne ad.

"Got a second?" he asks, as if we're friends. Were we ever?

"Busy," I say pleasantly. "But sure."

He steps in, closes the door—of course—and perches on the edge of a chair like a poised hawk. "You blindsided me," he says, still smiling. "In front of the department."

"You added an entire section at 8:02 a.m. and announced a verdict from the podium."

His smile thins. "You're smart, 'Sandra. Genuinely. Which is why it's a shame to watch you sell rigor for rhetoric."

A familiar heat rises up my neck. "I didn't sell anything. I named the frame. If you're going to use a Victorian to police what counts as 'real' in Homer, I'm going to ask who benefits."

He leans back, temple flexing. "This isn't Twitter."

"It's X now. And it's scholarship," I say softly. "Which is why I cited the text and you cited a man who thought hysteria was a diagnosis."

Aiden studies me for a long moment, as if recalibrating. Then, almost gently: "You know the committee chair likes me."

"I like the chair too," I say. "We go to the same yoga class."

He blinks at that, thrown off his axis for a heartbeat. Then the smile returns. "Just… be careful, Bennett. Trendy doesn't last."

He leaves the door open when he goes, which somehow feels more pointed than slamming it. I exhale into the empty room and start typing before the shake comes back: notes for my next class, a list of sources, a tidy constellation of bullet points. Control what you can control.

By late afternoon, the building thins. Fluorescents buzz. The hallway smells like lemon cleaner and dust. I pack my bag, sling it over my shoulder, and make it to the parking lot before my phone buzzes again.

APOLLO: Dinner tomorrow still on?

APOLLO: Sunset? I'll send the place.

My heart does the thing—stupid, traitorous. I type and erase three different versions of sounds great! before settling on:

ME: Yes. Sunset works.

The dots appear and vanish.

Appear.

Vanish.

When his message comes through, it's a pin-drop to a restaurant I've never heard of, tucked near the edge of the park where the city thins into trees. I zoom in. There's an olive tree icon on the map the city uses to mark historic plantings.

I swallow. It's nothing. It's a symbol on a map. It's just dinner.

A breeze scrapes across the lot and lifts the hair at my nape. For no good reason, I think of the owl that hooted outside my window when I was grading last week. I'd told myself it was a coincidence. My life is a string of coincidences lately, knotted into patterns I'm trying very hard not to see.

On impulse, I detour before going home. The sky is bruised purple; the streets, almost kind. I end up in front of the little bookstore without deciding to come here at all. The lights inside glow like a hearth. The bell jingles when I push the door, and the air smells like paper and honey.

"Back so soon?" Calliope asks, looking up from a stack of paperbacks. Her smile is bright, like she's been expecting me.

"I was…nearby," I lie badly.

She hums, a lilt of melody under her breath. "You have the look of someone who argued with a man and won."

I blink. "I—uh—"

"Dangerous habit," she says cheerfully, then slides a book across the counter without looking. Laments of the Ancient World: Ritual, Voice, and Public Grief. It's used, tabs peeking like little tongues. "This one sticks to the text, mostly. But it listens."

I stare at the cover. "Are you sure you work here?" I ask because it's easier than asking what I want to ask.

"Sometimes," she says, amused. Her gaze sharpens for a beat, gold catching gold. "Careful whose songs you let yourself be written into, Cassie."

Before I can find words, a couple wanders in asking about travel guides, and the spell breaks. I pay—she rings it up like any mortal cashier—and I step back onto the sidewalk clutching the book like a talisman.

Night had fallen hard by the time I reached my apartment. I set the book on the table, open to a chapter on women's ritual speech, and let the words wash over me until the tightness in my chest eases.

In bed, I draft and redraft tomorrow's lecture outline. I added a slide: Cassandra across Texts: Lament, Prophecy, Reception. I built the braid

Aiden refused to see, careful, clean, sourced within an inch of its life.

When I finally put the laptop aside, the room is quiet except for the hum of the AC. My phone glows faintly on the nightstand. I don't pick it up. I don't need another message to dictate my pulse.

I close my eyes.

Flame blooms behind my lids—marble and smoke, bronze doors buckling—then shifts, just as quickly, to something else: a stand of trees at dusk, the silhouette of a single olive bending in the wind, and a man with light in his hair waiting just beyond the edge of the path.

I wake, breath caught in my throat.

It was just a flicker, just a dream. Just a story I told myself.

Tomorrow, I have a department to face and a lecture to deliver, and a dinner at sunset on the edge of a park where the city thins into trees.

I tell myself I'm choosing it. I tell myself the story will be mine.

12

Cassandra

Ancient Troy

The council chamber smelled of oil and old cedar, of men who had argued in this room for longer than Cassandra had been alive. Maps lay unfurled across the long table—goat-skin parchment painted with rivers like veins and walls like careful scars. Bronze weights kept the corners from curling. A brazier hissed softly, eating its charcoal.

Cassandra stood at the margin where the firelight thinned. She had learned, over years of being told to watch and not speak, the power of the edge: to see the whole room at once; to note who reached for a cup without looking, who flinched at a name, who liked to hear himself. Tonight, her hands trembled despite that practiced stillness. Sleep had been a strip of torn cloth, too narrow to cover her. Every time she closed her eyes, the same image surged up: fire walking the walls, iron ringing the gates like a bell, smoke streaming past the towers as if the city were a single burning torch lifted to the indifferent sky.

Priam stood at the head of the table, gray threaded through his copper beard. He looked, Cassandra thought, not like a king so much as a father pretending at kingship for another weary hour—until he lifted his head, and the pretense hardened into rule. On his right, Antenor, old and careful, palmed his silence like a coin. On his left, Deiphobus tapped the haft of his spear against his foot, a small, relentless counting. Paris lounged near

71

the wine, ankle crossed over ankle, a smile that cut more than any blade. Hector, the city's shield, stood apart, fingers resting on the map's edge as if he could steady the world with a touch.

"Provisions," Priam was saying to a captain, "and the western gate's hinges. I want them greased before the month turns." He rapped a knuckle on the parchment. "If Mycenae's ships nose past Tenedos, I want to know the wind before they do."

Someone coughed; someone else murmured assent. The room moved with the low tide of business.

Cassandra stepped forward before her courage could remember to be afraid. The hem of her green chiton brushed the stone. "Pappá," she said, and the sound of the childhood name in that place drew more eyes than if she had shouted. "Father. Councilors. Hear me."

The small talk guttered. Even the brazier seemed to hold its breath. Hector's head came up sharply. Paris's smile grew interested; he leaned back as if to better enjoy a show.

"What is it, daughter?" Priam asked. He did not soften his voice—he was king here—but he did not sharpen it, either.

Cassandra kept her gaze on him and only him. It steadied her, the way his eyes stayed on hers, refusing to make her smaller. "I have seen the walls fall," she said, and the sentence left her mouth like a pomegranate seed, small and bright and full of stain. "I have seen our towers black with smoke. I have heard the gates groan like oxen, and then break." She swallowed. If she spoke quickly, the images tripped; if she spoke slowly, they gathered weight. She chose weight. "The Achaeans breach from the north and the west. The river runs with armor. The gods do not laugh."

Silence uncoiled. In it, a log collapsed in the brazier with a hush of ash.

"Seen," Paris repeated, the word tasting of wine in his mouth. "How useful, a sister who dreams."

"It is not a dream." Cassandra's voice thinned, then steadied again. "A god has—" She stopped. Instinct, or Athena's earlier counsel braided through her breath like thread, tugged the words back. She could not use Apollo to lend her speech authority; the room would hear only the scandal of it. "I have seen what comes. We must fortify the northern wall and store grain. We must send word to our allies to stand ready, and keep men off the towers when the wind runs east: the fire—" The image flared again. She swallowed it. "The fire will travel faster than feet."

Deiphobus snorted. "Women's tales."

"Deiphobus," Hector said, soft warning, without turning his head. Cassandra loved him for that small edge in his tone and hated that it had to be small.

Antenor cleared his throat, a diplomat's cough. "Princess, the northern wall is firm. We had the masons upon it in spring."

"Stone burns where pitch runs," Cassandra said. "Their ladders carry flame."

Paris clicked his tongue against his teeth. "Perhaps you should take up the loom again, sister. We would be safer wrapped in your embroidery than in your panic."

The room warmed; a few men smiled dutifully, the sort of laugh that is only a mouth moving. Cassandra felt something old and bright flash in her, not anger precisely but a refusal to let a line be drawn around her and called a cage.

"Hector," she said, turning toward him. It felt like turning toward a harbor. "You have watched the western hills. Have you seen the riders who ghost the ridge at dusk? Their scouts have pushed closer this fortnight."

Hector's jaw worked. "I have seen them," he admitted.

"And the river?" Cassandra said, and though she did not say the rest— When the bodies come, when the bronze drags the current—you could hear it threading the space between words.

"The river runs low," Hector said. He looked at Priam, not at her. "It will give a man footprints if he is unwary."

"Then you see—"

"I see the need for prudence," Priam cut in, not unkindly. He lifted a palm in a gesture that could bless or halt. "My daughter." The room shifted at the intimacy of the phrase; he went on anyway. "Your concern for Troy honors you. But fear eats a city faster than any fire. Speak to me in private, and I will hear you. Here—" He let the word hang. Here he was king; here he fed the city with displays of calm. "Here we must walk with measured steps."

Cassandra heard what lived under the measured: the council, the whisperers, the slow poison of rumor that a king let a woman steer his hand. She could feel the politics in the room as a draft under the door. She tasted bile.

"Measured steps into a pit are still steps," she said. "You ask me to carry water in a basket: be wise, but quiet; be loyal, but unseen. I cannot do it. Pappá, please—"

Paris laughed, delighted. "Did you hear? She cannot be quiet." He spread his hands as if in prayer. "O blessed news."

Deiphobus's spear-butt ticked against the stone: one, two, three. A captain near the door folded his arms. Antenor looked down, smoothing the edge of the map without smoothing anything at all.

Hector's fingers tightened on the parchment. "Cassandra," he said, pitched for her ear. "Enough. Not like this."

His eyes begged her—what? To swallow the fire. To be cunning rather than honest. To live.

Cassandra looked at him and thought of the olive tree beyond the far gate, of the god whose touch had pressed heat into her skull until the pictures broke open like ripe fruit. She thought of being believed, once, for a single instant. She thought that perhaps she would rather be burned than smothered.

"Not like this?" she repeated, and there was something of a laugh in it, though no one in the room would have called the sound laughter. "When? When the towers fall? When you count the dead by doorways?"

Priam's hand came down on the table. Not a blow—he would not strike in anger before them—but a king's period at the end of a sentence. "Cassandra."

He did not raise his voice, but it carried to the corners. The chamber took the breath he offered it and relaxed, almost audibly. He had saved them from a scene. He had saved himself.

Cassandra felt the quiet descend around her like a net. She stood in it for one heartbeat more—two—and then she bowed, shallow, not from the waist but from the neck, the motion a blade more than a courtesy.

"As you wish, my king," she said. She had not called him that since she was small enough to hide behind his knees. She watched the small hurt flick across his face and hated herself for placing it there, even as another part of her wanted to place it harder. "I will trouble your council no further."

She turned before anyone could answer and walked out. She did not hurry. She would not give them the flocking pleasure of her fleeing. Her sandals clicked—clean, even syllables—on the stone. The brazier's breath followed her like a hissed secret.

The hall outside was cooler, the stone drinking noise. She did not realize she was shaking until she braced a hand against the wall and felt the tremor travel up her arm to her teeth.

"Cassie."

Only Hector used the childhood name. He came after her alone—no clatter of guards, no chorus of advice—just his shadow lengthening beside hers. He did not reach for her. He knew she would not be touched right now by any hand but her own.

"You were right to speak," he said quietly.

"And you were right not to," she answered, and the bitterness in it startled them both. "Forgive me."

He breathed out. "If I must forgive you for being yourself, the city will need a second Hector to forgive me for not being enough."

Something in her loosened at his attempt; she almost smiled. "You are always enough."

"That," he said, and there was affection in his scold, "is a lie you tell to spare me."

She looked up at him, at the worry cut across his mouth like a scar that had not been earned in war but in rooms like the one they had left. "If I cannot bear your banners, what good am I?"

"You are the reason I know where to plant them." He hesitated. "But not everyone can hear you say where the wind will blow without thinking you mean to summon the storm."

"Then I will speak to winds and stones," she said. "They do less talking back."

He huffed what might have been a laugh if the day had been kinder. "Go to Mother," he said. "She will sit with you. Her hands are better for the shaking than mine."

"I cannot," Cassandra said, surprising herself with the truth of it. Hecuba's concern would be salt on this particular wound; her love was too heavy for this narrow ledge. "I need air."

Hector studied her for a beat, then nodded. "Take Stratokles," he said, motioning to the captain of her guard, to the man who was always a few paces away. "Take two men besides. Take the side gate. There are eyes on the main."

She almost argued—she wanted the city to leave her alone—but he addressed the blank space over her shoulder the way he did when he meant to be obeyed, and she sighed. "Very well."

He rested two fingers briefly against her shoulder—a benediction, not a command—and went back toward the room where the city ate its fear and called it policy.

Stratokles said nothing, merely fell in three steps behind her as she walked.

Troy changed in the later light. The markets thinned; the shouts gentled into bargaining instead of contest. The smiths' courtyards exhaled iron. Children chased each other between the knees of statues and were shooed, laughing, away from sanctuaries. Cassandra breathed it all in like a woman who had been held underwater too long and now tasted air that hurt.

They took the narrow streets that ran like seams beneath the main avenues, the ones she had learned from nurses and guards who liked to move without parading. At the side gate, the sentry bowed and pretended not to see the princess's flushed eyes. The olive groves lay beyond, dark green against the pale earth, leaves turned silver where the breeze lifted them.

"Here," Stratokles said, and his voice surprised her—always so small, compared to the man. "We will wait at the stones just below the rise. I will see your hair if you call, even if you whisper."

She nodded, grateful for his habit of pretending she chose what he had chosen. She walked on alone toward the low hill where the sacred olive bent as if listening.

The groves kept their own weather. Cool slid along the ground, the kind that made your ankles shiver. Bees threaded the air with a sound like thought. When she reached the tree, Cassandra stood with her hands at her sides, palms open, as if to show she was unarmed even to a god.

She had not planned to speak aloud—pride, perhaps, or dignity—but the day had scraped her raw. Words came without bidding. "They will not hear me," she said to the blue between the leaves. "Even when I stand in a room and hand them the shape of what is coming, they will not take it. I am a daughter and therefore a shadow, a sister and therefore a smaller echo. I am a woman and therefore a mouth to put work in and words out, but only the kind that comforts."

The tree did not answer. Leaves clicked gently against one another, the way bracelets do when a woman folds her arms to keep from reaching.

"I would be believed," Cassandra whispered. The confession tasted like theft. "Not for glory. Not even for triumph. Only so that when the fire comes, men do not say—ah, if only we had known." She scrubbed at her eyes with the heel of her hand, furious with the wet there. "I am so tired of speaking into rooms that eat my voice."

A warmth gathered behind her, as if the sun had rolled closer to the earth. She did not turn at once. She knew what the warmth meant now; she had learned the feeling of being near something that could turn her to gold or ash and would call both blessings.

"Cassandra," said Apollo's voice, from just at her back, and her name became the thing it had always been: not merely a word that meant "she who entangles men," as the little jest in the women's court went, but a summons. "You came."

She faced him. The light in his hair startled her even though she had expected it; you do not accustom yourself to lightning. He wore no crown now and no bow, but he needed neither to be terrible.

"I spoke," she said. "They did not hear." It was not an explanation; it was a verdict she offered up as if to a judge who might set it aside.

"Their ears are dulled by fear that looks like pride," he said, and the gentleness in it would have undone her if the day had not already done so. "Kings must pretend to be the wall that cannot fall. It makes them hard to warn." A brief, bright smile. "I have known a few."

"I thought—" She stopped. The words "I thought you would lend me your name" were unworthy; she swallowed them. "I thought if I said 'fire,' they would smell smoke."

"They will," he said. "When the door is already hot." He lifted a hand, not touching, just letting the warmth of it bathe her cheek. "This is why you have me."

Something in her flinched at that—mine to guide, he had said in the temple—and something else leaned forward like a plant seeking sun. "To be believed?" she asked.

"To be true," he said, and there was a terrible mercy in the distinction. "Truth ripens in the mouth whether it is eaten or spat out. Let me teach you to bear it."

Her lungs loosened; she had not known until then how tight she had held them. "Teach me," she said. It felt like kneeling without the pain of stone.

He stepped into the slant of evening and raised his hand. Not to bless; to begin. "Then listen."

Behind her, beyond the stones where Stratokles waited with his patience and his sword, Troy breathed as if asleep. In the trees, the bees stitched their small gold prayers. The god's voice slid into the spaces where the council's had tried to shear her down and found no purchase. Cassandra stood and let it fill her.

When he fell silent, the light had deepened. A chill ran its finger along her arms. She did not move.

"Tomorrow," Apollo said, quiet now, as if the grove itself might be eavesdropping, "you will see another piece. Do not try to give it to them whole. Too much bread chokes. Pin it where the wind can tug it. Work by inches. You will fail in rooms and still be right. Learn the difference between winning and keeping true."

"I do not like the lesson," she said, and he smiled as if she had pleased him.

"No one does."

He turned his head, listening to something she could not hear. "Go," he said finally. "Your guard will fret. Your brother will count the shadows. Do not teach them to look for you in groves."

She wanted to say his name and did not. She only bowed, the way the olive did, and stepped backward out of the little weather of him until the ordinary air touched her skin again.

On the hill below, Stratokles straightened from the stones, pretending he had not been leaning his weight there like a man who had stood too long. He took up his place three steps behind her. They walked back through the side gate as the lamps winked awake across the city.

When Cassandra reached the corridor outside her chamber, she paused. Her hands had stopped shaking. The vision still thrummed, barbed and bright, but it did not own her breath anymore.

There would be other rooms that would not hear. There would be councils that made a theater of their calm. But somewhere between the owl's cold eye and the god's warm hand, she had learned the line she would walk.

She crossed her threshold and closed the door softly, as if not to wake a sleeping future. Outside, night settled over Troy; inside, she sat with her back to the cool stone and let herself be still long enough to feel the shape of what she would carry.

13

Cassie

Present Day

The afternoon light filtered through the blinds, laying stripes of gold and shadow across the seminar table. I sat with my laptop closed, hands folded too tightly in my lap, while across from me, Aiden lounged with the smugness of someone already convinced of his victory.

"Ah, Cassandra," Dr. Hawthorne said as she entered, her gray gaze sweeping the room like an owl's. "It is a fine thing to have a prophetess among us, speaking of the forgotten women of myth."

Her voice steadied me for a breath. But then Aiden shifted in his chair, lips curving. I knew that he was teeing up his favorite topic.

"Every time I hear more about your research," he said, casual as a dagger tossed between fingers, "I can't help but laugh. Untold stories of mythological women? You might as well write a dissertation on the domestic habits of centaurs."

The laughter that followed was his alone. My throat burned.

"Surely you realize—" I began.

"Realize?" he cut across. "That you're projecting modern sentiment onto ancient texts? Revisionism dressed up as empathy. You're taking footnotes and pretending they're foundations."

That word—*footnotes*—struck like flint.

"Maybe it's you who missed the essence of those tales," I said evenly. "The strength of Andromache, the endurance of Penelope, the grief of Hecuba. Their stories matter."

"Sentimentality," Aiden scoffed. "You can weep for shadows if you want, but scholarship isn't therapy."

I could feel my face flushing, but I continued. "Is it sentimentality to name the silence? To ask why the so-called victors tell only half the tale?"

He leaned forward, elbows on the table. "It's naïveté. The epics were about glory, conquest, and men carving their names into eternity. Not about women sitting in corners, lamenting."

I wanted to strangle him. Instead, I clenched my hands in my lap until crescents bit into my skin.

"The extraordinary," I said, voice steadying, "is often found in the persistence of the overlooked. Their laments are blueprints of survival."

Aiden tilted his head, as if appraising a student paper he already intended to fail. "Romantic notions, 'Sandra. Charming, but unserious."

The nickname—Sandra—grated like sand in an open wound. "Don't call me that," I whispered.

He didn't even hear.

"You know the problem, *Sandra*?" he went on, savoring my name now like a cruel jest. "You care too much. You *identify* with your subject. You're not studying Cassandra. You're playing her. And *that*—" his smile widened, "isn't scholarship. It's cosplay."

The words landed harder than I expected. My own name is being used like a weapon.

For a moment, I glanced at Dr. Hawthorne. She sat inscrutable, as if carved in marble, refusing to intervene. Athena never fights the battle for you.

My pulse hammered. I forced my voice through the storm. "Funny," I said, low and sharp, "how you call them victims when it's men like you writing the crimes."

The silence that followed cracked the room. Aiden's smirk faltered for the barest second, then returned like a shield.

"Yet here you are," he murmured, "claiming victimhood."

The word detonated in me.

Victim.

My chair scraped back with the screech of bronze on stone. "Enough." It came out louder than I meant, but I didn't care. I gathered my bag and strode out, the heat of Aiden's grin burning between my shoulder blades, Dr. Hawthorne's silence like a lesson that stung worse than his barbs.

* * *

Hours later, I stood before the oak door of her office, my hand hovering. Before I knocked, her voice came through as if she'd been waiting: "Come in, Cassandra."

Her office was a sanctuary of tomes, the air smelling of paper and ink. I sank into the chair opposite her, heart still buzzing from the clash.

"That was a trial," she said, gray eyes steady.

"I was unprepared," I admitted, voice thinner than I liked. "He twists every word. Turns my emotions against me."

"Emotions aren't weakness," she said. "Athena waged war with reason and rage together. What matters is control—knowing when to sheathe, when to strike."

I traced the grain of her desk. "Would Athena have stayed silent?"

Her mouth tilted. "Athena rarely answers the questions mortals most want her to. But this much I'll say: next time, don't parry every blow. Cut through. Even heroes fall when someone aims below the shield."

I blinked. Her words coiled around me like prophecy, heavy and electric.

"You're not recounting myths, Cassandra. You're embodying them. Your work is a battlefield. Treat it like one."

Her eyes—gray like storm water—held mine until I felt steadier. Then, softly, almost as if betraying herself: "And I hate that he calls you Sandra."

A laugh escaped me, brittle and grateful at once. We sat in companionable silence until I finally murmured, "Thank you."

She only inclined her head, like a general releasing a soldier to the field.

* * *

By evening, I'd made it to the quiet alcove by the library windows. The spring campus outside buzzed with easy life, so at odds with the storm inside me. My phone buzzed. Theo's name.

"Cassie," he said, warmth in his voice, "got a minute?"

"For you? Always."

Papers shuffled in the background, the clink of tools. My eldest brother, forever multitasking. I could hear the office secretary on the phone behind him. "Kellie is finalizing the Greece trip. Tickets, itinerary, the whole deal."

Greece. My chest tightened. My brothers are going back to the land that still throbbed in our veins, while I remained chained to semesters and grading.

"I'm jealous," I said softly.

"I know," Theo admitted. "We'll walk the Acropolis, Olympus, and Delphi. Nik's already claiming he'll charm half of Athens. I'll keep him out of trouble. Well, I'll try."

A laugh broke out of me. "Nik causing trouble? I'm shocked."

"You'd scold him. I…patch the walls after." His tone gentled. "We all have our roles, Cass. That's why it works."

My throat thickened. "And mine?"

"You're the one who sees the fire before anyone else does," he said simply. "That's always been you."

I pressed my forehead to the cool glass of the window, watching students cross the quad, lives unburdened.

"Listen," Theo added, "don't let assholes like Rhodes twist you up. You're a Bennett. Descendants of Argonauts, remember? We don't shy from storms. We navigate them."

Tears pricked, hot and sudden. "Who told you?"

"Didn't need to be told. I could hear it in your voice."

Silence stretched easily between us.

"Thanks, Theo," I whispered.

"Argonauts," he reminded.

"Argonauts," I echoed, a smile tugging despite everything.

14

Cassandra

Ancient Troy

As the palace slept, Cassandra rose from her bed and slipped into a simple white chiton, the fabric whispering against her skin. Her bare feet made no sound on the cool marble floors. The corridors, usually loud with courtiers and servants, lay hushed, a labyrinth of shadows she had memorized since childhood. She knew which torches burned the longest, which tapestries hid doors in the stone. Tonight, she used that knowledge as if it were a weapon.

She pressed her hand against a concealed panel, pushing until the door yielded to her touch. The gardens exhaled night air, cool and sharp, wrapping her in scents of olive and laurel. Above, the stars scattered themselves in bright defiance, the same constellations she had traced as a child when she whispered questions to the gods and never received answers.

Until now.

The olive grove drew her like a tide. Its branches whispered as she passed, silvering in the moonlight. The trees had watched centuries unroll; they leaned toward her as though they recognized her steps. She followed the path deeper, until beneath the largest, most ancient tree, a figure stood waiting.

Even before she saw his face, she felt him—warmth radiating as if dawn had come early.

"My lord," she breathed, unable to stop herself.

Apollo turned. Moonlight glanced from his golden hair, and his smile was the kind that made mortals believe they had been chosen. "You came," he said.

Her heart leapt. "Of course I did." *You called. How could I not?*

He stepped closer. His hand rose, cradling her face with a gentleness that should have comforted her, but instead left her trembling. "You are a beacon in the dark," he murmured. "Do you know that? Every time I look, I find you burning brighter than the rest."

Her lips parted. "It's good to see you again."

"You do not need to call me 'my lord.'" His thumb traced the curve of her jaw, and his voice lost its warmth, taking on an edge. "Say my name."

She hesitated, her gaze falling to the ground. "Apollo."

He smiled—satisfaction gleaming like a blade sheathed in velvet. "Better. When you give me your voice, you give me yourself."

The words unsettled her, yet the thrill of being noticed by a god drowned her hesitation. He gestured, and she sat beside him on a stone bench beneath the tree. The grove exhaled silence around them, broken only by the chirp of night insects.

"You asked me once what I wanted," she said softly. "I want to be heard. In Troy, my words vanish like smoke. My father listens with love but little faith. My brothers...they laugh."

Apollo regarded her, his eyes like molten amber. "And yet you are here. You came because you know I will listen."

"Yes." Her voice cracked with the force of it. "I want more than a husband chosen for alliances. More than a life behind walls. I want...to matter."

His smile softened, though it did not reach his eyes. "You do matter, Cassandra. To me."

The words coiled inside her chest, warm and suffocating at once. "But why me?" she whispered. "Why would the god of prophecy seek out a mortal girl?"

"Because," Apollo said, leaning close, "I see in you the same fire that burns in me. The others dismiss you, but I do not. You speak the truth, and I crave truth, even when it wounds."

Cassandra's heart surged with something she could not name—pride, hunger, fear. "Then why do I feel as if my truth is a burden?"

He laughed softly, the sound bright but edged. "Mortals fear the truth. They hide behind feasts and battles and treaties. But with me, you need not hide. I will give your voice weight. I will bind it to my own."

The phrasing caught her: *bind it.* A shiver ran down her spine.

She turned her face toward the branches swaying above. "Sometimes I dream of music," she said, reaching for a safer thread. "Of a melody so strong it drowns out my fear. Music makes me feel free."

Apollo's eyes gleamed. "Music is my gift. A language above words. Perhaps one day we will play together, and the sound will echo through centuries."

Her lips curved despite herself. "That would be a dream come true."

"You see?" His gaze caught hers, burning. "Dreams are not so far from prophecy. Both are glimpses of what may yet be. And you, Cassandra—you are made for both."

They sat in silence for a moment, moonlight pooling around them. Then, with a suddenness that made her flinch, Apollo tilted her chin up. "Come to my temple tomorrow at sundown. Alone. The priests will have gone, and I want no ears but mine to hear your words."

She froze. "Alone? If I am seen—"

"If you are seen," he interrupted smoothly, "no one will dare question. Do you not trust me?"

"I…" The word lodged in her throat. *Do I?*

His hand tightened around hers. "Say yes."

The grove seemed to press in, expectant. She managed a nod. "Yes."

Relief and triumph mingled in his smile. "Good. I knew you would not refuse me."

The warmth of his presence enveloped her, but beneath it Cassandra felt a chill. She had come seeking comfort, answers, and she had found them—but also something larger, hungrier, than she had imagined.

When she finally rose to leave, Apollo's hand lingered a heartbeat too long against her skin. "Go," he said. "But remember: tomorrow, you are mine."

The words followed her through the olive grove, echoing louder than her own footsteps.

Back in the palace, slipping through the concealed door, Cassandra leaned against the cool stone wall of her chamber. Her pulse still raced, her skin still burned with his touch. And yet—beneath the thrill—unease coiled like smoke.

Was she blessed? Or had she just stepped into a snare of silver and fire?

15

Cassie

Modern Day

The soft chime of my phone interrupted my grading marathon. I'd been staring at a stack of student essays about the Trojan War. Apparently, it can all be boiled down to: Achilles always shouts, Hector always dies, and nobody has read beyond the *Troy* DVD case, when Apollo's name lit up the screen.

My pulse jumped.

I swiped to answer. "Hello, Apollo."

"Cassandra." Even through the speaker, his voice poured like warm honey. "I hope you're doing well. I was thinking of a small change for tomorrow. Instead of dinner at a restaurant…how about a picnic in the park? Something more relaxed. More…ours."

A smile tugged at my lips. "A picnic? That actually sounds perfect."

"I'll bring the food, the wine, everything we'll need," he promised. "All you must bring is yourself."

It was such a simple line, but something about the way he said *all you must bring* felt heavier than it should have. Still, my heart fluttered. "Then I'll see you there."

When we hung up, I stared down at the half-graded essays and laughed at myself. The fall of Troy could wait ten minutes.

Those ten minutes turned into calling my mother. I needed a voice steadier than mine.

Her contact read simply *Mom – Penelope.* I pressed it, pacing the length of my apartment until her voice answered, rich and familiar.

"Cassie, αγαπητέ. How are you?"

"Good," I lied automatically, then caught myself. "No, that's not why I called. I needed to tell you…about someone."

"Someone?" Her tone sharpened, but in a way that warmed me.

"Do you remember the man I told you about? From the coffee shop? His name's Apollo. We had our first date this week. And tomorrow—our second."

The pause on the other end stretched. Then she laughed, delighted. "Apollo! What a name. Only you, Cassandra, would find a man like that. And?"

"And…it was amazing," I confessed. "We shut down the restaurant, talking. He's—different. Confident. Charming. Smart. Honestly, Mom, I'm nervous."

"Why nervous? That sounds like everything you deserve."

"He changed our plan. Picnic instead of dinner. It sounds romantic, but…I don't know."

"Cassie," she soothed, "a picnic is intimacy. It shows thought. Relax into it. Enjoy."

Her words wrapped me like one of her shawls. Still, unease prickled at me. I am a grown woman. Why did I need her reassurance so badly?

* * *

Morning came bright and gold. I arrived early, my bag strap tight in my grip, scanning the park.

Then he appeared—his stride easy, smile bright enough to make heads turn. People moved aside without knowing why.

"Good morning." His fingers grazed my temple, and suddenly the sunlight dimmed. For half a heartbeat, I swore I heard women crying in the distance, a keening sound that didn't belong in this idyllic park. I laughed it off nervously, pretending it was just the wine going to my head. Apollo only smiled, eyes unreadable. "Ready for adventure?"

I laughed. "I thought this was a picnic."

"Trust me." His eyes glinted as he offered his arm. "It's more."

And I did.

We walked the city first—through winding streets, a hidden café, a street market alive with shouts and color. He bought me flowers before I could protest.

"You don't need to—"

"I *want* to." His tone left no room for refusal, though his smile softened the edge.

I pressed the blooms to my nose, the fragrance dizzying. "Thank you."

The air felt charged when he smiled back, almost rippling.

"Weren't we supposed to picnic?" I teased, trying to lighten the moment.

"Patience," he said, voice velvet but firm.

That word—patience—landed like a command, though I laughed it off.

Finally, we reached the park. Beneath an oak, a courier deposited a chilled basket with military precision. Apollo chuckled at my expression. "The cheese needed to be cold." Inside the basket was gourmet sandwiches, figs, olives, wine, and a plush blanket. I reached for the blanket, needing to help in some way, and fluffed it out beneath the ancient oak. I lowered onto the blanket, letting the laughter and food melt my nerves.

As we ate, he asked about music.

"What moves your soul?"

I snorted. "Hozier. Taylor Swift."

"Ah, a Swiftie?" His lips twitched.

"Don't laugh."

"I wouldn't dare." But his gaze lingered a second too long, unreadable, before softening again.

"I mean it," I said, suddenly defensive. "She's brilliant. A poet."

He inclined his head. "Then I'll believe you."

Something about the phrasing—*I'll believe you*—tightened my chest.

"She's brilliant, and I will not hear any critiques today, thank you."

After a second, we both burst out laughing.

"Seriously," he said, wiping his eyes. "That's wonderful. Did you ever play anything yourself?"

I nodded. "Yeah—flute, oboe, and a little piano. I was that kid in marching band who took it way too seriously. Thought about playing in college, but by then I was just burnt out on Sousa marches and ill-fitting uniforms."

"How unfortunate for the musical world," Apollo teased, his smile widening. "What about the lyre?"

"The lyre?" I blinked. "Isn't that like…the hipster ancestor of the guitar?"

His eyes glinted. "The lyre is a divine instrument." He said it with such weight that for a second I half-expected him to pull one out of thin air. "Perhaps one day, I'll play it for you."

Images of college boys strumming *Wonderwall* around a fire pit flooded my mind, except somehow Apollo's version felt like it would actually split the heavens open.

We talked movies, comedy, and Katharine Hepburn. He laughed at my Monty Python impressions, though again there was that strange weight in his phrasing:

"Laughter is a gift," he said. "But it only matters when shared with the right person."

Later, when books came up, I rambled about comfort reads and *Pride and Prejudice.*

"You're smiling," I accused.

"Because you light up when you speak," he said. "It feels as if your words were meant only for me."

Warmth flooded me—but a flicker of unease, too.

"What's your favorite?" I asked quickly.

He named *The Homeric Hymn to Hermes,* describing its wit and trickery.

"That's not what I expected."

"What did you expect?" he pressed, sharp interest in his eyes.

"Moby Dick? Hemingway? It's not a bad thing! It's just shocking, that's all. At least you didn't say *Catcher in the Rye* or, god forbid, *Mein Kampf* or something like that."

He chuckled, but his gaze didn't soften right away. "Never mistake me for ordinary, Cassie."

The day spilled into the museum, into stargazing, into dancing on cobblestones while a violinist played. Every moment felt stolen from a film.

Yet sometimes, mid-laughter, I caught his eyes fixed on me too intensely, as though he were memorizing, claiming. And each time, I ignored the chill that ran through me.

At my apartment door, he caught my gaze. The streetlight haloed him like some golden statue come to life.

"Cassie," he murmured, "today has been…everything. When you speak, it feels as if the words belong only to me."

Something fluttered low in my stomach—part thrill, part warning. *Too much, too soon.*

But then his hand brushed mine, warm and insistent, and the unease dissolved in the heat.

"I don't want this day to end," I admitted.

His answering smile held both tenderness and something sharper, as if ending were not an option at all.

16

Cassandra

Ancient Troy

The grand hall of the palace was a furnace of voices. Elders, nobles, and princes crowded around the long cedar table, their words colliding in a storm of ambition and caution. The torches guttered in the draft, smoke rising to the painted beams above, while at the head King Priam sat as immovable as a marble god.

Cassandra hid behind the heavy draperies near the edge of the chamber, her breath shallow, her palms damp. Women were not meant to be here. Not in this hall, not in this war council. But her dreams had shown her shadows gathering, and she could not stay away. Only one pair of eyes seemed to notice her behind the drapery. Aeneas, standing quiet as stone near the council's edge, caught her gaze for a moment and inclined his head the slightest degree before turning back. The gesture was small, but it kept her tethered to the room when every other voice sought to shut her out.

Priam's voice cut through the din. "A missive has come from King Agamemnon of Mycenae. An invitation for my sons, Hector and Paris, to visit his court. A gesture of friendship. Perhaps the seed of alliance."

The nobles murmured, some nodding, some frowning. Priam lifted a hand for silence. "It is no small offer. The bonds we forge may shape Troy's future security."

Cassandra clenched the curtain tighter. She had dreamt of ships black as vultures circling Troy's shores. Of smoke choking her throat. She wanted to shout, *Do not trust him!* but her tongue was bound by the invisible cords of her gender.

Hector stepped forward, solemn, measured. "Father, I do not deny the chance for peace. But Mycenae is a nest of serpents. Agamemnon is ambitious. Paris and I would be far from home, surrounded by those who wish us harm."

Paris's laugh rang out, bright and reckless. "Always the cautious one, brother. Where you see serpents, I see opportunity. Imagine it—Troy's reach stretching beyond the Aegean. Our names spoken in halls across Greece."

The council erupted, some siding with Hector's prudence, others dazzled by Paris's bravado. Cassandra pressed her forehead against the cool stone. The same dream flickered in her mind: a fire on the horizon, the screams of children.

They don't see it. They never see it.

At the far edge of the chamber, she felt a gaze upon her. Aeneas, quiet among the nobles, his dark eyes steady. Unlike the others, he did not sneer or look away. He saw her. Just a flicker of recognition, no more—but enough to remind her she was not entirely a ghost.

And yet no one called on her. No one asked what the princess thought.

Priam leaned forward, hands folded like stone weights. "Hector, Paris— you both speak true. But Troy cannot turn her back on opportunity. The world respects strength. And strength demands we show trust when it is offered."

Hector's jaw tightened. Paris grinned like a boy at festival games. The decision was clear.

From her shadowed corner, Cassandra bit her lip until she tasted blood. Her brothers' voices filled the hall. Hers never would.

* * *

Later, in Priam's private chambers, Cassandra at last found her chance. Her father dismissed his advisors, and the noise of the council faded behind them. In the hush of the lamplight, Cassandra knelt beside him.

"Pappá," she whispered, "I have had dreams."

Priam looked down at her, his lined face softened. "Tell me, child."

She hesitated. How could she describe it? The fire, the walls collapsing, Hector's arms empty of his child. The sea was crawling with ships like beetles.

"They are shadows," she said at last. "Storms on the horizon. I cannot see their shape clearly. Only that they come."

Priam's hand rested gently on her shoulder. "Dreams carry meaning, yes. But they can also be reflections of fear. Do not let them master you."

She searched his face, desperate for something more—for him to declare her visions as sacred, for him to bring her into the hall as an equal. But all she saw was love mixed with weariness. He would comfort her, but he would not champion her. Not in public.

"You trust Hector's counsel," she said softly. "Why not mine?"

He sighed, stroking her hair. "The city listens to Hector because he is a warrior. They would not hear you, even if your words shone brighter than Apollo's own oracle. In private, I will always listen. But in council…" He trailed off, the silence its own answer.

Cassandra swallowed the lump in her throat. Love was not enough. She needed belief.

When she left his chambers, rage boiled in her chest, hotter than any torch flame. The hall still smelled of incense and sweat, of men's voices echoing like war drums. Her dreams clung to her, their images too sharp to be dismissed as shadows.

It had begun after the garden. After Apollo.

The thought sent a shiver down her spine. If anyone could give her clarity, it was him—the god who had touched her mind and left it burning with visions. Her father's tenderness was not enough. She needed answers.

She called for her guards, her voice crisp, regal. "To the temple," she commanded.

The streets of Troy lay quiet in the dusk as she walked, her guards trailing at a respectful distance. Merchants were shuttering their stalls; children's laughter echoed in the alleys. Cassandra kept her eyes fixed on the marble columns rising in the distance.

Her dreams gnawed at her. The council had dismissed her before she even spoke. Her father had soothed but not believed. Her brothers had thundered, and only Aeneas had seen her at all.

By the time the Temple of Apollo loomed above her, Cassandra's fury had hardened into resolve. If mortals would not heed her, then she would drag the truth from the gods themselves.

She stepped across the threshold, the scent of incense thick, her heart pounding. "Apollo," she whispered into the still air, her voice shaking but fierce. "If you gave me this curse, then give me understanding. Speak. Answer me."

The silence that followed was unbearable.

And then, faint as a plucked string, she thought she heard laughter—warm, amused, unmistakably divine.

17

Cassie

Present Day

The morning sun streamed through the curtains, warm and golden, while I basked in the lingering glow of last night's date with Apollo. Every detail replayed in my mind—the easy laughter, the bouquet at the market, the way he looked at me like no one else existed. My stomach did an embarrassing flip as I reached for my phone and dialed Diana.

She answered on the second ring. "Well? Don't keep me waiting—how was it?"

I launched into a breathless recap, my words tumbling over each other: the café detour, the picnic in the park, the conversations that felt like they'd been waiting for us all along. Diana made all the right noises—gasps, giggles, delighted sighs—and each one fanned my giddy excitement.

"He's so charming, Di. We talked about books and music for *hours*. It felt like a dream."

Her laughter was infectious. "Oh, Cass. You sound like a teenager again. I love it."

We chatted aimlessly for another few minutes until another call buzzed on my screen. "Shoot—it's my dad. Can I call you later?"

"Go! But you're giving me the full play-by-play tonight."

I hung up and switched lines. "Hey, Dad."

"Hello, my beautiful daughter!" Dad's baritone practically rattled the speaker. He never had an indoor voice, even on the phone.

"Mom probably filled you in, but—I had a date. A real one. With an actual human man." I grinned, bracing for awkwardness. Talking about men was not Dad's strongest suit, but he was my favorite person in the world.

"All I want to know is that you had a good time and you were safe. You know how those city crazies can be."

I laughed. "Yes, Dad. I was safe. And it was wonderful. You'd like him—there's something about him I can't quite put my finger on." I grabbed a mug and started my coffee pot. "But enough about me. What's up?"

Our calls had always been like this: part update, part comfort, part detour into our favorite shared obsession—sports.

"Did you catch the game last night?" I asked, already smiling.

"Of course. How about those Rays, huh?"

We slid easily into analysis of the bullpen, batting averages, and playoff odds. I could picture him in his recliner at home, pacing his arguments with gestures the phone couldn't capture. From there, the conversation rolled into college football.

Dad chuckled. "Ran into Thomas the other day — said to tell you he hopes you're surviving midterms."

"He worries about everyone," I said, smiling despite myself. "That's his superpower."

"You know our Seminoles are gonna make a run this year," Dad declared, as he did every season.

"I'll believe it when I see it," I teased. "Even if they won the whole thing, I'd still be worried."

He chuckled, full of pride. "That's my girl. Always thinking like a coach."

We relived old stories—ball games he'd taken me to, late-night college matchups we'd stayed up to watch together. The distance between us blurred for a while, and I felt like I was back on the worn couch at home, his arm slung across the backrest, both of us shouting at the TV.

"Dad…I miss you," I admitted, softer now.

"I miss you, too, kiddo. You know you're always welcome home." He said it every time, and it never failed to put a lump in my throat.

But there was something else in his pause.

"Spit it out," I said. "What aren't you telling me?"

He sighed. "Your brothers—Theo and Nik—they're heading to Greece. Business trip."

"I know," I said quickly. "Theo mentioned it. I wish I could go too."

"I know, sweetheart. But it's a big deal. International partnerships, contracts in Athens. We just landed a huge build near the bayou in Tarpon Springs, and I need authentic Greek marble. The boys will negotiate with the supplier."

My stomach twisted. His explanation made sense, but his tone told another story. "Dad...that's not everything, is it?"

Another pause. I pictured him rubbing his temple, stalling. "Some details are...well, classified. Nothing you need to worry about. Just know they might be out of touch for a while. Support them, okay? That's what they'll need."

Concern burned in my chest. "Are you sure they'll be safe?"

"I trust them. You should too." His tone was final, soothing, but immovable.

When we finally hung up, I sat with my coffee, the unease gnawing at me. Apollo's name buzzed faintly in the back of my mind, but now Greece loomed larger, like a shadow creeping into the edges of my life.

* * *

By the time I reached campus, I'd tucked the worry away. My intro mythology class—mostly freshmen—was waiting, and they deserved the best version of me.

I launched into creation myths and the trickster streak of Prometheus, the feats of Hercules, and the trials of Odysseus. The lecture hall hummed with energy as students raised hands, debated the gods' motives, and even joked about which Olympian would win a modern reality show. (Zeus, obviously. He cheats.)

At the end, a freshman named Emma lingered. "Professor Bennett...did the Trojan War really happen? Or is it just a myth?"

I smiled. I loved this question. "That depends on who you ask. Some historians think it's pure legend. Others point to ruins at Hisarlik—what may have been Troy—and suggest there was at least *something* there. The truth is probably a tangled braid of myth and history."

Her eyes widened. "That's...fascinating."

"Yes," I agreed, warmth in my chest. "And that's why we keep asking the question."

After my lecture, when the last of my students filed out, I stacked my notes into my bag. The echo of my dad's voice still weighed on me, heavier than I wanted to admit.

"Cassie," came a voice from the doorway.

I looked up to find Thomas leaning casually against the frame, a clipboard tucked under his arm. His tie was loosened, the picture of someone who'd already been juggling numbers all morning.

"Budget check-in?" I guessed. He always seemed to be floating between departments like some kind of benevolent ghost of fiscal responsibility.

"Something like that." He stepped into the room, glancing at the board where my lecture outline still lingered in marker. "You make mythology look almost...practical. Even to us boring number types."

Despite myself, I smiled. "Almost?"

He grinned, but his eyes were careful. His head tiled to one side. "You okay?"

The question caught me. Not a casual *how's it going* but a real *I see something's off.* My throat tightened, and I ducked down to zip my bag. "Yeah. Just a lot on my mind."

"Fair enough." He shifted the clipboard to his other hand. "If you ever want someone to run numbers on all those Herculean labors, you know where to find me. Spoiler alert: none of them balance."

A laugh slipped out, shaky but real. "Noted."

"Take care, Cass," he said, with the kind of quiet sincerity that made me believe he meant it. Then he was gone, off to whatever meeting awaited him.

I exhaled, the room suddenly emptier than before.

* * *

That evening, I set out wine glasses and stirred pasta sauce while waiting for Diana. She swept in with a grin, a coat draped over one arm. "Okay, spill. Tell me everything."

I replayed the picnic, the laughter, the dizzying kiss goodnight. We drifted, as we always did, into tangents: *The Bachelor*, Taylor Swift, true crime podcasts, Florida State football. By the time the pasta bowls were empty, Apollo was a footnote.

But Diana eventually circled back. "So...was it kiss-kiss, or KISS?"

I blushed. "Electric."

She squealed. "Electric is good. I like electric."

We toasted with white wine (red was our mutual nemesis), watched a game show, shouted answers at the TV, and laughed until our cheeks hurt. For a few hours, I felt like college Cassie again—lighter, freer.

But later, as we sat with dessert plates in our laps, Diana noticed the silence stretching between us.

"What's wrong?"

I fiddled with my fork. "Apollo hasn't texted. Not since the date."

She squeezed my hand. "It's still early. Don't spiral. He'll call."

I tried to nod, tried to believe her.

* * *

When Diana left, the quiet hit harder than I expected. I slipped into bed, phone on the nightstand glowing like a watchful eye. No message.

I closed my eyes, Apollo's smile flashing against the darkness. For a moment, it felt warm, but unease twisted beneath it, stubborn and sharp.

Sleep came slowly, and with it the uneasy sense that something in my life—Apollo, Greece, the shadows in my dreams—was pulling me toward a place I didn't yet understand.

18

Cassandra

Ancient Troy

The sacred olive grove whispered as Cassandra walked beneath its branches, her sandals pressing silently into the earth. Her heart beat with a rhythm she could not quiet—visions haunted her sleep now, storm and fire seared behind her eyelids, and the looming departure of Hector and Paris gnawed at her like a curse.

When the god appeared, he stepped out of the dappled shadows as though he had always been there. Apollo's radiance caught on the leaves, painting him both sunlit and terrible.

"My lord…" Cassandra's voice was steadier than she felt. "Apollo. I need answers. My dreams—no, my visions—have grown darker since we first met. I see danger for my brothers. What do they mean?"

Apollo's golden gaze lingered on her, soft yet unyielding. "Visions," he corrected gently. "They are not mere dreams, Cassandra. They are glimpses of what must come. I chose you to see what others cannot."

Her breath hitched. "Then tell me why my family must suffer. Why must Hector, Paris—Troy itself—be pulled into destruction? Can nothing be changed?"

A breeze stirred the grove, carrying the faintest sigh from the god. "The future flows like a river. Even the gods may not dam its course. I gave you prophecy so you might navigate the current, not command it."

A flare of heat rose in her chest. "Then why bestow the gift at all, if I am helpless? Am I only a vessel for doom?"

Apollo touched her shoulder lightly. The warmth of him was unbearable—comforting, maddening. "You are not helpless. You may guide, you may warn. But altering the pattern comes at great cost. Some threads are woven tighter than you can imagine."

Cassandra lifted her chin, defiant. "Then let me pay that cost. I will not stand idle while my brothers walk into ruin."

His expression flickered—pride, sorrow, something more divine and unfathomable. "You are bold, seer. But know this: the more you struggle against fate, the more entangled you may become."

The grove shimmered faintly with his words, and Cassandra knew he would yield no further clarity. Rage smoldered beneath her ribs, though she bowed her head. If the gods would not save Troy, she must.

* * *

She found Paris later in a chamber bright with polished bronze and silk, his attendants fussing over him as though he were already a king. Aeneas stood quietly near the doorway, a silent shadow, his arms folded as he watched the proceedings with an expression that gave away nothing.

"Paris," Cassandra said sharply, sending the servants scattering. "You cannot go to Mycenae. You don't see what I see. It is perilous."

Paris finally looked up, his eyes filled with mild annoyance more than concern. "Always you and your portents, Cassandra. Father has judged it wise. Perhaps you should trust him instead of weaving riddles."

She clenched her fists. "It is not riddles. Mycenae is a nest of schemes, and you—impulsive, reckless—will not see the traps until they close around you."

Paris laughed softly, adjusting his cloak with careless vanity. "I go as a prince of Troy, not a fool. Leave politics to men."

Her rage flared. "Do not mistake my silence for ignorance, Paris. The threads of fate do not spare you because you swagger. They entangle princes as easily as washerwomen."

Paris waved her off like a gnat and swept from the room, attendants trailing in his wake.

For a long moment, Cassandra stood frozen, her chest heaving with unshed tears. She turned—and found Aeneas's eyes on her. Dark, steady, unreadable. He inclined his head the faintest degree, as though he had heard what no one else would. Then he, too, left in silence.

* * *

That night, she returned to the olive grove, fury fueling each step. The guards trailed at a distance, but as she passed through the gates, she caught sight of Aeneas again, speaking with one of the sentries. His eyes flicked briefly to hers as if he knew—knew she was going somewhere she should not. He said nothing. Only that same quiet acknowledgment, as if he bore witness to what others ignored.

She pressed on into the grove, and Apollo appeared once more, radiant and terrible in the twilight.

"You come again, seeking what you already know," he said.

"Then answer me plainly!" Her voice cracked, but she did not lower it. "Can I change anything, or am I condemned to watch my family fall?"

Apollo's expression softened into something infuriatingly kind. "Visions are glimpses, not certainties. You may influence, but not master. Wisdom lies in knowing which truths to speak, and when."

"So—vagueness," she bit out. "Another riddle. You gods play with lives and call it destiny."

A shadow crossed his features, but still he extended his hand. "You asked for this gift. Now you must bear it."

Her hand trembled as she placed it in his, divine heat rushing through her veins until the grove itself seemed to glow. The olive leaves whispered secrets, and the air shimmered with an ancient magic.

When she pulled her hand back, she was shaking—but resolved. The gods would not save Troy. Her father would not listen. Paris would not care.

But Aeneas had seen her.

And maybe, just maybe, that meant she was not entirely alone.

19

Cassie

Modern Day

I cleaned like a woman avoiding an email. Or, more accurately, avoiding a silence.

Apollo hadn't texted since our date a couple of days ago, and the empty stretch of nothing between then and now vibrated in my chest like a loose violin string. So I dusted the books (alphabetized by mythic dysfunction: House of Atreus, then House of "everyone is a swan"), scrubbed the counters, and reorganized my vinyl so Taylor Swift didn't have to shoulder the entire "breakup coping" section alone.

By the time I got to the kitchen floor, I'd graduated from "productive" to "feral." I set my speaker to an upbeat playlist and let the apartment fill with drums and bright synths until I could breathe without counting. The broom turned into a dance partner. The vacuum and I waltzed. Folding laundry became a choreography of sleeves. When a chorus hit, I used the spatula as a mic and took a bow to my invisible amphitheater. Ten out of ten bacchants approved.

I checked my phone. Black screen. I checked again. Still black. I set it face down and told myself very bravely that I did *not* care.

The phone chimed. I tackled the couch.

APOLLO: *Coffee and a walk? There's a place by the park I think you'll love. If you're free.*

It was such a normal text that my heart did a weird, relieved backflip. I typed, deleted, typed again.

ME: *Yes. When and where?*

* * *

I'd just finished tucking a tiny vase of grocery-store tulips on the coffee table when the knock came. Not a hurried knock. A confident *I belong to time* knock. I wiped my hands on my jeans and opened the door.

"Hey, Cassandra," he said, smiling like the sun was something he controlled.

"Hi," I said, and my brain, traitorous, added: *A god, a man, a walking sonnet.* Out loud: "Come in."

He stepped into my little museum of books and found a vantage point near the shelf where Penelope stood next to Medea, like the world's least compatible book club. He scanned the spines, amused. "You really are into mythology."

"I regret to inform you it is a terminal condition," I said, handing him water. "Symptoms include monologuing about Dionysus at parties."

As he traced the spines of my mythology books, Apollo suddenly reached into his coat pocket and pulled out a small box wrapped in soft linen.

"I thought you might appreciate this," he said casually, though his eyes gleamed with something more than casual intent.

I unwrapped it to find a delicate trinket box carved with scenes of olive branches and lyres, faintly weathered like something lifted straight from a museum case.

"It reminded me of you," Apollo added, almost too easily. "A safe place for your treasures…or your secrets."

My fingers traced the tiny carvings, and I laughed nervously. "You just happened to have an ancient-looking Greek jewelry box lying around?"

"You'd be surprised what I collect," he said with a shrug.

I set it carefully on the shelf beside my little Athena figurine, where it seemed to belong instantly.

He laughed, eyes catching on a painting. "What's that one?"

"A piece by my friend Kara. She works in watercolor and chaos. It's a wave, but it's also a spine."

"Beautiful," he said, and for a heartbeat his face went oddly still, like he was hearing something distant. The silence flickered, then eased.

We headed out into the afternoon, the city bright and wind-brushed. The coffee shop by the park was doing brisk business in midterms and oat milk. He ordered an Americano—"black as the night," which earned him a snort—and I got a caramel macchiato, extra caramel, because I reject austerity measures in all forms.

We took the drinks to a window table. Outside, the park trees stirred like they were whispering, and I tried not to stare at his hands when he set his cup down, our fingers slightly brushing. I couldn't decide if that light touch was intentional or accidentia. But, it didn't matter. It wasn't the first time his touch had hummed with something extra: the brush of his thumb across my knuckles at dinner that first night, when for half a second I'd seen torchlight lick a stone wall; the way the world had tilted when he tucked my hair behind my ear in the park, a keening way off where no keening should be. Little static pops of…something. I'd filed them under *anxiety + handsome man = brain glitches.*

"How's the grading?" he asked, leaning back.

"Let's just say if one more essay talks about Achilles's abs, I'm going to start handing out copies of *Rage, Goddess* like Gideon Bibles."

He grinned. "And how was the rest of your day?"

"Productive," I said. "My apartment is so clean the Furies could eat off the counters."

"Do they…eat off counters?"

"Only when someone procrastinates."

We walked our sarcasm out the door and into the park. Finches made suspect choices in the hedges. Somewhere, a kid squealed about a scooter. The paths were a scatter of joggers, dogs, and people experiencing public romance like a contact sport.

He pointed things out the way people from old places do—like every angle was a map to somewhere else. "That oak's older than the museum behind it," he said. "And over there, see the sycamore? Perfect for shade when the sun's aggressive."

"Apollo," I said dryly. "Do you have inside information on the sun?"

He glanced at me, amused, like I'd accidentally touched a hot stove. "I like light," he said, noncommittal, and we moved on.

We talked about books again—his allegedly eclectic reading somehow swung from Renaissance philosophy to contemporary poetry without stopping to pant. We talked about music. When I teased him about men and guitars, I braced for a defensive *Wonderwall* joke. Instead, he said, "I'm partial to strings that sing when you don't force them."

"Wow," I said. "What a mysterious sentence."

"Thank you," he said, utterly sincere.

We veered into the more personal: my mother's insistence that love is a choice you keep making, my father's play-by-play texts during baseball season, my brothers and their fully impractical definition of a "quick trip." He listened like the world had hit pause. I told myself not to imprint on that kindness like a baby duck.

By the time we reached the lake, the light had mellowed to honey. A street musician played something soft near the benches. We took one on the far side of the path, tucked under a stand of plane trees. A breeze came, lifted my hair, and the day felt briefly arranged—like the set had been dressed to look casual.

He was quiet, watching the water. I could feel the question rise before it showed on his face.

"Cassandra," he said, and the way he said my name was gentler than I'd expected. "May I—?"

He didn't finish the sentence, just lifted a hand and let it hover, asking. I nodded, trying for brave and landing somewhere near present. His fingers brushed my cheek, light as a moth's wing.

It was like the world clicked out of one gear and into another.

Not a big theatrical crash of sensation—no chimes, no earthquake. Just a widening, a pressure change, a doorway opening onto old air. In the space of a breath, the park tilted away, and behind it—layered, superimposed—stone and shadow and flame.

Torches guttered in sconces. A corridor breathed cool on my arms. I smelled olive wood and smoke and, under it, salt. Sound arrived next, wrong for a city park: bronze on bronze, the rhythmic murmur of many people breathing in close quarters, a woman's voice not pleading but *stating*, firm, unstoppable—and no one answering her.

I blinked, but the blink didn't shut anything off. The vision threaded tighter.

Laurel leaves shook in the wind I could not feel. An owl cut the air in two beats and was gone. A hand—my hand?—traced carved stone: an owl, an olive branch, a spear. I knew, and didn't know, the feel of the groove beneath my fingertips. Then fire quickened somewhere distant. A door. A fight started hours before anyone would call it that. A name rose in my throat, urgent, syllables ancient and familiar.

"—Cassandra," I whispered, except I hadn't meant to say it, and I wasn't sure if I meant me.

The park rushed back like surf. I was on the bench, breathless and thin. Apollo's hand had moved from my cheek to my shoulder, steadying. His eyes were worried, but not surprised. Not this time.

I swallowed. My coffee had become a poor choice. "What," I said, eloquently, "was that?"

He didn't answer right away. He sat with me in the returning ordinary: joggers, ducks, a dog trying to unionize for more treats. The musician shifted to a different key. My heartbeat did the slow work of turning from a running animal back into a person.

"You've felt it before," he said at last. Not a question.

"Something," I admitted. "At dinner—the torches. And in the park the other night—crying, I couldn't hear. I told myself it was low blood sugar. Or adrenaline. Or...you." I gestured vaguely at his face. "You're...a lot."

His mouth twitched. "I'm...aware."

"But that," I said. "That was a lot." I looked at him, and all the questions I'd been too polite to ask in the glow of his handsome and charming face lined up. "Is this going to be a thing that happens when you touch me? Because I— I like you, and I also like not fainting in public."

Something complicated passed over his face—pride, worry, a private argument with a very old memory. He dropped his hand, giving me back my shoulder, and folded his fingers together like he was remembering how to be careful.

"I didn't mean to let it go that far," he said quietly. "I've been…trying to be gentle."

The sentence slid into me like a key. *Trying to be gentle.* It sounded learned, not natural. A lesson carved by loss.

"What is it?" I asked. "Not metaphorically. Not 'chemistry' or 'instant connection' or 'we're both really into Homer so we hallucinate together.' What is it, Apollo?"

He looked at the lake, then back at me, eyes almost painfully clear. "You have always had a good intuition," he said. "A way of noticing what other people don't. That is yours; it didn't start today. Sometimes proximity—the right proximity—makes it sharper."

"Proximity," I repeated. "Like…to you."

His smile was rueful. "Like to me."

I huffed out a laugh that wasn't quite a laugh. "Good to know I'm not allergic to the caramel in my coffee. Is there a way to…control it?"

"Yes," he said simply. Relief loosened my shoulders. "And no."

The relief re-tensed. "Helpful."

He tipped his head. "You control what you can. Breathe. Ground yourself. Decide what to look at. If it presses, name what you're seeing. If you need it to stop, tell me. If I need to stop, I will."

"Is *that* part," I said, carefully, "something you've had to learn?"

His gaze flickered away, then back. "Yes."

We sat with that for a moment. I studied his hands—still, finally—and felt something soberer than fear move through my chest. Not dread. Not exactly. Responsibility? For my own body, my own mind. Even if the rules were getting rewritten.

"What did you see?" he asked softly.

I told him the pieces I could hold without shaking: the torches, the cold of stone under my palm, laurel leaves, the owl's two silent wingbeats. I didn't tell him the voice, the way the word *Cassandra* had rung like a bell struck from two times at once. That felt like something to keep, for now. To test against the quiet.

He listened. When I finished, he nodded, not in teacherly approval but in recognition, like the landmarks made sense on his map. "That was well done," he said. "Coming back."

"I didn't exactly *go* anywhere," I said, then grimaced. "Except I did."

"You anchored." He gestured at my shoes, my breath, the bench. "You held on to this."

"And if I hadn't?"

"Then I would have pulled you back." A beat. "But it's better if you can do it."

"So you aren't…doing this *to* me." I lifted a hand, cautious. "You're…what? A catalyst?"

"That's a good word," he said, and something like pride warmed his tone. "I'm not your source. I am…a tuning fork. I make the note you already heard, clearer."

I sat with that. It was a kinder idea than the alternative. It also made me want to reread every dream journal entry since I was twelve.

A jogger tripped, saved himself with a heroic arm-windmill, and carried on, dignity restored. I felt the absurd urge to clap.

"Okay," I said finally. "Proximity. Tuning fork. Gentleness. I can work with that. But I'm going to set some rules."

His smile curved like sunlight off water. "Please."

"Rule one," I said, holding up a finger. "No surprise…doorways…in crowded spaces. If I'm going to go full Oracle, I'd like to do it somewhere with fewer toddlers and Labradors."

"Agreed."

"Rule two. If I say stop, we stop. No…poetically ignoring my boundaries."

"Of course," he said, immediately.

"Rule three." I squinted at the lake, marshaling courage. "Don't lie to me."

He didn't flinch. "I won't."

"Even if the truth is weird."

"Especially then."

I exhaled. The musician near us slid into a minor key and then out of it again, like he'd thought about melancholy and decided against it.

"Do you want to walk?" Apollo asked, standing but not offering his hand this time. I appreciated it more than he could know.

We traced the long loop back under the plane trees, past the statue of the man forever pointing at a horizon he'd never reach. Twice my arm brushed his, and twice nothing happened except a pleasant shiver. He kept a sensible space, the kind of space men learn in good classes and gods learn the hard way.

By the time the skyline shouldered up above the branches, I felt steadier. The vision wasn't gone—it hovered at the edge of my sight like a word I almost remembered—but it no longer tugged. We made small talk: my student who had bravely asked if the Oracle was "basically high," his opinion that cities are best at dusk, my firm stance that the correct answer to "pineapple on pizza" is "yes, you cowards."

At my building's stoop, he stopped. The streetlight caught in his hair, making a halo I refused to comment on for the sake of my dignity.

"Thank you for trusting me," he said. Not a throwaway line. A real thing, placed in my hands.

"Thank you for...not blowing my mind into a thousand little myth fragments," I said. "And for the coffee."

He hesitated, then leaned in. Not a kiss. Just his forehead to mine for a second, a warmth that didn't push. The hum was there—faint as a remembered song—but it stayed where we left it.

"Goodnight, Cassie."

"Goodnight, Apollo."

I climbed the stairs on mostly functional legs and let myself into my apartment. It smelled like tulips and lemon cleaner and a life I recognized. I set my bag down and stood in the quiet, listening for anything that didn't belong. The fridge hummed. A car passed. Somewhere, a neighbor's laugh.

On my desk, the copy of *The Iliad* lay open, a ribbon marking the moment Achilles decides wrath is better than wisdom. I touched the ribbon like a talisman and then pulled out my notebook.

Observations:

— Touch = amplification, not origin.

— Images: laurel, owl, stone, torches, *salt*.

— Sound: voice stating, not begging. (Find parallels?)

— Ask Diana nothing. (Yet.)

— Breathe. Anchor. Name what I see.

I thought about texting him. *Thank you for not melting my brain* didn't have the cadence of romance. I settled for:

ME: *Home safe. Coffee was great. Rule compliance: A+.*

His reply came a minute later.

APOLLO: *Home safe. Likewise. I'll be better at rules if you keep making good ones.*

I smiled, turned off the lamp, and let the dark come. Behind my eyelids, the owl lifted and vanished into a sky that wasn't mine, and the laurel leaves whispered something I couldn't translate yet.

Not yet. But soon.

20

Cassandra

Ancient Troy

The horizon bled gold into violet as Cassandra left the Temple of Apollo, her steps quick but unsteady. The god's words still pressed against her ribs, a weight heavier than the gilded crown her father wore. *You have been given sight. You will not be believed.*

Visions. Prophecy. The future, like a river she could not dam, was now a sound she could not silence.

She walked through Troy as the city lived on, oblivious. Merchants called their wares — bright fabric, honeyed figs, fish glinting silver. Children shrieked in play, their bare feet slapping the stones. A flute trilled somewhere, sweet and careless. The pulse of Troy beat steady, unchanged, while her own heart thrashed against the knowledge that the weave of fate had already begun to twist.

For a moment, she lingered in the marketplace, watching an old sculptor chip away at marble. Each careful tap of the chisel rang like a heartbeat. She wondered if the gods felt such patience — carving mortals into shapes of their own choosing, indifferent to the cracks. Would her warnings become anything more lasting than that dust? Would her words endure, or crumble with her voice?

She moved on, unseen, unheard.

By the time she reached the palace, the sun had vanished and shadows had gathered in the courtyards. Bronze braziers flickered to life, their flames bending in the dusk breeze. Cassandra slipped through the colonnade, her reflection trailing long across the polished floor. In her chamber, oil lamps cast restless shapes across the walls, shadows that seemed to breathe when she did.

She pressed her palms to the cool stone, willing it to ground her — to remind her she still belonged to the mortal world. But the silence only amplified the god's echo in her mind.

You have been given sight. You will not be believed.

The words coiled around her, inexorable, until the door opened behind her.

Her mother entered, robes rustling like the wingbeats of a hawk. Queen Hecuba's poise was immaculate, her expression composed, yet the faint crease at her brow betrayed unease.

"Cassandra," she said, voice smooth as water over marble. "You are of age. Suitors petition daily. Troy's safety lies in alliances. Have you considered them?"

Cassandra turned slowly, the lamplight painting fire in her eyes. "I see shadows in our palace, Mother," she said. "False smiles. Treachery beneath silken words. If we trust blindly, we will invite ruin through our own gates."

Hecuba studied her — torn between belief and the necessity of disbelief. "Your instincts are keen, child," she said carefully. "But the throne cannot bend to every whisper. Marriage binds kingdoms; suspicion cannot anchor a dynasty."

Cassandra's voice frayed, desperate. "These are not whispers. They are visions — unbidden, unshakable. Danger coils within these halls. It waits, it watches. I can feel it moving already."

Hecuba's gaze softened. For an instant, the mask of the queen slipped, revealing the mother beneath. She reached out, her fingers brushing Cassandra's shoulder — light, trembling.

"Then I will tread with care," she said. "But we cannot rule by fear. Nor can we refuse every suitor. The gods may send you dreams, my daughter, but the people need something solid. They need stability."

Cassandra swallowed hard. "And when the gods demand the price for that stability?" she whispered. "What then?"

Her mother did not answer. The question lingered, unclaimed, between them. Hecuba's hand fell away, the warmth fading with it.

When she left, the scent of her perfume — myrrh and rose — clung to the air, heavy and bittersweet.

* * *

Alone again, Cassandra sank onto her divan. The oil lamps flickered low, their glow turning the chamber amber and strange. Exhaustion tugged at her, but her mind refused peace. Her breath came shallow, uneven.

She tried to steady herself — to remember the weight of her body, the cool weave of linen beneath her palms, the distant sound of guards changing watch — small mortal anchors in a world that felt increasingly divine and dangerous.

But sleep came for her anyway, sudden and deep.

* * *

She stood in a garden not her own. The air was thick with perfume; roses hung heavy with dew. Petals brushed her bare arms, cold and wet.

At the garden's heart stood Paris — her brother, radiant, proud, his smile sharp as sunlight on bronze. Opposite him moved a woman whose beauty stole breath from the air itself. Her skin shimmered with the faint glow of dawn, her every step a promise.

Their eyes met — desire flaring like a spark leaping to dry grass. Cassandra's chest constricted with dread. She knew, with the certainty of divine sight, that this moment would unmake them.

She tried to speak — to call his name, to warn him — but no sound left her lips. Her voice had turned to smoke.

The scene cracked apart. Roses blackened. The perfume became the stench of burning. The garden dissolved into fire and ruin. She saw ramparts collapsing, bodies strewn upon the stones, her father's crown crushed beneath ash. Whispers rose from the flames — war, ruin, destiny.

And then she was falling. Down, down, through smoke and screaming, until her own voice tore through the darkness.

* * *

"NO!"

Cassandra lurched upright, tangled in her sheets. The air burned her lungs. Sweat slicked her temples; her pulse thundered in her ears. The scent of smoke still clung to her, though the chamber was dark and still.

"Paris…" she gasped. "A woman… a choice…" The words broke, scattered by terror. "It will damn us all."

Her hands shook as she pressed them to her eyes, forcing away the vision's afterimage — the flash of golden hair, the fall of a city not yet lost.

The door creaked. Cassandra started, half expecting her mother's silhouette.

Instead, it was Aeneas — the guard who had walked a half-step behind her that morning, the one whose silence had seemed more understanding than most men's words. The torchlight caught the angles of his face, solemn and steady.

"I heard you cry out," he said, his tone careful but not cold. He did not mock. He did not pity. He simply stood there, as if ready to bear some of the weight she carried.

Cassandra struggled to speak. "A dream," she managed at last, though the word felt too small for what she had seen.

Aeneas inclined his head. "Dreams," he said quietly, "can be more than dreams."

Their eyes met — hers wild and glassy, his calm as still water. For a moment, she saw belief there. Not fear, not dismissal, but something gentler — a willingness to see her as more than cursed.

He bowed slightly and stepped back into the corridor, leaving her in the flickering lamplight.

Cassandra sat motionless long after he was gone, her heart still racing, her breath unsteady. Yet beneath the fear, something new stirred — faint but undeniable.

For the first time since Apollo had named her a seer, someone had not turned away. It was a small thing — a fragile thing — but it glowed within her like an ember refusing to die.

And as dawn's first light crept across the floor, Cassandra whispered into the stillness, half in prayer, half in defiance:

"I will not be silent."

21

Cassie

Modern Day

The city was already awake when I stepped onto the sidewalk, satchel slung across my shoulder. Sunlight caught the tops of glass buildings, gilding everything in gold, while a crisp autumn breeze slipped beneath my scarf and made me quicken my pace. Two days had passed since my date with Apollo, and though I'd tucked the memory of his touch safely away, it kept resurfacing with inconvenient timing—like now, as I rehearsed my lecture for the day.

Hercules. Twelve labors. Hera's patented brand of goddess-level pettiness.

Normally, I would have been buzzing with teacher energy, but my thoughts kept detouring. Apollo hadn't texted since the picnic. He wasn't the kind of guy you expected to follow dating "rules" (what god consults Cosmo?), but still.

I shook myself and cut through the quad. Coffee would help.

At the campus cart, Grace—last year's star student, the one I'd mentally adopted—looked up from the espresso machine and beamed.

"Professor Bennett!"

"Grace," I grinned. "Perfect timing. I've got to wrangle Hercules today, and caffeine is the only way I survive Hera's vendettas."

She laughed. "Man, that woman was bonkers. I kind of miss your class."

"You should sign up for Norse Myth next semester. Trade Hera's grudge for Loki's chaos."

"Pre-med's eating me alive," she said, steaming milk. "But maybe. Can I email you?"

"You'd better," I said, handing her a tip before she could protest.

As I turned from the cart, balancing my cup, I nearly collided with a tall figure cutting across the courtyard.

"Careful there, Professor Bennett," Thomas Sinclair said, steadying the lid of my drink with one quick hand before it could topple. "We finance people don't survive scalding. We're fragile."

I huffed a laugh, more relief than humor. "Oh, right. Wouldn't want to take down the entire university budget with one poorly timed mocha spill."

His mouth quirked. "Exactly. Think of the tuition hikes. Students would revolt."

The joke was small, but it grounded me in a way I didn't expect. He tipped his head toward my folder of notes. "Hercules today?"

"Yep. Trials, tribulations, the usual."

"Sounds familiar," he said wryly, but his eyes softened. "Hey—don't let Rhodes get under your skin. Some of us actually enjoy your work, even if we don't understand half of it."

I blinked, caught off guard by the casual sincerity. "Thanks, Thomas."

"Anytime," he said simply, and stepped back toward his building. "See you around, Cass."

I stood there a moment longer, mocha warming my hands, the brief encounter lingering like a reminder that not everyone dismissed me.

Continuing on my own quest, I pushed through the classroom doors, already flipping into professor mode. Today was special—an escape-room style lesson I hadn't tried since I taught high school years ago. Students loved it. I loved it. It reminded me why I stayed in academia despite the headaches.

I was halfway through taping clues to the walls when the world lurched sideways.

Sunset smeared the sky above an unfamiliar street. A foreign city pressed in around me, its alleys sharp with shadow and neon. My pulse kicked like a cornered rabbit.

And then—I saw him. Nik. My brother, standing with a stranger in a leather jacket. Nik's posture was wrong: shoulders tight, hands restless.

The stranger gestured sharply. Nik's jaw clenched.

I tried to step closer, but when I reached for my phone, nothing. No weight in my pocket, no phone at all.

Panic flared.

"Nik," I whispered.

He glanced up—and looked right through me.

The conversation ended abruptly; Nik gave a stiff nod, then walked away. The man melted into the alley's darkness. I stepped forward, desperate to stop him—only for Nik to pass straight through me.

The world snapped like a rubber band.

I was back in my classroom, hand still raised, tape stuck to my finger.

"What the fuck," I muttered, staggering to the nearest chair. One minute gone. Maybe less.

My breath rattled. This wasn't a dream. Not like the burning city weeks ago. This was sharper. Realer.

I dug my nails into my palm. *Compartmentalize.* I had ninety minutes to fake normal.

* * *

And thank Hera for teaching instincts. My students' laughter as they puzzled through the escape room pulled me through, kept me smiling, and even let me forget for stretches of time.

"Professor Bennett?" A boy caught me as he packed his bag.

"Yes?"

"That was awesome. Thanks."

It was nothing, but it steadied me.

Until Dr. Hawthorne stepped into the room, all presence and sharp gray eyes.

"I heard about your Hercules escape room before I even got to my office," she said. "Good work."

"Dr. H," I pressed a hand to my chest. "Nearly gave me a heart attack sneaking in like that."

She smiled faintly, then studied me longer than I liked. "Something's on your mind."

I froze. Family business wasn't exactly hallway chat. But she already knew my tells.

"It's…Nik." My voice sounded small even to me. "He and Theo are in Greece. Dad says it's about marble imports. But I had—"

I bit my lip. I wasn't ready to say *vision.*

"Why don't we get some tea?" she said, the phrase that always meant: *My office. Now.*

* * *

Her office smelled like incense and old paper. I sank into the chair opposite her desk, clutching my cup like it might explain the universe.

"I saw Nik," I said finally. "Not here. Somewhere else. A city I didn't recognize. He was meeting some guy in an alley. Shady. Pressuring him. And—he didn't see me. He walked right through me."

Dr. Hawthorne didn't blink.

"It felt the same as a dream I had weeks ago. The one with the burning city. Except worse. Because it was Nik. And it felt real."

Still nothing from her. Not disbelief. Not laughter. Just that hawk-eyed silence.

"And then—" My throat tightened. "Apollo. He…when he touched me the other night, I saw something. Felt something. It was like being plugged into a lightning strike. And now these visions keep coming."

Evelyn leaned forward. "Describe the object he gave you."

I frowned. "Object?"

"The relic."

I hesitated. I'd told myself I wouldn't bring it up, but her eyes pinned me. "A carved box. Greek. Apollo said it belonged to Delphi."

Her gaze sharpened. "And when you opened it?"

"I didn't." My hands twisted in my lap. "That's the thing. I didn't need to. He touched me, and it just…happened. Like the visions were already waiting."

She studied me for a long moment, then—very softly—"The oracles at Delphi spoke in riddles no one believed. But history still bent around their words."

A chill slid down my spine.

"So you don't think I'm crazy?"

She gave the faintest of smiles. "Cassandra, I've taught too long to dismiss the uncanny outright. But you're carrying a dangerous weight. Be careful who you tell."

Her hand landed briefly on my arm. "And don't underestimate Nik. Or yourself."

Something flickered across her face then, something private. She murmured something—too quiet for me to catch.

"Your what?" I asked.

"Nothing," she said briskly. "Go call your father."

* * *

Outside, I dialed Dad before I lost my nerve.

"Hello, my beautiful daughter!" he boomed, volume at "stadium announcer" as always.

"Dad." My throat closed around the word. "I saw something. With Nik. I think—"

"Cass," he said gently, instantly serious. "Start at the beginning."

I told him. About the vision, about Nik's posture, about the danger I couldn't name.

He was quiet for a long time. "Cassie, dreams aren't always the truth. But thank you for telling me. I'll talk to him."

"Should I call Theo?"

"No. He's knee-deep in tax meetings. Let me handle this."

"Dad, what if I'm right?" My voice cracked. "What if Nik screws this up?"

"Then we deal with it," he said firmly. "Together."

I closed my eyes, breathing against the ache in my chest. "Okay."

"Now stop pacing," he added. "You'll wear out your shoes."

I froze mid-step. Damn him.

I shoved my phone into my bag and let my feet carry me, mind still buzzing. I didn't realize where I'd ended up until the smell of espresso hit me. A cozy café, tucked at the corner of the block. Perfect.

I almost smiled—until I froze in the doorway.

Apollo.

Arm draped casually around a woman's shoulders, leaning close as he laughed at something she said.

Not just any woman.

Diana.

My best friend.

<h1 style="text-align:center">22</h1>

<h1 style="text-align:center">Cassandra</h1>

Ancient Troy

The gardens of Troy glowed with molten light as the sun dipped toward the horizon. The marble walls caught the last golden rays, and the air was heavy with the fragrance of roses and flowering olive branches. Servants moved through the grounds at a respectful distance, their voices hushed, though Cassandra suspected more than one ear tilted subtly toward her. Word traveled quickly in the palace, and even the rustle of silk could carry secrets.

Cassandra paced the gravel paths, sandals crunching with restless rhythm. Her heart was still hammering from the visions that had haunted her sleep the night before. Each time she closed her eyes, she saw flickers of fire, ships cresting waves, and the shadow of her brother Paris entwined with a foreign woman whose beauty shone like a trap.

Helenus stood at the edge of the fountain, watching the rippling water as though it alone would yield truth. In the fading light, he looked older than his seventeen years — more priest than boy, his posture stiff with the self-importance he had acquired since Apollo's priests had claimed him for training. His white robes carried the faint trace of incense, and around his neck hung the laurel branch of the augurs, a token of his new station.

He did not look like her twin anymore.

"The signs are clear," Helenus said at last, his voice carrying the cadence of a sermon. "Our treaties with Phrygia and Lycia will ensure Troy's prosperity. These alliances strengthen us, Cassandra. They are not to be feared."

Cassandra stopped pacing. Her fingers curled into her palms, nails pressing crescents into her skin. "And yet in my visions, I see their ships aflame. Their banners do not march beside ours, Helenus — they march against us. I hear their war songs. I see Troy's walls shrouded in smoke."

Helenus turned, brows knitting. "You and your visions again." His tone was not cruel, but laced with a sibling's weary exasperation — the kind that always cut deeper than an enemy's blade. "Sister, I respect your gifts, but I cannot run a kingdom on shadows."

She felt her face burn. "They are not shadows. They are truths given by the gods. You call yourself augur, but do you think Apollo would only speak to you?"

His jaw tightened, the muscle flickering in irritation. "I have been trained. I have learned to read the entrails, to study the flights of birds, to divine from flame and bone. That is Apollo's chosen art, Cassandra — not these… fevered dreams that torment you at night."

"They are more than dreams!" she snapped.

Helenus lifted his chin, the sun catching the copper of his hair. "Then why do they contradict what I have seen? I have cast the lots. I have performed the auguries with the high priests. They foretell prosperity in these alliances."

Cassandra wanted to laugh, to scream. "Prosperity? I saw Paris standing on a foreign shore with a woman at his side — and behind them, a thousand ships. Do you call that prosperity?"

Helenus blinked, unsettled for a heartbeat before recovering. "You let your fears twist your sight. Paris is reckless, yes, but he is not destiny itself."

Cassandra pressed forward, voice rising. "You think me blind? You think I do not know what the gods have given me? I see more clearly than any augury from ashes or entrails!"

From across the colonnade, a figure paused. Aeneas, son of Anchises, leaned against a column, his spear still in hand from training in the yard. He had been silent, half-shrouded in shadow, watching the quarrel unfold.

His eyes flicked from Helenus to Cassandra and lingered — just for a breath too long — on her. Recognition. Sympathy. He said nothing, but the acknowledgement was enough to loosen something tight in Cassandra's chest.

Helenus followed her gaze, saw Aeneas, and bristled. "Do you see? You make yourself a spectacle. You undermine Father by airing these visions in the open."

Cassandra spun back to him. "And you undermine me every time you dismiss them. You are not the only one touched by the divine, brother. Do you think the gods speak only to men?"

For a heartbeat, the garden seemed to still. The wind stirred the rose petals, scattering crimson across the marble paving stones. Cassandra's voice trembled, but not with fear. With fury.

Helenus stepped closer, lowering his tone, though his eyes burned. "I believe you think what you see is real. But belief does not make it truth."

Before Cassandra could reply, her knees buckled. The fountain, the gardens, her brother's furious face — all tilted, all blurred. The sunlight bled away, replaced by an infernal glow. She clutched the stone balustrade, gasping as the vision seized her.

She saw:

Paris. His hands tangled in the golden hair of a foreign woman.

Ships crowding the horizon, sails like white wings blotting out the sky.

Fire eating the wooden gates of Troy.

Hector's child crying in the smoke.

Her own voice screaming — unheard, unheard, unheard.

"Cassandra!" Helenus's voice dragged her back. His hands gripped her shoulders. She blinked, breath ragged, and the gardens returned. Only the tremor in her knees betrayed what she had seen.

"You see?" she whispered hoarsely. "The gods show me truth."

Helenus's face twisted, conflict warring across it. For a moment, the boy she had grown up with — the one who had once caught fireflies with her in these very gardens — flickered through. Then the priest's mask descended again.

"Or the gods torment you," he said quietly. "Not every gift is a blessing. Sometimes Apollo tests mortals to see if they can endure madness."

The words struck her like a slap. She pulled away, eyes flashing. "Better madness than blindness! You think entrails in a bowl outweigh the blood I see spilling through our streets? You would rather trust the hollow rituals of old men than your own sister?"

He flinched but held his ground. "I trust discipline. I trust the ways handed down to us since before Troy's walls were raised. And yes — I trust Father's wisdom. I will not throw the city into chaos based on your nightmares."

"They are not nightmares," she hissed.

"Then prove it!" Helenus's voice cracked out like a whip. The nearby servants froze. Even the birds startled from the hedges. He lowered his voice, but the fury remained. "If your visions are truly divine, then persuade Father. Convince Hector. But do not come to me demanding I cast aside auguries that the entire priesthood affirms."

Cassandra's breath hitched. For a heartbeat, silence stretched between them, thick and unbearable. Then Helenus turned, robes whispering against the gravel, and walked toward the colonnade.

Aeneas straightened, his spear glinting in the dying light. For a moment, his gaze met Cassandra's — steady, dark, unspoken. He inclined his head, a gesture so slight she wondered if she imagined it. Then he fell into step behind Helenus, silent as shadow.

Cassandra remained, trembling, the roses' perfume now cloying in her throat. The sun sank below the walls, painting the garden in copper and blood. She pressed her fists to her eyes, choking back the scream that clawed at her.

No one listened. Not her brother, not her father, not even her mother. Only Apollo had given her truth, and even he warned that changing fate carried a cost.

She sank onto the fountain's edge, the stone cool beneath her palms. The reflection of her face wavered in the rippling water — red hair aflame in the last light, green eyes wild with the weight of visions.

For the first time, she hated those eyes.

And in the stillness that followed, only the whisper of the olive leaves answered her — the gods themselves listening, silent and merciless, as Troy's doom gathered on the horizon.

23

Cassie

Modern Day

I couldn't think. Every muscle in my body locked where I stood.

There, framed by the cafe's big window, was Apollo with his arm around Diana, laughing as they stepped through the door together. My best friend and the man I was dating, shoulder to shoulder like they'd known each other for years—because apparently they had.

I hovered at the threshold, half in the city air and half in the warm coffee smell, trying to decide whether to bolt or walk straight in and invent a new Greek tragedy on the spot. My brain scrolled through every possible explanation and landed on exactly none.

Diana spotted me first. She lifted her hand, smile bright and easy. "Cass!" she called, like this was not the world's worst timing.

I pasted on a smile that felt like it had been ironed onto my face and stepped inside. The little bell above the door jangled, way too cheerfully.

"Hey," Apollo said, turning toward me. His smile was warm—too warm—and it only made my stomach drop farther.

"Hey," I echoed, voice thinner than I wanted. I didn't trust myself to say more without either sobbing or starting a ten-minute TED Talk titled Betrayal: A Case Study.

Diana's eyes flicked over my face, and I watched the instant she read me. She slid out from under Apollo's arm. "You know what," she said lightly,

"I'm gonna run. Apollo, I'll talk to you soon. Cass—" her brows raised in that are-you-okay way— "I'll call you later?"

"Sure," I said, somehow. Translation: *absolutely not.* Translation of the translation: *yes, and bring wine.*

Diana squeezed my elbow as she passed. "Don't murder him in public," she whispered. "It's bad for your tenure packet."

I didn't laugh. Apollo and I stepped out onto the sidewalk like two actors who'd rehearsed separate scripts.

He glanced at me, then at the street, then back. "There's… something I should tell you about Diana."

"This should be good," I said, which is Cassie for *I'm barely holding it together.*

He studied my face. "She's my sister."

I blinked. "I'm sorry—what?"

"My twin," he added calmly, like this was a fun fact about zucchini.

I stared. Then I snorted, because apparently my coping mechanism is incredulity. "Diana. My Diana. Your twin. As in the Diana I've known for fifteen years, who has never once said, 'By the way, my brother's name is Apollo, like the actual sun guy, no big deal'?"

"She doesn't like people treating her differently because of me," he said. "She enjoys being known for herself."

"Wow," I said. "Relatable. I spent most of high school as 'Theo Bennett's little sister.'" The words tumbled out before I could stop them. "Still! Maybe mention the twin sibling who shares a name with a goddess?"

He shifted his weight. "It's… complicated."

"Twins. Complicated. Imagine." A beat. "Divine chaos, even."

Something flinched behind his eyes. "Let me explain, but maybe… not here?" He tipped his head toward the alley next to the cafe, the one with the peeling mural of a phoenix and the dumpster that always smelled like lemons and espresso.

I should have said no. I stepped into the alley anyway.

The moment the city noise dimmed, the silence pressed close. He stood across from me, the late light catching in his hair. I folded my arms because otherwise I might throttle him, which seemed unwise considering the… everything.

"I need to talk to you about something," I said, words coming out steadier than I felt. "I've been doing a lot of thinking."

"Go on," he said carefully.

"I've been rereading source material about Delphi," I said, "and falling down rabbit holes because of the little lyre box you gave me." I saw his mouth twitch. "It sent me on a research bender, okay? And the more I read, the less your whole… existence made sense as purely 'guy with a cool name.'"

He didn't speak.

I took a breath. "You're not just named Apollo. You're *Apollo Apollo.*"

A sliver of something—relief? resignation?—moved across his face. He didn't deny it. He didn't smile. He just held my gaze and said, quietly, "Yes."

The alley tilted. The mural's painted flames flickered in my peripheral vision, and my heartbeat kicked into some heroic meter Homer would have appreciated.

"Okay," I said, because I am nothing if not articulate. "Okay."

"I was going to tell you," he added, voice low. "I hate lying."

"You didn't lie," I said. "You just… left out a lot and let me connect dots with a dry-erase marker and no supervision."

He winced. "That's fair."

"And Diana?" I asked. "Is Diana…*Diana?*"

"She calls herself that," he said. "Most people do. In another age, in another tongue, they called her something else." He met my eyes. "You don't owe either of us your belief. But I owe you honesty."

I shook my head, almost laughed. "You know what's wild? I teach this stuff. I stand up three times a week and tell a hundred undergrads that gods are messy metaphors for power and weather and our impulses, and now you're here in my alley telling me you share a lease with the sun."

A tiny smile tugged at his mouth. "I don't pay rent."

"Of course you don't," I muttered. "Must be nice."

We stood there, letting the air settle. I found my voice again. "There's one more thing. I had a… thing today before class. Time went slippery—like I was standing on a moving walkway and the rest of the world wasn't—and I saw my brother, Nik. He didn't see me. It felt like I stepped sideways into something."

His expression sharpened. "When?"

"Right before my lecture." I hesitated. "I don't think it was because of the little box—before you get excited. It felt like—" I swallowed. "It felt like you. Like electricity, when you touched my wrist at the park. Like *something* waking up."

He looked down, jaw tight. "Sometimes proximity thins the distance between what is and what might be. I… should have been more careful."

"Careful," I repeated, and a flare of anger lit up my chest. "Right. Careful would have included, I don't know, telling me the truth before my frontal lobe signed a lease with you."

The smile vanished. He nodded once, like he agreed to be stabbed. "You remind me of someone," he said after a beat. "Someone I failed."

The syllables hit like a thrown stone.

"Cassandra," I said softly.

He lifted a hand, almost like he'd touch my hair, then let it fall. "You even look like her sometimes," he said, voice roughened. "Stubborn. Bright."

"Didn't she die because of you?" slipped out before I could catch it.

His eyes snapped to mine. Something dark moved through them—rage, shame, the scary kind of grief you can't turn away from. He stepped back like he'd remembered what distance was for.

"I have to go," he said.

"Seriously?" I said. "You finally tell me you're you and your twin is my best friend, and I tell you I'm seeing visions like a malfunctioning Roomba, and your response is an Irish goodbye?"

He flinched again, then forced a breath. "I don't want to say something I can't unsay." He touched two fingers to his own chest, then to mine, a little gesture that felt older than language. "Please don't be alone tonight."

"Diana will be at my place in forty minutes with sauv blanc and judgment," I said. "I'm covered."

His mouth quirked. He looked like he might say something else, then didn't. The alley swallowed him in three strides.

I stayed there a full minute, staring at the firebird mural and counting backwards from fifty in ancient Greek because that's what one does when one's life detours into myth. Then I headed home.

Diana was already waiting at my door, arms folded, an expression that practiced mix of concern and defensiveness she uses when she knows she's about to get yelled at by someone she loves.

I unlocked the door, walked in, and let her close it behind us.

"Diana," I said, and even I heard the crackle under my voice, "we need to talk."

She nodded, quick and guilty. "Yes."

"You knew," I said. "You've always known. And you said nothing."

She winced. "Cass—"

"Don't," I said. "Don't call me *Cass* like that's a free pass. You hid your entire self from me."

"I wanted to tell you," she said, voice low. "I also wanted you to have a life that wasn't—" she gestured vaguely "—this."

"I study this," I snapped. "I've literally spent a decade constructing frameworks for this."

"It's different when it can bruise you," she said. "Trust me."

"I would have," I said. "If you'd given me the chance."

We stared at each other across my living room, over the coffee table and the vase of flowers Apollo bought me, and the little box glinting on a shelf like a punchline.

"Is Diana even your name?" I finally asked, and I was tempted to pick up the box, just to have something to throw.

"Yes," she said. Then, a beat. "And no."

"That's not helpful," I muttered.

"In your language, it's the one I've used the longest," she said. "In another, it was Artemis. It still is. Names stretch. The person stays."

Something in my chest sagged, some old pillar I didn't know was holding the roof up. "Great," I said, too bright. "So I've been best friends with a goddess since sophomore year, and the only time you lied was every single time."

"Don't do that," she said quietly. "You know it wasn't like that."

I did. And I hated that I did.

"I need time," I said, throat tight. "I need to stop shaking."

Diana nodded, eyes softening. "Okay." She stepped toward me and stopped when I flinched. "Okay," she repeated, like a promise. "Text me when you want. Or don't. I'll… wait."

She left. The lock clicked. The silence was enormous.

I sat on the floor and leaned my head against the couch, staring at the ceiling until the lines in the paint made constellations I didn't want to name. I tried to be angry in a clean, tidy way. Anger refused to be tidy. It swelled and ebbed and left me with the worst of it: grief.

After a while, I got up, put the little box inside the cabinet behind a stack of paperbacks, and shut the door.

I wasn't throwing it away. I just wasn't looking at it tonight.

Outside, the city lights blinked like a thousand tiny omens. I ignored them, washed my face, and got in bed. Sleep felt like the only neutral thing left.

I didn't sleep.

24

Cassandra

Ancient Troy

The palace was never quiet. Even at night, its marble bones hummed with voices—the whispers of attendants, the footfalls of guards, the restless rustle of courtiers who found sleep elusive. Cassandra had grown up in this noise, and yet tonight it grated against her nerves like sand beneath silk.

Her visions had grown stronger since her last meeting with Apollo, vivid in ways that left her gasping awake, the sheets damp with sweat. Fire licking Troy's walls. The cry of a child wrenched from his mother's arms. A shipyard thick with sails, a tide of black hulls pressing the horizon. Each time she tried to push the images away, they only returned sharper, like shards of glass.

She had told Helenus. He dismissed her with an augur's solemnity, insisting that omens must be weighed against ritual, that her images were "too raw, too untamed" to be trusted. She had tried to speak to her mother; Hecuba heard her out but turned the conversation to suitors. And her father—her dear, patient Pappá—would listen in private but never let her words reach the council.

So she paced the gardens alone, her sandals whispering over the gravel. Moonlight pooled over the olive leaves and spilled across her white chiton. She clutched her shawl tighter around her shoulders, but it did nothing to chase the chill that had settled in her bones.

"Restless again?"

The voice startled her. From behind a stone column emerged Aeneas, torchlight catching the planes of his face. He bowed his head respectfully, though there was a softness in his eyes.

"I might ask you the same," Cassandra said, forcing a wry smile.

"I am on watch," he replied simply. "But you... You wander like one haunted."

"I am haunted." Her voice cracked more than she intended. "The gods have given me sight, Aeneas. Visions that will not leave me."

He studied her carefully. Unlike her brothers, he did not scoff. Unlike her parents, he did not hush her. He said only, "Then speak, princess. If the gods have placed a burden upon you, perhaps they mean it to be shared."

The kindness undid her. Words tumbled out—ships, flames, betrayal wrapped in silk. The dream of Paris in a foreign garden, reaching for a woman more beautiful than any she had seen, a woman whose very presence promised ruin.

When she finished, her breath came ragged, and her hands trembled at her sides.

Aeneas was silent for a long moment. The torch sputtered in the breeze. At last, he said, "I cannot tell you what these images mean. But I believe you saw them."

"Believe," Cassandra whispered, tasting the word like honey and salt. "You are the first to say it."

"I am not a fool," Aeneas said gently. "The gods do not waste their voices. If they have chosen you as their vessel, we would be fools to ignore it. Though..." His mouth tightened. "It is not easy to speak truths others do not wish to hear."

Cassandra laughed, bitter and low. "You think I do not know this? My brothers call me mad. My mother pushes suitors at me like medicine. My father..." Her throat closed. "Even he only listens in secret, never before the council."

Aeneas shifted closer, lowering his voice. "Then perhaps you must find another way to be heard."

"Another way?"

"You know the palace as well as any man," he said. "You know who listens in corners, who whispers in the corridors. Truth can spread as quickly as rumor, if planted in the right ear. And if not… then prepare. Build your strength. When the tide comes, you will stand ready even if the rest of Troy does not."

His faith, measured and practical, steadied her. She nodded slowly. "You speak like a soldier, Aeneas."

"I am one." He smiled faintly. "And soldiers survive by trusting both sword and instinct."

Before she could reply, a sound drifted over the garden walls—the low thrum of a lyre, notes weaving through the night air like threads of gold. Cassandra froze. She knew that melody. It tugged at her heart, pulled her feet toward the shadows of the olive grove.

Apollo.

She glanced at Aeneas, her mouth dry. "I must… walk a little farther. Do not follow."

He looked as though he might protest, then bowed. "Be careful, princess."

She left him at the garden's edge and slipped into the grove.

The god was waiting, seated beneath the great laurel, his instrument glowing faintly in the moonlight. He strummed a final chord and looked up at her with a smile that could have thawed stone.

"You came."

"You knew I would," Cassandra said, though her heart hammered.

"Your visions grow stronger," Apollo said, rising to meet her. "I can feel it."

"I don't want them," she blurted. The words startled even her. "I want peace. I want to sleep without fire behind my eyes. I want my family to listen."

Apollo tilted his head, studying her with that infuriating calm. "Prophecy is never peace. It is the burden of sight where others are blind. But it is also power, Cassandra. Do you not feel it?"

"I feel only isolation," she snapped. "You gave me a gift no one believes. What good is sight if every word I speak is drowned in laughter?"

His expression softened. He stepped closer, fingers brushing a strand of her hair back from her face. "Then speak not to them. Speak to me. I will believe you."

Something in his touch burned—comfort, longing, the echo of something she did not want to name. She pulled back, shaking her head. "Belief from a god is not the same as belief from my kin."

"Perhaps not," Apollo conceded. "But your kin are mortal. Their vision ends where the horizon meets the sky. Yours does not. In time, they will see."

"They will see too late," Cassandra whispered. "That is what terrifies me."

Silence stretched. The olive leaves whispered overhead.

At last, Apollo said, "Then defy them. Defy fate itself, if you must. Use your gift to prepare, whether they heed you or not."

"And if I fail?"

"Then Troy will fall," he said simply. "But you will not have been silent."

The words rang like a sentence and a promise all at once.

She wrapped her arms around herself, staring at the god who had both cursed and comforted her. "I don't know if I can bear it."

"You can," Apollo said, with a certainty that made her ache. He touched her chin, lifting her gaze to his. "Because you are Cassandra. And you were never meant to be invisible."

* * *

Cassandra returned to her chamber that night with his words echoing like thunder. She wrote them into her memory, carved them into her resolve: if no one else would heed her, she would still speak.

And if Troy burned, at least she would not go down without a fight.

25

Cassie

Present Day

At 3:12 a.m., I gave up, hauled myself out of bed, and made tea like the Greek aunties who raised me had taught me: water absolutely boiling, honey generous, stare at the mug until you can taste your own patience. The apartment was too quiet, the kind of quiet that makes you start narrating your movements to yourself like a nature documentary.

DIANA: *Home. I'm sorry. I meant what I said. I'll wait.*

No text from Apollo.

Fine.

By morning, my resolve had crusted into something brittle and useful. I braided my hair, put on the professor uniform (cardigan, pencil skirt, mildly intimidating eyeliner), and told myself I could compartmentalize like a champion. My students did not need the saga. They needed Theseus and the Minotaur.

I made it to campus on autopilot. Grace at the coffee cart grinned and comped my mocha like a benevolent oracle. "You look like you wrestled a chimera," she said.

"Hydra," I said. "It keeps growing heads."

"That's extra credit, right?" she called as I hurried away.

My lecture was mercifully loud, fast, and funny. I cracked jokes, the class laughed, and for seventy-five minutes, I remembered why I love this job:

because myths are how we talk about the stuff we can't handle head-on. Labors, curses, stolen cattle—it's all grief and desire in costumes.

After class, while I was erasing the board, my hands went cold. Not vision-cold, just oh right reality-cold. I sat on the edge of the desk and stared at nothing until a student named Emma—sweet, bright, the one who last week asked if the Trojan War "actually happened"—hovered near the door.

"Professor Bennett?"

"Yeah?" I said, blinking back into my body.

"This is the best class I've had in college," she said shyly. "Thanks."

The knot in my chest loosened a fraction. "You're welcome," I said, and meant it.

I packed up my bag, marched to my office, and shut the door. Phone. Dad. Now.

He answered on the second ring, voice booming and familiar. "Hello, my beautiful daughter!"

"Hi," I said, and then, "I need you to promise you'll listen and not tell me I'm dramatic."

Silence. "All right," he said, tone shifting to the one he used after little league games when I'd missed pop flies. "Talk to me."

"I had a… moment yesterday. Like a premonition. It felt like more than a dream." I swallowed. "It was about Nik."

He didn't sigh. Points for Dad. "What did you see?"

"Back alley, sketchy guy, Nik looking jumpy," I said. "I know it sounds ridiculous, but it felt real. Just—keep an eye on him? Please?"

"I always do," Dad said gently. "I'll call the boys later. If I hear anything off, I'll let you know."

I exhaled. "Thanks."

"And Cassie?"

"Yeah?"

"You're a Bennett," he said. "We navigate storms."

I smiled, helpless. "Thanks, Dad."

We hung up. I set the phone down and stared at it like it might spit out a prophecy. It didn't.

By late afternoon, I'd finished grading the stack of essays that could have been titled *We Watched Troy (2004) and Then Wrote Feelings About Men With Swords.* I sent Diana one text—*I'm not ready to talk. I don't hate you.*—and got back a heart and a moon.

Still nothing from Apollo.

Good, I told myself for exactly one second, and then immediately: unfair. He owed me space; he also owed me words.

Around six, I left campus and walked without choosing a direction, the way you do when your brain is a storage room you can't get into. The city was softening toward evening, streetlights fuzzing the edges of things. I ended up, of course, near the small park where we'd had our picnic. Because the universe enjoys reruns.

I wasn't expecting him. Which is probably why he was there.

He stood beneath the same oak, hands in his pockets, looking—annoyingly—exactly like someone you'd trust with your secrets. When he saw me, something like relief moved over his face. He didn't come closer.

"I texted you," he said quietly. "Twice. Then deleted both."

"You made the right choice," I said, crossing my arms to keep from shaking. "I was composing a very long speech in which I am both reasonable and devastating."

He half-smiled. "I deserve devastating."

"Good," I said automatically, and watched the smile die. Great. Gold star for me.

He nodded at a bench. "Can we—?"

"We can," I said. "No guarantees I won't storm off like a reality TV contestant."

We sat at opposite ends, like that would help. It didn't.

He took a breath. "I meant to tell you from the beginning. I didn't because—" He grimaced. "Every time I do, the story stops being ours and starts being mine. People either fall to their knees or run."

"I'm fresh out of kneeling," I said. "Running's tempting."

"I don't want you to run," he said.

"I don't want you to lie by omission," I shot back. "And I don't want to be compared to someone you failed two thousand years ago, like I'm a replacement part."

His head dropped. "That's not what I meant."

"Then don't say it again," I said, voice steady, finally. "Say the thing you're actually afraid to say."

Silence. The wind nudged leaves along the path like small animals.

"I am not good with mortals," he said finally, each word like it cost him. "I loved badly once. I made everything worse. I don't know how to be with someone without breaking them."

I stared at him. "Then why start?"

"Because you looked at me like I was a person," he said, almost a laugh and not. "Not a statue, not a story. A person."

"You are," I said, then immediately, "and also very much not."

"Both can be true," he said.

We sat with that. For a long minute, it felt like a truce.

Then the other thing rose like a wave. "Why didn't you tell me about Diana?"

He blew out a breath. "She asked me not to be the one. She wanted to choose if and when you knew. I didn't think I had the right to take that choice from her."

"That," I said, "is the first thing you've said that makes sense."

He looked up, surprised. "Really?"

"Don't get cocky," I said. "I'm still mad. But I... get the part where someone wants to be known for herself."

His shoulders lowered a fraction. "Thank you."

I stood. "We're not fine," I said. "You don't get to glide back in with a poetic apology and dimples."

He had the nerve to look wounded. "Not the dimples."

"Don't test me," I warned, and caught the quick, involuntary laugh that escaped him. It loosened something between us, and I hated that I liked it.

"I need time," I said. "We'll text. *Maybe*. Don't show up unannounced. Don't touch me unless I ask." I paused. "And if these... vision episodes escalate, you tell me what to do to keep from short-circuiting in front of a hundred students."

His face sobered. "Yes," he said. "Of course."

I nodded once. "I'll let you know."

We walked out of the park side by side, not touching. At the corner, we stopped. He lifted his hand in a small wave. I didn't wave back, but I didn't turn away first. Small victories.

Back home, I showered until the water ran cold and stood in my kitchen in a towel, staring at the cabinet where I'd hidden the little lyre box. I left it where it was.

DIANA: *Safe home?*

ME: *Yes. Still need space.*

DIANA: *Understood. Love you.*

I breathed. Then, finally, a text from Apollo.

APOLLO: *I won't show up. I'll answer when you want. I'm sorry I made you feel cornered.*

ME: *Thank you. Boundaries matter.*

APOLLO: *They do. Good night, Cassandra.*

I put my phone facedown, crawled into bed, and whispered out loud—to the air, to the gods, to myself—"I am nobody's replacement. I'm writing my own story."

For once, sleep came quickly.

26

Cassandra

Ancient Troy

The torches along the corridor breathed and hissed, their light a wavering veil that turned every column into a sentinel. Cassandra sat alone in her chamber, a scroll unrolled but unread across her lap. The hush of the palace—soft footfalls, a distant lyre, the low creak of timber settling—usually soothed her. Tonight, it set her skin aflame.

It began as it always did, that warning prickle under the breastbone—the gods tugging a taut string only she could feel. Cassandra pressed her palms to her eyes until stars swarmed, but the thread only tightened. She stood, meaning to pace, to shake it off with motion. Instead, the room fell away.

Moonlight.

A garden—hers, yet not. The same laurel alleys, the same low murmur of water over stone, yet the air carried a strange sweetness, thick as overripe figs. Apollo stood beneath a bower, light collecting around him as if the night bent itself to please him. He did not look toward Cassandra. His gaze—beloved, ruinous—was turned to a figure whose outline the shadows kept.

A woman, cloaked and still.

"You," Cassandra said—or thought she said. The word drifted like ash and vanished. She reached out. Her hand passed through a cypress trunk that wasn't there.

Apollo leaned closer. His mouth shaped a private smile. He lifted a lock of the woman's hair as if it were a sunbeam he might braid. Cassandra knew the gesture; he had used it to make her laugh when she was trying not to. The air rang. Or was that her own blood thrumming?

"No," she breathed, and the garden trembled like water struck by a thrown stone.

The vision shattered—not cleanly, not like fired clay, but like sugar: a thousand bright shards skittering, reforming. Cassandra reeled in her body on her chamber's rug, one palm braced on the cool tile, her breath a scrape. She might have blamed weariness, or the heat, or even a fever—but the thread pulled again before she could name her denial.

The room dimmed; the moon grew a throat and sang.

Back to the garden, but closer. This time the fragrance was sharper, resin and crushed bay; she could taste it, could taste the salt on the air as if the sea had crept up the slope to eavesdrop. Apollo's profile was cut like a coin. The woman's hood slipped—not enough to give Cassandra a full face, only a glint: a cheekbone, a curve of mouth that might have been any mouth under heaven. Mortal? Divine? Herself?

The thought knifed her.

Not myself. Not me.

Apollo's hand rose. Not her hair this time—her throat. Not grasping, but the curl of fingers at the hollow, an intimate claim. The woman tilted her head to him as if to a cup.

"Stop." Cassandra's voice rang in her skull. "Stop." But the gods do not stop for mortal syllables, and neither do visions. She tried to step forward, to strike him, to wrench the night-girl away, and slammed into a wall of air that would not yield. She could not move; she could only witness.

It is a picture, she told herself. A symbol. Some trick. Prophecy speaks in masks.

But when Apollo's breath brushed the stranger's cheek and the stranger's shoulder lifted, Cassandra's stomach turned as if she had fallen from a height. The hood slipped a little more; a shine of auburn there—no, it was only the moonlight. Or was it?

The scene dissolved. The thread snapped. Cassandra was on her knees, hands splayed, a taste of iron under her tongue. Her lamplight made a honeyed pool about her feet; beyond that, darkness. She rose, her legs unsteady, and crossed to the narrow window. Troy slept: a quilt of roofs and terraces, a scatter of late fires, the high black line of the walls. Somewhere, a night-singer answered another across a garden. Somewhere, a child cried, and a nurse soothed.

And somewhere, in a place like and unlike her own garden, the god who had touched her thoughts had bent toward another.

A child's lesson rose—one of Hecuba's: Not all pictures show the thing they name. An omen may dress itself as a fox and mean a fire. A dream may be a warning, not a record. But the ache in Cassandra's ribs argued for the simplest meaning. The gods could tell truths without mercy.

She pressed her forehead to the cool stone of the embrasure. Rage and shame warred in her, then braided—two snakes twining. She wanted to storm the temple and demand: Answer me. She wanted to tear the laurel from the grove and set it alight. Instead, she stood very still and listened to her own breath stumble and smooth.

When she could trust her legs, she dressed for walking: a plain chiton, a cloak against the hour's dampness. She did not call for a lamp. The palace had known her feet since childhood; the dark did not refuse her. Past the storerooms and the sleeping hearths, past the court where the fountain's voice went on telling itself its old story, to a postern gate she and Helenus had used as children to slip out and dare each other to eat green almonds before the gardeners chased them.

Outside, Troy's night sighed. She took the path that skirted the walls, that cut through kitchen gardens and between quiet houses. The town gave way to the sacred rise of the gods' precinct. She did not turn toward Apollo's temple, its bright steps a pale geometry against the slope. She climbed instead to the owl-goddess.

The Temple of Athena was all angles and patience. Its columns rose not so much to impress as to make a place where thought could take shelter. The bronze doors were closed; the portico held shadows like a cup. Cassandra kept to the marble edge and put her palm to the seam. It was cool, dew-slick.

"Lady," she whispered to the threshold, to the bronze, to the stone listening inside itself. "Daughter of Zeus. Keeper of cities. Hear me."

No voice answered. A wind came up from the plain and lifted the hair at her neck. She let her forehead touch the door, just once, then stepped back. If the goddess would not open to her, she would make her plea under the open sky.

The olive trees beyond the temple wall were older than memory, their trunks spiral-twisted as if the tree within had wrung itself against an iron cuff. Between them, the earth lay silvered with moon. Cassandra moved among the shadows until she found a space where she could see both the dark of the sea and the small, steadfast light that was the moon caught in Athena's bronze spear-tip.

She knelt. Not as a priestess. Not as a petitioner with an offering cut and ready. As a woman with a wound.

"Lady," she said again, and her voice did not break. "I will not ask you for a lover's fidelity. I know what the poets sing and what the old women say at their looms. Gods are winds; they go where they list. But I have seen something—and whether it is an event or an emblem, it has struck me through. If I am being warned, teach me to read what is written. If I am being broken, show me how to set the bone so it heals strong."

Leaves answered. Not speech—leaf-speech, dry whisper on dry whisper. Something heavy moved on a branch, weight and balance, and regard. Cassandra lifted her head.

An owl sat two arm-lengths away, more shadow than bird. Its face was a pale coin; its eyes were two wells into which a woman might pour her questions until dawn.

"You came once," Cassandra said to it, remembering a softer day and a kinder wind. "Come again."

The owl tipped its head. It did not blink.

"Show me if I am deceived," she said. "Or show me how to bear the truth."

Silence, then the smallest answer: the bird's throat fluttered. A sound—so soft a mouse might have missed it. A breath of a note. Yet the hair on

Cassandra's arms lifted, and not with cold.

The wind shifted; the scent of crushed olive, of dust, of a distant, clean forge came with it. Cassandra closed her eyes. The garden again, for an instant—not the moon-garden of her vision, but this grove: Athena's shade. Within that breath-long overlay, she felt a different pattern of the threads— how one could pull and another could slacken without the whole weaving tearing. A picture broke and re-formed. In the temple of her ribs, the clamor quieted.

"Not a command," she murmured, because Athena did not command as some gods did; she reasoned. "A lesson."

When she opened her eyes, the owl was gone. Or it had always been nothing more than a shadow blooming into a shape her need could use. Either way, Cassandra rose with a bone-deep steadiness she had not brought into the grove.

"I will not run to him and wail," she said to the quiet trees. "I will not accuse the sun with smoke for proof."

She would watch. She would test. She would keep counsel like a tactician, not spend her heart like a reckless soldier in the first charge. If the vision was a mask, she would learn what face it wore. If it were true, she would not let it unmake her.

By the time the first gull cried out toward the morning, Cassandra had made her way down the slope and back along the shadow of the wall. Aeneas passed her in the gray light—cloak thrown back, jaw dark with a night's growth, the look of a man who had been at the watch and had found the city still there when dawn came. He inclined his head, not courtly, but with that soldier's acknowledgment that takes the other in as an equal in need.

"Princess," he said, voice low in the hour.

"Aeneas," she returned.

He glanced—a quick sweep that took in her cloak, her bare hair, her hands empty of offering—and said only, "Clear roads." It was a wish and prayer both, from one who knew how seldom either was granted.

"And steady oars," she answered, for sailors, and the corner of his mouth eased.

Back in her chamber, the lamps guttered. She washed her face in the water that had kept its night-cool, braided her hair with a briskness that left no room for shaking fingers, and greeted Bee, her handmaid, with a nod that asked for silence and received it. The palace woke around her—fire carried, bread cut, the first clash of practice spears in the yard below—and Cassandra felt herself settle into the day like a blade into a whetstone's groove.

She did not go to Apollo's temple. Not yet. She went about the morning's obligations with the alert attention of a hunter, and where she might have drifted in thought, she listened. Servants spoke. Guards compared idle stories. Priests passed in twos and threes, their sandals slapping marble. She sifted words the way a gold-washer sifts river grit.

A name recurred. Not a woman's—no lover gossiped from the kitchens— but a place: the north garden, the one beyond the laurel hedge, the one rarely tended because it had been planted in her grandmother's day and left to its own ideas of beauty. "Lovely for a tryst," one serving-girl said, rolling her eyes as another giggled. "Lovely for turtle-doves," a guard replied, and both laughed and glanced to be sure no overseer had heard.

Lovely for a tryst. Lovely for turtle-doves. Lovely for a god who liked old trees and spaces where the city did not expect to see him.

She kept her face mild. Inside, she pinned those phrases to a board. The owl's regard stayed with her. Measure first. Then move.

In the noon hour, when the palace thinned—men to training, women to their looms, children to whatever mischief they could invent—she crossed to Hecuba's apartments. Her mother sat with two matrons and a bronze worker's wife, choosing designs for a set of wedding cups. Gold thread spilled from a basket like sun-water. The Queen's face was all sweetness to her guests, all iron under it. Cassandra knew both faces and loved both, even when the iron cut her.

"Daughter," Hecuba said. "Sit. See this vine-work. Is it too bold?"

"It is perfect," Cassandra said, and meant it.

They spoke of cups and the number of lambs to be marked for the next festival. The matrons rose with carefully calibrated laughter and withdrew.

Hecuba repositioned a thread with the tip of her nail and said, without looking up, "You did not sleep."

"No."

"Is it a vision?"

"Yes."

Hecuba's hand paused. "Will you tell me?"

"I am not sure what it is," Cassandra said carefully. She was not lying. Not anymore. "Only that it cut."

Her mother's gaze lifted then—those flint-dark eyes, the ones that saw through boys' bravado and men's public faces to the soft and selfish beneath. "Then bind it," Hecuba said. "And do not show it bleeding to those who would salt the wound."

Cassandra almost smiled. The counsel was not Athena's, but it was wisdom of its kind. "Yes, Mother."

"And if this is about a god," Hecuba added, as if discussing a stain that would not come out of linen, "remember that gods are like storms. If you cannot bar the door against them, you secure your stores and wait them out."

"Even a sun-storm?" Cassandra said, too quickly, betraying more than she had meant to. Hecuba's eyes sharpened; she sat back.

"So," the Queen said softly. "So. A storm that thinks itself as fair weather." She considered her daughter for a long moment. "Be clever," she said at last. "Not loud."

Cassandra kissed her mother's hand and left with her spine straighter and her mouth arranged. She sought her father next and found him where she often did at midday when there was no war council: in a small loggia that overlooked the city, alone, his crown set aside on the bench beside him. Age had written new lines around Priam's eyes; grief had inked its signature at his mouth. But he still had the look of a man who would walk a wall at night rather than ask another to do it for him.

"Pappá," she said.

"Daughter." He smiled, and the lines softened.

They spoke of small things first: a crack in the eastern cistern, a shipment of cedar late from the north. Then Cassandra said, as if remarking on the weather: "If a picture is shown to you—one that may be a thing that will be, or only a warning—what do you do with your day?"

Priam did not ask what picture. He had raised too many children to hack at the hedge when a gentle hand would part it. He sat quietly long enough that a swallow stitched three flights between the loggia's arches.

"I remind myself," he said, "that a king is not a seer. And that a daughter is not a god. We have our labors. We set stones where they hold best. We do not build on clouds."

She nodded. "And if the cloud is lovely?"

"We enjoy its shade," he said, and then, with a rueful half-smile, "and we keep our rain-casks ready."

He reached and cupped her cheek, not asking, not pressing, only touching the face that was Hecuba's face at fifteen and his sister's face at twelve and his own mother's face in the look she carried when she climbed the citadel stairs faster than decorum allowed. "I love you, daughter," he said.

In the late afternoon, when the sun had a lazier slant and the gardeners set aside their tools, Cassandra took the long way to her favorite balcony—by the north garden. She did not skulk; she walked as a princess walks, with her veil half-drawn and her mind apparently on nothing more dangerous than shade. The laurel hedge breathed its green breath. Beyond it, the old garden lay: unmannered, gorgeous, a theater of bees.

No god stood there. No cloaked woman. A pair of doves quarrelled decorously on a fallen column. Someone—gods or children—had left a twist of ribbon on an olive twig.

The ribbon made her pulse jump. Then cool reason returned. It was red, a child's, not the gold she had worn the night she'd first spoken with him.

Measure first. Then move.

She did not stay to brood. She let the garden know that she had seen it and that she would not be haunted there. She returned to the public rooms, to Andromache's laughing baby, to Helenus's solemn new gravitas as he corrected a priest's citation, to Paris's perfumed chatter about lions and dancers from abroad. She was a sister again, a daughter, a woman of a house that did not yet know the shape of its end. She let life's noise lap at her ankles and felt her anger settle into a colder, more useful form.

That night—only then—she went to the olive grove where she had first met Apollo. Not at the hour of trysts. Late, when even the sprites yawn. She stood under the oldest tree, its bark ridged like an elder's knuckles, and said—not loudly, but with a clarity that gave the air a bright edge:

"I have seen a picture. If you painted it for me to hurt me, you have succeeded, and I am not softened by it. If you showed me a symbol, then speak to me as you promised you would, in truth, not in riddles you admire for their cleverness. I will not be kept ignorant and grateful. I am a daughter of kings, and I have a city to guard."

The leaves went on whispering. The grove held its breath and then exhaled it. No blaze of presence came; no heat rippled the ground. She waited, counting slowly to one hundred. When the count was done and the world remained the world, Cassandra nodded once—the small bow a duelist offered before the bout—and turned for home.

She did not know yet whether the vision foretold a lover or a lesson. She knew only this: whatever thread it was, she would not let it wrap her throat. She would learn the weave. And when the time came to pull, she would choose her strand and draw it with a steady hand.

27

Cassie

Modern Day

I slept terribly. My neck and shoulders were stiff from holding tension, like I'd clenched myself through every dream. I had never been so angry — especially at Diana — and the remnants of that fury still hummed in my body like static. My head throbbed as I rolled, literally rolled, out of bed and stumbled toward the shower.

I didn't check my phone. I didn't need to see the unread texts and voicemails from Diana that I knew would be waiting. My day needed to start on *my* terms, not hers.

I turned on the shower as hot as it would go, rummaged through the bathroom cabinet, and pulled out a lavender-eucalyptus steamer I'd been hoarding for weeks. Today called for everything in my self-care arsenal — aromatherapy, masks, lotions, the works. Thank God it was Friday and I didn't teach. I could hide from the world in reruns and bubble baths if I wanted.

Steam filled the bathroom. The water poured down in a rhythm so steady it nearly hypnotized me, pounding away the ache in my shoulders, drowning out the looping reel of last night's fight. I focused on the small things: shampoo lather, the sharp cold rinse at the end (which I still hated but stubbornly did because some article swore it was "good for your hair").

By the time I stepped out, wrapped in my softest robe, I felt half human again.

That lasted until I walked into the kitchen.

On the counter sat a to-go cup, a donut bag, and a note in Diana's neat, loopy handwriting.

My dearest Cassandra,
　Forgive me.
　I would never intentionally do anything to hurt you.
　Please know I had my reasons.
　All my love, Di.

I stared at the note, throat tight. For a moment, the anger ebbed. This was so like Diana — contrite, soft, offering sugar as an apology. But beneath the guilt, another feeling bubbled up: shame.

Because if I was honest with myself, I wasn't just mad at her. I was mad at myself.

I'd told myself last night that I was betrayed. That my best friend had lied, that Apollo had humiliated me. But pacing my apartment now, I saw the truth clearly: jealousy. Ugly, green-eyed jealousy.

I'd seen Apollo with Diana — beautiful, radiant Diana — and every insecurity I thought I'd buried in my teens rose like hydra heads. I was the funny friend, the late bloomer, the one who watched other girls get chosen first. And for one raw second, I thought maybe Apollo had chosen her over me.

And that was on me, not her.

By the time I picked up my phone to call, my hands shook with regret more than anger.

She answered instantly. "I'm glad you're okay," Diana said, calm as ever.

"I was an ass to you."

"No," she soothed. "You could never—"

"Yes, I was. I got…jealous. Thinking Apollo looked at you and thought, *yep, better option.* And I hated myself for it." The words burned coming out.

There was a pause on her end. Then: "Cass…"

"Can you forgive me?"

"There isn't anything to forgive."

I laughed, broken and soft. "There is. But..." A knock at my door interrupted me.

When I opened it, she was there. We hung up our phones at the same time and just hugged.

"I'm sorry," I whispered into her hair.

"I know." She squeezed me tighter.

We drifted to the couch. She told me a little about her "complicated" relationship with Apollo, about their strange upbringing, about her wish for normalcy. She still didn't say *everything*, and I didn't push. Our laughter came easier than I expected, but beneath it, something felt...fragile. We weren't fully mended. Not yet.

* * *

The apartment was quiet after she left. I had a face mask drying on my skin when the now-familiar hum began in my veins.

Another vision.

I braced myself and let it take me.

This time, the world formed in sharper detail than ever before: a dim chamber, moonlight spilling across marble. And there was Apollo. Golden, radiant, magnetic. Only he wasn't alone.

A woman stood close beside him, her face blurred by shadow, but the intimacy was unmistakable. The way he leaned in, the way his smile softened just for her — gestures I thought were mine.

My stomach lurched. The air in the vision thickened, charged, until I swore I could taste betrayal on my tongue.

When the vision snapped away, I barely made it to the bathroom before vomiting.

I knew what I had seen. And I knew who had made me see it.

* * *

That evening, Apollo sat across from me in my living room, his presence filling every corner — too much light, too much warmth. Even the shadows seemed to flinch from him. I clenched my mug between my hands like armor, the ceramic searing against my palms.

"Can we talk?" My voice cracked before I could stop it. I forced it steady. "I had another vision."

His head lifted, a faint smile ghosting across his lips. "Another?"

"This one felt different."

He leaned forward, interest sharpened. "What kind of vision?"

I hesitated, searching his face. "I saw you."

Something flickered behind his eyes — curiosity, then caution. "And?"

I swallowed. "You weren't alone. You were with someone else. Too close. Too…intimate."

The warmth in the room wavered, like a candle in wind. His expression froze. For a heartbeat, silence pressed heavy between us.

"Cassie," he said finally, too softly. "There's no one else."

I wanted to believe him. Gods, I wanted to. But the vision still burned behind my eyes — his hand on another's face, that same light spilling across skin not mine.

"I trust you," I said, my voice small. "But I also trust what I saw. You gave me these visions. They're not dreams. They're you."

His jaw tightened. "Mortals dream fears all the time." He leaned closer, tone honeyed, almost coaxing. "Don't let shadows trick you."

Something in me snapped. "Don't gaslight me."

His eyes widened slightly at the word — modern, sharp, human — then narrowed, molten.

"These aren't shadows," I continued, my voice rising. "If the visions are lies, then you are lying."

The air changed. It thickened, humming with static. His light flared, no longer gentle but edged with violence, gold hardening into white.

"Careful," he said, and the word cracked like thunder.

Heat rushed up my neck. "Careful? I'm telling you what *you* showed me."

He rose so fast the mug slipped from my hands, shattering on the floor.

His glow filled the room — too bright, too real. The walls seemed to bow under it.

"You are just like *her*," he hissed.

My breath caught. I knew who he was talking about, but something in me needed to hear it directly from his lips. "Like...who?"

His smile was sharp as glass. "The first Cassandra. The one who dared accuse me. Who refused me. Who saw too much." He stepped closer, and I felt it — the divine weight, the impossible gravity that made air itself a prison.

"Always doubting. Always ungrateful," he whispered. "And still pretending you are *blameless*."

My heart pounded so violently it hurt. "You're frightening me," I whispered.

"Good."

His eyes burned — sunlight turned to fire. The room smelled of ozone and scorched air.

"You mortals never learn," he said, voice breaking from human to something vast and echoing. "You beg for gifts, then curse the hands that grant them."

My throat closed; panic clawed up my chest. I wanted to move, to flee, but my legs refused.

"So suffer like she did," he said.

Then the light vanished.

The slam of the door came a breath later, so hard the shelves rattled and the pictures tilted, glass trembling in their frames. The echo hung there, a hollow vibration that filled the silence he left behind.

I sat frozen, the smell of burnt dust still in the air, my pulse screaming in my ears. My hands shook — one cut from the shattered mug, blood threading down to the floor.

I had angered a god.

And somewhere in the golden afterimage that clung to my walls, I swore I heard him whisper my name — not with love, but with promise.

I would pay the price.

28

Cassandra

Ancient Troy

The late afternoon light poured through the high columns of the Temple of Athena, painting the marble floors in streaks of gold. Cassandra lingered there more often these days, drawn not by duty but by need. The quiet order of the temple soothed her mind in a way the bustling palace never could.

She was no priestess, but the senior women welcomed her as a daughter seeking wisdom. They allowed her to sweep petals before the statue, to join in the hymns, to read the scrolls when her hands were steady enough to hold them. Among them, Cassandra could forget the sharp eyes of her mother and the heavy expectations of her birth. Here, she was not a pawn in a marriage game, not a princess bound by duty, but a young woman searching for answers.

In the gardens, she found moments of peace: the sound of bees in the thyme, the scent of incense clinging to her hair, the steady rhythm of prayers that promised a wisdom greater than her own. And for a time, it was enough to anchor her.

Until she saw him again.

It was as the sun dipped toward the horizon. Her guards had gathered at the base of the temple steps to escort her home when, just beyond them, she spotted him. Apollo, standing casually as though he were any other man, his gaze locked only on her. He said nothing — he couldn't, not with mortals so close — but he tipped his head ever so slightly toward the temple gardens. A signal. A summons.

Her stomach tightened.

She nodded once, barely perceptible, and allowed her guards to lead her away.

* * *

Later that night, Cassandra returned.

The Temple of Apollo was empty, its incense still burning from evening prayers. She had told Leander — her most trusted guard, the boy who had grown up at her side — that she wished for solitude. He had bowed, worry flickering in his dark eyes, and stationed himself outside the door. Cassandra hated deceiving him, but this meeting could not wait.

She slipped into the garden, and there he was.

"Lord Apollo," she whispered, her voice catching.

The god stepped from the shadows, radiant even in the moonlight. "You came."

"I always come," she said, though the words tasted bitter.

For a moment, they simply looked at one another. The air between them hummed with everything unspoken — awe, longing, doubt, anger.

Finally, Cassandra broke the silence. "I have seen visions." Her voice trembled, but she did not falter. "Visions of you. With another."

Apollo's smile faltered.

Cassandra pressed on, the words spilling faster now. "At first I thought it was me — a memory of that night in the olive grove. But no. Her shape was different. Her presence..." Her throat tightened. "I saw your face, your tenderness, turned not to me but to her. And then, again — another vision. Perhaps the same woman, perhaps not. But the meaning was clear. You were unfaithful."

The silence stretched long enough that the cicadas in the garden seemed deafening. Cassandra shifted, nails digging into her palms.

Finally, she demanded, "Is it true?"

Apollo looked away. His usual brilliance dimmed, his eyes flickering everywhere but hers — the sky, the temple walls, the flowers swaying at their feet. He, the god who never broke his gaze, could not meet her eyes.

That was enough.

Her voice broke. "You do not deny it."

He flinched, as though her words had struck him. "Cassandra…"

"You told me my visions were true," she cut him off, her voice rising, trembling with fury. "And now you dare tell me this one lies?"

He stepped forward, hands raised in a half-plea. "The threads of fate are tangled. What you see may not always mean what you think—"

"No," she snapped. Tears blurred her eyes, but her voice was iron. "Do not twist my gift into riddles. I trusted you. I loved you." The word slipped out before she could swallow it back, and she saw it hit him like a spear.

"You—" he began, but she barreled on.

"Yes. While there had only been a handful of meetings, I was foolish enough to think it was love. I, a princess who is never allowed to choose. I had chosen you. And now…" She swallowed the lump in her throat. "Now I see I was wrong."

Apollo's composure cracked. Rage flared bright in his eyes. "How *dare* you doubt me! I blessed you. I gave you prophecy. I gave you *myself.*"

"You gave me visions," Cassandra shot back, voice breaking. "And the visions showed me the truth. You stand before me, unable to deny it. That is all the answer I need."

Her chest heaved with sobs she refused to release. She turned, lifting her skirts, intent on leaving the garden.

"Cassandra!" His voice thundered, shaking the leaves.

She froze.

"If you walk away," Apollo said, every word vibrating with power, "you will suffer. You think your gift is heavy now? I will make it a curse. You will still see true visions — but no one, not your father, not your brothers, not even your beloved Hector, will ever believe you again."

Her blood ran cold. She thought of Hector's new baby, of Andromache's kind smile, of the city she longed to protect. Without her visions, how could she save them? If no one believed her, what use was the truth?

A war raged inside her: beg forgiveness and maybe keep her power intact — or hold her ground and lose everything.

Slowly, Cassandra clenched her fists until her nails bit flesh. She did not turn back to face him.

Her tears spilled hot down her cheeks, but her voice steadied. "Then curse me, Apollo. I will not be your plaything."

And with that, she stepped out of the garden, into the shadowed halls of Troy, carrying her doom like a crown.

29

Cassie

Modern Day

After Apollo slammed my door that Friday night, it was as if the world had tilted on its axis. Colors looked the same, sounds carried the same, but everything felt…off. The curse clung to me like smoke.

By Monday, I noticed the shift. A colleague muttered about going down Rome Avenue because of construction delays, but did not want to be stuck in traffic. "Don't go down Rome Ave. today," I warned automatically. He smiled, humored me, and took that route anyway. An hour later, he was late to the seminar, fuming about a car wreck blocking traffic.

"Lucky guess," he said when I reminded him.

Lucky guess. My teeth ached from grinding them.

I tried again on Tuesday, with Grace at the coffee cart. She was always sweet, always chatty. As she handed me my latte, she warned, "Careful—the lid's loose."

Without thinking, I replied, "Thanks, but the wind's going to knock that whole napkin stack over in about ten seconds."

She gave me a bemused look. "Uh-huh."

And then, right on cue, a gust ripped across the quad, scattering napkins everywhere like confetti. Grace laughed, but not in amazement—just that indulgent kind of laugh people use with kids who say silly things.

"You're a trip, Professor B," she said, shaking her head. "Always guessing the weirdest stuff."

Guessing. My stomach dropped. No matter what I said, no one believed me. The curse was working.

* * *

By Wednesday, I canceled my classes. One email, a quick apology about "illness," and then I just…stopped. The blinds stayed half-shut, light carving diagonal slashes across my apartment while I sat like a ghost in the corner.

Even Diana's calls went unanswered.

Especially Diana's.

When I finally reached out, it was to Eloise. She taught high school now, tenth-grade intensive reading, but we'd survived grad school coursework together. She had always been pragmatic, the type who kept planners color-coded and reminded me to eat when I forgot. If anyone could steady me, it would be her.

"Cassie, I'm worried about you," Eloise said through the glow of my phone screen. Her background was the classroom whiteboard, half-wiped annotations behind her like unfinished ghosts. I sat on my couch in leggings and an oversized hoodie, a glass of wine sweating in my hand. Too much wine, if I were being honest.

"I've been having visions," I blurted. "Not just dreams, El. They're real. They show me things before they happen. Two weeks now. And I can't stop them."

She sighed, and I could tell she was doing the mental calculus of how to phrase the next sentence without offending me. "Cass, I think you're under a ton of stress. Apollo ghosting you, your dissertation, midterms coming up. And your brothers in Greece? That's a lot."

"It's not stress." My voice was sharper than I meant. "I know what stress dreams feel like, and these are different. They're too vivid, too exact. They terrify me."

Eloise tilted her camera down, fiddling with something offscreen—

stalling. When she looked back up, her expression was gentle, the kind people use when talking someone down from a ledge. "I believe that *you* believe it. But, Cass, your mind can play tricks when it's overloaded. Maybe you should take a week, step back. Sleep. Write for yourself instead of your students."

Her sympathy hurt more than outright dismissal. It felt like being handled. Like my visions were fragile delusions she could tuck neatly into a box labeled "burnout."

I traced the stem of my wineglass with my finger. "Thanks for listening," I said, hoping she'd change the subject.

She obliged. "Distraction time. Want to hear about the ridiculously cute new football coach they hired? I think half the faculty suddenly cares about Friday night games."

I forced a smile, grateful for her normalcy, even as my chest ached with loneliness.

* * *

The rest of the week bled together. My apartment mirrored me—disheveled, adrift. Books lay in uneven piles across the table, some spines cracked mid-paragraph, abandoned. The calendar on my fridge, once a riot of neon sticky notes, was wiped nearly bare.

When colleagues texted, I ignored the buzz. For once, I let the red notification bubble sit, glaring from the corner of my phone. After forty-eight hours, I stopped even feeling guilty. Better to cocoon.

By Friday, I scribbled another half-drawn nightmare in my journal. Fire. Voices screaming. A shadow reaching for me before it dissolved to ash. My handwriting was jagged, illegible. My stomach twisted when I realized the vision was identical to the one from last week. They weren't fading. They were compounding.

I needed my dad.

* * *

"Hey, beautiful," came his baritone greeting when he picked up.

"Hey, Dad," I said softly. "Do you have a minute?"

"For you? I've got several." His warmth, always steady, loosened something in my chest. For a heartbeat, I believed he'd hear me.

"It's about Nik," I rushed. "Please don't interrupt. Just…let me finish."

I told him everything—the vision of Nik in the alley, the shady deal, the dread that had coiled in my stomach since. Words tumbled out fast and hot, as if speed alone might make them sound credible. When I finished, silence stretched, weighted and heavy.

Finally, Dad exhaled, a sound like gravel shifting. "Cassie…I just talked to Theo and Nik this morning. Theo double-checked the imports—he swears everything is clean, above board. You have to understand, this is a serious accusation. Are you sure you're not…imagining things?"

The dismissal stung sharper than Eloise's. "I'm sure," I snapped. "I *know* what I saw."

"Cassie," he said slowly, careful like I was glass, "I know you and Nik butt heads. But please don't sabotage this because you're mad at him. This deal is huge for the family business."

It felt like the floor dropped. Sabotage. As if warning him meant betrayal.

My throat burned. "I'm not trying to sabotage anything! I'm trying to protect us!"

He sighed again, weary. "I'll keep an eye on things. But don't do anything rash. Don't call your brothers. Promise me."

"I won't do anything rash," I whispered, tears pricking my eyes. "But please, Dad. Be careful."

"I will, Cassie. I promise. Sorry, gotta go, kid. Kellie is standing in the doorway waiting for our next meeting."

We hung up. I clutched my pillow, muffling the scream that tore out of me. The curse was working—no one believed me. Not Eloise. Not Dad. Maybe not anyone, ever again.

* * *

Later that night, my phone buzzed. A short email from Thomas, subject line: *Faculty Budget Update.* Just numbers, boring logistics. But he added a line at the bottom: *Hope you're hanging in there, Cassie. Let me know if you need a sounding board.*

It was nothing.

It was everything.

Proof someone, at least, still thought I was worth hearing.

30

Cassandra

The rolling hills of Troy no longer held any joy for Cassandra. Since the night she defied Apollo, visions plagued her without mercy. They came like waves: small ones—"turn left toward the agora," "avoid the beach"—and great storms, scenes of fire and ruin that left her trembling on the floor.

Her handmaids whispered she had gone mad. Guards exchanged looks behind her back. In a palace overflowing with voices, Cassandra had never felt so alone.

For a week, she remained in bed. The once-vibrant princess of Troy was now a hollow figure beneath tangled sheets. Shadows stretched across her chamber, the ivory effigy of Athena clutched to her breast, her lips moving in silent prayer.

But the goddess did not answer.

Only silence.

* * *

"Daughter."

King Priam's voice broke the stillness. Cassandra startled as the door opened and his tall figure filled the threshold.

"Pappá, please," she whispered. "Leave me be."

He stepped inside, his expression lined with worry. "I cannot ignore you any longer, Cassandra. Rumors are spreading like wildfire. They say you have gone mad."

Her laugh was sharp, bitter. "Mad? No, Pappá. Cursed. Apollo has laid a curse upon me. My visions are true—yet no one will ever believe them."

Priam sat beside her bed, lowering himself with the heaviness of both king and father. His gaze softened. "What visions trouble you, child?"

Cassandra's throat tightened. She knew he would not believe—but she could not stay silent. "Paris has done something reckless. Something that will bring ruin upon us all. Hector and Paris will return to Troy in a day or two, and when they do, you will see."

Priam's brow furrowed. "Enough," he said quietly, though his voice held steel. "Do not speak ill of your brother. I will not hear it."

"Pappá, please—"

"Enough," he repeated, rising sharply. Anger flashed in his eyes, but beneath it, Cassandra glimpsed sorrow. "You disgrace yourself with these ravings. Put these dark thoughts to rest before they consume you."

His words struck her like a blow. He left, the door closing with finality, and Cassandra collapsed against the pillows. Tears blurred her sight as she clutched Athena's effigy tighter.

"Oh, goddess," she whispered. "Help me. I cannot bear this burden alone."

But the only reply was more silence.

* * *

The following morning, Cassandra forced herself into the palace gardens. The air smelled of rosemary and sea-wind, the gravel crunching beneath her sandals. She traced her fingers along the bark of an olive tree, trying to still her mind.

But the vision struck without warning.

The gardens vanished.

She stood upon the deck of a ship, salt spray stinging her skin. Hector's voice thundered in her ears:

"Brother, what have you done?"

Paris turned, guilt flashing across his handsome face. "Nothing that cannot be undone."

"Paris—"

"She is here," he said, gesturing toward the cabin.

From below deck emerged a woman whose beauty seared Cassandra's eyes. Golden hair spilling over ivory shoulders, her gaze luminous and terrible. Helen of Sparta.

"Dear gods," Hector whispered, horror breaking his voice. "You've stolen the wife of a king. You've doomed us all."

The sea roared. Fire bloomed on the horizon. Cassandra saw Greek ships gathering like storm clouds, saw the walls of Troy bathed in flame. Screams filled her ears until she choked.

She gasped awake in the gardens, knees buckling beneath her. The world swam.

"No," she whispered. "It cannot be."

But the curse allowed no mercy.

* * *

That night, she stood trembling before her father's chambers. The torches sputtered in the corridor as she forced her hand to knock.

"Pappá?" Her voice cracked. "Please. I must speak with you."

From within came his weary reply. "Leave me be, Cassandra. I have no patience for your ravings tonight."

She pushed the door open anyway. Priam sat at his table, maps of the Aegean spread before him. His face, stern and tired, lifted to hers.

"What calamity have you seen now?"

"Paris," Cassandra whispered, stepping closer. "He has stolen Helen, wife of Menelaus. I saw her—her face, her beauty beyond compare. Hector tried to stop him, but it was too late. Father, the Greeks will come. They will come for her, and they will not stop until Troy is ash."

For a long moment, Priam only stared. The silence stretched like a taut string.

Then, softly, "Do you hear yourself? My son, a thief of kings' wives? Cassandra, you shame him with these tales."

"It is no tale!" Her voice broke, but she pressed on. "Pappá, please. You must believe me. A war is coming. I saw the flames. I heard the screams. Troy will fall—unless we act."

Something flickered in his gaze—doubt, fear. For half a heartbeat, she thought she had reached him.

But then his jaw hardened. His king's mask returned. "I cannot, daughter. I will not condemn Paris on the word of visions. You ask me to tear my family apart with no proof."

"Because proof will come too late," Cassandra cried.

"Enough!" His voice rang like a hammer. "You poison this house with your despair. I forbid you to speak of this again."

Her knees trembled, her heart fracturing under his words. "Pappá…"

But he turned away, gathering his scrolls, his shoulders heavy with sorrow.

"Go, Cassandra." His voice was weary now. "Leave me."

She stumbled from the chamber, tears burning hot trails down her cheeks. The door closed behind her with a sound like finality.

Back in her room, she collapsed before the window, the marble cold beneath her palms. She lifted her face to the night sky, whispering desperately:

"Athena, guide me. Please."

But the heavens gave no answer.

Cassandra bowed her head, tears falling into her lap. She understood, finally, what Apollo's curse truly meant: to speak truth into the void, unheard, unheeded, forever.

Yet as despair crushed her chest, another truth burned beneath it.

She would not stop.

Even if no one believed her—even if it killed her—Cassandra of Troy would not be silent.

31

Cassie

Modern Day

The air around me shimmered, and images of a sunlit Grecian coast materialized before my eyes. I blinked against the brightness, salt in the air, sand grinding beneath my feet—yet I wasn't really there. Nik stood on a cliffside above the Aegean, his usual cocky grin softened into something unfamiliar. Beside him was a woman with long, dark hair that glinted like copper in the sun. Her smile was warm but nervous, the kind of smile that carried more fear than joy.

Her name floated to me on the wind, though I hadn't heard it aloud yet. *Helen.*

Nik clasped her hands too tightly, like he was afraid she'd disappear if he let go. "It doesn't matter what anyone says," he told her. "You're mine. You've always been mine."

A chill crept up my arms.

The waves crashed violently below them, foam spraying like shattered glass. No priest, no witnesses—just the two of them whispering vows as though the sea itself were their audience. It wasn't a ceremony; it was an elopement. Desperate. Dangerous.

And when they sealed it with a kiss, my stomach dropped.

What in the fresh hell are you doing, Nikolaos?

The vision dissolved. Suddenly, I was back in my apartment, breath shallow, heart pounding. The shadows of my tiny living room seemed too sharp, too close. Theo would *lose his mind* if he knew. Dad's marble deal with Helen's father—*the* Dimitri Kostas—was supposed to secure our future. Dimitri didn't just run the Hellenic Marble Supply Company; he ruled it. The only thing tougher than his stone was his reputation, and the only thing he guarded more fiercely than his marble was his daughter.

And Nik had just made her his wife.

My throat tightened. *This is Paris stealing Helen all over again.* And I was Cassandra—watching, knowing, powerless.

I snatched my phone off the counter. "Pick up, Dad. Come on. Pick up."

Finally, his voice—steady, deep, gruff—answered. "Hello? Cassie?"

"Dad," I rushed, pacing my living room. "Nik…he—he married Helen Kostas. In secret. I saw it."

The silence was heavy before his voice exploded like thunder. "Damn it, Cassie! Not this again."

I froze, stunned by the anger in his tone.

"You can't go around accusing your brother of this kind of recklessness because of some…some *dream,*" he snapped. "You're not six years old anymore, running tattletale stories because you're mad at Nik."

I swallowed hard, tears burning. "It wasn't a dream. It was real, Dad. I saw it. You *have* to believe me—if Dimitri finds out, the deal's over, everything's over—"

"Enough." His voice went cold, clipped. "Nik knows what's at stake. He wouldn't be that stupid. Don't call me with this again."

The line went dead.

I stood there, phone in hand, my father's dismissal ringing louder than his words. *You're not six years old anymore.*

My chest ached as I scrolled through my contacts. One unread message blinked back at me.

THOMAS SINCLAIR: *Hey, Cass, just checking in. Want to grab lunch next week?*

I stared at it, the contrast twisting the knife deeper. Dad thought I was a child. Theo probably would too. And Thomas—who always believed me, who *saw* me—was still waiting on a reply I hadn't dared to give.

But I couldn't ignore Theo. Not now.

I dialed.

"Hey, Cassie!" Theo answered, warmth in his voice, a balm after Dad's coldness. "What's up?"

I inhaled shakily. "It's Nik. I had a vision. He married Helen. Secretly. In Greece."

Silence stretched, then a half-laugh. "Wait. What?" His voice lowered, muffled, like he was moving. I heard him excuse himself before he came back clearer. "Cass…are you sure? Nik's been—honestly, he's been incredible on this trip. Holding things together. Helping me. He wouldn't do something this reckless."

"Please, Theo," I begged. "I've never been so sure. I saw it all—the waves, the vows, the kiss. It wasn't a dream. It was real."

Another silence. When he spoke again, his voice was tired, fraying at the edges. "Cass…I love you. You know I do. And I want to believe you. But you have to see how this sounds. Nobody will take this seriously. Not Dad. Not Dimitri. Not Nik. And if you start spreading this, it could ruin everything before we even have marble on the ship."

The words stung worse than if he'd shouted at me.

"But Theo—"

"I have to go," he cut me off, pained. "We'll sort this out when we get home. Just…hang tight, okay?"

And then he was gone too.

The room spun. No one believed me. Not Dad. Not Theo. Not anyone.

A scream ripped from my throat as I hurled my phone against the wall. It cracked, clattering to the floor. My gaze landed on the little ivory Athena figurine sitting on my bookshelf—the one I'd bought in Athens, the one I whispered to when I needed strength. My hand trembled as I reached for it.

And then, with a sob, I threw it too. The sound of it shattering against the hardwood floor broke something inside me.

I collapsed among the shards, clutching a pillow to my chest, screaming into the fabric until my throat was raw. Feathers or glass—it didn't matter.

I was alone.

A knock came at the door. Soft. Hesitant.

I dragged myself up, wiping my face with the sleeve of my sweatshirt. "Who is it?" My voice cracked.

"It's Diana," came the reply.

Relief, sharp and cutting, stole my breath. I opened the door, just a crack. She stood there in the hallway, moonlight catching in her silver eyes. Without a word, she stepped in, saw the wreckage, and crossed the room to pick up the largest shard of Athena's broken form. She set it gently on the counter, then turned back to me.

"Tell me," she said simply, pulling me into her arms.

The words poured out—Nik, Helen, Dad's dismissal, Theo's doubt. The curse. The loneliness.

When I finished, her answer was quiet but steady. "I believe you. I always have."

The weight of it crushed me and saved me all at once.

"Thank you," I whispered into her shoulder, my tears wetting her shirt.

"Then here's what you do," she said, pulling back, her gaze unwavering. "Go to Tarpon Springs. Confront Nik yourself. Make them see. I'll come with you if you want—you don't have to face this alone."

Fall break. I'd already planned to go home. Now I knew why.

"Okay," I whispered. "Okay."

Her hand found mine, warm and unyielding. "We'll face it together."

And for the first time since the curse began, I didn't feel completely alone.

32

Cassandra

Ancient Troy

The cliffs above the sea had become Cassandra's refuge, though she found no peace there anymore. The wind carried brine and the cries of gulls, but even nature's song could not drown the voices in her head. Every morning since her confrontation with Apollo, she woke already weary, her body heavy as though she'd walked miles in her sleep. Visions came without warning, snapping into her mind like lightning splitting the night: a face in the crowd, the turn of a soldier's spear, the taste of smoke. Some were small warnings about the market road or an overturned cart. Others were catastrophic—the city aflame, her brothers lying broken at her feet.

She had stopped going to Athena's temple, too ashamed that the goddess never answered her prayers. She stayed in her chamber for days at a time, curtains drawn, hands clenched around her wooden amulet until her knuckles whitened. Even her handmaids began to whisper, their pitying looks sharper than open scorn. The curse Apollo had laid on her was working. Cassandra could see the threads, but her words unraveled before they reached another's ear.

This morning, though, she had felt the pull of the sea. She knew, before any herald could cry it, that the ships were coming home. Hector's ship. Paris's ship. And the woman.

Cassandra stood at the edge of the precipice, her hair lashing in the salt wind, and stared at the sails on the horizon. They came gliding like wings of gulls — white canvas flashing in the sunlight, oars biting into the waves with perfect rhythm. To anyone else, the sight was triumphant. To Cassandra, it was doom clothed in splendor.

Her vision flared again: for one dizzying heartbeat, she saw the same ships not gilded by dawn but by fire. Their masts were snapped, their hulls blackened, the sea choked with corpses and wreckage. She staggered back a step, clutching the edge of her robe to her mouth until the present snapped back into place.

Her brothers' silhouettes appeared as the ships docked. Hector, tall and grave, already weighted by the command of men. Paris, golden as a god, his chin lifted in arrogance. And behind them, walking hesitantly onto Trojan sand for the first time, came Helen.

Her hair caught the sun like molten bronze, and even from this distance, Cassandra understood the stories — why Paris had risked everything, why men whispered her beauty would sunder kingdoms. But Cassandra also saw the fear in Helen's face, the way her hand clutched the edge of her cloak as though she wished to hide. The crowd at the harbor roared its welcome, deaf to the shadow already coiling around them.

"Paris, you foolish man," Cassandra whispered into the wind, her voice shredded by the waves. "What have you done?"

* * *

The palace courtyards bloomed with celebration. Citizens crowded the walls and streets, pressing forward for a glimpse of the princes' return. Flowers were scattered on the flagstones; garlands were draped from columns. The air swelled with pipe music and the deep roll of drums.

Cassandra slipped among them unseen, her veil pulled low over her brow. She watched as Hector dismounted first, bowing to their father with the composure of a soldier who had long carried duty like a shield. He said little, his eyes darting to Paris with a darkness Cassandra recognized.

Paris dismounted more slowly, but with the practiced grace of someone certain of his welcome. He extended a hand to Helen, drawing her into the light. Gasps rippled through the crowd, followed by a roar of approval. To the people, it was romance, a victory greater than plunder — the most beautiful woman in the world, now theirs.

Cassandra's nails dug into her palms. In her mind, the cheers bent into screams. Flowers underfoot blackened into ash. She blinked hard, fighting the vision back, and shoved her way toward the steps of the palace.

Within the palace hall, the celebration thinned to a brittle calm. Servants bustled, guards took their posts, and King Priam descended from his throne to greet his sons.

Cassandra lingered in the shadows, watching.

Hector faced Paris first. His voice was low, but Cassandra caught the iron edge beneath it.

"Do you have any idea what you have done?" Hector's jaw was clenched, his fists tight at his sides. "You have stolen the wife of a king. You have brought war to our gates with your own hands."

"She came willingly," Paris shot back, his eyes gleaming with defiance. "Ask her. Helen chose me."

Helen's lips parted, but no words came. She kept her gaze fixed on the floor, as though her silence might shield her.

"Whether she chose you or not," Hector said, his voice rough, "you have dishonored us all. Menelaus will not rest. And Agamemnon—" He broke off, fury strangling his words.

Paris lifted his chin. "Let them come. I will defend her with my life. Is that not honor?"

"Honor?" Hector barked, his composure cracking. "You confuse pride for honor, brother. And we will all bleed for it."

Cassandra could not stay silent. She stepped into the light of the torches, her veil slipping from her hair.

"Hector is right," she said, her voice trembling but strong enough to carry. "I have seen it. The Greeks will come. They will bring fire and ruin to Troy, all for Helen. I beg you, listen to me."

The hall stilled. For a moment, eyes turned to her with something like hope. Then the silence broke — a murmur rippling, skeptical, pitying. Paris's face twisted into scorn.

"Not you again," he muttered. "Always with your visions of doom. Do you never tire of casting shadows?"

"I do not tire of truth," Cassandra snapped, stepping forward until she stood before them all. "I saw the ships. I saw the fields soaked with blood. I saw our city burning. If you bring her here, none of us are safe."

Paris turned away with a laugh, his arm tightening around Helen's waist. "Madness. She envies me, that is all. She envies what I have won."

Cassandra's breath caught in her throat, but Hector's eyes met hers. For one heartbeat, she thought he might believe. His hand twitched at his side, as if he longed to reach for her. But then he lowered his gaze, and the moment passed.

King Priam raised a hand, silencing them all. His face was grave, his voice heavy with the weariness of age.

"We will not tear this family apart by shouting," he said. "Paris, you have brought us both a treasure and a burden. Hector, your caution is wise, as ever. Cassandra…" His eyes lingered on her, kind but resigned. "You are beloved, daughter, but your visions bring only despair. We cannot govern a city on shadows."

The words cut deeper than any blade. Cassandra bowed her head, her cheeks burning with humiliation. She knew this was Apollo's curse — her truth twisted into folly by every ear that heard it.

As the men resumed their debate, Cassandra turned to leave. A hand caught her sleeve. She looked up, startled, to see Helen.

Helen, who until now had stood a pace behind Paris, lifted her chin and stepped forward. Golden hair spilled over her shoulders like sunlight on marble, but it was her eyes that struck Cassandra — not docile or ashamed, but steady, the eyes of a woman who had lived among kings and had learned to see through them.

She ignored the murmurs of the court and went straight to Cassandra, closing the space until only a breath separated them. "They will say I was stolen," Helen said, her voice low but carrying, silencing the room. "But I walked onto that ship with my eyes open. My life in Sparta was gilded, yes — but gilded like a cage. I chose to leave it."

Cassandra's breath caught. The curse clawed at her throat, threatening to choke her words before they formed. But Helen's gaze didn't waver.

"You've seen something," Helen pressed, as though she *knew*. "Your eyes are not the eyes of mockery, but of warning. Tell me, princess of Troy — what did you see?"

The court bristled at the intimacy of her words, the scandal of Helen daring to ask Cassandra what the men dismissed. But for the first time since Apollo's curse, Cassandra felt a spark of kinship: someone was asking, *and listening*.

"I saw fire," Cassandra whispered, her voice trembling as the gods twisted it into madness. "I saw ships like locusts, blotting out the sea. Blood running in rivers. And you—" Her words faltered. "You, at the center, whether you will it or not."

Helen held her gaze, and for a moment, something like sorrow flickered across her perfect features. Then she nodded once, firm and unflinching.

"Then let us face it with eyes open," Helen said quietly, pressing Cassandra's hand once before retreating to Paris' side.

Paris scoffed at the gesture, but the image hung in the air: Helen, radiant and unashamed, choosing not just Paris, but *to hear Cassandra*.

The torches in the hall wavered. Cassandra's vision seized her like a storm. She saw the same hall years from now, its marble blackened, its roof collapsing in flame. She saw Hector sprawled in the dust, Paris pierced through, Priam cut down at the altar. And Helen — Helen standing with her hair unbound, her face a mask of grief, as men dragged her from the smoke.

The roar of war filled her ears. She gasped and stumbled back, clutching the wall until the vision receded. When her eyes cleared, no one else reacted. They hadn't seen. They never saw.

Paris laughed again, already boasting to those around him. Hector's silence was colder than anger. Priam spoke of alliances, of diplomacy, of appeasing the Greeks. No one looked at Cassandra.

She turned and fled into the corridors, tears streaking her cheeks. Her bare feet slapped against the stone, echoing her heartbeat. She ran until the voices faded, until she found herself in the dark garden outside, the stars wheeling overhead.

She sank to her knees in the grass, pressing her fists against her eyes. "Why give me this gift only to bind my tongue? Why make me see if no one will hear?"

There was no answer but the wind in the olive trees.

When Cassandra finally rose, dawn was breaking. The city was awake with celebration, but to her the trumpets sounded like funeral bells. She looked toward the sea, where the waves foamed against the shore as if hungry for blood.

"Forgive me, my people," she whispered, clutching her amulet of Athena to her chest. "I have tried. The gods have cursed me, and all I love will fall."

And with that, Cassandra turned back toward the palace, her heart already carrying the weight of Troy's ashes.

33

Cassie

Modern Day

As my footsteps crunched over fallen leaves, I felt a sense of liberation wash over me. Fall break had finally arrived, and with it, a much-needed respite from the endless grind of the semester. I glanced over at Diana, her eyes bright as she took in the view of the bay.

"Tarpon Springs is such an interesting place," I told her, gesturing at the sponge boats docked along the waterfront. "So much Greek history here. My grandparents used to bring us every year for the Epiphany festival."

Diana smiled, her gaze lingering on the small shrine by the docks. "I haven't been back to a town that feels this Greek in…ages."

The slip in her voice made me laugh out loud. For the first time in weeks, it wasn't bitter laughter but warm, full-bodied. Diana joined me, her silver necklace glinting in the late-afternoon sun.

Our first stop was Hellas Restaurant and Bakery, a local landmark. The air was thick with the smell of cinnamon, honey, and freshly brewed coffee. We slid into an outdoor table, the Mediterranean-blue awnings shading us from the sun.

"You have to try the bougatsa," I said, already ordering for both of us. "My favorite here."

Diana bit into the flaky pastry, eyes closing. "You're right. This is divine."

We wandered afterward through streets lined with sponge shops and blue-trimmed white buildings that looked more Santorini than Florida. A man played bouzouki in the Sponge Exchange courtyard while women danced with arms raised high.

"My sister Athena was always better at weaving than dancing," Diana mused as we passed an old man working a loom. "Turned a woman into a spider once. Long story."

I snorted. I knew the story. But to hear Diana mention it so casually was another thing.

By evening, the sky was streaked with pink as we pulled up in front of my parents' house, its porch light casting a golden halo through swaying palm fronds.

My father opened the door, tall and broad-shouldered, his green eyes twinkling. "Κόρη μου!" he boomed, pulling me into a crushing hug.

"You remember Diana," I added as I caught my breath.

"Of course," he said, shaking her hand warmly. "Welcome."

Inside, the smell of lamb and oregano wrapped around us like a blanket. My mother, Penelope, appeared in the kitchen doorway, her braid falling over her shoulder. "Cassandra!" she cried, kissing my forehead, then hugging Diana. "Diana, you are always welcome here."

The front door opened again, and in came Theo, Nik, and—my eyes widened—Helen Kostas herself. Nik's hand rested possessively at the small of her back.

"Little sister!" Theo swept me into a hug that left my feet dangling.

"Hey, Cassie," Nik said, smiling in an almost boyish way. He gestured to Helen.

She stepped forward, embracing me before I could react. Her perfume was warm and grounding, vanilla laced with sandalwood. "I've heard so much about you," she said, her Greek accent lilting. Then, squeezing my hand, she added quietly, "Sisters see more than brothers ever will."

Her words startled me. But her grip was firm, her gaze steady—this woman was no ornament. She was steel wrapped in silk.

Before I could respond, my attention snagged on Blair, Theo's wife, standing just behind him. Her hand rested on a pronounced bump.

"Wait—what?!" I shoved Theo playfully aside. "You weren't going to tell me you're having a baby?"

Blair laughed, letting me lay a hand on her stomach. "Sebastian Peter," she said softly. "We'll call him Bash."

"Oh my god, Bash Bennett is the best name ever." Right on cue, a tiny kick pressed against my palm. "See? He loves me already."

We were ushered to the table, where dishes crowded every inch: spanakopita, lamb, roasted potatoes, bowls of olives glistening with oil. Conversation flowed as easily as the wine. Diana fit in effortlessly, teasing Theo about fatherhood and making my mother laugh.

At one point, Diana raised her glass toward Nik. "And what exactly did you trade for this marble deal, Nik? I hope not a horse. You Greeks have a history with those."

Everyone laughed. Except me—and Diana, whose eyes met mine knowingly.

Later, Theo tugged me onto the lanai, away from the din. We sat under the faint scent of my mother's marigolds while he told me about Greece, his voice full of excitement.

"The marble is incredible, Cass. Dimitri Kostas is tough, but fair. We're set up to build mansions all over Tampa Bay. Even Sinclair—you know, that numbers guy in your finance department—looked at the deal and said it was airtight."

"Thomas?" I asked, startled.

"Yeah. Good guy. He saved us thousands in taxes with one spreadsheet." Theo clapped me on the shoulder. "We're golden."

But his words only twisted the knot in my stomach tighter. I told him about my vision—Nik marrying Helen in secret, the danger it would unleash.

Theo's smile faltered. "Cass...come on. Nik finally settled down. Helen's amazing. This is a good thing."

"It's not," I insisted. "Theo, you have to believe me."

"I love you," he said quietly, "but sometimes dreams are just dreams. Don't let fear ruin this moment."

Inside, laughter swelled again. Through the open door, I saw Helen touching my mother's arm as they laughed, her presence already woven into the family like she had always belonged. Nik hovered at her side, protective, his jaw tight as if he'd overheard us.

"Cassie," he said later, when I approached him in the hall, "don't start. Not tonight."

"Nik—"

"No." His eyes were sharp, warning. "Don't." He turned away, pulling Helen gently along with him.

The rejection cut sharper than I expected.

I stood frozen until Diana's hand slipped into mine. "Stop torturing yourself," she whispered, her voice low.

"They look so happy," I murmured, unable to stop staring at the pair of them.

"Isn't that what you wanted?"

"Yes. But I know it won't last."

"Then talk to him," Diana said firmly. "Even if he won't believe you. Especially then."

Her eyes shone like silver in the lamplight. And I believed her.

For now, though, I followed her back to the table, where my family laughed, Helen's voice bright among them. For one fleeting moment, I let myself sit in the warmth of it all, knowing the storm was coming.

34

Cassandra

Ancient Troy

The sea smelled of iron that morning.

From her balcony, Cassandra gripped the marble balustrade until her fingers ached, her eyes fixed on the horizon where the Aegean bled into the sky. The air was heavy with brine and incense drifting up from the harbor shrines; somewhere in the distance, a blacksmith's hammer rang against bronze, and the clamor of merchants haggling echoed faintly from the agora. The city breathed and bustled, blissfully unaware.

But Cassandra felt the tension, a storm thrumming beneath the skin of Troy. She could almost hear the sea whispering her name.

Her eyes, sharper than most, caught the shapes long before the watchtowers cried out. Dark triangles of sail cut across the water, slicing steadily toward the harbor. She knew whose ships they were. She had seen them in her dreams — Hector standing grim, Paris with his smug smile, and beside them, the face that would topple empires.

Helen.

Her chest tightened. Troy's people crowded the docks, their cheers rising on the morning wind as if Paris returned with a hero's prize rather than a harbinger of war.

Cassandra's knuckles whitened. "By the gods, Paris, what have you done?" she whispered into the wind, but the gulls were her only answer.

The palace thrummed with celebration by the time she descended from her tower. The golden walls echoed with laughter, with the trilling of flutes and the pounding of drums as dancers spun in the courtyards. Servants scattered flower petals before Paris and his new companion as they strode through the gates, and the scent of roses and crushed rosemary clung to everything.

Paris basked in it. He moved like a man crowned with victory, Helen beside him radiant in white, her golden hair catching every shaft of light. Even Cassandra felt the pull of her beauty — no mortal could help it. Helen's eyes flicked to Cassandra in that moment, a fleeting exchange that made Cassandra pause. There was strength there, beneath the uncertainty. A Spartan daughter, not a stolen lamb.

But Cassandra's vision still clung to her like smoke: the city burning, walls collapsing, her people screaming in the streets.

She pushed forward through the throng, ignoring the sidelong glances and whispers that followed her — *mad Cassandra, cursed Cassandra.* Hector stood at the edge of the hall, grim and silent, his hand resting on the pommel of his sword. She caught his arm, her voice low but urgent.

"Brother, listen to me. You must send her back. Return Helen to Menelaus before it is too late."

Hector's jaw tightened. He looked at her, and for a moment she saw the brother who had once shielded her from their tutors' sharp words, the man who had knelt beside her when she scraped her knees as a child. But now there was weariness in his eyes — and doubt.

"You think I haven't tried?" His voice was steel wrapped in exhaustion. "Paris hears nothing but the sound of his own triumph. Father sees only the chance for alliance. And the people—" he gestured toward the courtyard, where laughter rang out — "they believe he has brought Troy a gift, not a curse."

"Because they will not believe me," Cassandra shot back, bitterness cracking her voice. "Because the god saw fit to make me truth-teller and liar both."

Hector's gaze softened, but he shook his head. "Even if you were right, sister, what would you have me do? Return her like a parcel and admit we are cowards? No. Troy does not bow to Greece. If they come, we will meet them with spears."

Her throat tightened. "You speak of honor while I see only fire and blood."

He squeezed her shoulder, not unkindly. "Then pray your visions are false, Cassandra. Pray you are wrong."

* * *

The council met at dusk, the torches in Priam's hall sputtering as though uneasy with the weight of the gathering. Cassandra slipped in behind Hector, her heart pounding. The chamber was filled with the heavy scent of oil and sweat, and the air buzzed with voices — young nobles clamoring for war, older men urging caution.

King Priam sat upon his throne, his silver hair glinting in the lamplight. Beside him stood Paris, preening like a rooster, and Helen — quiet, but her chin lifted, the bearing of Sparta still in her spine.

Cassandra could not hold her tongue. She stepped forward, her voice carrying through the hall:

"Father, lords of Troy — hear me! Paris has brought not a bride but a blade to our throats. I have seen it: ships upon our shores, fire in our streets, the blood of our sons staining the sand. If Helen remains, war will follow. Return her before the gods themselves strike us down!"

The hall erupted.

"She is mad!" cried a young lord, his voice rising above the din. "Always with her doom-songs and nightmares!"

"She speaks treason against her own brother!" another barked.

Hector's voice cut through like a blade: "Enough!" He looked at Priam. "Father, I will not dismiss her words outright. She has spoken true before."

A murmur swept the chamber, half in agreement, half in scorn.

Then Darius, the eldest councilor, rose. His voice was slow, heavy with years. "My king, I have served since the days of your father Laomedon. And never — *never* — have we taken counsel from a woman. Will we begin now, with one plagued by madness? She sees shadows and calls them fate. Are we to chain the future of Troy to the ramblings of a girl?"

The words fell like stones. Priam's face tightened. His eyes flicked to Cassandra — and for a heartbeat she thought she saw sorrow there, even shame. But when he spoke, his voice was weary and final.

"Cassandra, daughter, enough. I cannot let your visions tear this council apart. War has been declared. We will prepare our defenses. You are dismissed."

Her mouth opened, but no words came. Her father's gaze slid from hers. The guards shifted. And Cassandra — princess, prophetess, cursed — was ushered from the chamber like an errant child.

She stumbled into the darkened corridors, her body trembling. Rage and grief warred in her chest until she thought her ribs might crack. She pressed her forehead against the cool stone and whispered to herself: *I tried. I tried.*

A soft voice startled her.

"Cassandra."

Helen stood there, her white gown trailing like moonlight, her face pale but her eyes fierce.

Cassandra's breath hitched. "You… you heard me."

Helen stepped closer, lowering her voice. "I believe you."

The words were so unexpected that Cassandra almost wept. "Then help me convince them!"

Helen stepped closer, her voice low enough that only Cassandra could hear. Her golden hair caught the lamplight, but her eyes burned darker, sharper, more resolute than Cassandra expected.

"You think I don't know what I've done?" Helen said quietly. "You think I don't hear the whispers already circling Troy? That I don't feel the weight of a thousand eyes judging me?"

Cassandra held her gaze, but Helen pressed on, fiercer now.

"Yes, I came with Paris. Willingly. But not for the reasons you believe. Menelaus may be king, but he was no husband. I was a prize to him, a body to command, a name to polish his throne. In Sparta, I had no voice. No choice. No peace."

Her voice broke for just a moment, then hardened again, laced with steel.

"Paris was a fool, yes—but he asked. He looked at me not as property but as a woman who could choose. Do you understand what that means, Cassandra? For once in my life, the decision was mine. Not Sparta's. Not Menelaus'. Mine."

Cassandra's lips parted, but Helen shook her head, her grip tightening on Cassandra's arm.

"I know the cost. I know the war that follows me. But I will not apologize for seizing one moment of freedom, even if it burns this city to the ground. Better one choice of my own than a lifetime of being ruled by others."

Cassandra's heart clenched. She grasped Helen's hands. "Then we are both prisoners of men's pride."

Helen's lips curved into a bitter smile. "Yes. But prisoners can still whisper to each other through the bars." She squeezed Cassandra's fingers. "You are not mad. You are not alone."

Cassandra held onto that warmth as long as she could, even as Helen was pulled back into the hall by Paris's hand on her arm.

* * *

That night, Cassandra roamed her chambers like a caged lion. Sleep would not come. The visions bled into her waking sight: flames licking the walls, corpses lining the streets, her brothers lying broken.

She thought of the old tunnels beneath Troy — half-forgotten stories from childhood, when she and Helenus had dared each other to sneak through dusty passages that smelled of earth and bones. One, she remembered, led beyond the walls toward the beaches. Another, perhaps, toward the foreign quarter where traders docked. Could one lead farther still? To the Greek camp?

Hope flickered. If no one would listen here, perhaps she could reach the enemy and barter peace herself.

She slipped from her chamber, skirts gathered in her fists, heart pounding with each step. The palace was quiet, save for the crackle of torches.

192

Then — "Cassandra."

Helenus emerged from the shadows, his twin's eyes mirroring her own anguish. He caught her wrist, firm but not cruel. "I know where you go. I will not let you."

"Let me? Since when have you been my gaoler?" Her voice cracked. "I cannot sit idle while Troy burns."

He swallowed hard. "And if you run into the jaws of the Greeks? If you die alone in some dark trench? No. Better my anger than your funeral."

He summoned Leander, a loyal guard, and gave the order. "Do not let her leave these chambers."

Cassandra struggled, tears spilling hot and furious. "You would cage me, brother?"

Helenus's face twisted, grief-stricken. "I would keep you alive." He turned away, his voice breaking. "Forgive me."

* * *

By dawn, Cassandra stood again on her balcony, her body taut with exhaustion. Below, the city stirred with preparations for war — smiths hammering, boys running messages, soldiers tightening cuirasses. Troy's walls gleamed in the rising light, proud and doomed.

She pressed her hands together until her nails bit her skin. "Athena, hear me. If they will not believe me, then give me the strength to endure. Let me speak, again and again, even if the world calls me mad. Let me fight with the only weapon I have — my voice."

Somewhere beyond the walls, the Greek fleet gathered, sails like a storm cloud on the horizon.

And still, no one listened.

35

Cassie

Modern Day

The Florida sun slid low over the bayou, throwing golden streaks across the porch where I paced, barefoot on the weathered boards. Laughter drifted from the neighborhood, Thanksgiving kitchens bursting with turkey and cinnamon. But I couldn't taste the holiday warmth. My chest carried only the bitter tang of the vision I had woken to at dawn.

Helen's hands—red with blood. Her mouth opened in a silent scream. A life crumbling into ruin around her.

Not a dream. Not imagination. The curse.

The same one that once destroyed Cassandra of Troy now lived in me. And like her, no one would believe.

When the door creaked open, Nik appeared, Helen tucked protectively at his side. He looked irritatingly relaxed, suntanned from Greece, his arm heavy around her waist. Helen smiled — the kind of luminous smile that makes you understand why men launch wars.

"Hey, sis," Nik grinned.

But my stomach dropped. It was Helen's eyes, wide and uncertain, that struck me. Somewhere, she already sensed what Nik refused to see.

"We need to talk," I said. My voice shook more than I wanted it to. "Nik. Alone."

Helen stopped, but she didn't pull away. She tilted her head, studying me, that hint of Spartan strength in her posture. "I don't mind hearing," she offered.

Nik's grin faltered. "Cassie, not tonight. No doom and gloom. We're here for dinner, not more of your—"

"Prophecies?" I snapped, harsher than I intended. "Nik, I saw her. Covered in blood." My voice dropped to a whisper. "Your Helen."

The air shifted. Helen's hand flexed where it rested on his chest.

Nik's jaw tightened. "Enough."

"She's in danger!" I pushed. "From Dimitri. He will never forgive you for this marriage. He'll—"

"Stop." Nik's voice cracked like thunder. "You don't know him. You think because you've read some myths, you can predict the future. This isn't Troy, Cassie. This is Tarpon Springs. We'll handle it."

I looked to Helen. "Do you believe me?"

Her lips parted, uncertainty flickering in her eyes. She didn't answer.

Nik pulled her toward the kitchen. "Later," he promised, already dismissing me.

The door shut behind them, leaving me with the sound of cicadas and my heartbeat like a war drum.

Family first. Always family first. But how could I protect them if no one would listen?

That night, while my brothers drank and laughed inside, I stood outside with my phone pressed to my ear.

"Alexis?" My voice cracked. "It's Cassie Bennett."

A groggy groan on the other end. "Cassie, do you know what time it is in Athens?"

"I don't care," I hissed. "It's life or death. Dimitri Kostas — I need everything you know about him. Now."

A silence. Then a sigh. "Alright. But if you're wrong—"

"I'm not," I cut in. "I never am."

When the line clicked off, my reflection stared back at me in the kitchen window — pale, frantic, green eyes too wide. I looked exactly like the woman I'd spent years studying. Cassandra of Troy, screaming at her family as fire rose over the walls.

* * *

Days later, back on campus, I buried myself in research, but nothing could quiet the visions. Night after night, Troy burned in my dreams. Helen screamed. Nik ignored me. Apollo laughed.

At last, one vision bled into waking life.

I was in the campus café when the world shifted. One blink, and I was standing in a different café, the air thick with Greek tobacco and tension.

Dimitri Kostas sat at a corner table, his black hair slicked back, his gaze sharp as a blade. Across from him, a long-haired man leaned in, whispering. I couldn't catch every word — my Greek was rusty — but I didn't need to.

"…cannot trust him," Dimitri snarled.

"He took something from you," the man said.

Dimitri's hand slammed the table. Glasses rattled. "He will pay."

The man leaned closer. "Then you must go to Florida."

The words struck like an arrow to the chest. Florida. Tarpon Springs. My family.

A waitress appeared, and Dimitri looked up. For one breathless second, his eyes met mine. Could he see me? My skin went cold.

Then the café blinked away, and I was back in line at the student union coffee shop, heart pounding, fingers trembling around my phone.

I called Nik immediately.

"Nik, listen to me. Dimitri's coming. He's planning something. Please, take Helen and get away."

He laughed. He actually laughed. "Cassie, do you hear yourself? He's her father. A businessman, not a monster."

"Nik, you don't understand," I whispered, tears choking my throat. "I saw it. He'll destroy you. Please, just believe me."

His voice hardened. "Enough. You sound insane."

The line went dead.

My phone screen blurred through my tears. In my chest, the curse burned like fire.

I whispered the only words that came: "Oh gods… It's happening again."

36

Cassandra

Ancient Troy

The clang of bronze on bronze rang out across Troy like a cruel hymn. Even within the thick stone walls of her chamber, Cassandra could not escape the sound of war sharpening itself for the feast. Black smoke curled above the rooftops where smiths hammered swords, spearheads, and shields. The smell of burning pitch mixed with the salt tang of the sea and the faint perfume of her mother's rose gardens, cloying and acrid all at once.

Cassandra pressed her palms against the cool stone of the windowsill. Her knuckles were white, her shoulders taut. She had barely slept since the council dismissed her pleas. Every time her eyes closed, she saw Troy in flames. Every time she opened them, she was still trapped in a palace that felt more like a cage than a home.

The door creaked. She stiffened.

"Cassandra," Hector's voice rumbled softly.

She turned. He stood framed by the torchlight in the doorway, taller than ever, his armor half-laced as though he had abandoned preparations midway. The sight of him—the steady rock of her childhood—was almost her undoing. Her throat tightened.

"You should not be shut away like this," Hector said, stepping inside. His expression was stern, but his eyes betrayed worry. "It is not fitting for a princess. Nor for my sister."

"I am no princess," Cassandra whispered bitterly. "Only the madwoman of Troy."

Hector's jaw clenched. He crossed the chamber in three long strides and drew her into an embrace. His chest smelled of leather, oil, and smoke. For a moment, she let herself sag into his strength, though she kept her eyes squeezed shut. If she opened them, she might see the vision again: Hector's corpse dragged behind a Greek chariot.

"You are not mad," he murmured against her hair. "And you are not alone. I've brought someone."

He pulled back, guiding her toward the corridor. Confused, she followed. Their footsteps echoed in the hushed halls, the sounds of war muted at this distance.

"Someone?" she asked, wary.

"Aeneas," Hector replied simply.

She had spoken with Aeneas on more than one occasion—brief exchanges in palace corridors, moments stolen in the training fields when Hector was nearby, quiet conversations that lingered in her mind long after. She knew him to be steadfast and deliberate, a man who weighed his words as carefully as he wielded his sword. Unlike Paris, he was not reckless; unlike many in Priam's court, he was not vain. His lineage—descended from Anchises and said to be favored by Aphrodite—was often whispered about in reverence, but what struck Cassandra most was not his bloodline; it was the quiet gravity with which he carried himself. Even Hector, who trusted few beyond his own shield, spoke of Aeneas with respect.

And now Hector was leading her to him.

They emerged into the outer courtyard, where the last rays of the sun bathed the training ground in red-gold light. The clang of weapons was muted here, replaced by the low murmur of men at rest. Aeneas stood apart, tightening the straps of his greaves, his broad shoulders bent in focus. When he straightened, his dark eyes caught hers instantly, as though he had been waiting.

Cassandra faltered. Something in his gaze was different from the others—

no suspicion, no mockery. Only steadiness.

Hector beckoned. "Cousin."

Aeneas approached, bowing with grave respect. "Princess."

"Please," Cassandra said quickly, voice catching. "Do not call me that. I am simply Cassandra."

His lips curved, almost imperceptibly. "Then Cassandra."

Her heart skittered in her chest. She folded her hands tightly to still them.

"I brought you here," Hector said, his voice careful, "because you carry this burden alone. Perhaps you should not. Aeneas is not a man who takes words lightly. If you trust him, he will guard what you say."

Cassandra glanced at Hector, startled. Was this…a chance? Her brother had always been her champion, but even he had not said he *believed* her. Only that he loved her.

She turned back to Aeneas. His face gave nothing away, but the patience in his eyes steadied her.

"I…" Cassandra faltered. How to speak what had been festering in her heart? To risk once more the sting of ridicule?

"Say it," Aeneas said quietly. "Whatever truth weighs on you."

Her throat burned. She closed her eyes, and the vision returned with terrible clarity:

The black shore, smoke rising like a shroud. Helen was weeping as she was dragged by Paris through the gates. The sea churning with a thousand Greek ships, their sails fat with wind, their prows sharp as knives. Troy ablaze. Her brothers dead. Her father fallen.

Her voice shook as she forced the words into the air. "Paris has brought doom into our walls. I see it—the Greeks will not forgive. They will come with fire and swords, and Troy will fall. All I love will burn."

Silence. The courtyard noises faded until only her own breathing remained.

Cassandra opened her eyes, braced for derision. For pity. For that tight smile that said *yes, yes, of course, poor girl.*

But Aeneas did not look away. His gaze was steady, heavy, and utterly unflinching.

"I believe you," he said.

The world tilted. She staggered.

"You—what?"

"I believe you," Aeneas repeated, voice as even as the sea. "I have seen enough battles to know omens when they appear. And you…your eyes do not lie."

Her vision blurred. Tears pricked hot behind her lashes. For so long, her words had been daggers turned against her, proof of madness, fuel for scorn. Now, with three simple words, Aeneas had transformed them into something else: truth.

Hector exhaled, shoulders loosening as if some weight had shifted. "Then you see why I brought him," he said softly.

Cassandra turned back to Aeneas, desperate and trembling. "But belief is not enough. I cannot stop it. I see the flames and the blood, and no one listens—"

"Then I will," Aeneas interrupted. His tone was not dramatic, not oath-sworn or flowery. Just solid. "Tell me what you see, and I will carry it into action where I can. If the council dismisses you, then let them dismiss me too."

Her breath caught. He meant it.

No words came. Only a sob, half-choked, rising from her chest.

Aeneas did not flinch. He simply inclined his head, as though she had just given him a command he would obey without question.

The torchlight flickered across the planes of his face, highlighting the strength carved there by war and discipline. And Cassandra, for the first time in what felt like eternity, felt the crushing weight on her shoulders lift—just a little.

Hector touched her arm gently. "Come, sister. You've said enough for one evening."

Reluctantly, she let him lead her back toward the palace. But as she passed Aeneas, she dared to glance up at him again. He was still watching her, calm, unwavering.

And in his eyes, she saw it: not mockery. Not fear. Not pity.

Belief.

It lodged in her chest like a spark struck in dry kindling.

That night, as she lay sleepless on her bed, Cassandra pressed her hands to her heart and whispered into the darkness:

"He believes me."

For the first time since the curse, the words did not taste like madness. They tasted like hope.

<h1 style="text-align:center">37</h1>

<h1 style="text-align:center">Cassie</h1>

Modern Day

The night in downtown Tarpon Springs was damp, the streets slick with an earlier rain. A hush had fallen over the town's sponge docks, broken only by the faint creak of boats rocking in their slips. Kellie drew her blazer tighter around her shoulders as she stepped from the black car idling at the curb. She had always hated this place: the smell of salt, the stubborn Greek pride in every stone, the way the Bennetts acted like royalty here. Tonight, she would finally begin to erase it.

The restaurant across the street was still lit, Hellas' blue neon flickering against the puddles. Families laughed over baklava and wine, oblivious to the storm gathering. Kellie turned her back on them and entered the darkened office two doors down, where Dimitri's envoy was waiting.

A tall man with a scar bisecting his lip leaned against the file cabinet, arms folded. "You're late," he said in Greek-accented English.

"I'm careful," Kellie snapped. She set her leather bag on the desk and pulled out a thick folder of Bennett Construction shipping manifests. "The first marble shipment arrives next month. I've marked which containers you'll need to compromise. If they break in transit, the entire deal collapses."

The man smirked. "You want Kostas's wrath to fall on them."

Kellie's eyes glittered. "I want ruin. Dimitri gets his leverage. I get satisfaction."

He leafed through the documents, then looked up. "And if they find out this came from you?"

"They won't," Kellie said sharply. "They've never believed Cassandra before. They won't believe her now."

The words tasted bitter, but she relished them. Cassie Bennett, with her knowing little smiles, her habit of quoting myths like they mattered in the real world, Kellie had hated her from the start. Always so sure of herself, always in the middle of things. Just like her brothers.

"Do it," she said. "Make sure the Bennetts regret crossing me."

The scarred man closed the folder. "It will be done."

* * *

On the other side of town, I sat cross-legged on my apartment floor, surrounded by scattered papers, books on Greek trade law, and a half-empty glass of wine. My phone buzzed violently against a pile of notebooks, and I lunged for it.

"Alexis?" I whispered.

"Cassie," came the familiar voice, low and urgent. "You were right to worry."

My throat went dry. "What did you find?"

"Dimitri Kostas is more than marble. He's tied to... other ventures. Smuggling, laundering. Dangerous men in Thessaloniki and Athens. I shouldn't even be telling you this." He paused, his breath quick. "But if your brother married Helen without his blessing, he'll see it as betrayal. He will use business as a weapon. He will make an example."

I pressed a hand to her temple. The room spun. "An example... Nik?"

"Yes. Nik. Theo. Your father. All of them. Kostas doesn't just cut deals, Cassie. He destroys reputations. He buries families."

My stomach churned. The echoes were unmistakable: Troy welcoming the horse into its walls, thinking it a gift, never realizing it carried death. I had seen it before—in Hector's fall, in my dreams of burning roofs—and now I was living it again.

"Alexis, listen to me," I said, my voice breaking. "You have to send me everything. Documents. Proof. If I can show them—"

"Cassie…" His sigh was heavy with pity. "Even with proof, will they believe you?"

I closed my eyes. My brother's voice rang in her ears: *You sound insane, Cassie.*

"No," I whispered, mostly to myself. "They won't. But I'll try anyway."

* * *

The Bennetts' office smelled of cedar and dust, the last interns long gone for the holiday weekend. Kellie moved through it like a ghost, her heels silent on the polished floor. She paused at Theo's framed family photo—Blair radiant in her pregnancy, Theo's arm around her shoulders, Peter standing proudly beside them. Cassie smiled in the corner, head tilted, red hair catching the light.

Kellie felt the sharp edge of rage cut through her. They had everything. They had cast her out as if she were nothing. She traced Cassie's face in the glass with one manicured nail.

"You should have stayed out of my way," she hissed.

Then she flipped the photo facedown and returned to her work.

* * *

Back in my childhood bedroom, I typed furiously, pulling together notes, Alexis's whispered warnings still ringing in my ears. The air outside was heavy, storm clouds gathering over the Gulf.

My phone buzzed again—Nik.

I snatched it up. "Nik, thank god. Please listen to me. I found out—"

"Cassie," he cut me off, weary irritation in his tone. "Not this again."

"It's not a vision this time!" I cried. "It's real. I have proof. Dimitri's involved with criminals—if this marble deal collapses, he'll come for you and Helen. Please, just let me show you the files."

Silence. Then: "Do you hear yourself? Do you have any idea how paranoid you sound? Always seeing doom around every corner. Helen and I are fine."

My heart clenched. "Nik—"

"No more, Cassie. You're obsessed. You need help."

The line went dead.

I sat frozen, phone limp in my hand, every nerve screaming. It was happening all over again: a woman shouting warnings into the void, family choosing to ignore her until the fire was already at their door.

The curse lived.

I whispered into the silence, voice trembling. "Why won't anyone believe me?"

* * *

Meanwhile, Kellie slid into the waiting car outside Bennett Construction, the folder of stolen manifests gone, handed off to Dimitri's men. She lit a cigarette, exhaling a thin plume of smoke into the damp night.

"It's done," she murmured. Her reflection in the window looked nothing like the woman she used to be—ambitious, eager to belong. No, she thought now, she had become something else entirely.

A spark in the dark. A match waiting to fall on a house soaked in oil.

* * *

I stayed awake until dawn, the glow of my laptop painting my face in pale blue. I drafted emails to Theo, to my father, attaching what little Alexis had managed to send. My words bled desperation: *Listen. Please. Don't let this deal go through. It will destroy us.*

My finger hovered over send.

Would they even open it? Or would my warnings join all the others, dismissed as hysteria?

Somewhere far across the ocean, in the ruins of Troy, Cassandra's voice seemed to whisper: *You already know the answer.*

I pressed send anyway.

And then I whispered, to the empty apartment, to the storm rolling in off the Gulf:

"If I have to burn with you to make you see…then so be it."

38

Cassandra

Ancient Troy

Cassandra's heart raced as the vision unfolded before her eyes, a nightmare of blood and steel. The battlefield between Greeks and Trojans stretched out like a tapestry woven by the Fates themselves. She saw a man, his golden armor glinting in the sunlight, his spear thirsting for Trojan blood. And in the palace, surveying the chaos and carnage, were her brothers: Hector, the valiant defender of Troy, and Paris, the cause of it all.

"Will they survive this?" she whispered, feeling the weight of her gift—no, her curse—pressing down upon her. If only others believed her prophecies, perhaps this war could have been avoided. But as always, her words fell on deaf ears, leaving her to bear witness to the horrifying outcome. She clenched her fists, nails biting her palms, as the vision faded.

With a heavy sigh, she turned to the window. Below, Greek soldiers swarmed the shoreline like ants, their black sails snapping violently in the wind. The sight sent a shiver down her spine. Soon, the horror she'd seen would be real.

"Such a terrible sight, isn't it?" came a soft voice.

Startled, Cassandra turned to see Helen approaching, her beauty radiant even in the shadow of impending doom. Cassandra couldn't help but feel a pang of envy; Helen, after all, was the reason the Greeks had come to Troy.

Yet, she remained unscathed by the burden of prophecy, her life untouched by the dark visions that haunted Cassandra's every waking moment.

"Yes," Cassandra replied, her voice barely audible. "It seems the gods are determined to see our city fall."

Helen nodded solemnly, her eyes clouded with sorrow as she looked out at the beach below. "I never wanted any of this, you know."

Cassandra believed her. Helen was no more the cause of the war than Cassandra was. And yet, both of them would be remembered as harbingers of Troy's doom.

"Sometimes I wonder," Cassandra murmured, "if the gods play with us like children with their dolls—sending us down paths we cannot escape, all for their own amusement."

"Perhaps," Helen agreed softly. "But even dolls can endure. We must find a way, even when it seems all is lost."

They stood in silence, watching the gathering army. Wind whistled through the window, carrying salt and distant cries. Cassandra prayed—though no god listened—that she and Helen might weather what was to come.

Another gust blew through the chamber, scattering Cassandra's red hair. She studied Helen more closely. Rumor named her the daughter of Zeus, and in her presence, Cassandra could almost believe it.

"Growing up in Sparta," Helen said, her voice low with memory, "I knew nothing but freedom and strength. Our people taught that women could be warriors too—fierce and unyielding."

A wistful smile touched her lips. "I trained with my brothers and sisters for hours. Combat, strategy, racing, hunting. We were encouraged to excel in all things, not only those deemed 'proper' for women."

Cassandra's heart ached with envy. Troy, for all its beauty, clung to its traditions. A princess's worth was her marriage, her obedience. Even she, daughter of Priam, was not free.

"Such freedom," she murmured.

Helen reached for her hand. "Do not envy me. My birthright led me to Menelaus—and to this. Your chains may look different, but they are chains all the same."

Cassandra's voice sharpened with pain. "And yours brought you here."

Helen nodded. "Yes. But Sparta's lessons gave me endurance. And perhaps the courage to imagine a better future."

For a long moment, they held hands in silence. One cursed by prophecy, the other burdened by beauty and lineage—both women shackled by the choices of men.

"Perhaps it is not too late for us to find our own freedom," Cassandra mused, her eyes fixed on the horizon, where the sea met the sky in an endless embrace. "We may be bound by the whims of others, but we can choose how we face our destiny."

"Indeed," Helen agreed, squeezing Cassandra's hand. "Together, we will find our way through this storm and emerge stronger for it."

As the wind continued to whip around them, carrying the scent of salt and the distant cries of soldiers preparing for battle, Cassandra held tightly to Helen's hand, drawing strength from her newfound ally. And within her heart, a small flame of hope was kindled, a beacon to guide her through the dark days ahead.

As the waves crashed against the shore, a melancholic melody that echoed through the halls of the palace, Helen's voice trembled, barely audible above the cacophony of the sea. "Menelaus," she whispered, her gaze cast downward as if revealing a secret too painful to look upon. "My husband was not the man I thought he was."

Intrigued and concerned by this sudden turn in their conversation, Cassandra leaned closer, urging Helen to continue. Helen hesitated for a moment, then exhaled slowly, steeling herself for the confession to come.

"His rage was like a tempest, uncontrollable and destructive," Helen began, her voice growing stronger as she spoke. "He would berate me for the smallest perceived slight, his words like barbs designed to wound my spirit. And when his anger flared, it would manifest physically, leaving bruises upon my skin that served as a constant reminder of his cruelty."

Cassandra's heart ached at the thought of this radiant woman, a daughter of Zeus, subjected to such torment. She reached out to take Helen's hand, offering solace the only way she could. Together, they moved to a more secluded corner of Cassandra's chambers, where the sounds of the outside world faded into the background, replaced by the soft rustle of silk as they sat down on a plush divan.

"Many nights, I would lie awake, tears streaming down my face, praying to my father Zeus to take me away from Menelaus and the life I had been forced into," Helen continued, her eyes filling with unshed tears. "I long to return to Sparta, to the freedom I had known as a child, but I know that my fate was sealed."

Cassandra listened intently, her heart heavy with empathy and sorrow. She, too, knew the bitter taste of a destiny not chosen, a life that seemed to be dictated by the whims of others, and the gods themselves. And in Helen's tale, she recognized a kindred spirit, someone who understood the burden of powerlessness.

As the wind picked up and blew into the window where Cassandra and Helen stood, the flames in the hearth flickered and danced, casting long shadows across the room. Helen turned to look at Cassandra, her gaze filled with a newfound resolve. "I will not allow myself to be a pawn in the gods' cruel game any longer," she declared, her voice steady and unwavering. "I will find a way to break free from this prison of duty and expectation, to reclaim my independence and forge my own path."

Cassandra felt a surge of admiration for Helen's determination, a flicker of hope igniting within her own heart. Together, they shared a silent vow to defy the fates that sought to bind them, to rise above the constraints of their circumstances and seize control of their destinies.

In that moment, as the wind howled outside and the flames crackled in the hearth, Cassandra and Helen stood side by side, united in their strength and resilience. They knew that the road ahead would be fraught with challenges and uncertainties, but they also understood that they were not alone in their struggle. The bond that had formed between them, like an invisible thread woven by the hands of fate, gave them the courage to face whatever trials lay ahead. As the night deepened and the stars began to twinkle in the dark velvet sky, casting a soft glow over the room, Cassandra and Helen shared a rare moment of peace amidst the chaos that surrounded them.

"Cassandra," Helen said, her voice filled with quiet determination, "I refuse to be a victim of my circumstances any longer. Together, we will find a way to break free from the chains that bind us and carve out our own paths."

Cassandra gazed at Helen, her heart swelling with pride for the woman who had endured so much yet still possessed an unyielding spirit. In that shared gaze, they found a silent promise to uplift each other in times of darkness and to celebrate together in moments of triumph.

Cassandra hooked her arm in Helen's elbow and led her new sister towards warmer chambers, hoping to find privacy - and maybe some olives, meat, and wine. Cassandra wanted to continue speaking with Helen, learning more about the woman from across the sea.

* * *

Secluded within the confines of Cassandra's chambers, a tapestry of shadows danced upon the walls as candlelight flickered, casting an ethereal glow over Helen and Cassandra. They sat across from one another, their hearts laid bare in the dim light, finding solace and understanding in each other's presence.

"Perhaps it is by the will of the gods that we find ourselves here, together," mused Cassandra, her gaze introspective. "For though our paths have been fraught with pain and sorrow, they have also led us to this moment of shared understanding and companionship."

"Indeed," agreed Helen, her eyes brimming with sincerity. "And while I know my presence here has brought great suffering to your people, I cannot help but feel grateful for the friendship we are forging amidst these terrible times."

As they spoke, the weight of years of isolation and disbelief seemed to lift from their shoulders, replaced instead by the comforting warmth of newfound kinship. For both women had long struggled against the tide of ignorance and dismissal - one cursed by the gods to see the future yet remain unheard; the other bearing the mark of divine parentage yet condemned to a life of torment at the hands of a cruel husband.

"Tell me more," Cassandra asked gently, her voice laced with curiosity, "about your life in Sparta before Paris."

A wistful smile graced Helen's lips as she delved into memories of her homeland. "Like I mentioned, Sparta was a place of freedom, especially for women. We were encouraged to learn, to fight, and to speak our minds. My family and I were close – even to the man I thought was my father, King Tyndareus. He always doted on me," she paused briefly, her eyes clouded with longing. "I miss them dearly."

"Your story speaks of a life that I can barely imagine," admitted Cassandra, feeling a twinge of envy. "Here, in Troy, the expectations placed upon women are far more restrictive. But I, too, have found solace in the bonds of family, particularly with my brothers."

"Ah, your brothers," Helen murmured, a flicker of guilt passing over her features. "Hector and Paris. It grieves me that my presence here has caused great suffering for them and your people - my people, now."

"Your heart is kind, Helen," Cassandra reassured her, reaching out to grasp her hand gently. "But it is not you alone who bears responsibility for this war. The whims of the gods play their part, as does the hubris of men."

The two women stared at each other.

"It is the men who start wars," Cassandra started, moving closer to her new sister - her new friend. "And yet..."

"And yet, I am blamed."

Silence stretched, broken only by the crackle of fire. Then Helen leaned closer. "I will not allow myself to be a pawn in the gods' cruel game any longer. I will find a way to break free. To reclaim my independence."

Cassandra's heart swelled with admiration. "Then we will face it together. Whatever storms come."

"Promise me," Helen said, gripping her hands. "Promise that you'll stand with me."

"I promise," Cassandra whispered.

They sat there, two women bound by fate yet forging their own pact. And though war loomed, and Cassandra knew her visions would not be heeded, for the first time in years, she felt the spark of hope.

Together, they would endure.

39

Cassie

Modern Day

The December air had a bite to it as I crossed campus, my scarf whipping against my chin. The symposium loomed in my mind like a thundercloud—my chance to be heard before faculty and peers, or to be dismissed outright like Cassandra herself.

I nearly dropped my notes when I heard a voice behind me.

"Cassie, you're walking like you're headed to war."

I turned to see Thomas Sinclair keeping pace, hands shoved in his coat pockets, the faintest smile on his face. He'd always carried himself with a steadiness that felt unshakable, even when Aiden was baiting him in faculty meetings. I had known Thomas for years, but today it hit me how tall – very tall – he was, and his dark hair framed his golden-brown eyes like a celestial canvas. There was something undeniably handsome about him, something I hadn't noticed before.

"Feels like it," I admitted. "If I get through today without throttling someone, it'll be a miracle."

He chuckled. "I'd bet on you over any of them." His words weren't casual flattery. They carried the weight of someone who had watched me fight for my research in rooms where I wasn't taken seriously.

"Is your lecture on Cassandra and the lost women of Greek mythology right now? I've heard it's quite captivating."

"Y-yes," I managed, surprised by his knowledge of my work. "It's just a dress rehearsal with some of my more advanced students. How did you hear about it?"

"Word travels fast around here," he chuckled softly. "Mind if I sit in on your lecture?"

"Of course not." Flattered, I led him into the lecture hall, feeling my heart race as he settled into a seat near the front row.

I kept watching him out of the corner of my eye throughout the whole lecture. When the students streamed out after my lecture, Thomas stayed behind, leaning against the desk with that patient expression of his.

"You've been wound tight for weeks," he said softly. "Do you want to tell me what's really going on?"

The question lodged in my chest. I had spent months hiding this part of myself, even from people who cared. But the way he said it—not prying, just open—made something in me unravel.

"Promise you won't think I'm insane?" I whispered.

"Cassie." His gaze locked with mine, steady and unwavering. "I already think you're one of the sanest people in this department. Try me."

"Well, considering this department is a total of 10 people, one of them Aiden, it's not saying much."

He laughed and then turned serious. "Please."

So I told him. About the visions. The dreams. The way they haunted me. My voice trembled, but I kept talking, afraid that if I stopped, I'd lose my nerve.

He didn't laugh. He didn't interrupt. He just listened.

When I finally trailed off, he said, "I can't pretend I understand it. But I believe you believe it—and I've seen enough of this world to know that not everything fits neatly into a ledger. So if you say these visions are real, then I'm with you."

The knot in my chest loosened. His belief wasn't dramatic. It wasn't some cinematic declaration. It was steady, like him—like an anchor.

And for the first time in weeks, I felt seen.

That evening, Thomas and I found ourselves in a cozy corner of a quaint little restaurant. The flickering candlelight created an intimate atmosphere, casting shadows on the walls as we spoke of every topic that came to mind—myths, sports, music—it didn't matter. Our conversation flowed effortlessly, accompanied by the soft clink of silverware against porcelain plates.

"Did you always know you wanted to study Greek mythology?" Thomas asked, studying me with genuine curiosity.

"Ever since I was young, I've been fascinated with stories and mythology. I think it helps that my mom is Greek," I confessed, my heart swelling with joy to share this part of myself with someone who understood. "The idea of uncovering lost truths and finding meaning in ancient tales has always spoken to me."

"Your enthusiasm is infectious," Thomas replied warmly, his golden-brown eyes sparkling in the dim light. "I can see why your students find your lectures so engaging."

As the night wore on, it became clear that there was something special between us and not just a shared hatred for one man. Thomas's unwavering curiosity, intelligence, and dedication to understanding the world around him captivated me in ways I had never imagined possible.

* * *

The air was crisp as we walked hand in hand through the park, snowflakes drifting down to dust the ground in white. Thomas's fingers tightened around mine, steady and grounding, and for a moment, the chaos in my head eased.

"Your visions," he said carefully, "they're both a blessing and a curse, aren't they?"

"Exactly." My breath puffed into the cold night air. "They give me glimpses of what's coming, but what good is that if no one believes me? Most days, it just feels… useless. Powerless."

We stopped beneath the bare arms of an old oak tree. Its branches reached upward against the night sky, stark and skeletal. Thomas's gaze was steady, though I could see the weight of his thoughts in the tight line of his jaw.

"I think I understand more than you realize," he said. "I've always been a skeptic. But yesterday—" He hesitated, as though saying it aloud might make it less real. "I ran into Diana while she was practicing archery. She told me who she really was. Artemis. And when I laughed, she showed me things… things I can't explain away."

I only nodded. I remembered that same hollow, dizzy feeling when my own world cracked open.

"I felt insane," he admitted. "But then—well, Sherlock Holmes said it best: when you've eliminated the impossible, whatever remains, however improbable, has to be the truth."

I squeezed his hand, needing him to feel that I was real, that we were both standing here.

"She showed me enough that I can't deny it anymore," he continued, his voice softer now. "And it made me think of you. Your visions. Your warnings. I may not understand them, but I believe you, Cassie. I believe in you."

The weight I'd carried for months loosened, like someone had finally cut me free. My throat tightened. "Thank you," I whispered. "You don't know what that means."

"Whatever comes next," Thomas said, "we'll face it together."

I leaned into him, overwhelmed by the simple truth of those words. He wasn't dismissing me, mocking me, or brushing me aside like everyone else. He believed.

And in that moment, standing in the cold under the skeletal oak, I realized how much I needed someone like Thomas at my side. Not just a partner, but someone who saw me—really saw me—and still chose to stay.

The snow kept falling, silent and soft, and for the first time in weeks, I felt warm.

* * *

The December chill had settled into the bones of campus, the old university halls colder than usual. Inside the lecture room, though, my blood was running hot. I'd been preparing for weeks—the symposium was my chance to present my research before my defense, to prove that my work on women in myth was more than a footnote.

Aiden, of course, couldn't resist.

"Really, Sandra," he said, voice dripping with condescension. "The heroes are what shaped civilization. Odysseus. Achilles. Men whose names echo across history. And yet you insist on wasting time digging into their wives, their lovers, their victims. Do you honestly believe Andromache or Penelope matters more than Achilles' rage? It's quaint, but let's be serious—your focus is inconsequential."

The room went still. My pulse hammered in my ears.

"Inconsequential?" I repeated, my voice low but steady.

He blinked, maybe surprised I didn't just shrink back like usual.

I stood taller, letting the silence stretch until every eye in the room was on me. "Let me explain something, Aiden. Without those women you dismiss— those so-called 'supporting characters'—your precious heroes don't even have stories."

My words sharpened, cutting through the air. "Penelope held Ithaca together for twenty years while Odysseus played soldier. Andromache lived through a war that killed her husband and enslaved her son, and she still endured. Cassandra saw the truth and was cursed never to be believed. These women weren't side notes. They were the spine holding the story upright. They navigated the same horrors as your men, without glory, without armor, without an audience—and they *survived.*"

Aiden shifted, but I wasn't finished. Not by a long shot.

"You want to talk about *inconsequential?* Your perspective is what's outdated. You glorify violence and ignore the quiet resilience that actually carried civilizations forward. You're so obsessed with echoing the same old stories about men and their swords, you've missed the heartbeat underneath them. The women whose voices were silenced."

I leaned forward, locking eyes with him, every word ringing clear. "And let me make one thing absolutely clear: do. not. call. me. Sandra. My name is Cassandra. We are not friends. We will never be colleagues. You don't get to minimize me—or them—ever again."

The room was silent, the kind of silence that comes after a thunderclap. Aiden's face flushed red, his mouth opening and closing, but no words came. For once, the man who always had something to say had nothing.

He gathered his papers with shaking hands and left, the scrape of his chair the only sound as the door closed behind him.

I stood there, heart pounding, every nerve in my body electric.

Then—applause. It started soft, then built. Dr. Hawthorne's voice rose above it: "Brava, *Doctor Bennett.*"

Her words quieted the room. She stepped forward, her gaze fixed on me with something that felt like pride and kinship all at once.

"You did more than defend your work today," she said, her voice carrying like a verdict. "You defended every silenced woman whose name was reduced to a footnote. You gave them back their place in the story. That is scholarship. That is the *truth.*"

Her eyes softened, but her words struck deep. "For years, Cassandra's curse was to speak and never be heard. But you—you made them listen. Remember this moment, Cassie. Carry it. Because today you broke the spell. Consider this your defense presentation. I'll have to meet with the rest of your committee, but as far as I am concerned, you've done it."

The applause rose again, but I barely heard it. I felt my throat tighten, a sting of tears threatening. For the first time, I wasn't Cassandra, doomed to go unheard. I was Dr. Cassie Bennett—and today, I was believed.

When the room cleared, I packed my notes with trembling hands. That's when Thomas appeared in the doorway. He hadn't clapped or called out, but his eyes said everything.

"You know," he said quietly, "I think you just burned Achilles and Odysseus to ash in front of the entire department."

I let out a shaky laugh. "Too much?"

"Not enough." His smile was warm but steady. "You were brilliant, *Doctor.* Every word. You didn't just defend your research—you made them listen."

The weight I'd carried for months eased, just a little. "Thank you for believing me."

"I always will." He squeezed my hand, grounding me the way only Thomas could.

221

40

Cassandra

Ancient Troy

A year had passed since the war began.

From her balcony, Cassandra gazed out at the city walls, gilded red in the sinking sun. The air carried the tang of smoke from distant fires, carried across the Aegean on the wind. Below, soldiers patrolled the ramparts, their laughter sharp, edged with weariness. They still toasted Hector's victories, but Cassandra could not share in their mirth. Every laugh seemed to mock her visions.

Paris entered her chamber without knocking, his stride confident, his smile infuriatingly smug. "Another victory. Hector routed them again today. Even the Greeks must admit his greatness now."

Cassandra turned from the balcony. The shadows caught Paris's face, gilding his beauty in gold, but also revealing something else—an unease in his eyes he tried to hide. "Is it truly cause for celebration?" she asked softly. "How many victories until this ends? How many more lives?"

Paris's smile faltered. "I don't know," he admitted, shifting. "But we have Hector. He keeps us safe."

"Safe," Cassandra echoed, her chest tight. She had seen too much blood, too many pyres burning outside the gates. "Hector may keep us breathing, but we are already dying, Paris. Every vision tells me so."

He flinched at her words, as though the curse itself pricked him. "Do not speak so. You frighten people when you talk of doom. Keep your shadows, Cassandra. Let Hector and Father carry the rest."

And then he was gone, leaving her staring at the fading light, her heart a stone in her chest.

That night, Troy celebrated. Torches blazed in the courtyards, goblets overflowed, music thundered. Cassandra slipped through the crowd in a gown of deep blue, the color of midnight seas. Everywhere she turned, she saw joy — wine-stained mouths, dancers spinning in wild circles, Paris preening at the center of it all.

"Ah, there you are," King Priam called, his voice rising above the din. He gestured her forward, his hand warm on her shoulder when she reached him. "Stand with me, daughter. Let all see how proud I am."

Her father's rare pride warmed her, though it also cut — for it was not her prophecies he admired, only her silence.

"Pappá," she began, hesitating. Her gaze slid toward Aeneas, standing near Hector at the edge of the firelight, solemn even amidst celebration. "I…have grown close to Aeneas these past months."

The words hung between them like an unstrung bow.

Hecuba was the first to break the silence. "At last," she said, her smile tired but sincere. "He is loyal, pious, beloved of the people. A good match."

Priam's expression was harder to read. His eyes flicked toward Cassandra — not the proud king's daughter tonight, but the girl too often branded mad. For a moment, she feared his rebuke. But then he nodded slowly. "If he gives you steadiness, I cannot forbid it. Troy needs hope wherever it can be found."

Her breath shuddered with relief. For once, her parents had not dismissed her. She turned, meeting Aeneas's eyes across the court. He inclined his head, almost imperceptibly, but the meaning was clear. She was not alone.

* * *

Weeks folded into months, and still Troy stood. Achilles had withdrawn from battle, sulking in his tent after some quarrel with Agamemnon. For the first time since the war began, hope stirred in the city like spring after winter. The Greeks faltered. Priam ordered a feast.

Wine poured, laughter soared, dancers stamped the courtyard stones. Priam lifted his goblet high. "Tonight, we give thanks to the gods! They have turned their favor from the Greeks. Without Achilles, they are nothing!"

The crowd roared.

Cassandra forced herself to smile, to lift her own cup. She felt Aeneas's steady presence at her side, his hand brushing hers, a silent anchor in the chaos. She clung to that warmth, but inside her chest something cold coiled.

When the feast ended, she slipped away to her chamber. The celebration echoed dimly down the halls, muffled by stone. She sank onto her bed, exhaustion heavy in her bones.

And then the vision came.

Flame. Smoke. The crash of timbers splitting. Troy burning.

She stood on the shoreline, the sea stained crimson, the roar of fire behind her. Ships lined the water, sails swollen with a triumphant wind. On the prow of one, she saw Aeneas — his face grim, determined — steering away from the inferno.

"No," she cried, her voice breaking. She stumbled toward the water, hands outstretched. "Take me with you! Don't leave me here!"

But he did not hear. Or would not. His ship cut through the waves, carrying him into the horizon until even the sail was gone, leaving only smoke.

Cassandra fell to her knees, sobs tearing her throat raw. "Please," she whispered to the indifferent night. "Please, let this not be true."

But the vision lingered, etched into her soul like a scar.

* * *

When she woke, her pillow was wet with tears. The echoes of fire still clung to her ears. She pressed her fists to her eyes, wishing she could rip the images free.

The celebration outside carried on, but Cassandra knew the truth.

Achilles' absence was no reprieve. It was the calm before the storm.

And in the storm, Troy would burn.

225

41

Cassie

Modern Day

The winter sun in Tarpon Springs wasn't like the winter sun on campus. It had a sharper brightness, bouncing off the water of the bayou until it hurt your eyes, and it smelled of salt and frying oil and damp earth. I'd grown up under this sky, the warmth of it woven into my bones, but coming back now—after the storm that had been the symposium—felt different. I wasn't the same Cassie who had slunk away from arguments, who had swallowed down the curse of disbelief like a bitter pill.

I was finally ready to speak.

The Bennett family home glowed like it always did, porch light on even though the Florida sun still hung high, jasmine twining up the railings, Christmas lights strung unevenly because Theo had insisted on "helping" but never bothered with measuring tape. It was familiar, safe. And yet my chest was tight as I climbed the steps.

"Κόρη μου!" My dad's booming voice met me the moment the door swung open. His arms engulfed me before I could protest, pulling me in against the scratch of his salt-and-pepper beard. "You're home! Did you bring hunger? Your mother made enough lamb to feed all of Tarpon Springs."

I laughed—really laughed—because of course he'd open with food. "I missed you too, Dad."

The living room was a mess in the way only a Greek-American household can be during the holidays. My mom, apron still tied, was ferrying trays of spanakopita like a general commanding troops. Theo stood by the fireplace, hand protectively on Blair's shoulder, who was radiant and round with pregnancy. And then there was Nik—smirking, casual, arm looped confidently around Helen as if the two of them hadn't detonated a land mine in the middle of our family's future.

Helen herself looked like she'd stepped out of a myth. Even in jeans and a simple sweater, she carried herself like royalty, like a woman who had been raised with Sparta's discipline in her blood. She caught my eye, gave a small nod, and in that instant, I remembered the dream: her hands stained in blood, her face broken by grief.

The weight of my gift pressed hard against my ribcage.

"Cass!" Theo was the first to notice I'd gone still. He crossed to hug me, squeezing so hard my ribs protested. "You survived the semester. We're proud of you, little sister."

I almost said it then—almost blurted out the whole thing about Dimitri, about visions of ruin, about marble shipments and blood on Helen's hands. But I swallowed it. Not yet.

Dinner came first.

We gathered around the long oak table, plates overflowing, wine flowing even faster. The house rang with laughter, with Blair telling stories about Theo's half-finished baby-proofing attempts, with my dad booming prayers half in Greek, half in English, with Nik bragging about deals made in Athens.

I watched. I waited.

Finally, when plates were cleared and dessert had been set down—galaktoboureko steaming with cinnamon and custard—I spoke.

"I need to say something."

The room quieted. That was new. Normally, my warnings were met with sighs or immediate interruptions. But tonight, my voice carried differently. Maybe the symposium had changed me more than I realized.

"It's about Dimitri Kostas," I said, steady and sure. "About Helen. About what's coming."

Helen stiffened at her name, her fingers curling against Nik's. My father frowned, setting down his wine. "Cassie…"

"No, Dad. Please. Listen." My hands shook, but I kept going. "You think I'm obsessed, that I'm just the little girl who used to play-pretend in the backyard. But I have seen things. Not dreams. Not imagination. Visions. And they've already started coming true."

Theo shifted uncomfortably, rubbing at his jaw. "Cass—"

"No, let me finish!" My voice cracked like a whip across the table. Everyone blinked. I'd never shouted like that at them before. "I saw Helen before Nik even told me she existed. I knew. I saw the two of them together, and no one believed me. And now here she is. Sitting at our table."

A silence fell, heavy and strange.

Helen's gaze locked onto mine. Her expression wasn't offended—it was haunted. She believed me. Or at least part of her wanted to.

Nik, however, rolled his eyes. "Cassie, don't start this again. You don't know Dimitri like I do. He's tough, but he's not a monster. You're spinning mythology into reality again—"

"Am I?" I snapped. "Because I saw blood, Nik. I saw Helen weeping. I saw everything you've built with Dimitri crumble to dust. You think this is a game? You think your marriage is some romantic rebellion? It's not. It's war. And you've dragged all of us into it."

"Cassandra!" My father's voice boomed. "That's enough."

I turned on him, fire in my chest. "No, Dad, it's not enough. You have ignored me my whole life. Every warning, every vision—dismissed. Like Priam ignoring Cassandra while Troy burned. Well, guess what? I'm not going to be silent anymore. You will hear me, even if you don't believe me."

The room crackled with the echo of my words.

Nik pushed back his chair, jaw tight. "You sound insane."

"Maybe," I shot back. "But I'd rather be insane and right than smug and blind."

The air between us vibrated with anger, but then Helen's voice cut through. Soft, deliberate.

"Cassie."

We all turned. She was pale, but steady, her chin lifted. "I don't know what I believe about your visions. But I do know my father. And you're right about one thing: he will not forgive us for marrying without his blessing. He is… dangerous."

Nik's face drained of color. "Helen…"

She laid a hand over his. "I love you. But we can't pretend Cassie's fears are baseless."

It was the opening I needed, the glimmer of solidarity across centuries of echoes.

I looked around the table, meeting each of their eyes. My voice dropped to a near-whisper, but the conviction in it was steel. "Something is coming. And when it happens, don't say I didn't warn you."

* * *

Later that night, as laughter and conversation picked back up in forced cheer, I slipped outside into the jasmine-scented air. The stars were sharp over the bayou, mirrored in the dark water. My breath steamed in the cool Florida night.

The screen door creaked, and I turned to find Helen joining me, her arms folded against the chill.

"I don't know what you are," she said quietly. "Prophet. Dreamer. Madwoman. But I do know this—" She met my gaze, her blue eyes bright as sea glass. "I will listen. Even if no one else does."

The weight in my chest loosened. Just a fraction.

"Thank you," I whispered.

For the first time all evening, I felt like maybe I wasn't completely alone.

42

Cassandra

Ancient Troy

The citadel of Troy lay restless behind her as Cassandra climbed the long marble steps to Athena's temple. Her stomach turned with that familiar churning—half dread, half anticipation—that had accompanied every visit here since her curse began.

Leander, a guard and shadow, walked silently at her side. His bronze armor caught the morning sun, polished as though he could polish away the soot of war clinging to the city. When they reached the topmost step, he glanced at her face, searching, but said nothing. That was Leander's way—constant, protective, always a step behind her, yet never prying.

Inside, the temple's cool shadows embraced her. Incense curled like smoke from a battlefield pyre, filling the vast chamber with a thick, otherworldly sweetness. Candles flickered, casting long columns of light across the marble floor. The statue of Athena loomed in the sanctum—helmeted, spear raised, eyes sharp and unblinking. Cassandra's throat tightened. Of all the gods, Athena should have been the one to help her.

"O Athena," she whispered, sinking to her knees before the altar. The stone was cool beneath her palms, as though the goddess's marble flesh carried its own steady breath. "I come to you in desperation. Grant me your wisdom. Show me the path."

A shuffle of fabric. A voice.

"My child."

Cassandra turned to find Eunice, the high priestess. Her hair was silver now, her lined face etched with years of prayer, sacrifice, and disappointment. She studied Cassandra a long moment before speaking.

"It has been too long since you last stood here," Eunice said, voice soft but edged with reproach.

Cassandra bowed her head. "I am sorry. My duties as Princess…" She stopped. The excuse tasted false even on her tongue. The truth was harder: *I was afraid to know what I would see here.*

Eunice's gaze softened. "I know you, Cassandra. You were meant for more than silks and feasts. Had you remained with us, had your parents allowed it, you might have been one of my successors."

Something cracked inside Cassandra's chest. "I wish it," she confessed. "I wish I had been left here to serve Athena instead of…this." She gestured helplessly, meaning the palace, the war, the curse.

The priestess laid a hand on her shoulder, papery skin but steady pressure. "You carry both gift and curse, yes. But you are still hers, child. Always hers."

Her throat tightened again, but this time with longing. "Then tell me, Eunice—why does no one believe me?"

Eunice's smile was bitter, knowing. "Athena's wisdom is feared as much as it is honored. Men prefer omens they can twist to their liking. A clear prophecy, a woman's voice—these they reject, for they cannot bend them." She leaned closer. "But I believe you. Always."

The words warmed Cassandra more than any blanket. She nodded, tears stinging her eyes, and turned back to the statue.

She prayed again, lips trembling: "O Goddess of Wisdom, grant me courage. Guide me in this darkness. Show me how to protect them—Hector, Aeneas, Helen, even Paris. Even Troy."

For a heartbeat, silence. Then warmth. Not imagined warmth, but something that seemed to rise from the stone itself, humming through her bones. The scent of myrrh grew stronger, almost cloying. And in her mind, as clearly as if it had been spoken aloud, she heard:

All will be well.

Her heart surged. It was not detailed, not the map she craved—but it was something. The first time since her curse that a god had answered with comfort instead of cruelty.

When she opened her eyes, the glow was gone. Eunice stood several paces away, her head bowed, as though she had not seen.

* * *

Leander waited at the temple steps, spear planted in the ground. When Cassandra emerged, her eyes distant, he straightened.

"My lady?" His voice was cautious, like a man approaching a skittish horse.

She took his arm gratefully. Their silence as they descended was companionable, broken only when he asked, "Did she answer?"

Cassandra looked at him, startled. Leander never asked. His dark eyes held hers, steady.

"…Yes," she said finally. "She did."

They walked through the streets of Troy. The city was quieter now than she remembered from her childhood: no vendors calling wares, no children darting between market stalls. Shuttered homes, abandoned shops, the air carrying smoke from distant pyres. Cassandra noticed everything, the way one notices a scar they know will never fade.

Leander must have noticed her grim expression. "We are still standing, Princess. That is something."

Cassandra managed a small smile. "You sound like Hector."

"I will take that as praise."

She let herself laugh—quiet, fleeting, but real.

* * *

That evening, Cassandra sat at her writing desk, quill scratching furiously across parchment. The memory of Athena's warmth still lingered, urging her on.

We cannot save Troy, she wrote. *But perhaps we can save a piece of it.*

Her plan was desperate, dangerous, but it gave her purpose: select Aeneas and a small band of loyal men, slip them out of the city by night, and guide them toward the secret mountain passes. Let them carry Troy's bloodline, Troy's story, beyond the ruin she knew was coming.

She was so absorbed she didn't notice the time until a servant knocked to bring supper. Cassandra waved her off, heart hammering. She had to bring the plan to her father. Tonight.

The king's private room smelled of parchment, smoke, and age. Priam sat by the fire, a scroll in his hand, his expression weary. When Cassandra entered, he looked up, eyes softening.

"My daughter," he said warmly. "What brings you here at this hour?"

Cassandra bowed her head, then lifted her chin. "Pappá. I have been granted a vision by Athena. Troy cannot be saved—but some of our people might. I have devised a plan."

He gestured for her to continue. Cassandra outlined every detail: the men, the route, the secrecy, the hope of rebuilding elsewhere. Her voice was steady, passion burning through her words.

When she finished, silence. Priam's lined face betrayed nothing. At last, he sighed, and the weight of kingship filled his tone.

"My dear child. You are brave. You are clever. But you are wrong."

Cassandra's breath caught. "Wrong?"

"Troy stands. Hector still fights. If I give up now, if I send away one of our strongest commanders, what message does that send to our people? That their king has already surrendered? No." He shook his head. "I will not allow it."

"Pappá, please," Cassandra begged, stepping closer. "This is not surrender. It is survival! If Aeneas lives, Troy lives. If we do nothing, we all die."

Hecuba entered then, silent until she caught Cassandra's last words. Her eyes narrowed. "And what would you have us do? Whisper our defeat in the ears of our children before the city has even fallen?"

"It is not defeat, Mother, it is foresight—"

"It is madness," Hecuba snapped. "Your madness, Cassandra. Enough."

The sting cut deep, but Cassandra forced herself to look back at Priam. His expression was sorrowful, but his decision was final.

"My love for you is boundless, daughter," he said softly. "But I cannot give in to despair. Not yet."

A knock at the chamber door. Leander entered, face grave. He bowed to the king, then spoke quickly.

"My lord. Word from the walls. Achilles has returned to battle. He demands a duel with Hector."

The room stilled. Cassandra's blood ran cold. Her vision of Hector's death surged up, vivid as flame. She swayed on her feet.

"No," she whispered. "No, it cannot be."

Priam's jaw tightened. "We must prepare. Have Hector summoned."

And as Leander hurried out, Cassandra clutched the edge of the table, nails digging into the wood. She could already hear the cries of mourning, the clash of bronze on bronze.

She turned to her father, tears burning her eyes. "Pappá, stop him. For once, listen—"

But Priam's silence was answer enough.

Moments later, Hector himself entered. Armor half-fastened, face calm but resolute. He looked between his sister and his father.

"I have heard," he said simply.

Cassandra rushed to him, clutching his arm. "Brother, please. Do not go. You will not return."

Hector's eyes softened with love, even as he gently pried her fingers loose. "You see shadows, sister. But I see duty. If Achilles calls, I must answer. For Troy. For all of us."

Cassandra shook her head violently. "Then I will go in your place!"

A rare smile touched Hector's lips. He kissed her forehead. "If only it could be so. But this is mine to bear."

And with that, he turned and strode from the chamber, his figure framed in torchlight, leaving Cassandra trembling in the silence he left behind.

Cassandra sank to her knees. Athena's warmth still echoed faintly in her chest, but it could not ease the knowledge that her brother walked toward death.

"Please," she whispered into the empty air. "Please, let me be wrong."

43

Cassie

Modern Day

The next morning, Tarpon Springs stirred like any holiday town: bakery doors thrown open, tourists wandering past sponge shops, the tang of saltwater and powdered sugar thick in the air. On the surface, everything was normal. But inside me, everything vibrated with unease.

Sleep had been restless, broken by flashes of visions: marble crates split open, shadows moving through warehouses, Helen's face pale beneath fluorescent lights. Each time I bolted upright, my chest heaving, the image of Dimitri Kostas hovered like smoke.

I needed answers.

I pulled on a jacket and left the house before anyone else was awake. The streets smelled of coffee and seawater, the chatter of sponge divers rising from the docks. I ducked into a small café near the waterfront, ordered something bitter and black, and opened my laptop. My inbox was a mess— student emails, drafts of my symposium notes—but one message caught my eye. Alexis.

Subject line: Kostas. Urgent.

My pulse skittered as I clicked.

Cassie—

You were right to be worried. I asked some old friends in Athens to do digging. Dimitri's finances aren't clean. He's got ties to an importer in Italy, yes, but also connections to groups far darker. I won't say names in writing, but think organized crime. Arms. Trafficking. Not just marble.

And the marriage? He's furious. People overheard him say he'll "reclaim what was taken" no matter the cost.

You need to be careful. He's not a man to forgive betrayal.

—Alexis

The words blurred. Organized crime. Reclaim what was taken.

I slammed the laptop shut, my hands trembling.

"Bad news?" a voice asked.

I jumped so violently that my coffee sloshed. Across the table slid Thomas, his scarf askew, concern written all over his face.

"You scared me half to death," I hissed.

"Sorry. You left the house like it was on fire. I followed." His voice softened. "Cass, what's wrong?"

I slid the laptop toward him, open again, letting him read the email. His brow furrowed as he scrolled.

"This is… bad," he said finally. "Very bad."

"No kidding," I muttered, running a hand through my hair. "This isn't just about family politics or Dimitri throwing his weight around. He's dangerous, Thomas. If Nik thinks love will protect him from this—"

"He's blind," Thomas finished grimly. "So what do we do?"

Before I could answer, my phone buzzed. Unknown number. Against my better judgment, I answered.

"Cassandra Bennett?" The voice was male, low, thick with an accent. Greek.

"Yes," I said cautiously.

"This is a warning. Tell your brother: enjoy his pretty wife while he can.

The Kostas family reclaims what belongs to it."

My blood ran ice cold. "Who is this? How did you get this number?"

But the line went dead.

I stared at the phone, my knuckles white.

Thomas reached across the table, gripping my wrist. "Cassie, you need to go to the police."

I barked a laugh, high and bitter. "What do I say? 'Hi, I had a prophetic vision and also some shady guy just threatened me over the phone, please arrest one of the most powerful men in Greece?' They'll laugh me out of the station."

"They won't laugh if you tell them about the call," he pressed.

But I was already shaking my head. "Even if they take it seriously, Dimitri's reach is too long. He'll find out. And that will just put a target on my back. On all of us."

The café door opened then, bell jingling, and I froze. A tall man with an angular face and pale blue eyes walked in. He didn't order. Didn't look around. Just stood, scanning the room like he was cataloging exits. His gaze swept over me, lingered a beat too long, then moved on.

My stomach dropped. Mr. Ivanov.

I recognized him from the description Alexis had given me in an old message—an "associate" Dimitri had been rumored to meet in Thessaloniki. Eastern European ties. Ruthless.

"Thomas," I whispered, grabbing my laptop and shoving it into my bag. "We need to leave. Now."

We slipped out the back before Ivanov could make another sweep, my heart hammering against my ribs. The Florida sunlight hit me like a slap, too bright, too ordinary for the dread curling in my gut.

* * *

Back at the house, chaos was in full swing. My mother was yelling at Theo to move the crib parts out of the living room, Blair was perched on the sofa with her swollen feet in a bowl of warm water, and my dad was gesturing wildly with a spatula as he ranted about someone forgetting to buy more olive oil.

It was safe. Loud. Normal.

And it would all come crashing down if I didn't act.

"Cass?" Helen's voice pulled me aside as I set my bag down. She looked pale, lips pressed tight. "What did you find?"

I hesitated. She deserved the truth. "Your father isn't just angry. He's dangerous. He's tied to people who don't just fight in courtrooms—they fight in alleys and ports. If he knows about you and Nik…"

Her hand flew to her chest. "Then it's worse than I thought."

I nodded grimly. "I got a call this morning. A threat."

Helen's eyes flicked toward the kitchen where Nik stood, oblivious, laughing with Theo. Her expression hardened. "You'll never convince him. He loves me, but he thinks love makes him untouchable. It doesn't."

"I know," I said. And for the first time, I saw in her what the ancients must have seen in Sparta's princess: steel beneath beauty, a survivor's spine.

"Then we prepare," Helen whispered. "Because when Dimitri comes, he won't come alone."

* * *

That night, as the family gathered around the table again, I sat silent, listening to Nik boast about marble shipments arriving next week, about how Dimitri had finally agreed to "a meeting in Florida."

Every word was a countdown clock.

I caught Helen's eye across the table. She nodded once, small, deliberate.

We were the only ones who understood what storm was gathering.

And this time, I swore to myself, I would not be silent.

44

Cassandra

Ancient Troy

The sun hung low, a molten disk sinking toward the western horizon, painting the walls of Troy in burnished gold. In the palace gardens, roses spilled from trellises, their fragrance mingling with the salt-stung breeze drifting up from the sea. Cassandra and Helen walked among them, their silken dresses whispering across the grass, two women bound together by circumstance, by guilt, and by something far deeper than either dared admit.

Helen reached for a pale bloom and traced its petals with delicate fingers. "Tell me again of Aeneas," she said, her voice softer than the murmur of the fountains. "You speak of him with such reverence. He must be remarkable."

Cassandra smiled despite herself. Aeneas's name was a balm on her tongue. "He is steady, noble. He bears his duties like a shield, never wavering. In him I see the strength of Anchises and the favor of Aphrodite—but also something more. A gentleness, a devotion. He fights because he must, not because he craves glory."

Helen tilted her head, studying Cassandra. "Strange, is it not, how the men most fit to rule seldom seek it?"

A faint smile touched Cassandra's lips. "And those who crave it most—" She didn't finish. Both knew whose name lingered unspoken.

Silence stretched between them. Cassandra could hear the distant clang of smiths hammering bronze, the voices of soldiers calling to one another on the walls, the eternal drumbeat of war. She turned her face to the sea, where dark sails marred the horizon. The hairs on her arms prickled.

Her breath caught. A vision surged upon her with the force of a storm. The gardens dissolved; the sky bled into crimson; the earth split open beneath her feet.

Hector stood in gleaming armor, the crest of his helm catching the sun like a golden flame. Across from him, Achilles glowed like something more than mortal, his rage burning so hot it seemed to warp the very air around him. Their spears met with a thunderous crack. Cassandra's chest tightened—she could feel the blows as though each struck her ribs. She watched Hector stumble, his face streaked with sweat and dust, while Achilles's eyes blazed with inexorable wrath. And then—blood, screams, sand stained red. Hector's body was dragged through the dust by merciless horses.

Cassandra gasped and stumbled back, clutching at her chest as if to keep her heart from bursting.

"Cassandra?" Helen's hands gripped her shoulders, steady and warm.

Her voice came raw. "It is Hector. He will meet Achilles this day—and he will not return alive."

Helen's eyes widened, her lips parting in disbelief. "No. That cannot be. Hector is the pride of Troy—he has never faltered. Even Achilles cannot best him."

But Cassandra shook her head, tears spilling hot down her cheeks. "The Fates have already cut the thread. I saw it. The gods will not let him live."

Helen's golden brows drew together, anguish flashing across her face. "Then why must it be so? Why can the gods not be sated with all the blood already spilled?"

"Because cruelty is their sport," Cassandra spat. Her fists curled, nails biting into her palms. "Apollo gave me sight only to watch me drown in it. He revels in my torment."

Helen's lips trembled, and for once her beauty seemed almost fragile. "Then if he cannot be saved...what becomes of us?"

Cassandra had no answer. Only silence, heavy as the sea.

Cassandra ran through the palace corridors, her sandals slapping against the stone. She found Hector in his chamber, tightening the straps of his cuirass. The lamplight turned his armor into a river of molten bronze.

"Brother!" she cried, rushing to seize his arm. "You must not go. I have seen it—you will face Achilles, and you will fall."

Hector's dark eyes softened with sorrow. "Little sister." He set aside his helmet and cupped her face with one calloused hand. "Your heart is heavy with visions. You always beg me to turn aside. But what honor would I have if I refused my duty? If I do not face Achilles, he will tear through our gates unchecked."

"You are our heart, Hector!" Cassandra sobbed. "Without you, Troy cannot stand. Stay behind the walls. Let others fight. Live—for Andromache, for Astyanax."

His lips quirked in a bittersweet smile at the mention of his wife and son. "Every father longs to watch his child grow. Every husband longs to grow old with his wife. But I am more than a man—I am Troy's shield. I cannot abandon my place."

He pressed a kiss to her forehead and pulled the helmet over his head, the great horsehair crest shivering like flame. "If the gods decree my death, then so be it. I will meet it with courage."

"That's what I am afraid of."

Cassandra's knees nearly buckled as he strode past her, his broad shoulders filling the doorway. She wanted to hurl herself across the threshold, to bar his path, to scream until he yielded. But she could only sag against the wall, weeping, as destiny pulled him inexorably forward.

The family gathered atop the walls, the whole city pressing shoulder to shoulder to witness the duel. The air was a hive of murmurs, prayers, and muffled sobs. Cassandra stood between her parents, Priam's trembling hand resting on her arm, Hecuba's veil pressed to her mouth. Paris hovered nearby, restless, his eyes fixed on the field where Hector approached Achilles with steady, deliberate steps. Helen stood apart, her face pale, her hands knotted together.

Below, the champions circled one another. Achilles shone like the wrath of Helios itself, his armor newly forged by Hephaestus. Hector looked human by contrast, mortal, vulnerable—but resolute. The clash began with the scream of bronze on bronze, the ring of shield on shield. The Trojans on the wall roared encouragement, and Cassandra's heart twisted at the cruel irony.

"Please, Father," she whispered urgently, clutching Priam's sleeve. "Call him back. He cannot win. You will lose your son."

Priam's jaw tightened. "This is his choice, daughter. He fights for us all. Do not shame his courage."

"Courage will not save him!" Cassandra cried, her voice breaking. "The gods have decreed it—he cannot prevail!"

Hecuba sobbed beside her, her hands trembling. "Hush, child. Do not curse him with your words."

Cassandra bit her tongue until she tasted blood. Rage boiled within her—at her father's blindness, her mother's resignation, the gods' merciless cruelty. She lifted her gaze to the heavens, eyes burning. "Damn you, Apollo," she whispered. "Is this my punishment still? To watch him die and know no one will believe?"

The battle below raged on. Hector lunged, his spear grazing Achilles's shield. For a moment, Cassandra dared to hope—perhaps fate could be defied. But Achilles whirled, driving Hector back. His blade sang, relentless as the tide.

Then the fatal moment. Hector stumbled. His spear splintered. Achilles seized the opening, plunging his sword deep into Hector's throat. Blood fountained, scarlet against bronze.

A sound tore from Cassandra's throat, raw and animal. On the wall, women wailed, men groaned, Priam's face crumpled in horror. Hecuba collapsed against her daughters, keening like a wounded beast. Paris's lips curled in rage, but his eyes flickered with terror.

Achilles stood triumphant over Hector's fallen body, his chest heaving. With brutal calm, he lashed Hector's ankles with leather thongs, binding them to his chariot. Then, with a crack of his whip, he dragged his enemy's corpse across the sand. Dust and blood rose in a choking cloud as Hector's lifeless form was hauled around the walls of his own city.

Cassandra fell to her knees, her nails clawing the stone parapet. "No," she sobbed. "No, no, no!" Her cries mingled with the city's collective scream, a chorus of grief that shook the very stones.

She buried her face in her hands, but the visions came anyway—rushing in like floodwater. She saw the Greeks at their forges, hammering together planks, shaping timbers into the form of a horse vast enough to rival the city gates. She saw soldiers hidden in its belly, cramped and silent, their breath hot against the wood. She saw the horse wheeled to Troy's gates, the Trojans' cheers of victory, her own screams drowned out by their joy. And then—fire, everywhere, devouring her beloved city.

The vision shattered, leaving her trembling on the wall.

"Father!" she cried hoarsely, staggering to her feet. "Listen to me! They will build a horse, a great wooden horse—they will hide inside it, and it will be the end of us!"

Priam turned, his face ravaged with grief. His eyes, red and wet, met hers with pity. "My daughter," he murmured, "you are broken by sorrow. Do not add madness to your grief."

"It is no madness!" she shrieked, gripping his arm. "It is true! They will destroy us from within—"

"Enough, Cassandra!" he thundered, shoving her hand away. "Do not blaspheme Hector's courage with your ravings. Leave us to mourn in peace."

She swayed, stunned, her mouth working soundlessly. Around her, her brothers and sisters looked away, ashamed, afraid, unwilling to meet her gaze. Even Helen, eyes wide with pity, said nothing.

Cassandra's chest rose and fell in ragged sobs. The curse pressed down on her like chains, suffocating her, silencing her. She sank back to her knees as the fires of the funeral pyres were lit, smoke curling into the darkening sky.

Above the wails of mourning, Cassandra whispered to herself, broken but unyielding: "I will not stop. Even if they never believe, I will not stop."

45

Cassie

Modern Day

The first weeks of the spring semester had blurred together in a haze of lectures, grading, and endless departmental meetings. My title had officially changed—*Professor Cassandra Bennett*—a small miracle I still didn't quite believe. The plaque on my office door gleamed brighter than it should have, as though mocking the sleepless nights, the tears, the sacrifices that had gone into earning it.

But even the triumph couldn't settle the storm inside me. Visions came more frequently now—shards of memory and prophecy mixed, impossible to untangle. Each one was sharper, cutting closer to the bone, and each one featured the same shadow looming larger: Dimitri Kostas.

Thomas had noticed. He always noticed. He was the anchor I hadn't known I needed, his patience a quiet balm against the sharpness of my curse. Where Aiden had sneered, where my brothers doubted, Thomas believed. That was enough to keep me moving forward, even when my stomach twisted with dread.

Now, looking up at the famous (infamous?) giant flamingo in the middle of Tampa International Airport, I wondered if it would be enough.

"Cass," Thomas said softly, placing a steadying hand on my elbow as the automatic doors parted, spilling us into Florida's heavy winter air. "Breathe."

I obeyed, though the knot in my chest remained. "I saw it again," I murmured. "The fire. The ruin. Helen in blood. Nik—"

"Hey." He stopped me with a firm shake of his head. "You told me. I heard you. That's why we're here. You're not carrying this alone anymore."

I wanted to believe him. But a small, poisonous voice whispered otherwise: *you will always be alone in this.*

* * *

The stucco walls of my childhood home came into view as the sun dipped low, gilding the palms and the crosshatch of power lines in molten light. My mother had decorated the porch with garlands, leftover from Christmas, but still stubbornly twinkling. From the driveway, I could hear voices—the overlapping tones of Theo and my father, the softer timbre of Helen, and another, deeper register that made my skin crawl.

Dimitri Kostas was already here.

Inside, the house smelled of roasted lamb and rosemary. My mother had gone all-out, of course; no Bennett family gathering was ever casual. But the moment I stepped across the threshold, I felt the tension humming, electric and invisible, pulling at the walls.

Theo greeted me stiffly, his hug brief. "Glad you made it." His eyes flicked to Thomas but offered no welcome, only a nod.

Nik was seated at the dining table with Helen beside him. She rose to embrace me, her eyes luminous, her perfume faint but steady—a blend of sandalwood and vanilla that reminded me too much of my last vision.

And then Dimitri rose. He was taller than I remembered from our brief encounters, his silver hair slicked neatly back, his posture radiating command. His tailored suit was dark, expensive, and understated. He extended his hand like a diplomat, like a man who knew the world bent to his will.

"Cassandra," he said warmly, too warmly. "At last. I hear so much about you."

"Likewise," I managed, my throat tight.

Beside me, Thomas's hand brushed mine, subtle and grounding. My father clapped Dimitri on the back as though they were old friends. My mother gestured toward the table, urging us to sit, as though this were a normal dinner and not a meeting with fate.

The meal stretched long and uneasy. Conversation circled in shallow loops: Theo's projects at the company, Helen's adjustment to Florida, the weather. Dimitri laughed in the right places, nodded at the right times, his charm a mask as flawless as polished stone.

But I saw the fissures.

The way his gaze lingered on Helen, possessive, proprietary. The faint curl of disdain when Nik spoke. The predator's patience coiled beneath the mask of geniality.

At last, Dimitri set down his glass with deliberate care. The sound of crystal meeting wood was soft, but the room seemed to fall silent around it.

"Nikolaos," he began, his voice smooth but cutting, "you have taken my daughter. Without blessing. Without thought for the family she left behind."

Nik straightened. His hand slipped into Helen's, their fingers intertwining, but his jaw was tight. "Mr. Kostas, I love your daughter. I married her because I couldn't imagine my life without her."

Dimitri's smile was all teeth. "Love." He tasted the word like it was bitter. "A noble sentiment. But love does not build empires. Love does not protect families. Respect does. Honor does." His gaze slid, serpent-like, to me. "Loyalty does."

Something in me snapped.

"You don't mean loyalty," I said, my voice sharp as glass. "You mean obedience."

The room froze. Theo's brow furrowed, my father's lips pressed thin, my mother fidgeted with her napkin. Only Helen looked at me with a flicker of gratitude, though she said nothing.

Dimitri chuckled, low and dismissive. "You speak boldly, Professor. But perhaps you should keep to your books."

My pulse pounded. "Books tell the truth. They show us what happens when men put pride above reason. When they treat women like pawns instead of people. You think you're Zeus, Dimitri—but you're just another tyrant rewriting the story to suit yourself."

"Cassie," Theo hissed, his tone edged with warning.

But I couldn't stop. Not now. "I know what you're planning. You think no one sees it, but I do. And if you keep pushing this family, you'll bring us all down with you."

For a long moment, Dimitri said nothing. He lifted his napkin, dabbed politely at his lips, then placed it neatly beside his plate. When he finally spoke, his voice was almost tender.

"You remind me of my daughter when she was a child," he said, turning to Helen. "Always questioning, always rebelling. But in the end, she understood the importance of family. Of loyalty."

Helen flinched as though struck.

Nik's hand tightened around hers. "Helen isn't your property," he said, his voice steel.

Dimitri's gaze turned to him. "She is my blood. That is more binding than marriage papers signed in secret."

Theo broke in, his tone sharp. "This isn't productive. We're here to build a partnership, not tear each other apart."

"Partnership?" I echoed, incredulous. "You can't partner with a man who sees his daughter as a bargaining chip. You're walking straight into a trap."

"Cassie, enough!" My father's voice cracked across the table. His eyes were heavy with exhaustion, with shame. "You are not helping."

I turned to him, my throat raw. "Dad, I'm *trying*. You don't see it now, but you will. And by then, it'll be too late."

He shook his head, refusing to meet my eyes.

Dimitri rose. The scrape of his chair against tile was like thunder. He circled the table with slow, measured steps until he stood behind Nik. His hand fell to my brother's shoulder, heavy, proprietary.

"You have spirit," he said. "That I respect. But spirit must be tempered with wisdom, Nikolaos. With obedience. If you honor my daughter, you will honor me. Do you understand?"

Nik swallowed hard. "I will honor Helen. Always. But my life, my choices—those are mine."

Dimitri's smile didn't falter, but his grip tightened. "Defiance runs in this family." His gaze flicked to me, dark and unyielding. "Dangerous."

The room felt suffocating, the air thick with smoke though no fire burned. My hands trembled on the edge of the table, desperate to claw through the silence.

"Let him go," I whispered.

For a heartbeat, Dimitri's eyes locked with mine. Something cold and ancient passed between us, as though he could see every vision I'd ever had, every curse that had ever branded me Cassandra.

Then, with a laugh as sudden as it was false, he released Nik and clapped him on the back. "A good man," he declared loudly, raising his glass. "And I am proud to call you son."

Laughter rippled around the table, brittle and hollow. Relief, forced and fragile. My parents smiled, my brothers exhaled, Helen's shoulders sagged.

But I knew better.

Later, when the house had quieted and the dishes were stacked in the sink, Theo cornered me on the lanai. Nik hovered nearby, arms crossed, Helen lingering like a shadow.

"What the hell was that?" Theo demanded. "You embarrassed us in front of him."

"I was protecting you," I shot back. "He's dangerous. Can't you see it?"

"What I see," Nik said tightly, "is you inserting yourself where you don't belong. Helen and I—we can handle Dimitri. We don't need your visions dictating our lives."

Helen opened her mouth, but no sound came. Her silence was answer enough.

Theo's jaw clenched. "Cassie, we love you. But this has to stop. You're turning Dad against Nik, making Mom anxious, and dragging Thomas into this circus. And for what? Nothing ever happens."

The words burned. "Nothing happens because I warn you. Because I see what's coming and try to stop it."

"Or maybe nothing happens because there's nothing there." Theo's voice was sharp enough to cut.

And with that, they left me on the porch, the cicadas humming louder than my heartbeat.

* * *

The night pressed in heavily. I gripped the railing until my knuckles whitened.

"Please," I whispered to the dark. "Give me something undeniable. Something they can't ignore."

The world tilted.

Suddenly, I was at the Port of Tampa, the air thick with diesel and salt. Containers stacked like looming walls stretched as far as the eye could see. Men in dark uniforms pried one open, their flashlights cutting through the gloom. Inside: marble, gleaming under the beam. But wedged between the slabs were packages wrapped in unmarked plastic.

"Jesus Christ," one agent muttered. "Get Nikolaos Bennett on the phone. Now. This will bury him."

The vision snapped shut.

I staggered, bile rising in my throat.

"Cassie?" Thomas's voice broke through the dark. He had followed me outside, concern etched in every line of his face.

I turned to him, my voice hoarse but steady. "The shipment. Dimitri's marble. It's a trap. Nik's name is all over it."

Thomas stepped closer, cupping my face in his hands. "Then we act. Whatever it takes."

I clung to him, the storm still raging, but no longer mine alone to bear. And as I stared into the night, toward the Gulf, I knew: this was only the beginning.

46

Cassandra

Ancient Troy

The city mourned. Smoke from Hector's pyre still clung to the air, heavy and acrid, settling in Cassandra's lungs until every breath felt like ash. The palace was shrouded in grief; its corridors echoed not with laughter but with the low keening of women, the shuffle of men too weary to speak. Cassandra moved like a ghost among them, her eyes hollow, her lips raw from silent prayers that went unanswered.

But her curse did not relent. Even as her people wailed for Hector, visions struck her like blows to the skull. She saw it—always the same: the hollow belly of the wooden beast, the shadowed faces of Greek soldiers, the fire consuming stone, timber, flesh. She screamed it to anyone who would listen. And as always, none believed.

They looked at her with pity now, not scorn. That was worse.

The day dawned clear, cruelly bright, when the Greeks abandoned their camp. From the city walls, Trojans watched in stunned disbelief as the enemy torched their tents, dragged ships into the surf, and vanished over the horizon. Only a colossal wooden horse remained on the plain, gleaming in the sun like a god's plaything.

The people surged to the gates. Some shouted in triumph, others in suspicion. But all were drawn toward it, this towering marvel of pine and cedar, wheels beneath its hooves, its carved flanks etched with patterns like waves. Its head arched high, proud and terrible, and its eyes—two polished stones—seemed almost alive.

Cassandra's stomach turned. The sight of it made bile rise in her throat. She saw, superimposed upon the polished wood, the truth: armed men crouched in darkness, their blades gleaming faintly in the slivers of torchlight. She staggered back from the parapet, clutching her temples.

"No!" Her voice tore through the crowd. "Do not bring it inside! Burn it where it stands, drown it in the sea! It is no offering—it is our doom!"

The murmurs swelled, unease rippling through the crowd. But then Priam's voice rose, regal and steady despite the tremor beneath it. "My daughter is undone by grief. Do not heed her ravings. The Greeks have fled—they leave this horse as tribute to Athena, in atonement for their desecrations."

Cassandra whirled on him, her hair wild, her eyes blazing. "Father, please. Listen! It is not a gift—it is a trap!"

But already the crowd was turning. Paris, smug as ever, waved to the masses. "The gods smile upon us at last. Let us not insult them with Cassandra's madness. Bring the horse to the citadel!"

Cheers erupted. Men strained at ropes, dragging the enormous structure toward the gates. Children ran alongside it, laughing, tossing garlands of flowers that snagged in the horse's carved mane.

Cassandra fell to her knees on the stones of the wall, her hands outstretched. "Please," she sobbed, her voice raw, "please don't." But the city thundered around her, deaf to her words.

Beside her, Helen laid a hand on her shoulder, her own face pale. "I believe you," she whispered. "But what can we do?"

Cassandra clutched her hand like a drowning woman clings to driftwood. "Pray. If the gods will not save us, then perhaps they will save the children."

By twilight, the horse stood in the heart of Troy, a giant shadow looming over the streets. Torches cast flickering light across its surface, making it seem to breathe, to shift, to crouch in readiness. The city feasted that night, celebrating the Greeks' departure. Wine flowed, laughter rang through the streets, music soared from lyres and pipes.

Cassandra sat apart, on the palace steps, her eyes never leaving the monstrous figure. To her, it pulsed with malice, each creak of its timbers like a heartbeat. She whispered under her breath, prayers and curses interwoven: to Athena, to Apollo, to anyone who might listen. But no answer came.

Helen slipped down beside her, draped in a cloak against the night air. Her beauty was muted now, her eyes hollow, her smile a ghost. "They will not listen," she murmured.

"They never have," Cassandra replied bitterly. "Not when I warned of Paris's folly. Not when I begged Hector to stay within the walls. Not even now, when the trap is plain before their eyes."

Helen's gaze flicked to the horse, her jaw tightening. "And yet, if you are right, we are both to be blamed. My beauty, your visions—two women condemned by the choices of men."

Cassandra turned to her, tears stinging her eyes. "Not blamed. Bound." She reached for Helen's hand. "And if the city falls tonight, then at least we will fall together."

Helen squeezed her fingers. No words were needed.

***

Midnight.

The fires of revelry guttered out. One by one, the Trojans collapsed into sleep, their bellies heavy with wine, their heads fogged with celebration. The streets lay silent but for the sigh of the sea and the restless shifting of the giant horse.

Cassandra had not slept. She sat by her window, her heart thudding with dread. And then—she heard it. A faint scrape of wood, the groan of timbers. Her blood ran cold.

The belly of the horse opened.

One by one, shadows slid down ropes into the sleeping city. Men in bronze, their helmets glinting faintly in the starlight, blades drawn, eyes hard. Cassandra's scream caught in her throat. She watched, frozen, as they fanned out through the streets.

Then came the flames.

Torches flared, hurled into homes, into thatched roofs, into storerooms. Fire raced greedily through the city, leaping from beam to beam. Screams shattered the night as Trojans woke to smoke and slaughter.

Cassandra bolted into the corridor, her feet pounding marble slick with ash. "Up! Wake up!" she shouted, banging on doors. "The Greeks are here! To arms!"

Doors cracked open, confused faces peering out, only to twist into terror as smoke billowed in. The wail of children, the shouts of men groping for weapons, filled the palace.

She burst into the hall where her parents huddled with their daughters. Hecuba clutched Priam's arm, her veil soaked with tears. "What is happening?"

"They came out of the horse," Cassandra gasped. "I told you! I told you!"

Priam's face sagged with disbelief, grief breaking him anew. He stumbled to a seat, his crown askew. "The gods…they have betrayed us."

"No!" Cassandra cried, seizing his hands. "It was Apollo. Always Apollo. He cursed me so you would never believe. And now—now we are undone."

Hecuba's sobs shook her frame. Priam buried his face in his hands. Cassandra spun away, fury boiling in her chest. "I will not forgive him," she spat. "If Troy burns, let Apollo's temples burn too."

The night became a nightmare.

Cassandra ran through smoke-choked corridors, dragging Helen with her. Together, they saw men cut down where they stood, mothers clutching infants cut down without mercy, the marble floors slick with blood. Statues toppled, tapestries burned, the shrieks of the dying echoing against the stone.

On the walls, Trojan soldiers tried to rally, but the gates were already thrown wide. The Greek fleet had returned, and now the city swarmed with enemies—Odysseus with his cunning eyes, Menelaus with his face twisted in fury, Ajax roaring like a beast.

In the square, Cassandra glimpsed Paris, arrow in hand, his face stricken. He shouted for his men, but his voice was drowned by the chaos. She turned away, unwilling to waste even hatred on him.

"Cassandra!" Helen tugged her arm. "This way!"

They stumbled into the temple of Athena, its sanctuary thick with the stench of incense and fear. Dozens of women huddled there, clutching the statue of the goddess, their prayers a babble of desperation. Cassandra pressed herself against the cold marble, her whole body trembling.

"O Athena," she whispered. "You gave me wisdom once. Give me strength now."

But the statue was silent.

Above the din, Cassandra heard the crash of doors breaking. A storm of footsteps filled the temple. Greek soldiers burst in, their swords flashing in the lamplight.

"No," she gasped. "Not here."

But the men surged forward, cutting down women where they knelt. Blood spattered across Athena's statue. Cassandra screamed until her throat tore, throwing herself before the altar, but rough hands seized her arms. She kicked, fought, clawed, but they wrenched her upright.

Her eyes found Helen across the temple. Soldiers seized her too, Menelaus himself among them, his face twisted with triumph and loathing. Helen struggled, her hair a golden snare around her captors' hands, but when her eyes met Cassandra's, there was no shame—only fury, and something like love.

Cassandra thrashed in her captor's grip. "Damn you!" she screamed, not at the men but at the heavens. "Do you see? Is this your sport? Our lives, our bodies, our city—nothing but your game?"

The rafters shook with fire. Smoke poured down in black waves. Somewhere outside, the towers of Troy groaned and collapsed, their stones tumbling into ruin.

And still the gods were silent.

They dragged Cassandra through the burning streets, past corpses she could not bear to recognize. The once-proud citadel roared with fire, its domes cracking, its walls bleeding smoke into the sky. The city she had loved since childhood—its markets, its gardens, its temples—died around her.

The soldiers jeered as they hauled her toward the palace gates, their armor gleaming in the firelight. "The mad princess," one sneered. "Let's keep her for the generals. Let them laugh at her ravings before the night is done." Another spat at her feet. "Lock her away. Let her choke on her prophecies while her city burns."

The iron doors of the palace cell slammed shut with a reverberating clang, the sound echoing like a death knell through the stone corridors. Cassandra stumbled as the guards shoved her forward, her bare feet scraping against the damp floor. The air was thick with mildew and ash, stinking of despair, as if the walls themselves had absorbed centuries of sorrow.

She caught herself against the rough stone, her palms scraping against it, and turned to glare at the soldiers. "You do this because you fear me," she spat, her voice hoarse but burning with venom. "You think to silence prophecy by locking me in shadows. But the truth does not yield to chains."

The men said nothing, their eyes sliding away from her like cowards, as though meeting her gaze would invite the madness they so readily accused her of. One muttered a prayer to the gods under his breath. Then they were gone, the echo of their boots fading into the depths of the palace until silence pressed in close, suffocating.

Cassandra pressed her forehead to the cold wall, her chest heaving. For a moment, despair clawed at her ribs, whispering that all was lost — Hector gone, Paris wounded, Priam broken, Troy in flames. Her visions, her curses, had brought her to this place: a prophetess abandoned in a tomb of stone.

She sank to her knees, clutching at her shift. "Athena, if ever you heard me, hear me now," she whispered. "Take this gift from me. Take it back, or let me die with my people. Do not make me linger, watching them burn."

The silence stretched, heavy and cruel. Then, slowly, the air shifted. The flickering torchlight bent strangely, elongating shadows across the stone. A golden warmth seeped into the chill of the chamber, a glow too pure for such a place.

Cassandra's breath caught. She lifted her head.

He was there.

Apollo stood before her, luminous even in this dungeon, the faint gleam of dawn clinging to his hair and skin. His presence turned the dank chamber into a shrine, yet the light did nothing to comfort her. She recoiled, fists clenched, heart pounding with fury.

"You," she hissed, her voice echoing off the stone. "You dare come here?"

47

Cassie

Modern Day

The hum of domestic life was in full swing. Bridal magazines and scraps of paper littered the dining table, the clatter of teacups punctuating bursts of laughter. My mother and Blair debated napkin colors, while Helen—glowing in her new role as Nik's wife—described fairy lights and linen-draped tables as though conjuring them by will alone.

Their voices should have soothed me. Instead, they reminded me of Troy's courtyards, where women planned feasts while warriors sharpened their spears. I knew too well how quickly joy could turn to ashes.

I tried to smile, to let Helen's excitement anchor me. She turned to me suddenly, clasping my hand.

"Cassie, will you be my…what's the phrase…Maid of Honor? I know it's not a real wedding, just a reception, but… I'd like you by my side."

Her eyes were luminous, and for once, I didn't hesitate. "Of course, Helen. I'd be honored."

The table erupted in cheers. For a moment, it almost felt normal—family, food, celebration.

Then laughter rang from the hallway: Theo and Thomas, their arms full of fishing rods, teasing each other like brothers.

"Coming with us, Cass?" Theo grinned. "Could use my good luck charm to land a big one."

I waved them off. "You don't need me to catch bait fish."

Thomas bent to kiss my hair. "We'll be back for dinner." His steadiness, his ease with my family—even that should have calmed me. Instead, unease crawled up my spine.

Nik hadn't joined them. And Nik never passed up fishing.

* * *

The knock came while I was chopping tomatoes, Helen humming beside me. Sharp. Impatient.

When I opened the door, dread settled instantly. Gus. One of Nik's old high school friends—the kind my mother used to warn us about. His crooked grin hadn't changed, nor the way his eyes slid past me like I was already dismissed.

"Nik home?"

"In the office," I said reluctantly, stepping aside. He brushed past me without thanks.

Every instinct screamed to stop him. Instead, I trailed behind, silent as a shadow.

Nik barely looked up when we entered, his face lit by the glow of spreadsheets and emails. His shoulders hunched with stress I hadn't seen in years.

"Hey, Gus," he muttered.

They shut the door. I lingered.

Through the wood, I caught fragments:

"—the shipment—"

"—Port of Tampa—"

"—feds are all over it—"

"—hidden inside the marble—"

My stomach flipped.

I pressed closer, desperate.

"You'll get a call, Nik," Gus said, low and urgent. "They think you're mixed up in something. Drugs, weapons, I don't know. But it's bad."

My hand flew to my mouth. *The Horse. The horse is inside our gates.*

When Gus finally slipped out, avoiding my eyes, I didn't hesitate. I stormed in, slamming the door behind me.

"What the hell was that, Nikolaos?"

Nik froze, guilt flashing across his features before anger settled in its place. "Cassie, don't start."

"Don't start? You've dragged our family into something criminal, and you want me to *stay quiet?*" My voice shook. "What's in that shipment?"

"Marble. For the company. That's it."

"Don't lie to me."

"I'm not lying!" He shoved back his chair, pacing. "Cassie, I swear—I didn't put anything in that container but marble. If something else is in there, it's Dimitri's doing. Not mine."

The name chilled me. Dimitri Kostas. Always Dimitri.

"Then why are the feds circling *you?*" I hissed. "Because you signed for it. Because you tied yourself to him. And now? Now they'll bury you with him."

His face crumpled for a moment, just a moment, into fear. "I was trying to build something. For Helen. For us."

"You were trying to play king," I snapped. "And you've just brought a Trojan Horse through our gates."

Before he could reply, the office door burst open. Our father, Peter, filled the doorway, his face grim.

"Nik. We have to go. The Port called."

"The Port?" Nik's voice cracked.

"They're holding the shipment. We need to be there." His gaze flicked to me, heavy with unspoken questions. "Now."

For a heartbeat, time hung suspended. I saw the ruins already—the marble cracked open like ribs, secrets spilling onto the dock, our family's name dragged through fire.

Still, I nodded. "I'm coming with you."

Nik's jaw tightened. He grabbed his jacket.

* * *

As we walked to the car, Helen's laughter drifted faintly from the kitchen, still bright, still unknowing. My mother's voice rose in gentle reply, planning floral arrangements as though fate weren't already carving epitaphs into stone.

I wanted to stop. To scream. To tear the sky open until they believed me.

Instead, I slid into the backseat beside Nik, my heart pounding like a funeral drum.

"Cassie," he muttered, barely audible, "you've got to believe me. I didn't know."

I searched his eyes—the same green as our mother's, wide and pleading. For the first time, I wondered if he might be telling the truth.

But belief had never been my luxury.

At the Port of Tampa, the truth would reveal itself. And I feared it would devour us all.

48

Cassandra

Ancient Troy

The cell stank of ash and iron. Smoke from the burning city seeped through the narrow grate high above, carrying with it the cries of Troy's dying. Cassandra crouched in the corner, her dress torn and blackened, her throat raw from screaming warnings no one had heeded. Her hands trembled, but not from fear. Rage, pure and unyielding, coiled within her chest like a living flame.

She pressed her forehead against the cold stone, whispering a prayer not to the gods but against them. *You have destroyed me. You have destroyed us all.*

The air shimmered. Light — golden, blinding — filled the narrow cell, swallowing the gloom. Cassandra did not need to look to know who had come.

"Apollo." His name left her lips like a curse.

The god appeared unmarked by the smoke, radiant and flawless, his beauty a mockery of everything burning outside these walls. His eyes lingered on her, filled with something between pity and pride. "Cassandra," he said, his voice like the pluck of a lyre string. "You survived."

Her laugh was bitter, scraped raw from her throat. "Survived? My brothers are dead, my father broken, my city burning. This is what survival looks like?" She rose unsteadily, her chains clattering against the stone. "You call this mercy?"

Apollo stepped closer, the glow of his form softening the jagged shadows of the cell. "I warned you. I offered you my love, my protection. You spurned me, and so the curse was sealed. This is not of my making alone, Cassandra — it is the will of Olympus."

"Do not speak to me of Olympus," she spat, standing tall despite the grime on her face and the ruin of her gown. "This is *your* doing. Your pride. Your wounded vanity. You gave me a gift and made it poison because I dared say no to you. You could not bear to be denied by a mortal girl."

Apollo's expression darkened. "Careful."

"No." Her voice rang against the stone, clear and fierce. "You will listen. Look around you, Apollo. This is what your curse has wrought. Troy burns. My family dies. And all because you could not endure rejection." She stepped closer, so close she could see the flicker of flame in his irises. "You call yourself a god, but you are smaller than any man I know."

Apollo reached out, but she slapped his hand away with her shackled wrist. Her defiance blazed hotter than his glow.

"One day," she hissed, "you will meet another. She will have my hair, my eyes. She will remind you of me. You will try again — to charm, to seduce, to possess — and you will fail again. She will see through you, as I did. She will call you out, as I do now. And you will suffer, Apollo, because the truth you cannot escape is this: you never learn."

For a heartbeat, silence hung between them, heavy as iron.

Apollo's jaw tightened, his radiance flaring like the sun at its zenith. "Then let it be so," he said, his voice low with fury. "If another should bear your likeness, she too shall carry your curse. To speak the truth that no one will believe. To see doom and be powerless to stop it. As you suffer, so shall she."

Cassandra's breath hitched, but she forced herself to stand unflinching. "Then curse her. Curse her as you cursed me. But remember this — she will outlast you. My name will live in her, and through her, the truth will rise again. Even if no one believes, still it will be spoken."

For the first time, Apollo looked away. His light dimmed, just slightly, a shadow crossing his divine face. Without another word, he vanished, leaving behind only the faint smell of myrrh and smoke.

Cassandra sank back against the wall, her chest heaving, her throat raw. The flames of Troy still roared beyond her prison, but within her, a strange calm settled. She had cursed a god in turn, and through her defiance, had carved a promise into fate itself.

* * *

The cell door groaned open in the dead of night. Cassandra startled awake, her head lolling against the damp stone wall, the acrid taste of smoke clinging to her throat. She braced for Greek soldiers, for jeers and rough hands dragging her to some cruel end.

Instead, a whisper cut through the darkness.

"My lady."

Lila.

The handmaiden's face was smeared with soot, her braid half-unraveled, but her eyes burned with the same loyalty Cassandra had seen since childhood. She carried a stolen torch, its flame stuttering as if afraid of the destruction surrounding them.

"How—?" Cassandra rasped.

"No questions," Lila urged, slipping a key into the manacle lock. "I bribed a guard with the last of my jewelry. You must come. Now."

The chains fell with a dull clang. Cassandra rubbed her raw wrists and swayed on her feet, her body weak, but her heart surged with a fragile hope. "Lila, if they catch you—"

"They will think me you," Lila said simply, steadying her mistress by the arm. "It is better that way."

The torch cast long shadows as they slipped through the corridors. The palace shook with distant battle cries; Greek soldiers had breached the outer courts. Once-proud walls, painted with scenes of Troy's victories, now trembled with every blow of enemy steel.

"Where is my father?" Cassandra whispered as they passed the shattered remnants of her childhood — overturned vases, crushed laurel crowns, broken marble busts.

"The throne room," Lila said. "The last place left to defend."

They pushed open the massive bronze doors, their hinges shrieking in protest. The sight within rooted Cassandra to the ground.

King Priam sat upon his throne, not in regality but in ruin. His robes were torn, his crown discarded at his feet. His face was hollowed, streaked with ash and grief. Around him, a few loyal guards held the line, though their shields dented and their eyes weary, told the truth: Troy's end was minutes, not hours, away.

"Father." Cassandra's voice cracked. She rushed forward, falling to her knees before him.

Priam's dulled gaze sharpened at the sight of her. His hand, trembling, cupped her cheek. "Cassandra." His voice broke like brittle stone. "My child. I should have believed you."

Her chest tightened, tears spilling hot onto his hand. "Pappá—"

"I called you mad," he whispered. "When all along, it was I who was blind. Forgive me, daughter. Forgive me, though my words come too late."

She laid her forehead against his hand. "I forgive you," she said, her voice barely more than a breath. "But the gods do not."

The doors burst open again. Cassandra whirled, heart lurching — until she saw Aeneas. He strode in, smoke clinging to his armor, his eyes fever-bright with urgency.

"My lord, my lady," he said, bowing briefly to Priam before turning to Cassandra. "There is no time. The Greeks have broken the gates. I've gathered a handful of survivors. We must flee now."

"Go with him," Priam said at once, his hand tightening on Cassandra's. His gaze, proud even in despair, burned with command. "Go, my daughter. Live. Bear witness. Troy must have a voice even in ruin."

"I cannot leave you!" Cassandra sobbed.

"You must." He pressed her hands together and pushed them toward Aeneas. "Take her. Take her where the fire cannot reach."

At that moment, Helen entered, her golden hair tangled, her gown streaked with blood and soot. She went to Priam's side, her beauty dimmed by grief yet still undeniable. Her eyes met Cassandra's — steady, strong. "I will remain," she said softly. "Paris asked me to stay, and I will. I will not run while your city burns."

Cassandra shook her head, torn between fury and awe. Helen was no longer the face that launched a thousand ships, but the steel that endured their wrath.

And then Lila stepped forward, placing a steadying hand on Cassandra's arm. "My lady. It is time."

Cassandra turned — and froze. Lila was already unclasping Cassandra's torn, soot-streaked gown. "No," Cassandra whispered, realizing. "Lila, you cannot—"

"I must." Lila's smile was tired but radiant. "If the Greeks take me, they will think me you. It will buy you time to escape with Aeneas. Time enough to live."

Cassandra grabbed her hands, shaking her head violently. "I will not let you do this."

"You must." Lila pressed the circlet of gold — Cassandra's circlet — into her mistress's hands. "Please. Let me give meaning to my life. You once told me the gods see every sacrifice. Let them see mine."

Helen's voice broke the silence. "She is right. This is the only way."

Aeneas, his jaw tight with anguish, nodded. "The Greeks will be upon us any moment. Choose, Cassandra."

Her chest heaved as she looked from her father to Aeneas, to Helen, and finally back to Lila. Her heart screamed no, but her soul knew the truth.

Slowly, she slipped the circlet back onto Lila's brow. "You honor me beyond words," she whispered. She pulled Lila into a fierce embrace, breathing in her scent one last time. "Elysium awaits you, sister of my heart."

When they pulled apart, Lila now wore Cassandra's finery, her chin lifted in quiet defiance. Cassandra stood in a simple shift, suddenly a shadow, no longer a princess.

"Go," Priam commanded. His broken voice cracked like a whip. "Before all is lost."

Aeneas seized Cassandra's hand. Together, they hurried toward the secret passage beneath the palace, Helen at their side. Behind them, the throne room's doors rattled under the assault of Greek shields and spears.

Cassandra glanced back only once. She saw her father, regal even in defeat, and Lila — her Lila — standing before him in her place, her head high, ready to face the conquerors.

The doors splintered. The Greeks surged inside.

Cassandra's scream was swallowed by the roar of fire and steel as Aeneas dragged her into the shadows of escape.

49

Troy

The throne room stank of smoke and blood. The Greeks surged through the shattered bronze doors like a tide of steel, their spears catching the firelight, their cries echoing in the vast hall. Marble floors, once polished to a gleam, were smeared with ash and gore.

Odysseus was first through the breach, his clever eyes scanning every shadow. Behind him came Diomedes, breathing hard, sword slick with Trojan blood. And then Agamemnon himself, king of men, his armor gleaming like a dark promise.

At the far end of the chamber sat Priam, the ancient king of Troy, still upon his throne. He looked less like a ruler than a statue, his face carved from grief, his eyes hollow. And before him stood a figure they all knew by reputation: Cassandra, princess and prophetess, cursed with foresight and madness.

Or so they believed.

Her golden circlet glinted in the firelight, her gown torn but regal. She did not run. She did not beg. She stood tall, her chin lifted, defiance written in every line of her bearing.

Agamemnon's lips curled into a cold smile. "So. The jewel of Troy remains."

Priam rose with sudden fire, his old body trembling with rage. "Touch

268

her and may the gods strike you down, Greek!"

Diomedes barked a laugh. "The gods abandoned this place long ago."

Before Priam could take another step, Odysseus raised his hand, signaling the soldiers to hold. His eyes narrowed as he studied Cassandra. She looked… smaller than he had imagined. A girl in borrowed finery, eyes wide but unyielding. Something tugged at the edges of his suspicion — but the chaos of conquest drowned it out.

"Alive," Agamemnon commanded, striding forward. "She is mine. Cassandra will ride with me, a prize for my house. The Fates themselves decree it."

Two soldiers rushed forward, seizing her arms. She struggled — not wildly, but with a desperate dignity, twisting against their grip. Her voice rang through the chamber, cracked with smoke but steady: "You may chain my body, but you will never chain my truth."

The Greeks jeered. To them, it was the ravings of a madwoman, nothing more.

Priam lunged forward, tears streaming down his face. "Take me instead! By all the gods, she is but a child—"

Diomedes' blade flashed. The old king crumpled to the ground, lifeless, his blood spreading across the cracked marble at Cassandra's — at Lila's — feet.

Agamemnon did not flinch. He grabbed her chin roughly, forcing her to meet his eyes. "Troy has fallen," he said, his voice like iron. "And its prophetess will serve in Mycenae."

Her eyes burned with unspoken words, but she said nothing. She only stared past him, beyond him, to something none of them could see.

Odysseus felt the weight of her gaze and shivered, though he told himself it was the smoke.

"Bind her," Agamemnon ordered. "She sails at dawn."

The soldiers dragged her away, her circlet slipping sideways, her gown streaked with ash. She did not cry out. She did not weep. She only walked with head high, as though the ruin of Troy itself could not bend her spirit.

Behind them, the throne of Priam lay empty, the last light of the fires glinting on its polished arms.

Odysseus lingered, uneasy. Something about the girl gnawed at him. She had spoken no prophecy, offered no warning, save that silent stare. But as he turned to follow the others, he wondered if, in claiming Cassandra of Troy, they had truly claimed what they believed.

And in the shadows of the ruined hall, the truth remained hidden: Cassandra had already fled.

50

Cassandra

Ancient Troy

The night breathed fire.

Troy's streets — once filled with laughter, lyres, and the scent of roasted figs — now crackled under the weight of flame and ruin. The air shimmered with heat; smoke clawed at Cassandra's throat as she stumbled beside Aeneas, every step dragging her farther from everything she loved — her father, her sister, her home.

Her heart did not beat with the rhythm of escape. It beat with the rhythm of grief.

Behind her, she could still hear echoes — her father's voice, broken but proud, bidding her to flee. The slam of bronze doors. Lila's last glance through the smoke, her golden circlet catching the light as she whispered a promise Cassandra could not hear but somehow understood: *Live.*

"Keep moving," Aeneas urged, his hand firm at her back. His armor was streaked with ash, his jaw tight, but his eyes flicked constantly toward her — not the flames, not the enemy, *her.*

"The tunnels," he said. "They'll take us to the river."

Cassandra faltered. "Lila—"

"She chose," Aeneas said. His voice was low but unyielding, the tone of a man who had already lost too much. "Honor her by living."

The words struck like a spear — and stuck. Cassandra pressed her lips together, tasting soot and salt, and forced her body to obey.

They slipped through a narrow corridor where the walls sweated heat. Firelight seeped through the cracks in the stone, painting everything in bleeding red. Once, these had been storage halls, lined with amphorae of oil and wine. Now they were tombs. The jars lay shattered, their contents feeding the hungry flames.

Every few steps, she stumbled — not just over debris, but over her visions. They came in flashes: soldiers storming the palace, her father's crown falling from his brow, her brothers' bodies sprawled across marble floors. Sometimes the images aligned with the world before her; sometimes they didn't. It no longer mattered. The line between vision and reality had burned away.

Aeneas caught her elbow as she faltered. "Stay with me," he said.

"I'm trying," she breathed.

They emerged into an open courtyard. The night above them was a bruise of red and black, the constellations swallowed by smoke. Arrows whistled overhead. Across the rooftops, Cassandra saw figures with torches — Greek soldiers moving like wraiths, their shadows leaping across the walls like demons tasting victory.

She pressed herself against a colonnade, heart hammering so hard she thought the sound might betray them.

Aeneas crouched beside her, his arm sliding around her shoulders — protective, grounding. "We're close. Just a little farther."

But Cassandra couldn't move. The world tilted, hot and unreal. "I saw it," she whispered. "All of it. My father. My brothers. Troy's walls collapsing. I saw myself taken in chains." Her breath hitched. "And no one ever believed me."

Aeneas turned to her, catching her chin gently between his fingers. His eyes, dark and steady even in the firelight, anchored her.

"I believe you," he said simply.

The words cracked something inside her — not despair, but the brittle shell she had carried since Apollo's curse. Her throat ached; tears carved streaks through the soot on her cheeks.

Her voice broke. "Then help me believe there's still something left to save."

Aeneas's hand tightened around hers. "Believe in this," he said. "We're not done yet. You and I — we walk out of here alive. Do you see that in your visions?"

She pressed her palm against his chest, feeling the thunder of his heartbeat beneath the armor. For the first time since Apollo had touched her, the future was silent. No flames. No screams. Just that single, steady pulse.

"No," she whispered. "But maybe that means it hasn't been written yet."

His lips curved faintly. "Then we'll write it ourselves."

They moved.

Across the courtyard, shadows lunged — Greek soldiers, their blades catching the firelight. Aeneas's sword sang as it met the first. The sound was sharp and metallic, slicing through the roar of burning timber. Cassandra flinched at the spray of blood, but she didn't turn away. Not this time.

Another soldier advanced. Aeneas blocked, pivoted, drove his blade clean through the man's chest. His movements were efficient, brutal, almost ritual. Cassandra could see the exhaustion trembling in his shoulders — and the resolve that would not break.

When the last man fell, the courtyard fell silent again except for the hiss of fire and Cassandra's ragged breathing.

"This way," Aeneas said, grabbing her hand. They slipped behind an overturned cart, ducking through a narrow opening in the wall — the mouth of a tunnel half-hidden by rubble. The air changed at once: cooler, damp, heavy with earth instead of ash.

Cassandra hesitated at the threshold, glancing back.

Through the rising smoke, the palace loomed — or what was left of it. Flames climbed the dome, devouring it from within. The light turned molten, collapsing inward until sparks burst outward like dying stars.

"Goodbye," she whispered. The word barely left her lips. "To my father. To Lila. To Troy."

Aeneas turned, his face streaked with soot, eyes gleaming faintly in the firelight. "Not goodbye," he said. "Not yet."

Cassandra swallowed, her throat raw. "You sound so certain."

He gave a small, grim smile. "Certainty is all we have left."

She took one last look at the burning city. Somewhere out there, she imagined Apollo watching — his fire consuming the world he had once promised her she'd save. For a heartbeat, she thought she saw him in the smoke, radiant and pitiless, and she whispered under her breath, not in prayer but in defiance:

"You don't own the ending."

Then Aeneas pulled her into the tunnel.

The world above roared as Troy collapsed, but down in the earth, the sound became muffled — distant, like the heartbeat of something dying. They stumbled through the dark, breath echoing against the stone, their hands never letting go.

Behind them, the city screamed its last.

Ahead, somewhere beyond the black and the river's whisper, the future waited — unwritten, fragile, terrifyingly theirs.

51

Cassie

Modern Day

The drive south from Tarpon Springs was silent except for the low hum of the tires and the ragged rhythm of my breath. I sat in the backseat, staring out at the dark ribbon of highway unspooling under the Florida night, the Gulf's salt still lingering faintly in the air. Every streetlight we passed flickered across Nik's face, revealing the war raging inside him: fear, guilt, denial.

Beside him in the passenger seat, our father was rigid, hands gripping the steering wheel as if the force alone could keep his family intact. His green eyes — my eyes — were shadowed, unreadable.

Theo drove his truck behind us, headlights steady in the rearview, his presence a silent shield.

I clutched my phone in my lap, Thomas's last text still glowing on the screen: *"Call me if anything goes wrong. I'll come."*

Something *would* go wrong. I could feel it, as surely as Cassandra had felt Troy's walls trembling when the Horse rolled inside.

The Port of Tampa was a cathedral of industry: towering cranes, endless stacks of shipping containers, the metallic tang of machinery lacing the night air. Floodlights glared down like artificial suns, casting the docks in harsh shadows.

Uniformed customs officers and federal agents clustered near a single container, its steel sides sweating under the humid night. Men spoke in clipped tones, their radios hissing static.

The sight twisted my stomach. *This is it. This is the Horse.*

We parked near the cluster. Our father strode forward, shoulders squared, a king walking into council. Nik followed, slower, his hands trembling at his sides.

I trailed behind, dread crawling up my spine. Every footstep echoed like prophecy.

"Mr. Bennett?" A federal agent in a dark windbreaker approached, flashing a badge. He was middle-aged, hard-eyed, his tone brisk. "Peter Bennett?"

"Yes." My father's voice was steady, commanding, though I saw the slight tremor in his jaw.

The agent gestured toward the container. "We've flagged your shipment. Manifest says marble slabs. But we had cause to inspect. What we found..." He shook his head. "You'll want to see for yourself."

Nik swallowed hard. "It's marble. That's all."

The agent didn't even look at him.

The crane's gears groaned as the container door swung open. The smell hit us first: sharp, chemical, out of place against the usual salt and rust of the docks. A wrongness that made my throat close.

Inside, pale marble slabs gleamed under the floodlights, stacked in neat rows. For a moment, relief flickered across Nik's face.

Then the agents slid one slab aside. Beneath it, hidden in the hollowed-out crate, were bricks. Dozens of them. Wrapped tight in black plastic, stamped with symbols I didn't recognize.

Not marble. Not stone.

Drugs.

The world tilted.

Nik staggered back, horror blanching his face. "No. No, no, no... this isn't mine. I didn't—"

The agent cut him off. "Mr. Bennett, your name's on the manifest. You signed for this shipment."

"I swear—I didn't know!" His voice cracked, raw with panic. "I didn't put that there!"

I grabbed his arm, my own fury boiling over. "Nik, this is the Trojan Horse! I told you something was coming — and now it's here!"

"Cassie, shut *up!*" he barked, desperation twisting his features.

But I couldn't. I wouldn't.

Our father stepped forward, his voice iron. "You expect me to believe my son arranged this? We built this company on sweat and stone, not this filth."

The agent's face was unmoved. "Doesn't matter what *I* believe. This container came in under your family's name. Someone's setting you up, or you're in deeper than you admit. Either way, it's federal."

I saw Theo's headlights cut across the dock as he pulled up, hurrying over with his jaw set. He froze at the sight inside the container. "Jesus, Nik."

"It's not me!" Nik cried. His eyes darted to Helen's father's name on the paperwork, stamped bold in Greek letters. "It's Dimitri. It has to be him. He set me up."

Dimitri. Always Dimitri. The Zeus-figure pulling strings from Greece, thundering from afar.

"Then prove it," Theo said coldly.

My vision blurred, the air vibrating with the onslaught of another prophecy.

I saw the Horse again, but not wood — steel. I saw our family's name carved into the container's side, consumed by fire. I saw agents storming through our offices, seizing papers, dragging our name into the headlines. *Bennett Construction, complicit. Bennett sons, disgraced. Cassie Bennett, the mad sister who knew and was ignored.*

The curse, alive and well.

I stumbled, clutching the cold steel edge of the container, my nails scraping metal. "If you don't listen now, you'll all fall. Just like Troy. Just like before."

"Enough!" Nik roared, his face twisted. "Stop with the mythology! This is real life, Cassie. You can't save us with stories!"

The words sliced me open. He was Hector and Paris all at once — proud, blind, doomed.

The agent barked orders, men moving in to photograph, catalog, bag the evidence. Floodlights glared, and the night closed in around us.

Our father turned on Nik, his voice quiet, dangerous. "You brought this into our house. Into our family."

Nik shook his head frantically. "No, Dad, listen—it wasn't me! I didn't know!"

But his words sounded hollow, even to my ears.

Theo's eyes flicked to me, pity and anger tangled in equal measure. "And you knew something was coming. Didn't you, Cass?"

"Yes," I whispered, the admission thick with salt and shame. "I saw it. But you never believe me."

"And why should we?" Nik snapped. "You're always seeing disasters, always crying doom. One time you're right, and you expect us to bow to you? You're a fool, Cassie."

I wanted to scream. To tear the sky open. To make them *see*.

Instead, I just stood there, trembling, as my family fractured in the shadow of the container.

The agents began sealing the evidence, radios crackling. The night smelled of oil, salt, and ruin.

I looked up at the floodlights, their beams stabbing the dark like accusing fingers.

"This is only the beginning," I whispered, half to them, half to myself.

No one answered.

* * *

The Port still clung to me. The smell of diesel and salt, the way the floodlights turned my family into shadows, tearing at each other — it lingered even as we drove back to Tarpon Springs. Nobody spoke. Nik stared out the window like a man condemned. My father sat in the passenger seat, silent, his profile carved in stone. It was a miracle that neither of them was taken away in handcuffs.

By the time we reached the house, my mother had laid the table, candles flickering against platters of roasted chicken and vegetables. The normalcy was almost obscene.

"Finally," she said, relief in her voice. "Sit, eat. Tell me what happened."

Nobody moved at first. Then Theo pulled out a chair for Blair, who looked pale and uncertain, one hand protectively on her stomach. Helen hovered near the sideboard, eyes darting between Nik and her father-in-law. My mother's gaze flicked from face to face, sensing the storm.

We sat. The clink of silverware was deafening in the silence.

It was Theo who spoke first. "There were drugs, Mom. Hidden in the marble."

The fork fell from my mother's hand, clattering against porcelain. "No. No, that can't—"

"It's true." My father's voice was flat, final.

All eyes swung to Nik. His face was flushed, his hands trembling as he gripped his glass. "I didn't know. I swear to you, I didn't know!"

"That's not enough," Theo said coldly. "You signed for it. Your name is on everything. You've dragged all of us into this."

"I didn't do it!" Nik slammed his fist on the table, rattling the dishes. "You think I'd risk Dad's company? Blair's future? Our family?"

"You already did," Theo shot back.

Blair's voice was soft, pleading. "Please, both of you—stop."

Helen reached for Nik's hand. "We'll fix this. We'll find a way." Her accent thickened with desperation.

But my father cut her off. "This is no longer just business. This is federal. This is ruin." He turned his gaze to Nik, his green eyes burning. "You have humiliated my name."

Nik crumpled, the weight of those words crushing him more than any indictment.

I couldn't sit silent anymore. "It isn't Nik's fault!" My voice rose, shrill even to my own ears. "This is Dimitri Kostas. He planted it. He's been circling us since the beginning. I *told* you—"

"Cassie." Theo's voice cracked like a whip. "Not now."

"Yes, now!" My fists clenched against the tablecloth. "You never listen until it's too late. Just like Troy. Just like before. And you'll sit here, laughing, drinking, pretending everything is fine until the fire is at our door!"

"Enough with your stories!" Nik's face was twisted with anguish. "Do you hear yourself? You sound insane. Always seeing visions, always talking about curses. You want me to be guilty so your prophecy makes sense."

My mother gasped. "Nik—"

But he wasn't finished. "You've wanted me to fail since we were kids. You think you're better than me, with your degrees and your lectures. You think your visions make you special. But they just make you crazy, Cassie. Crazy!"

The word cut deeper than any blade.

The room froze. Even the candles seemed to hold their breath.

My father's jaw was tight, unreadable. Theo stared at his plate. Blair closed her eyes. Helen reached for Nik again, whispering his name, but he pulled away.

I swallowed hard, forcing back the tears that burned behind my eyes. "You don't have to believe me," I whispered. "The truth doesn't need your belief."

No one answered.

I pushed back from the table, the scrape of the chair loud in the stillness. "Enjoy your feast," I spat. "While it lasts."

And I walked out, leaving the candles, the wine, the broken pieces of my family behind.

Outside, the Florida night wrapped around me like a shroud. The cicadas sang their endless dirge. I leaned against the porch railing, my chest heaving, staring out at the bayou.

I saw it all so clearly: the wooden horse rolled inside Troy's gates, Cassandra screaming at the walls, no one listening. And now me, standing in the dark, unheard, my family eating dinner as if nothing were crumbling.

I pressed my palms against my eyes. "What do you want from me?" I whispered to the night. "What good is a gift if it only destroys?"

The silence pressed close, thick as prophecy.

Somewhere in that silence, I thought I heard it: a low, distant hum, like the first note of a song.

Not yet, Apollo.

But something was stirring.

52

Modern Day

Offices of Bennett Construction

In the dim light of the office, shadows crawled across the walls as a lone figure sat hunched over a cluttered desk. The rhythmic ticking of an old clock was the only sound, marking time as if waiting for something to snap. Papers whispered as she moved them aside, scribbling notes with sharp, impatient strokes.

The company name glowed faintly on the back wall: *Bennett Construction.* The sight of it twisted something inside her chest. Peter Bennett and his sons had just signed their lucrative partnership with Hellenic Marble Supply — a deal that would expand their empire. To outsiders, it looked like success, legacy, and family. To Kellie, it was another insult carved on her skin.

Her eyes flicked to a framed photo on the wall: Peter with his three children, smiling, untouchable. Kellie's hand twitched. She wanted to rip it down, smash the glass, leave her mark on their perfect lives. But she stopped herself. That was too obvious. Too easy. What she wanted was far worse than broken glass. She wanted them ruined.

She turned toward Theo's office. The thought of him made her jaw tighten. It hadn't been her fault, really. Theo Bennett was handsome, intelligent, effortlessly kind — the sort of man women noticed. She had noticed. One night, when they'd been working late, she'd made her move. She had chosen her best perfume, the dress that left little to the imagination, and the perfect smile. In her mind, if she could catch a Bennett, she could secure her place in the company forever.

But Theo hadn't taken the bait. Instead, he had shut her down with sharp words and sharper boundaries. Hours later, Peter himself had called her into his office. *Inappropriate behavior,* he'd said, his voice full of that sanctimonious Bennett righteousness. She had walked out humiliated, branded, dismissed.

From that night forward, Kellie had vowed to destroy them all.

She drifted through the office now, each familiar object pulling memories out of her like splinters. The Bennetts had built this place into a fortress of respectability, pouring profits into their employees, their community, their legacy. Every detail reeked of self-righteousness. To Kellie, it wasn't generosity; it was arrogance. And arrogance deserved to fall.

Sliding into Peter's old chair, she leaned back and surveyed the desk, a storm of documents spread before her. She knew the Bennett-Kostas deal inside out. She'd followed every marble shipment, every contract revision, every handshake. Some might call her obsession unhinged. She called it preparation.

"Such a shame," she murmured, a dark smile curling her lips. "All this hard work… just to watch it crumble."

She stood, drifting to the window. Moonlight spilled across her tailored suit, casting sharp lines on her face. Below, the street glowed under lamplight. A sleek black car rolled to the curb. Her pulse quickened.

"Perfect," she whispered. "Let the games begin."

The door creaked open. A man entered, tall and broad, moving with the ease of someone accustomed to violence. His pale blue eyes swept the office before fixing on her.

"Mr. Ivanov, I presume?" Kellie asked smoothly, extending a hand as though she belonged here.

"Indeed." His accent was thick, his grip unyielding. "You have the details?"

She slid a folder across the desk. Inside were pages of sabotage plans, each precise, each cruel. Routes, shipment times, contingencies. Ivanov skimmed the papers, the faintest nod of approval crossing his face.

"Impressive," he said. "You want the marble shipments compromised. That will hurt your Bennetts badly."

"My Bennetts," she sneered. "Yes. They need to learn that nothing they build is untouchable."

Ivanov smiled, thin and dangerous. "We can make that happen. We have dealt with far worse than stone."

"Good. Discretion is key. I don't want this traced back."

"Discretion is our middle name," he said, though the smile that followed betrayed how little he believed in words like *trust.*

She inclined her head, satisfied. "Then we're finished. I'll expect confirmation when it's done."

Ivanov tucked the folder beneath his arm and turned for the door. "Pleasure doing business."

"Likewise," she replied, her voice steady.

When the door clicked shut, Kellie let out a slow breath. Her heart was still racing, but the fear that coursed through her veins felt intoxicating. She had done it. The first stone had been pulled loose from the Bennetts' wall.

And yet… as she turned back toward the window, her reflection caught in the glass. Her own eyes stared back, hard and unblinking. *Is this truly the right thing?*

The question lingered, unwanted. She shoved it aside.

"The bigger they are," she whispered to her reflection, her lips curling, "the harder they fall."

53

Cassie

Modern Day

The Port of Tampa was alive with noise.

Metal screamed against metal; cranes clattered like titans shifting in their sleep. The low moan of ship horns vibrated through the air, through my bones. Diesel fumes mingled with salt and tar, and gulls wheeled overhead, shrieking like omens.

I should have been invisible among the workers in their neon vests. But my pulse betrayed me. My hands shook. My heart stuttered against my ribs, frantic as a trapped bird.

My father was already talking to a port agent, papers in hand. Nik hovered nearby, jaw tight, the muscle there ticking like a clock winding toward disaster. I wanted to stay, to listen, to pretend everything was normal—but the weight in my chest was suffocating. I *knew* something was wrong. I could feel it, humming in my teeth.

So I slipped away.

The noise faded as I moved deeper into the maze of shipping containers. Steel walls rose on either side—rusted, red, immense—swallowing sound, swallowing light. It was a canyon of metal and memory, the air thick and still, vibrating with the ghost hum of engines.

When I spoke, my voice barely carried.

"Apollo."

No answer. Only the creak of steel and the distant thud of cargo.

I clenched my fists. "Apollo, I need your help. My brother is in danger. If you have *ever* listened to me…if you've ever cared, even a little, please answer me now."

The air shifted.

A warm gust curled around me, and with it came that familiar scent — laurel and sun-warmed stone. When I opened my eyes, he was there.

Apollo leaned against a container as if he had been waiting, as if he always knew I'd crawl back. Light clung to him, too bright for this place. His smile was thin, curved like a blade.

"Cassandra Bennett," he drawled, voice like honey over broken glass. "Summoning me in the shadow of a port authority container. Hardly a temple worthy of my presence."

"I'm not here to worship you," I said. My voice trembled but didn't break. "I'm here because my brother's in trouble. There's a shipment—something dangerous. If someone doesn't stop it, he'll be destroyed."

He tilted his head, lazy and cruel. "Why should I care?"

"Because you're a god," I snapped. "Because you could stop it."

His mouth twisted. "Do you think a few desperate words erase centuries of contempt? My Cassandra cursed me with her defiance. And now here you stand: another mortal with her name, her fire—presuming to order me."

I stepped closer, fury burning through the fear. "Order you? No. Beg you. Isn't that what you always wanted?"

The air between us cracked, heat rising like from an open furnace.

"You think you're clever," he said softly, too softly. "But do you know what I see when I look at you?" His gaze sharpened, cutting straight through me. "*Her.* The first Cassandra. Raging, accusing, calling me a coward for letting Troy burn. She saw too much and still blamed me."

His words hit like a lash, but I refused to look away. "Maybe you should hear it again."

He blinked. "What?"

"That you're a coward." My voice shook, but not from fear but from fury.

"Because I am her, Apollo. I am every woman you silenced. Every truth you refused to face. And I will not stop screaming."

His smile vanished. "Careful, mortal."

"No," I said, stepping into his light until it seared my skin. "*You* be careful. You call yourself the god of light, of truth — but you curse women for telling the truth you don't like. You punished Cassandra of Troy because she embarrassed you. You let her city burn to prove a point. And now you stand here, doing nothing while my family is about to be destroyed. What kind of god does that make you?"

For the first time, his composure broke. His glow flared, wild and uneven, gold burning into white.

"Do. Not. Speak. Her. Name."

"Why?" I shot back. "Because you're afraid? Because you can't stand to remember the woman who saw you for what you were?"

He moved toward me, the air trembling. His heat pressed against my skin like sunlight turned weapon.

I met him halfway.

"You don't get to bury us," I said, voice low, shaking. "You don't get to rewrite the story."

He reached for me, maybe to silence me, maybe to strike, but I caught his wrist, nails biting into his skin. The light beneath my fingers burned, but I didn't let go.

"What's the matter?" I hissed. "Don't like being reminded? Does it sting to know you failed her? That you'll fail me, too?"

The ground trembled. The world warped.

And suddenly —

I wasn't just Cassie Bennett standing in a shipping yard.

I was Cassandra of Troy, standing in a crumbling palace, smoke rising, stone splitting. Fire roared around me. I saw hi —younger, beautiful, terrible—standing untouched amid ruin.

"You cursed me," I spat in Greek, my voice hers, hers mine. "Because I told you the truth. And now you'll watch me fall. But one day, you'll meet another with my face, my fire. And you'll fail her too."

The vision ripped through me. Troy's walls collapsing, women screaming, a city dying…then shattered. I gasped back into the present, the air thick with diesel and salt.

Apollo's face had gone pale, his eyes wide, almost human.

"You felt that," I whispered. "Didn't you?"

He said nothing.

"That was her. That was *us*. You can't run from it anymore."

He wrenched free of my hand, chest heaving, rage and shame battling across his features.

"Enough," he snapped.

The air shifted again but this time, it grew colder. From the shadow between containers, a silver light bloomed.

And out of it stepped Artemis.

Diana. My Diana.

She was all sharp edges and stillness, bow in hand, her presence cutting through the chaos like moonlight through smoke. Her hair caught the glow of the sodium lamps, turning it soft, almost holy.

She came to stand beside me, close enough that her shoulder brushed mine.

"Brother," she said, her voice like ice cracking on stone. "Do you know what I saw just now? A woman begging for mercy while you turned away. And then another, centuries later, begging for the same. You call yourself the god of truth, but all I see is a coward afraid of it."

Apollo's aura flared. "Stay out of this."

"I will not," Artemis said. "You owe Cassandra more than excuses. You owe her atonement."

The silence that followed was heavy enough to crush air. The twin gods stared at one another—sun and moon, pride and judgment—and I stood between them, trembling but unbroken.

Finally, Apollo exhaled, light dimming. His shoulders sagged beneath the weight of something ancient. "I will do what I can," he said, voice rough. His gaze flicked to me — bitter, reluctant. "For your brother. But don't mistake this for forgiveness."

"Forgiveness?" I spat. "You'll never have it. Not from me. Not from *her.*"

His eyes flashed—not anger, this time, but pain. Then he was gone, dissolving into sunlight that never reached the ground.

The port fell quiet. The gulls wheeled above us again, their cries suddenly small.

I was shaking, every nerve raw. Artemis placed a hand on my shoulder, cool as moonlight.

"You reminded him," she said softly. "Of what he did. Of who he lost. He cannot unhear it now. And that is why he listened."

Tears stung my eyes. "Do you think… that means she won? Cassandra?"

Artemis's expression softened. "You are her victory, Cassie. The voice that was once dismissed is now undeniable. That is how the curse ends."

Her words hit deeper than any prophecy ever had. For the first time, I didn't feel haunted. I felt *holy.*

When I returned to my father and Nik, the port agent was waiting with paperwork. The shipment—that cursed shipment—was being sent back to Greece, unopened, due to a "clerical error." Nik sagged with relief. My father muttered thanks to the officer, but his eyes kept flicking to me, wary, searching, as if he sensed something unseen had shifted in the world.

He wasn't wrong.

Only I knew the truth.

Apollo had finally listened.

And this time, the god of truth had *heard* a woman.

54

Modern Day

The Offices of Bennett Construction

The glass doors of Bennett Construction slid open on a breath of refrigerated air and lemon cleaner. Theo had let the last of the admin staff go early; the place felt unnaturally quiet, a hive emptied mid-flight. Fluorescents hummed. Somewhere, a printer sighed itself to sleep.

Nik stood in the doorway of the reception bay and gave a low whistle. "Hard to believe Kellie used to hold court in here."

Theo didn't answer. He'd already moved behind the reception desk—Kellie's old desk—opening drawers, stacking documents into neat piles, forcing order on the chaos she'd left. The spot still smelled vaguely of her perfume, something sugary that clung to paper and plastic like a dare.

He spoke without looking up. "We're not leaving until we account for every invoice, every bill of lading, every import declaration tied to the Kostas shipments. If there's a gap, we find it."

Nik came around the counter, rolling up his sleeves. "You think the problem started here?"

"I think," Theo said, flipping a file and stabbing a finger at a red-ink notation in the margin, "that the 'problem' sent itself flowers and ate lunch at this desk every day for a year."

They worked in clipped silence—Theo sorting, Nik cross-checking

290

container numbers against an Excel printout. Stacks grew, then toppled, then grew again. Lines of black text turned into patterns: the first Kostas shipment, clean. The second, mostly clean. The third—

"Here." Nik tapped a page. "Declaration stamp looks off. It's darker than the others, and—look, the date format. Day-month-year on the first two. Month-day-year on this one."

Theo held the paper to the light. "Who filed this?"

"Signature block says 'P. Bennett.' But that's not Dad's signature."

The fluorescent hum seemed to sharpen. Theo's stomach tightened. "Someone forged it."

"Someone who knows what our signatures look like," Nik said quietly.

He didn't add the name. He didn't have to.

A shadow slid across the frosted glass of the front doors.

Theo's eyes flicked up. "You locked those after we came in, right?"

Nik frowned. "Yeah."

The latch clicked. The door swung inward.

Kellie stepped into the foyer like she'd never left—heels precise, hair glossy, smile small and sharp. She closed the door behind her without looking, then glided across the marble to her old post.

"Evening, boys," she said, as if she'd wandered in from a coffee run. "Miss me?"

Nik's jaw clenched. Theo set his palms flat on the desk to keep from balling them into fists. The surprise passed; irritation flooded in behind it. This was their space now. She had no right—

"How did you get in?" Theo asked.

Kellie set her purse down on the counter, as if she'd been asked for her appointment time. "You never changed the keypad code."

"We did," Theo said.

Her smile widened by a single millimeter. "You changed the obvious one. You didn't change the backup maintenance code you gave me when the lock broke in April."

Theo felt heat rise under his collar. "You don't work here anymore."

"Trust me," she said lightly, "I got the memo."

Nik's voice came out more brittle than he intended. "You need to leave."

She folded her arms on the counter and tipped her head. "And miss the reunion? Don't be cruel."

Theo forced his heartbeat to slow. "You were terminated for cause. You're trespassing."

"Then call the police," she said pleasantly. "I'll wait."

Nik took out his phone. Kellie's smile didn't falter. "Before you do," she added, "you might want to hear why I'm here. It's relevant to that little… snag at the port."

Both men went still.

Kellie glanced down at the carved wooden nameplate she'd once polished like a talisman. She ran a fingertip along the edge and then flicked it. The little block thunked against the desk and rattled to a stop.

"You don't get to talk about the port," Nik said. "You don't know anything about the port."

"Don't I?" she asked softly.

Theo's voice flattened. "What do you want, Kellie?"

"Clarity," she said, eyes bright. "And credit. Two things I never seemed to get here."

She reached into her bag and pulled out a thin folder, not the slapdash kind they'd been sorting all afternoon, but a precise, tabbed thing with corner protectors. She opened it, selected a page, and slid it across the desk with manicured fingers.

A photocopy of the third Kostas import declaration stared up at them—black stamp, misformatted date, Peter Bennett's forged signature—only this version had a faint watermark beneath the text: a two-headed eagle inked so pale you had to tilt the page to catch it. Theo looked. Nik looked.

"Not ours," Nik said.

"No," Kellie agreed. "It's theirs."

Theo made himself ask, "Whose?"

"People with appetites," she said. "And networks. People, your new friends in Athens, told you not to worry about it because their bank wires cleared on time." She cocked her head. "But you worried anyway, didn't you? You worry so well, Theo."

He shifted his weight. "This isn't a game."

"It's never been a game." Her tone cooled. "Which is why I tried a dozen times to get you to look past your neat little spreadsheets and see the currents underneath. But you were always so sure your 'ethics' would insulate you. That Peter's name on a form was a kind of talisman. A charm. You thought the world would respect it." She gave a small, almost tender shrug. "It doesn't."

Nik swallowed. "What did you do?"

"Me?" She widened her eyes with feigned innocence. "I became useful to people who don't make me fetch coffee."

Theo slid the page back across the desk. "You queued the forged declaration, didn't you? You used Dad's name to hustle something through the port. What was in the crate, Kellie?"

She looked delighted. "Would you like the story version or the part where you call 911 and the nice dispatcher asks you to keep me busy while a patrol car drives over?"

Nik's phone buzzed in his hand. He flinched and glanced down. A text from Cassie lit his screen: **on my way. DO NOT LET KELLIE LEAVE.** Another followed: **don't be idiots.**

He didn't answer.

"Story version," Theo said.

Kellie's smile thinned. "Fine. Once upon a time, a hardworking immigrant company built by a decent man got complacent. The sons thought they could handle a bigger league without learning the rules. The daughter"—she didn't say Cassie's name, but the air seemed to say it for her—"couldn't keep her nose out of a book. The secretary you tossed away for being a problem discovered she was finally very good at being a problem." She folded her hands. "And a certain shipment stopped in Tampa for three extra days, long enough to attract interest and hands, long enough to become more than marble."

"Drugs," Nik said, because the word was already in the room.

Kellie lifted a shoulder. "Or cash. Or electronic components that don't like sunlight. The precise noun isn't the point. The point is: the horse was already inside your walls."

Something cold slid down Theo's spine. The phrase yanked at a memory—Cassie on the lanai last night, white-faced and shaking, saying, *Don't let the horse in,* and Peter chuckling, *We're not in your myths, kiddo.* He'd brushed it away as nerves. Better to believe in clerical errors than hidden warriors.

Kellie watched understanding move behind his eyes. "You were warned, weren't you?" she asked, almost kindly. "That sister of yours. She always looks like she's arrived breathless from the edge of a storm."

Theo stared at her. "How do you know what Cassie said?"

Kellie's amusement came back in a small, bright flash. "Because the people who pay attention heard her, even if you didn't."

The outer door opened again. "Then maybe you'll enjoy hearing her in person."

Cassie stepped into the reception bay with Thomas a pace behind her. She carried no folder, no proof, no rehearsed speech—only a face set in a clean, hard line that Theo had seen maybe twice in his life. She didn't look at him. She didn't look at Nik. She walked straight to the desk and looked at Kellie as if taking a measure.

"You're in our office," Cassie said. "Walk out now."

Kellie's head tipped, curious. "Hello, Cassandra."

"Leave," Cassie said. "Before you make me angrier."

"Your family fired me," Kellie said. "They humiliated me. I told the truth about what I wanted and got punished for it. Isn't that your line? Always crying that your brothers never took you seriously."

Thomas's hand found the small of Cassie's back. "Cass."

Cassie didn't move. "You weren't fired because you wanted something. You were fired because you cornered my brother in his office while his wife was pregnant and tried to leverage your body into a promotion. You were warned, and you ignored it. You broke every rule we have, and then you broke a few I didn't think we'd ever need to write down." She curled a hand around the desk edge. "And now you've come back as if the thing you didn't get gives you license to burn this building down."

Kellie's expression didn't flicker. "License? No. Consequence, yes." She slid the forged declaration back toward Cassie with two fingers. "You all wanted the Kostas deal because it made you feel big. You needed Greece like a mirror to tell you what you already believed about yourselves. I asked to sit at the table. Your father said no. Your brothers said no. You looked through me like glass." Her lip lifted. "When people make you invisible long enough, Cassandra, you become a ghost. And ghosts are very good at walking through walls."

"I told them you were the ghost," Cassie said, voice steady. "I told them you were our horse. They laughed."

"Men love a laugh," Kellie said.

Thomas shifted his weight. "You forged a federal declaration. That's prison time."

"Cute," Kellie said. "You're the new boyfriend? You practice lines like that in the mirror?"

"Enough," Theo said. He couldn't stand the back-and-forth another second. "Kellie, here's what's going to happen. You're going to give me the name of your contact who added contraband to our container. You're going to give me every email, every burner number, every screenshot of every chat that lives on that folder you just flashed like a magician's silk. You're going to sit down with the police and then a federal agent, and you're going to explain how you were manipulated and used and got in over your head. Then you're going to ask for a deal. And if you're smart, you'll take it."

For the first time since she'd walked in, something like uncertainty crossed Kellie's face. Fleeting, but there. Then it smoothed away. "You're very good at sounding like your father," she said, "It's very sexy."

Cassie stepped forward until she and Kellie were the same breath's width apart. "I don't care what story you tell yourself to make this feel righteous," she said, low. "You targeted my family. You put our men's names on your crime because you wanted to watch us burn. You walked our halls and memorized the way the locks sound and kept a code you weren't supposed to have because you thought you'd need it, and you did." Her eyes didn't blink. "You don't get to stand in my father's office and talk about invisibility like you invented it. You don't get to act like the victim here."

Kellie's smile split, not into humor but into something rawer, briefly human. "He didn't fire you," she said, so softly Theo almost missed it. "When you cry in a bathroom and wipe mascara with printer paper, people see you."

Cassie's mouth tightened. "When you can't get what you want one way, you don't get to become a weapon."

Silence pressed around them. The air hummed with the fluorescent lights and the grinding of old hurts.

Then Kellie sighed, as if bored, and reached into her purse. Every muscle in Thomas's arm tensed. Nik's phone came halfway up, as if a screen could be a shield. Kellie withdrew not a gun, not a knife, only another crisp folder. She opened it, plucked out two more tabbed sheets, and set them on the desk side by side.

One was a printout of a Signal chat, the kind with disappearing messages, except someone (Kellie) had screen-recorded them before they blinked out. A username with a ship's wheel emoji sent a container number and a port schedule; another user sent a wire confirmation and an address in Clearwater for a "thank-you envelope." The second page was a scan of a warehouse badge application with Nik's photo at the bottom.

Nik recoiled like he'd been slapped. "I never filed that."

"Of course you didn't," Kellie said. "But that badge would have been printed. And if something ugly came out of that container, and if anything tied to that badge was near it, and if your name was on a visitor log—" She didn't finish. She didn't need to.

Theo felt the floor tilt. Cassie's jaw set. Thomas swore under his breath.

"That's the play," Kellie said, almost gently. "Not to sell drugs, not really. To put the rot in your walls and then let people wonder who opened the door."

"Why are you showing us this?" Cassie asked.

Kellie's eyes flicked to her. For a heartbeat, there was something almost like respect. "Because someone—" she waggled a hand "—made a call you were never supposed to receive. Your shipment got turned around on a paperwork technicality so clean I almost applauded. Which means the party I promised is going to be very, very angry that they paid for music and never heard it. I like a fight, Cassandra. I like revenge. I don't like being disposable." Her voice was like glass.

Theo reached for the pages. "We'll take those."

Kellie's hand closed over them first. "Of course you will. But I don't hand over leverage for free." She reached back into her purse and this time produced a small black phone, ancient and anonymous. "You're going to call 727—" she rattled off a number "—and you're going to tell the voice on the other end that the container turned around because of a clerical error. You're going to say you'll fix the error in Athens and try again in two months. You're going to buy me time."

"And in exchange?" Theo asked, already knowing.

"In exchange," she said, "I text you the names I know and the numbers I can burn and screenshots of every single time someone tried to use your family like a doormat. And I walk out that door tonight on my own two feet."

"No," Cassie said.

Kellie didn't look away. "You'll still call. Not because you like me. Because you love your father." She let the words hang, then added softly, "Because you love your brother."

The front door opened again. This time, Peter stood in the frame, wind-tousled and stern, a familiar figure in a world that had tilted. His gaze swept the scene—the desk, the papers, the rigid lines of his sons' shoulders. It found Kellie, and his jaw tightened.

"What is she doing here?" he asked.

"Closing her loop," Cassie said.

Peter looked at his daughter, then at the folder under Kellie's palm. "You give us those," he said to Kellie, "and you leave. We do it clean. No deals with devils. No calls."

Kellie considered him, head angling, eyes narrowing. "You always did like a sermon, Peter."

"And you always did like playing with matches," he said evenly. "You're done in this building."

Her smile turned almost wistful. "Am I? Or am I only done being honest about wanting what you all keep for yourselves?"

Peter didn't flinch. "You want to be seen? Here I am seeing you: a bright woman who could have had a future here if she'd honored the people in this room instead of trying to own them. You made yourself a Trojan horse because you thought that was the only way anyone would open a gate for you." He gestured at the stacks of files, the printouts. "But a horse only works once. Everyone learns the sound of wheels after the first fire."

The room seemed to shrink for a beat. Then Kellie's eyes slid to Cassie. "There it is," she said lightly. "The speech. The father. The lesson." She tapped the folder. "Fine. A trade then. Call your cop or your customs friend; I don't care. But you know as well as I do—this doesn't end with me." She lifted the printouts. "The people behind me don't care about revenge or love. They care about frictionless corridors."

Cassie reached into her own bag and took out her phone. She didn't dial Kellie's number. She dialed the local police. She put it on speaker.

"Tarpon Springs Police, what's your emergency?"

Cassie's voice was calm. "This is Cassandra Bennett. We need to report criminal tampering with import documentation and an attempted conspiracy to defraud customs. The suspect is on site and willing to provide evidence in exchange for protection and cooperation with federal authorities. We will also require patrol units to secure the location."

Kellie's mouth quirked. "You really are who you say you are."

Cassie kept the phone steady. "We're done playing with matches."

Kellie considered the door. She considered the four Bennetts and Thomas standing between her and it. She considered the weight of whatever she'd felt at the port—the sudden swivel of the world, the turned container, the whispered *not this time*. When the dispatcher asked for the address, Kellie herself recited it, crisp and correct.

They waited. Nobody spoke. Somewhere down the corridor, a printer woke and yawned and went back to sleep.

Sirens bled into the silence a minute later—thin at first, then fuller, rolling closer. Cassie felt a thud in her chest that didn't feel like fear. It felt like a stone being set back into a wall, true and square.

Kellie's composure didn't crack. She stacked the two pages and slid them across the desk toward Theo. She set the little black phone next to them. Then she shoved the tabbed folder toward Cassie and tapped it twice, a wordless: *this is the map you'll need.*

"Last lesson, professor," she said. "When you tell the truth, they won't believe you. You need to find a way to make it expensive not to."

The glass doors opened. Two officers stepped in, alert but not aggressive. Cassie gave her name. Peter did the same. Kellie folded her hands and said clearly, "I'd like to cooperate."

They cuffed her without drama. As they turned her toward the door, Kellie looked back, not at Theo or Nik or Peter, but at Cassie.

"You'll never stop them from playing with you," she said, not gloating now, only certain. "But maybe you can make them play nice."

"Maybe I can," Cassie said. "Maybe I already did."

Kellie's smile, the real one, small and human, flared for a heartbeat. Then she was gone into the twilight and siren-sound.

The doors shut. Silence inked back into the room. Theo let out a breath he didn't know he'd been holding and sagged against the desk. Nik scrubbed a hand down his face. Peter looked old and not old, like a statue someone had just polished—lines deeper, edges sharper.

Thomas pinched the bridge of his nose, then looked at Cassie. "Are you okay?"

Cassie stared at the folder Kellie had left. For a moment, all she could see was an old, cracked wall and a girl with red hair pounding on it with both fists while men on the other side shouted to ignore her. Then the image shivered and split, and she saw a clean, empty bay at the Port of Tampa and a container sailing back into light.

"I'm tired," she said honestly. "But I'm okay."

Nik edged closer. He looked wrecked. "I should've listened last night."

Cassie cut him off with a small shake of her head. "You will next time."

Peter stepped around the desk and put a hand on his daughter's shoulder—

the same weight he'd used when teaching her to ride a bike on the cracked driveway, guide and anchor both. "We will," he said, and his voice didn't wobble.

Theo gathered the pages into a stack, slid them into a new folder, labeled it with a single word in his neat block letters: **HORSE**. He set it on top of the other evidence, as if naming the thing could keep any new version of it from creeping through a gate they forgot to guard.

Outside, the sirens faded. In the office, the fluorescent hum softened to an ordinary insistence.

"Okay," Cassie said, straightening. The pragmatic tone made Peter smile despite himself; it sounded like her mother. "We call the port attorney. We call the Feds. We call our insurance. We call Alexis in Athens. And we buy new locks. Different codes."

Theo nodded. "Done."

Nik swallowed. "And we tell Helen?"

Cassie's gaze softened, but her answer didn't. "We tell Helen. We tell Mom. We tell Blair. No more keeping the horse in shadow because we're afraid of how it looks."

Thomas reached for Cassie's hand. She took it. The small warmth of it traveled farther than it had any right to.

As they moved toward Peter's office to start a list—names to contact, statements to prepare, locks to change—the sun slid down behind the sponge docks and threw a last sheet of gold across the lobby. It clipped the edge of Kellie's old desk and the sharp acrylic nameplate and the folder labeled **HORSE**, and it lit them up briefly, like a warning flare or a benediction.

Cassie paused, looking at the light, at the shadow it cast behind, long and straight.

In some other century, a girl had watched a wooden animal roll past her and had known, with the bone-deep certainty you don't learn so much as are born with, that the wheels meant fire. She'd screamed herself hoarse. Men had smiled and patted her hair and said the gods were appeased.

Now, Cassie touched the folder with two fingers and found her voice didn't tremble at all.

"Not this time," she said.

No one laughed. No one humored. Three men she loved nodded—and then moved, all of them, the way people move when they finally believe the person who told them what was coming all along.

55

Cassie

Modern Day

The wedding celebration of Nik and Helen unfolded before us like a living tapestry, woven with joy and laughter. Theo stood proudly as best man, resplendent in his suit, a fine fabric that glimmered in the candlelight. I, too, had dressed in my finery, a long beaded gown adorned with jasmine flowers woven through my hair—but it was Thomas that caught my eye, standing tall and steady at my side.

The room seemed to swell with music, a melody that breathed life into our limbs and set us dancing. We swayed in time, eyes meeting in brief moments of understanding, of shared delight. For the first time in months, I felt the tight knot of fear inside me loosen.

Nik and Helen had found their happily ever after. I could only be thankful—thankful for love, for survival, for family that had weathered storms together.

As Thomas spun me across the floor, I whispered up to him, "I can't believe it's over. Kellie...everything. I was so sure it would destroy us."

His hand tightened on mine. "It didn't. You stood up to all of it. And you were right, Cassie. Maybe not in the exact way you feared, but you were *right.*"

I swallowed back sudden tears. "Cassandra never got this moment," I murmured. "She warned, she screamed, she fought—and no one listened.

But tonight, I'm dancing in the middle of my family. They know I wasn't crazy. They know I loved them enough to try."

Thomas leaned down, his lips brushing my temple. "Then maybe you've broken her curse."

* * *

Kellie Anderson was in jail now. Within thirty minutes of interrogation, she crumbled, spilling every detail about the cartel she had worked with. It would take months for the DEA and Interpol to unravel it all, but her smug laughter had ended in handcuffs.

It wasn't just justice, it was vindication.

* * *

Months later, spring sunlight slanted across the campus halls as I stepped into Dr. Evelyn Hawthorne's office. I presented at the annual Boosters symposium; Aiden hadn't even bothered to show. Coward. Now, with a sabbatical granted, I finally had time to begin the book I'd always wanted to write.

Dr. Hawthorne greeted me with a smile, and something cradled in her hands. "For you," she said, setting it on the desk between us.

It was a statue—Athena, gleaming in bronze, owl perched at her shoulder, spear at the ready.

My throat tightened. "I smashed mine months ago," I admitted quietly.

"I know." Her wise eyes softened. "So, I thought you should have another. Athena protects truth-tellers, Cassie. Every scholar needs her guardian. And you've earned that protection."

I ran my fingertips over the goddess's helm. For the first time, I didn't feel like an impostor. I felt like someone who had taken Cassandra's story—the ancient one—and forced the world to listen.

"Ancient Cassandra's words died with her," I whispered. "But mine won't. I'll write her story, my story, *our* story. And this time, people will hear it."

Dr. Hawthorne's hand closed over mine, warm and grounding. "You've done what she never could. That is justice enough."

* * *

At home, Thomas and I unpacked boxes together. We had chosen to move in slowly, one book, one framed photograph at a time, until his apartment became *ours*.

"You know," he said as he carried in a stack of my dog-eared texts, "you could have gone the easy route. Kept your head down. Pretended you didn't see what you saw."

"And?" I asked, arching a brow.

He smiled faintly. "And instead, you fought. You risked your career, your family, your sanity. And you won."

I set Athena on the mantle, where she caught the evening light. "So did Cassandra," I said. "She survived. No one wrote it down, but I know she did. Maybe not in history books, but in the truth that outlasts them. And now, so have I."

Thomas stood there, arms folded, watching me with that steady gaze that never wavered. "So, Professor Cassandra," he teased, "what will the world say when your book comes out?"

"That I was right," I answered simply. No apology. No hesitation. The words rang with clarity I had never felt before.

Thomas walked forward and slid his arm around me, pressing his forehead to mine. "Then maybe the curse really is broken."

I didn't answer. I just held his gaze, the weight of centuries resting between us—and, for the first time, it didn't feel heavy. It felt like victory.

Cassandra of Troy had been silenced.

Cassandra Bennett would not be.

56

The Island of Delos

The golden light of sunset wrapped Delos in fire and honey, an ancient island that once saw gods born, now echoing only with their whispers. Apollo sat strumming his lyre, the melancholy notes winding through the myrtle trees.

"Ah, sister," he said without looking up, "I sensed your approach."

Artemis lowered herself onto the marble beside him, silver eyes steady. "You always do. And yet, with the Cassandras, you sensed nothing until it was too late."

His fingers faltered on the strings. "Both trouble me. One, long dead—unless the histories are more fragile than we think. The other… defied me in ways no mortal should. I cannot shake the thought that I've left them worse off."

"They left *you* changed," Artemis corrected. "The first refused you. The second grabbed your jaw and forced you to listen. Tell me, brother—when was the last time a mortal made you flinch?"

Apollo's smile was brittle. "My jaw still aches."

"And so it should," Artemis said, smirking. "Twice now, mortal women have marked you. That is their victory."

Apollo set the lyre aside, his hands tightening in his lap. "I am a god. Revered. Feared. And yet… tolerated, now, at best. I do not enjoy being humbled."

"None of us do," Artemis murmured. "But even gods can learn. Cassandra was never insignificant. Both of them carried truth heavier than bronze shields—and dared to place it at your feet. They endured what you could not bear: to be ignored."

He winced, remembering the fire in Cassie Bennett's voice, the scorn in Cassandra of Troy's eyes. *You will fail again.*

Artemis leaned closer, lowering her voice. "Truth is no longer yours, Apollo. It belongs to them. Athena guards it, Cassandra wields it. You only stand witness."

He stared toward the horizon, where the sun drowned in the indigo sea. "And what am I, if not the god of prophecy?"

"Perhaps," Artemis said, rising to her feet, "you are still learning what it means to listen."

The silence stretched between them, heavy as centuries. Finally, Apollo gave a low, rueful laugh. "Even gods can be humbled. By mortals. Twice cursed. Twice taught."

"Not cursed," Artemis corrected. "Victorious."

As the sky deepened to indigo, Artemis shifted on the marble bench, her gaze steady on her brother. The waves lapped quietly against Delos' shore, the night carrying the scent of salt and myrtle.

"Brother," she began, her voice low, nearly blending with the rustle of leaves, "have you ever wondered why so many of your loves ended in tragedy?"

Apollo's golden eyes narrowed. He knew the question was deserved, but answering it meant stepping into a place he rarely let himself go. "I loved them," he said finally, his tone defensive. "Each one deeply. Their ends…that was fate."

"Was it?" Artemis arched a brow. "Take Daphne."

Apollo flinched, remembering her sprint through the forest, her desperate prayer, her body twisting into bark and branches beneath his hands. "That wasn't me. She chose the laurel tree over me."

"She didn't exactly have much of a choice," Artemis muttered. Then, more firmly: "But ask yourself why she would rather root herself in soil than be rooted at your side."

He frowned, struggling for an answer. "Mortals fear the divine. They're fickle, fragile."

"No," she said softly, "they're not. And if we look at Coronis, at Clytie... even Hyacinthus...there's a pattern."

Apollo's jaw tightened. "What pattern?"

"Jealousy." Artemis didn't flinch. "You burn so hot when someone refuses you, or when another draws their affection. You scorch everything around you. And the ones you claim to love are always the first to turn to ash."

Her words dug deep. He thought of Hyacinthus, beautiful and laughing one moment, his lifeblood spilling into the grass the next. He thought of Marpessa, who had chosen a mortal rather than endure the storm of his possessiveness. Even Daphne, her terror forever carved into the twist of laurel branches.

Apollo exhaled, heavy as stone. "Perhaps you're right. I wanted love. Worship. Devotion. And in demanding it, I...destroyed it."

"Recognition is the first step," Artemis said gently, her hand brushing his shoulder. "And perhaps the hardest for you."

He stared at his lyre, fingers tightening over the strings. For once, no song rose to fill the silence. "I need to change," he admitted. "Not just with mortals, but in how I spend my days. I can't keep bending lives to fit my whims."

"Then find something else to bend," Artemis replied simply. "Your music, the hunt, something that doesn't leave broken bodies in its wake. Gods don't have to stay the same. Even you can choose a different pursuit."

For a long while, the only sound was the sea. Apollo finally nodded, a slow bow of his head. "Maybe you're right. Maybe I need...a new hobby." A faint, rueful smile touched his mouth. "I've heard whispers, you know—about a camp in the mortal world. A place where the half-blood children of gods are trained. Perhaps I could go there, teach archery, or music. Do something other than ruin everything I touch."

Artemis laughed, a sound like silver bells. "Imagine that. Apollo, humbled. Teaching."

He smiled faintly, plucking a gentler chord. "Stranger things have happened."

"Speaking of stranger things," Apollo said after a while, his mouth quirking, "our father seems determined to keep us entertained. Have you heard? He went after another mortal last week."

"As a swan again?" Artemis asked dryly.

"The very same trick." Apollo shook his head. "You'd think Hera would be used to it by now."

"She'll never be used to it." Artemis's laugh rang like windchimes. "But perhaps even Zeus proves the point: desire clouds even the sharpest minds. God or mortal, none of us is immune."

They shared a smile, rare and unguarded, before turning their eyes back to the dark horizon. On Delos, in the hush of the twilight, the two immortals sat together—siblings bound not just by eternity, but by the uneasy knowledge that even gods could be humbled, and perhaps remade.

Epilogue

Cassandra

I told you.

Afterword

Writing a book about Cassandra — seer of doom, ignorer of red flags, icon of unheeded warnings—is a bit like screaming into a thunderstorm and getting struck by your own lightning. It's dramatic. It's exhausting. It's occasionally divine. And I wouldn't have survived it without a host of absolute **legends** behind me.

To my husband, Patrick: thank you for encouraging me to finish this book, for holding space when I sobbed over fictional disasters, and for nodding along while I monologued about ancient mythology. I love you oceans, you patient, brave mortal.

To my dad—thank you for being my first coach, my loudest cheerleader, and for always reminding me of who I am.

To my sister—thank you for being steady and solid in a world full of shifting sands. You matter to me, even in silence.

To my nieces and nephews: You are my heart with legs. I love you more than the Trojans loved a good horse metaphor—which is saying something.

To my mother in heaven—thank you for planting the very first word. You've always been part of this story, even now.

To my Coven—you chaotic, magical wonders. You hex the nonsense, charm the good stuff, and conjure joy exactly when I need it. Your spells work. (Also: never stop.)

To all my English teachers, past and present: You taught me to love words, wield commas like weapons, and never underestimate a story's power to raise hell. You're the real heroes.

To Amanda and Kara—my writing sisters-in-arms: thank you for reading early drafts, laughing at my bad ideas until they got better, and for believing in this story even when I was ready to launch it into the sea.

And to you, dear reader: You made it. You picked up a book about a woman the world refused to believe, and you listened anyway. That's no small thing. You are heard. You are believed. Your voice matters. And may the gods finally listen.

P.S: My use of an em dash (—) doesn't mean I used AI (I didn't). It means I'm a millennial. And I won't stop using it.

About the Author

Kara Funcheon writes stories about women, wit, and the moments that shake us awake. She's a feminist, sports fan, and former teacher with a doctorate in education who believes in the power of humor and honesty.

Kara lives in Tampa, FL, with her husband, Patrick, and their tuxedo cat, Mr. Knightley—who has main-character energy and zero chill. When she's not writing, she's probably watching a game, reading a great book, or laughing at something wildly inappropriate.

Echoes of Prophecy is her first published novel, but not the last.

You can connect with me on:

↩ https://www.instagram.com/karafunbooks